Advance praise f

"*Better than Fiction* is great fun. Storylines past and present bob and weave, combining to deliver a story readers will love."

~Karen Ball, best-selling author of *The Breaking Point* and *What Lies Within*

"*Better than Fiction* is a fantastic bang-for-the-buck novel with a story within a story. It's deep and rich, full of lovely phrasing and superb characterization. The team of Massaro and Gardner have a stunning novel that touches on rekindling romance in your marriage and becoming the person God meant you to be. I hope to see more from this team of writers!"

~Angela Breidenbach,
ECPA and Amazon bestselling novelist
and Christian Authors Network president

"[In *Better than Fiction*] Meghan's feelings toward her husband, and the progression of her assumptions, were in line with what I see so often in counseling. The pastor's wife in me wanted to tell her to (respectfully) confront him and get things resolved! The emotional affair she was entering into was spot-on with how I've seen marriages destroyed again and again. Very well done."

~Nancy Kaser, wife of Pastor Brent Kaser
of Calvary Chapel Westgrove.

Since I'm partial to Corona history, I found *Better than Fiction* to be an especially captivating novel. The characters bring the 1916 era to life with their charming love story woven among details of the exciting 1916 Corona Road Race. The authors' historical accuracy is impeccable. Also cleverly integrated into the novel is a modern romance dilemma.

~ Mary Bryner Winn, Corona Historic Preservation Society
and author of *Corona (Then And Now)*

BETTER than *Fiction*

April W Gardner
&
Michelle Massaro

Cover design: Roseanna White Designs
Cover models: Samantha Crouch Wilson and Sam Lipot
Cover photography: Michael Massaro

Publisher's note: This novel is a work of fiction. Names, characters, places, and incidents are either products of the authors' imaginations or used fictitiously. All characters are fictional, and any similarity to people living or dead is purely coincidental.

ISBN-13: 978-0-9973797-0-9 (Trade Paper)
ISBN-10: 0997379707
LCCN: 2016935509

Published by Plaited Press
Printed in the United States of America.

To our sisters in Christ.
May our hearts seek shelter in His unconditional love.

"Above all else, guard your heart,
for everything you do flows from it."
Proverbs 4:23 (NIV)

Chapter One

Corona, CA, Present Day

Meghan laced her fingers in front of her face and listened to the ceiling fan whir. Looking past the dancing dust particles, she stared through the window behind her computer screen, vaguely aware of the hum of little-girl voices and the *thump-thump-thump* of the clothes dryer down the hall. Biting the inside of her cheek, she nested her chin atop her hands and closed her eyes.

The scene rolled behind her closed lids, like a movie. The camera of her mind panned across the 1916 Stutz Bearcat—the shiny red paint, the long steering column, the red wheel spokes. She focused on the hero until she saw the flecks of green in his eyes and the smudge of grease on his shirt. Watched him check the street sign as he walked down the sidewalk, searching for something. Desperate.

Determination shot through her own veins . . .

Okay, good. She felt it. Time to make her readers feel it too. She opened her eyes and positioned her fingers . . .

~~Walked. Strutted. Plodded~~

"Mommy!" The little voice came from behind. "Faith pinched me and called me a jerk."

> *Stomped.* Russell stomped down the street . . .

Ooh, wait! Meghan backspaced one more time.

> Slapped the pavement . . .

"Mom, are you listening? Tell her to stop being mean to me."

"Yeah, sweetie, give me a minute. I have to finish this line." Meghan tossed the words over her shoulder, keeping her eyes on the monitor. The perfect phrasing eluded her, like a needle in a . . . forget the cliché. She'd get the rough sketch down first, then go back and dress it up. Her eighty-word-per-minute fingers flew across the keyboard.

> Russell Keegan's loafers slapped the pavement. The only sound on that empty street. The town was dead by six p.m.

"Nobody ever listens to me! You don't even care!" Zoey's voice broke, and a whimper-and-sniff drifted to Meghan's ears.

"I do too care. Be patient." She raised her voice. "Faith, quit picking on your sister."

From the end of the hall, Faith wailed. "But that's not f-a-i-r! She's the one being mean to *me*. She took my fuzzy pencil that she *knows* I didn't want her to touch, and she didn't even ask."

Though tempted to charge to the bedroom and bust some heads, Meghan remained in her seat. She swiveled her chair and tightened her lips into a thin line. "You two better knock it off before I lose my patience! I'm trying to focus here."

"You always say that."

"I always mean it." Meghan tried to read the line she'd been working on a moment ago, before she lost her place in the haystack. The dryer buzzed. She blocked it out.

"I'm hungry."

"It's only four thirty." Meghan kept typing.

```
Dead like his chances of winning the
Corona Road Race . . . unless he could find
a mechanic.
```

As if burdened by the falling economy, a mortgage, and two car payments, Zoey dragged herself over to her mother's side. "I'm b-o-o-o-r-e-d." The whine curled like barbed tendrils around Meghan's eardrums.

Her shoulders and neck tightened, and a twitch threatened her left eyelid. She pinched the bridge of her nose. This child was going to be the death of her. Or at least the death of her novel.

Drawing in a slow, deliberate breath, Meghan looked her youngest daughter in the eye. "If you promise to be a good girl, I'll let you turn on the TV and watch two episodes of *Veggie Tales.* Then I'll start dinner, okay?"

Zoey's blue eyes brightened as she bobbed her little blonde head. "Okay, I promise."

With her five-year-old settled into the beanbag in the family room, giggling at Larry the Cucumber, Meghan plopped back into her office-in-the-dining-room chair, cracked her knuckles, and somehow found her way back into *Racing Hearts*.

Corona, CA, 1916

Sixteen months of rigid training, undone with a single vicious act.

Russell Keegan's loafers slapped the sidewalk and echoed through the deserted street. Corona was the same as every other small town in America—dead by six in the evening. Dead, like his dream of winning the Corona Road Race . . . unless this last mechanic proved helpful.

As he approached the garage, the smell of oil cozied up to his senses and triggered his Pop's baritone: *You're a racer, Son. It's in your blood.* The memory of his father's hand weighed on Russell's shoulder as well as his mind, igniting his stride.

A large sign hung lopsided above the building, the words Danny's Automotive discernible in the light cast by the dim street lamp across the intersection. *Danny's?* Had he been sent to the wrong establishment?

Through the open double-bay door came a faint glow. At least one employee was still at work, but with Russell's luck, it wouldn't be Fred. Russell's luck had pegged him with a car *and* a mechanic out of commission. Since bad things seemed to run in groups of threes, he was due another heartbreak.

He picked his way through the dark interior toward the flicker of a gas lantern precariously perched on the thick wheel well of a newer model Dodge. "Fire hazard," he muttered, grasping the lamp by the handle and arching it around him. "Hello? Anybody here?"

His muted lamplight washed over a mountain of stacked tires and a row of bicycles, all in various states of disassembly. A wagon wheel with a broken spoke and a tangle of cobwebs hung from a hook in the rafters.

The scream of hinges swung Russell's gaze to the back of the shop where a figure materialized in the shadows. "Hi, there. Can I help you?"

The warm, feminine voice jammed his thoughts. "Er, help me? Doubt it, but I'm told there's a Fred who might." Holding the lantern out before him, he moved toward her. "The sign says Danny's. Am I at the wrong place?"

She harrumphed. "Be useful and bring that over here." A chill frosted her words.

What had he said?

No matter. He obeyed.

His circle of light revealed a tiny woman wearing filthy, oversized coveralls. A large cap covered her head down to her ears, concealing beneath its shadow all but her smudged chin and pursed lips. She looked like a child playing dress-up in her father's clothes.

He grinned. "A little early for Halloween, isn't it?"

"I'm busy. Either tell me what you want, or leave me to my work."

Ouch. He had a lot of ground to make up after that remark. "Nice cap, though. It suits you." *Stupid, stupid.* Around the ladies, his intelligence dropped by several degrees. Apparently, it happened around semi-ladies, as well.

"Set the lantern there on your way out." She jabbed her thumb toward a cluttered counter then snatched a clipboard from a tall stack of tires.

He ground his molars to retain a biting remark. "Just got in yesterday. The name's Russell Keegan." He paused for the inevitable exclamation his name often produced, but she didn't so much as twitch. He told himself it didn't matter that this slip of an oil-stained girl didn't know who he was.

"My Stutz was torn up pretty bad. I was sent this way by a couple of gentlemen over at Thomas Drug."

She tossed the clipboard back on the tires and disappeared behind the raised hood of the Dodge.

"Look, I know you're busy with . . . whatever you're doing here, but I could use some help." He rounded the corner of the massive automobile.

Hands propped on her hips, she stared at the car's engine as though she'd dropped a hairpin into its black interior and was debating where to begin her search.

Russell took the opportunity to glance around for evidence anyone else was there, but the shadows revealed no other doors. His gaze swung to the ceiling. No bulb.

"You know, you should have electricity installed."

Her reply came in the form of a soft grunt as she stretched across the engine block and shoved her arm into a dark crevice.

"Whoa! What are you doing? You wanna get stuck in there?" He grabbed her around the waist, going through a sea of stiff fabric before finding a grip and giving a good tug.

"Get off me, you over-inflated dunce!"

The steel in her voice made him drop her like a hand-crank on a backfiring engine.

As she fought for balance, the cap tumbled from her head, uncovering a mass of corkscrew curls that collided in a knot of pins and spun copper. When he managed to pull his sight from the auburn glow, it landed on her narrowed eyes.

"Didn't I ask you to leave?" She plunged her arm back into the crevice.

Russell didn't budge.

Cheek pressed against the engine, she bit her lip, seeming to strain to reach something. "Was one of those gentlemen at Thomas Drug broad around the midriff and wearing a ratty engineer's cap? Playing checkers with another, who dribbled tobacco juice like a leaky Chevy?" She spoke in an easy tone, seeming to have forgotten her injured feelings.

Hope rose within him. "Yeah, how did you know?"

"Typical, is all. Got it." With a firm yank, she withdrew her arm—along with the corpse of a stiff, scorched rat. She held it up to the light by its tail, her nose wrinkling. A snap of her wrist sent it onto a pile of rubbish in the corner. "Don't guess he'll be making that mistake again." She brushed her hands together.

Russell laughed in spite of himself. What kind of woman dressed like a man and fearlessly fished rats out of engines?

She cracked a tiny smile, jiggled a hose, then spun and rummaged through a toolbox. What did she figure on doing?

"Well, I need the help. The guys at the drugstore said this shop is the best there is within a hundred-mile radius."

Her hand stilled on a pair of pliers. "Generous of them to say."

"They also say business is reserved for special customers."

She jutted a hip, a smile tipping one corner of her mouth, and for three skips of his heart, she looked pretty. "And Fred should do business with you, because *you're* special?"

Suddenly, all Russell saw was the grit stuck to the underside of her nose.

Before he could scramble for a retort, she smoothed her expression, crossed her arms over her chest, and leaned her posterior against the Dodge. "A Stutz you say?"

"That's right."

"The Bearcat stranded over on Victoria? It has a few flats and a busted monocle."

The street name would have sufficed. She needn't have reminded him of his baby's blemishes. "Yeah, that's her."

"So what happened to your mechanic? Did he bail on you?"

He wished that were all. "He's laid up. Same thugs that got to the Cat busted Chester up, too."

He expected compassion to soften her features. Instead, a fire sparked in her eyes. "Why, the low-down, rotten—" She jabbed a finger toward his chest. "If anyone asks you where the cheaters are in this town, you point them toward the guys who did this to your Chester."

Eyes widening, he made a mental note to never cross this woman.

She plucked her cap from atop the carburetor and crammed her curls under it. "All right, I'll have a look at it. But just a look, and I'll charge you for it. Ten bucks, and not a red cent less." She was already moving toward the door. "We'll take Lizzie."

He followed in her wake, confusion curling his lip. "What about Fred?"

"Oh, sorry." She spun, her hand extended. "I'm Fred. I'd say 'nice to make your acquaintance,' but I'd be telling a half-truth. Your Stutz, on the other hand, I'd be more than pleased to meet."

He chuckled, ignoring her hand. "You're joshin' me."

"I don't josh." The set of her jaw confirmed it.

"*You're* Fred?" Mechanically, he followed her out of the shop, then let her bump him aside so she could close the doors.

"Winifred Fisher, the best mechanic within a hundred-mile radius. Or so you say." She marched across the lot toward a 1908 Model T. "Let's go. I haven't got all night."

Present Day

A hissing splash pulled Meghan from the scene. *The potatoes!* She dashed into the kitchen, turned down the flame, and blew across the irritated foam. The spuds more than passed the fork-test, so she drained the mushy clumps and plopped a half stick of butter into the pot.

"I hate pork chops."

Meghan looked up to see Faith wandering into the Spanish-tiled kitchen. The nine-year-old's face scrunched up as though she'd taken her crimping iron to it.

"Can I have macaroni and cheese instead?"

"Nope. And you can put away that sneer, I'm not buyin' it. You'd think I was making you eat the scrapings from the bottom of your shoe."

"Eww. Mom, that's gross."

"Yes, it would be. But pork chops are fine and dandy, and they'll be done soon."

"Dandy? Come back to the twenty-first century, Mom."

"Pull the beaters out of the drawer and stick them on the mixer for me, would you? Then you and Zoey can wash up for dinner."

Meghan's cell phone sang a scale. She fished it out of her pocket with one hand while revving the electric mixer with the other. A text from Brooke.

How much did u write 2day? R we on 4 tomorrow?

Meghan smiled, powered down the beater, then thumbed in her reply.

Tons! Yes for tomorrow. 8:30 a.m. Making dinner, g2g.

Just then, the knob turned and Steve's frame filled the doorway between the kitchen and garage, sandy-colored hair sticking to his forehead. At six-foot-one, he dwarfed Meghan's five-foot-three, which was the way she'd always liked it. No evil could touch her when she was in his arms. But when was the last time he'd wrapped them around her?

His weary brown eyes paused on hers. "Hey." He tossed his keys on the overstock-granite counter and opened the fridge, cracked open a soda, and guzzled it.

Meghan replaced the pot lid and turned toward her husband. "How was your day?"

He shook his head. "I tell ya, the Johnson project is killing me. I'm working with a bunch of morons."

She pressed her lips together. "I'm so sorry, hon. Anything I can do to help?"

"No, don't worry about. How was your day?"

"Stressful. Long. But . . . " Meghan sidled up to her husband and reached her arms up around his neck with a smile. She pretended not to notice the way he stiffened as she pulled herself onto tiptoes for a kiss. "I started that project I told you about. A novel. Set right here in Corona. Wrote the whole first chapter. The premise is good. I think I have a real shot at making this happen." She beamed at him, searching his eyes for a reflection of her own exhilaration.

"Oh, good." He puffed out his cheeks in a tired exhale, the stubble on his unshaven face standing on end. After a perfunctory peck on her lips, he slipped out of her arms. "I'm gonna go change. Dinner smells great."

Meghan's chest fell but she smiled as she dropped her hands to her sides. "Okay."

Casting off her disappointment, she finished whipping the potatoes, stuck the peas in the microwave, and pulled the chops from the oven. She shoved off the gnawing awareness that she and Steve weren't in sync. Hadn't been for a long time.

She returned to the counter to dish up the food and pour milk for her daughters. Nearby stood a bowl of lemons from one of the few remaining city groves, and Meghan sliced one for her water. Ten minutes later, the family sat around the dining table.

Green Corel plates rattled, and Meghan cast an icy glare at the girls for kicking each other and making pests of themselves. "*Watch it.*" She worked too hard to make family dinner a bonding time. Weariness ate at her bones, and her patience met a swift end. "I didn't raise you to be little hellions."

"What's a hellion?" Zoey pulled her legs up under her.

Faith's caramel brown eyes narrowed. "What you are and I'm *not*."

"Nuh-uh. I'm not one of those things!"

"You don't even know what we're talking about, *baby*."

"That's enough!" Steve roared, and smacked the table.

Both girls fell silent and turned to their food, chins tucked toward their chests.

Meghan's eyes stung. The girls deserved a reprimand, but she wished they didn't have to hear their father raise his voice like that. And it was becoming too frequent a thing these days.

She set the saltshaker down in front of him. "You're home kinda late tonight, aren't you?"

Steve's eyes shifted to the left, fork paused in midair. "Not really." He cleared his throat. "Work's been a bear." He stuffed pork chops into his mouth and scooped up some peas.

Meghan shot him a sideways glance as a tingling sensation slid from her chest to her gut. She assessed him a moment, then shoved away her unease and savored a small bite of potatoes. Comfort food at its finest. Sounds of chewing and scraping pierced the quiet. "Faith, why don't you tell Dad about your day?" Meghan nodded to her daughter.

"I beat Abigail in spelling at school"—Faith straightened in her chair—"And now I get to represent our class in the big spelling bee two weeks from Friday. Can you come, Dad?"

Meghan followed Faith's gaze to her father. He looked from one to the other. "Friday? Sorry, don't think I can. I gotta work. But Mom'll tell me all about it."

Faith's face fell. "Oh... Okay." She pushed food around on her plate.

Meghan's chest tightened. She leaned toward Steve. "You can't get someone to cover the factory floor for a couple hours?" She glanced at Faith, at the disappointment in her daughter's eyes.

"I wish I could. We're behind schedule as it is. I told you this project is killing me."

"Yeah, I know. I just wish . . . " She eased back against her chair. "Well, that's okay." Meghan forced the bubbling resentment back under the surface. It had no place here; Steve was nothing like her dad. She offered a reassuring smile to Faith.

"Daddy, ask 'bout my day!" Zoey grinned with cheeks full of "smashed" potatoes.

"All right, tell me about your day, princess. But first, swallow your food." Steve cut into his pork chops, pulling his brows together as he shifted uncomfortably in his seat.

Meghan appraised him. "You okay?"

"Yeah. Fine. Go ahead, Zoey." He flashed a stiff grin.

Zoey began a detailed account of everything she'd done since waking up that morning—from getting dressed, to conducting her duties as Light Monitor, to being the last one picked up from kindergarten.

At that, Steve raised a knowing eyebrow at Meghan.

Meghan forced a smile. "I was writing. And I wasn't that late. Maybe five minutes. I just lost track of time." She took a sip of lemon water. "Remember when I almost made us miss our flight to Hawaii, and we had to sprint through the terminal to catch our plane?" She giggled.

"I remember." Steve's half-smile melted into that faraway expression Meghan still couldn't read, though she'd had plenty of practice these last months.

Her giggling dissipated, but the memory lingered. It had been a magnificent honeymoon—hiking, snorkeling, even biking down Maui's Haleakala Mountain. Of course, that was a long time ago.

Back when the adventure called life was a blank page waiting to be written. She sniffed against the sting in her nose.

Steve dropped his napkin onto his plate. "The pork chops were good, Meg."

"Thanks." She smiled, happy her cooking still got a thumbs-up.

With dinner finished, Faith and Zoey disappeared into their room, and Meghan cleared the table while her husband moved to the couch. He slumped onto it with a grunt, then stretched his long legs across the whole of it.

Meghan trailed in a moment later and settled into the nearby recliner. She ran a finger over her bottom lip and watched Steve read something on his smart phone, retreating into his own little world, wherever that may be. *She* was right here. No show-stopper, a little cellulite and a few split ends, but somewhere inside she was still the woman he'd pledged his heart to.

Wasn't she?

She tucked her hair behind her ears. "So, the Johnson project is turning into a train wreck, huh?"

"You have no idea."

"And Tony's no help?"

"Tony doesn't work for us anymore."

"Really? When did that happen?"

He shook his head and sighed. "I don't really want to get into work stuff right now."

"Oh. Sure, of course." She cleared her throat. "Wanna hear about my story?"

Once upon a time, after dinner was their time to have a cup of tea and sit together, sharing about their respective days. She'd love to get back to that. "I'm calling it *Racing Hearts*, and it's really captured my imagination. I'm so excited."

"That's great, Meg." He flicked a grin at her and reached for the remote. The TV blinked to life with a sports channel.

Meghan pulled in a wobbly breath and took her cue. "So . . ." She ran her palms down her thighs and stood. "I guess I'll work on that for a while, if you're busy."

"Yeah that's fine." He didn't even look up.

Meghan paused, waiting for him to glance her way. Connect with her for even one tick of the clock. But his gaze never left the screen. She turned and made her way to her computer, scolding herself for the ache in her chest.

But as she fired up her laptop amidst the racket of a basketball game, the ache only deepened. The sounds—and the silence—from the living room almost strangled her awakening muse.

She wanted to get up, to go back and talk with him, tell him how empty she felt, how lonely . . . but she shook her head. She wouldn't make an issue of it. She'd just tune out the TV and focus on the task at hand: making her way back to 1916.

1916

Thoughts collided inside Russell's head, leaving him able to do little more than stare as Winifred Fisher struck a match and bent to light the Tin Lizzie's gas headlamps. He'd never *heard* of a woman mechanic, much less come face-to-face with one. There had to be some mistake.

Lamps lit, she hopped behind the wheel and spotted him standing where she'd left him. "Do you want me to look at it or not?"

He tramped over and planted one foot on the Ford's runner. "And just what do you think you're gonna do?" No woman—regardless of how good the locals claimed her to be—would get her hands on his Cat.

Her fingers froze around the choke. "Are we going? I could use the ten, but I haven't got all night for you to decide whether your ego can handle a woman criticizing your engine."

A flash of anger curdled the blood in his veins. "Ego? Y-you—This has nothing to do with ego. Listen here, *Fred*, I'm man enough to handle just about anything—"

In one smooth move, she popped the choke and stomped the starter pedal. The engine roared to life, cutting his words short.

"Prove it and get in."

His fingers dug into the top of the closed door. How had this day gone so awry? He hadn't asked for much—just a reliable mechanic. A reliable *male* mechanic. But the *one* willing even to look at his injured baby was a woman with a runaway mouth who wouldn't know her place if a street sign were plastered above it.

"Fine! But I'm driving." He hoisted himself over the running board and sent her scrambling across the leather bench.

"Of all the ill-bred—"

"Hey, if you wanna run with the boys, you'll have to play by our rules." He adjusted the spark advance to the correct RPMs to smooth out the slight sputter. "Rule number one? The guy with the most brawn always makes the rules. That would be me. Second rule? No whining about the rules. Scoot over. You're hogging." He elbowed her in the arm, but she elbowed him right back. Hard.

With a crooked grin, he set the throttle to high and swerved out of the lot, taking a jolting dip into a rut in the dirt road. Fred's squeak and frantic scratching at anything for a grip brought Russell wicked satisfaction. He'd deal with some guilt later, but right then, he would have given any number of things to tear down the Corona Speedway with Little Miss Smudge clinging, white-knuckled, to the leather bucket seat of his Bearcat.

She whipped the cap off her head and walloped him with it. "Are you crazy? You'll warp the spokes!"

On the street now, he throttled down, maneuvered around a pile of horse manure, then turned to her, all wide-eyed innocence. "What's wrong, Miss Fisher? Afraid of a job tougher than extracting rats?"

She clamped her mouth and faced forward. He might have grown up without a mother, but he wasn't so clueless about women that he believed Winifred to be through with him.

Five minutes later, he pulled into the Hotel Del Rey's lot and parked in front of his racer. The Ford's headlamps bathed the Bearcat in light and, as it did every time, the sight of her constricted Russell's throat. There, next to her gleaming fender, stood a vision of Pop, his fingers stroking the flawless paint job, his wool cap flopping to the same side as the lopsided grin on his face. *Whatcha think, Russ? Will she do?*

A soft cry spun his head to the passenger's seat. One hand touching her mouth, Winifred sat statuesque, her gaze riveted to his Cat. "She's a real beauty." The awe in her voice took his breath away.

In actuality, the Cat had never looked worse. Three slit tires had her sitting at a pathetic tilt. The monocle windscreen, shattered and twisted on its stand, bowed over the steering column as if too ashamed to lift its head. Glass peppered the two seats. In some semblance of mercy, the vandals hadn't touched the body. Their work under the hood, however, was enough to make every mechanic in Corona shake his head and point to the door.

Russell couldn't stomach looking at the Stutz, but Winifred left the Ford and approached with slow, almost reverent steps.

He leaned forward, propping his arms on the smooth wood of the steering wheel. As she walked the circumference, studying every angle of his car, he studied her.

Washed in light, patches of clean skin glowed pale through the grime on her face and neck. A single curl hung forgotten against the side of her gaping mouth. Having made a complete circle, she came around the back of the Cat and took measured strides along its side. Her fingers hovered above the wheel and followed the curve in a worshipful caress.

If he didn't know her to be an unfeminine creature, he might think she were trying to seduce him.

Unbidden, the feel of her fingers ran a similar trail along his bare shoulders. He swallowed hard and squirmed in his seat. Something was wrong with him if a figureless woman in filthy coveralls set his mind on such an unchristian path. With a grunt, he shook off the images, jammed the handbrake into place, and jumped from the vehicle.

Present Day

Steve's game had ended long ago and Meghan was still tapping away on the laptop. Smiling, she closed her computer and nestled into her propped pillows with a dreamy sigh.

There was something about historical romance. A different time, a different way of life, but the same spark between a man and a woman.

And this story was becoming deliciously electric.

A sharp snorting broke her from her reverie. Her gaze traveled to her husband—snoring loud enough to send the city into evacuation—and to the unattractive loll of his gaping mouth.

After setting aside her laptop, Meghan turned and propped her head on her left hand. She studied the small creases of Steve's forehead, the strong angle of his nose, the outline of his lips—even if they were hanging slack and flapping with every rattling breath. To be fair, she'd been caught snoring on occasion as well. And he'd seen her looking less than stellar countless times over the years. In fact, she'd gotten pretty lax with her own appearance until a couple months ago, and Steve had never said a word. Of course, he hadn't looked at her the way he used to in a long time, either.

She reached out and ran a finger along his arm. Would he stir and pull her close? Make her blood race?

He smacked his tongue on the roof of his mouth a couple times, then turned to face the other way.

Dejected, Meghan rolled onto her back and stared at the popcorn ceiling.

Looked like all the sparks tonight were reserved for Winifred and Russell.

Chapter Two

Present Day

Meghan sped down Ontario Avenue, passing Lincoln and the "brown corner," as Zoey called it. The empty lot had been promising for years to bring an exciting shopping center to the neighborhood. Five years ago, that open space represented possibility. Today, barrenness.

She squeezed the steering wheel, hoping to force out the sadness. But she was the same as that five-thousand-square-foot spot. The passing of time had turned her from a woman with dreams, goals, and passion into a nearly invisible part of the landscape.

She cranked up the volume on the radio, tossing her bangs out of her eyes.

Everything was about to change. It had to.

Her chest pounded to the beat of the music—a song of new life. Pulling into the parking lot, she finished out the song before killing the engine.

Meghan stepped out of her Camry, hit the key fob for the car alarm, and headed for the double glass doors. The scent of warm pastries and early-morning fog teased her nose. Whose idea was it to put a cake shop two doors down from the gym? How she'd managed to make any progress was beyond her. She adjusted the duffle bag on her shoulder and crossed her fingers that today the scale would be her friend. Steve *had* to start noticing soon.

"Hey, stranger."

Meghan turned to see Brooke coming in right behind her, her glossy black hair looking as though she'd just stepped out of an Herbal Essences commercial—as always.

Meghan gave her a hug. "Good morning."

Had Brooke not been such a good friend, Meghan would find it difficult to be around the cover-model-in-the-flesh. But somehow, the girl had a way of making Meghan less aware of her own flaws. It defied logic, so Meghan just went with it.

"And how are we today?"

"Fine and dandy, like lemon candy. Ready to sweat off last night's potatoes." Oops—why did she let that slip? Brooke's look of horror made Meghan shrivel. "I went easy on the butter."

"Butter? Looks like I'm gonna have to go all Jillian Michaels on your—"

"Don't. Even. Say it."

They locked eyes for a full three seconds before bursting into laughter. Grinning, Brooke gripped her wrist and headed toward the cardio room. "Come on, love."

An hour later, the two finished their workout—Brooke glistening and Meghan sweating like a pig. But Meghan didn't mind because she was finally catching up to her friend on the dress rack. Or was that catching down? Either way, it was worth it.

Meghan emerged from the locker room, happy to check one item off her to-do list for the day.

"Come on, I'm buying lunch." Brooke slid her arm through Meghan's and steered her toward the exit.

"Have you looked at the clock? It's not even ten thirty. And my face is naked."

"I'm buying *brunch* then. And nobody else cares."

Meghan grimaced but gave in. "Fine, but I hope we don't see anyone we know."

They arrived at Hunny's for an egg-white omelet and O.J. The mascot bear greeted them with its armload of lollipops and the walls boasted an array of community photographs. The historic roots and down-home feel of the place filled Meghan with warm fuzzies. She'd take this place over a hoity-toity French Café any day.

Meghan skimmed the menu contents, stomach twisting at the sight of a Nutella crêpe. A rumbling sound emanated from across the table. She caught sight of Brooke's wide eyes and suppressed a laugh. "Girl, I don't think I've ever heard your stomach growl before!"

"Quiet, you." Brooke kept her gaze on her menu. "It was a big workout."

At least she wasn't the only one with an appetite today.

As she resigned herself to the veggie omelet, Meghan chewed the inside of her cheek. "Guess who my mom heard from last week." She glanced at Brooke. "My dad."

"Shut your face, seriously?"

She closed her eyes and nodded. "I guess I'm to expect a call from him soon. I have no idea why now, after three years with no more than a Christmas card." Hadn't he toyed with her heart enough as a child? She still felt the sting from every hastily scribbled note that came with the child support checks her mother received. One for Mom and one for her. Neither of them had gotten what they'd needed from the man.

"What on earth could he have to say? Think he wants to apologize and get a fluffy fresh start or something?"

Meghan had wondered that herself. She chewed her lip and stared at Brooke. "I don't know. And I'm not sure I'm ready to find out."

Brooke lifted one side of her mouth in a shrug. "Try not to worry about it for now. You're too stressed as it is, that's why you haven't been able to lose these last few pounds."

"Maybe." Stress hormones *should* take all the blame for that, shouldn't they? Although, she did have a bad snacking habit when she got immersed in a new writing project. Stupid Peanut Butter M&M's. But that was one confession Brooke wouldn't be hearing. At least she'd managed to avoid the bear claw that called her name at church last Sunday.

Meghan drew in a breath. "So anyway, what's new with you?"

"Oh, you know. Same ol', same ol'. The boys have been pestering Darren for a camping trip and finally wore him down. They've been scheming out their summer excursion ever since. I plan to spend that time at the beach or the pool so if you're gonna try to get me to read something, that'd be the time." She grinned right as their server arrived to take their orders.

As she returned her menu, Meghan leaned back in her seat and puffed out her cheeks, positive that after this meal she'd still be hungry.

"So, how's *your* book coming?"

Meghan perked up at that. "Great, actually. I'm so into this story. I can't stop thinking about it. I'm going to get the Corona Historical Preservation Society on board if I can. I just wish I could share it with Steve, ya know?"

"Yeah, I know. Men. He'll be more excited when he sees an email from the agent or something."

She paused and sent her naïve friend a bemused smile. "Yeah, I don't think so. If I make it to an endcap at Barnes and Noble, *maybe* he'll say 'Hey, good job' and pat my arm. These days he does his own thing and leaves me to mine."

Brooke reached out and squeezed Meghan's hand. "I'm sorry."

"It's fine, I guess." She shrugged. "I just wish . . . things feel . . . I don't know, *off*. We're barely a part of each other's lives anymore." She stopped and took a drink of water, swallowing down the uncomfortable truth that had somehow followed her to breakfast.

"Oh, I get it. Believe me. Darren used to take an interest in anything I talked about—including why Coach was better than

Prada. Now I have to do cartwheels naked to get his attention." She gave an exaggerated roll of her green eyes.

Meghan's cheek lifted in a half-smile. "Well, that oughtta do it."

"Brooke? Meghan?" A male voice drew her gaze.

"Tom! How are you?" Brooke smiled at the blond man Meghan recognized from church. As he and his dimples approached, all she wanted to do was hide.

Brooke smoothed her ponytail. "We just came from the gym. We must look a mess."

"Nah. Hey, are Steve and Darren planning to come to the Men's Workday at church on Saturday?" His hands slipped into his Dockers pockets.

"I know Darren is." Brooke glanced at her.

Meghan felt a tad warm under their waiting eyes. If she could pop off an answer like Brooke's, she'd gladly do it. But of course, she couldn't. "Uh, I don't think Steve even knows about it." How would he? Most often, they ran late for service, left immediately, and never looked at the bulletin.

Tom smiled, the fine lines around his eyes crinkling. "Tell him we need him, would ya?" He winked. "Those sets won't build themselves."

Though feeling far from hopeful, Meghan nodded. "I'll do my best."

Brooke glanced from Meghan to Tom. "Do you want to join us for breakfast?"

Oh, come on. Seriously? Meghan shot Brooke a covert death stare.

"No, I better not. But thanks." He rapped his knuckles on their table and grinned, showing off his dimples again. "Enjoy your food. See you Sunday."

"Tell Sonya we said hi." Brooke smiled and watched him as he lifted his hand and walked away.

Meghan waved, then gave her friend a pointed look. "I would have killed you had he stayed. I'm so embarrassed."

Brooke laughed. "Oh, hush. I didn't want to be rude."

Meghan shook her head. Brooke couldn't relate to the exposed feeling of unvarnished, pore-ridden skin. Hers was frozen in a perpetual state of peaches-and-cream.

"It could've been worse. I heard that Kiefer Sutherland was here with his band the other night."

"Kiefer Sutherland wouldn't have stopped at our table to say hi."

The waitress set down two mugs—coffee for Brooke, and hot tea for Meghan.

Brooke stirred in some Stevia while Meghan poured milk into her mug.

The rest of the day's to-do list snagged her thoughts. She had a daunting scene to tackle next and would spend half her morning on research. She set down her drink with a heavy sigh.

Brooke slurped her toxic waste. "What's up?"

Meghan shook her head. "Nothing. I just know zilch about cars in general, let alone old ones, and I need a lot of information on them for my next scene."

"Can't you just use the Internet?"

"For some of it, yes. But it's a lot of work. Wish I could skip ahead. It's much more fun writing the characters."

Brooke wiggled her eyebrows. "Especially the heroes? Hey, maybe you should give the main guy those dimples."

Meghan scrunched her forehead. "What dimples?"

Brooke cocked her head and gave her best 'are you kidding me?' look. "Uh, hello. Tom? *Mr.* Dimples? He'd make Mario Lopez jealous."

Meghan tucked in her chin and looked up at Brooke. "Uh, don't forget that ring on your finger, girlfriend." She glanced up as their food arrived. "Thanks."

Brooke arched one of her well-defined eyebrows as she placed her napkin on her lap. "Look but don't touch, I always say. And don't tell me you never noticed the dimples."

Meghan grinned from behind her mug. "Maybe I saw one of them."

"I knew it!"

She pursed her lips to reign in her smile. "So, you think I should give the hotshot racer dimples, then?"

"Well, *I* like them. But I don't read a ton of books. Are dimples hot in fiction?"

"Hot is hot in fiction." Meghan forked another bite of egg whites. What she craved was a stack of pancakes, but Brooke would have her head. The conversation slowed and quietness stretched between them as they ate.

"Shoulders."

"Huh?" Meghan looked up.

"Shoulders. I like broad shoulders. And strong hands." Brooke dabbed the corner of her mouth with her napkin. "For your story."

"Oh, gotcha." Meghan grinned. "Sounds good to me."

It all sounded good to her. Bringing characters to life was one of her favorite parts of writing. Was Russell sun-bleached-blond or dark and rugged? The girls exchanged their picks for the best leading men in Hollywood. Maybe Russell was a Tom Cruise type, a Maverick. Or a back-to-nature type like Matthew McConaughey. Antonio Banderas or Brad Pitt?

"Hey, was the US in the war yet in 1916?"

Brooke's forehead puckered. "The Civil War?"

"World War One!"

"How would I know? You're the history buff."

Meghan bit back a laugh, then shook her head. "Well, I gotta figure it out because if we were at war, it'll affect the plot for sure. Guess I'll add that to my list of research points. But it can wait until after I work on the hero."

Exercise—and all the talk of dimples—fueled Meghan's creativity. As she noshed on her breakfast, she chomped at the bit, eager to find out what Winifred thought of Russell.

Her leg bounced as the check arrived. "Hey listen, speaking of hot heroes, I gotta scoot. Writing calls!" She slung her purse over her shoulder and exited the booth.

Brooke signed the receipt. "Can't wait to read all about him. Keep me posted."

"Always." Meghan grinned. "Thanks for brunch."

1916

Winifred leaned over the Bearcat's doorless frame and dragged her fingertips across the driver's seat upholstery. A longing to brush aside the glass, climb aboard, and take the wheel between her hands almost overtook her. She imagined the Cat's six cylinders at peak speed vibrating the floorboards, the buzz of it traveling through the wheel to her palms, the wind whipping around the monocle and pressing the goggles into her cheeks.

"I know the feeling."

She snapped her gaze up.

Russell Keegan—*the* Russell Keegan, "racer extraordinaire" as the *Corona Herald* had coined him, not that she cared a flip for any of it—chuckled from the opposite side of the car, his eyes full on her.

She cleared her throat, dusted her hands against her legs, and told herself it was being caught drooling over his car that made her pulse kick up—not his striking face nor the way his shoulders strained at the seams of his tailored Norfolk jacket. No, it was that if he discovered how she yearned to get her mitts on this engine, it would be that much more embarrassing when she told him she wouldn't do it.

She'd coveted long enough. All business now, she directed her attention to the car's front end. The nearest side of the "dog house" hood lay at a warped angle, a detestable product of the vandalism. She *tsk*ed. "So tell me, pretty girl, what else did those bad men do to you?" She reached to lift away the sheet-metal cover.

Mr. Keegan came around the front of the car. "Let me."

It wasn't heavy, but for once she appreciated being treated like the lady her mother raised her to be—the lady beneath the mask of breadwinner. "Thank you." Her lashes fluttered.

What was wrong with her?

Maybe it was his darker features. She'd always been a sucker for a man with a hint of Italian heritage. Or was it the fame and fortune tacked onto his name? Nah, that couldn't be it. Whatever the cause, it had been a long time since the mere sight of a man had set her heart sputtering as Russell Keegan had as he'd sauntered toward her in the shop, the light from the lantern casting a warm glow across his olive-toned skin.

Thanks to the paper, she'd recognized his face in an instant. His bearing had betrayed his typical, cocky racer persona. She gave a low growl at the memory of his harsh treatment of her Dad's precious Lizzie.

Lifting the cover away created a breeze that bathed her in his scent—leather and the unmistakable, syrupy aroma of castor oil—a racecar's staple. It transported her to August 28, 1914, the day the Circle had last been cloaked in the white haze of exhaust and the stench of castor oil.

The day she'd made herself an unswerving promise.

Light from Lizzie's headlamps spilled across the massive engine, snapping Winifred back to the moment and sending her mind into suspension. "This . . . this is a . . . " She *knew* what she was seeing, but out of sheer disbelief, she looked to Mr. Keegan for verification.

A boyish grin lit his face. Hands in his pockets, he shrugged. "I never cared for the sky, but there's no reason the flyboys should have all the horsepower."

Her jaw hung at the sight before her. Where a factory-installed, Wisconsin T-head engine should be, sat one that belonged in an aeroplane. She swiveled to Mr. Keegan. What kind of man even *conceived* of such a thing? And what kind of results would it produce on a racecourse? "How much? A hundred?"

"Horsepower? Uh huh.

Winifred's low whistle was as long as the Lincoln Highway.

"Its RPMs top out at—"

"Twelve hundred. Yeah, I know. That's forty ponies over the average out on the track."

"Yeah, I know."

His flat tone prompted a smirk. Men hated it when they discovered she knew as much as they did. "I can't help wondering if this is even on the level. Do the officials know what you've got tucked under your hood?"

A suspicious pause was followed by hearty laughter. "How do you do it—talk engines in one breath and call a man a shyster in the next? And to his face!" He wagged his head. "I've never seen a lady quite like you." Sarcasm drowned his tone.

"What are you implying?"

He flipped up his palms, blocking her. "Hey, keep the war in Europe."

"You're avoiding the question. Did you mean to imply I'm not a lady?"

"I never said that."

"And I never called you a cheat."

"Fair enough."

"Your breeding leaves much to be desired, Mr. Keegan, but your Hall-Scott aero is quite the beauty."

Together, they leaned over the wheel and stared at the sleeping monster. Like a father soothing a hurt child, he stroked the rim of the grill, while she drank in the wonder of the engine itself, snipped sparkplug wires and all. Oh, the possibilities!

The deep whoosh of his steady breaths conked out in a great heave. "She's in a pretty bad way, huh?"

"Not as bad as you made it sound. Possible damage to the circulating pump." She pointed toward it, then shamed by the deplorable state of her nails, drew her hand back into the shadows. "Severed fuel lines, a couple cracked cylinder plugs."

He gave a slow shake of the head. "And add in the body repair—"

"What body repair?"

"The scratches. Didn't you see 'em?"

"Oh, well, yeah." She laughed. "But scratches won't keep a car off the Boulevard. Besides, the paint would never arrive in time. Mercedes Red, if I'm not mistaken."

Mouth ajar, he said nothing for a full three seconds, then found his tongue. "You're not, but that's beside the point. Chester said we'd need to order a new crank. Did you notice it's snapped at the base? Then there's the matter of managing to get the windscreen off, being warped as it is. The tires, and all the internal repair, to an *aero* engine, no less."

He ticked the flaws off on his fingers, unaffected by her contrived droll expression. "This is no joking matter, Miss Fisher. It's a doozie of a job for your average mechanic, much less for . . ." With a slow sweep of his hand, he took in all of her.

Angry heat licked up her cheeks. "For a woman?"

He grinned. "Is that what you are, beneath all that? I wasn't quite sure."

The words sliced clear to her core, and, heaven help her, tears pricked the backs of her lids. But could she blame the man? Seventeen months with a wrench in her grip had destroyed the young, carefree girl she'd once been. That girl was long buried beneath a mound of grease and the inescapable burden of responsibility.

She blinked away her humiliation and stiffened her back. "Insult me all you want, roadster. You're the one without wheels. Not me."

A glimmer of regret softened his features. He swept his newsboy cap from his head and twisted the wool between his hands. "Nine days. That's all I got, and my Cat's a heap of useless iron."

"She's still enchanting. Your dad was a fine motorist, and he had fine taste in cars. I was sorry to hear of his passing."

The statement gave him pause. "Yeah, he did. How'd you know about that?"

"Are you kidding? You're the talk of the town, you and your pathetic Bearcat. The car that 'made good in a day,'" she quoted the Stutz slogan, "but couldn't hold up its first night in Corona."

He crammed the cap back on his head and flicked up the tip with a finger. "That's what they're saying about her?" He worked his lips around a pucker.

Winifred stroked the glossy red hood, fingers picking up the rougher texture of the black number twenty-three occupying half its surface. "Of course, it isn't *her* fault men are beasts."

Her reply relaxed the ever-straining cords in his neck. It seemed he preferred the male gender be put down over his beloved Cat—a choice she couldn't disagree with.

"You're right about one thing."

His brows arched.

"It *is* a doozie of a job. But I'm not your average mechanic."

He propped an elbow against the fender. "Is that so? How do you suppose?"

"In addition to motor cars, I service crop dusters. It's been a couple years, but I don't guess much has changed. In my shop, your Cat would be up and running in under nine days."

"As if I would be crazy enough to offer you the job."

Air spurted from her nose. "As if you could afford me."

His instant grin suggested he was a man in love with a challenge. Judging by his choice of leather loafers and top-of-the-line cars, money wasn't an issue. Just the same, she toyed with a few numbers in her mind. How much could she get out of him, and, more important, how many debt collectors would it satisfy?

She shook the ridiculous notion from her head and nodded toward the engine. "Twelve cylinders." It was a job keeping the childish awe from her voice. "Nice addition. What did the extras set you back? Two bucks twenty-five? Fifty?"

He shrugged. "Knowing Pop, he wouldn't have blinked at a full three hundred. Nothing deterred him from what he wanted."

"Must be dandy to be rolling in the dough."

Gaze riveted to the driver's seat, Russell appeared not to hear.

"Mr. Keegan?"

"I'll give you three hundred."

"Excuse me?" Winifred's lungs halted mid-suck. Was the man offering her the job? For three hundred dollars?

"Three hundred, plus whatever you need for parts."

The sap was willing to pay her *nine months'* wages for the privilege of working on his car.

Russell squinted and scrubbed at his forehead. "Look, I'm desperate. So here's the deal. Half upfront, and if you manage it in time, I'll double it before I pull to the starting line." He looked her up and down with a slight shake of his head. "Naturally, I'll expect to be included in every decision. Not a wrench gets turned without my say-so."

Winifred's tongue went dry. She clicked her jaw shut. Arrogance and demeaning remarks aside, she had never been given a better offer. How could she turn it down?

Her mother's tear-streaked face flashed before her mind's eye, twisting Winifred's gut. *That's how.* "No. I won't do it."

Russell blinked several times before an easy smile shifted his cheeks. "A haggler, eh? I can admire that. Three-twenty-five. What do you say?"

Winifred closed her eyes. Her shoulders sagged under the weight of disappointment. She never should have agreed to come look at the Stutz. She'd understood it would be hard to walk away, but the temptation to get a close-up, to advise about the care of one of the nation's top racing machines, had been too much.

She turned her back on his Cat before opening her eyes and dragging her feet toward the Tin Lizzie.

"Where are you going?"

"I said I'd look at the car. Never said anything about fixing it." It might have been conniving of her, but then she'd never expected such a conceited prig to offer her the job. With a foot on Lizzie's runner, she gripped the frame.

He clamped a hand over her arm, halting her escape. "What? You specifically said you'd get it done in under nine days. Those were your exact words. Are you a liar, or is this some womanish scheme to weasel more money out of me? If that's the case, no need for theatrics. Just tell me. Is it four hundred you're after?"

"Could. I said *could*. Not would. And I'm not a liar. Ask any motorist around here. He'll tell you. I'm able to fix your car in the exact manner I said, but it doesn't mean I *will*. I've got standards, and supporting idiotic ventures that do nothing more than expand already over-inflated egos doesn't line up. I said I'd have a look, and I did. My assessment is it can be fixed in time. That doesn't mean I'll be the one doing it."

With a twist of her arm, Winifred freed it and lifted herself into the car. "I'm sorry if you feel misled. But—"

"If?" His voice rattled her eardrums.

"Fine! I'm sorry you feel misled, but I refuse to associate myself with this race or anyone participating in it. That's something else you can ask anyone around here, including the *gentlemen* down at Thomas Drug, who were probably slapping each other on the back and hooting with laughter, imagining this very moment." With shaking fingers, she fumbled for the choke.

Russell took a backward step, and she breathed a sigh of relief. She'd had no assurances he was a gentleman.

With the engine tuned and roaring, she chanced a last look at him. Their eyes met, and instead of anger and shock, as she'd expected, she found weariness and disappointment furrowing his brow. Guilt stabbed at her. "Mr. Keegan, I . . . "

He waited, his level gaze not condemning, yet not forgiving.

It was on her tongue to offer a sincere apology when he shoved his hands into his pockets and lifted his chin. "I've seen enough of the world to not be surprised by manipulative women, no matter the role they play. Get on home, Miss Fisher. Scrub off some of that filth and see if it inspires you to act like a lady."

Present Day

Woo hoo hoo! Did he really just say that? Meghan shook her head, laughing at the torment she had put her characters through. What would it be like to have the guts to blurt out whatever she wanted to? To say exactly what she felt?

Rex was barking. Probably had been for a long time. Squeals and screeches sounded from the other side of the sliding glass door. The girls on the trampoline.

"Yes!" Steve sat nearby, another game on the screen. "That's how you do it!"

When Meghan was fifteen, basketball season meant blushing as varsity point guard Steve Townsend pointed to her in the stands after each shot he made. Then being seen holding hands with the senior in front of her freshman class. Now, basketball was one more thing to compete against for Steve's attention.

The halftime buzzer sounded as Faith and Zoey tumbled in, all out of breath with giggles. Meghan's heart smiled seeing them play together. They could be sweet when they wanted to. Faith leaned down and whispered to Zoey, who covered her grin with her hands and bobbed her head.

Meghan narrowed her eyes at them. What were those girls up to? She watched them count with fingers.

One. Two . . .

On three, both girls ran and leapt onto Steve, squealing with laughter.

"Hey! Knock it off! Get down," Steve snapped, widening Meghan's eyes.

The girls slid off the couch to their feet as Meghan sucked in a breath.

"We want to play with you, Daddy," came Zoey's little voice.

"Not now, okay? Maybe later."

Faith ran a piece of hair through her fingers as she glanced at the screen. "But, it's halftime. You always say wait 'til halftime."

"I know, but I can't right now. Sorry. Go play something else. We'll read a book later."

"Okay," they said in unison, then slunk away down the hall.

Meghan's throat clamped and in a breath, she was nine years old again, walking up her dad's driveway, eager for a weekend with his undivided attention. She couldn't wait to show him the surprise she'd brought—*Black Beauty*. They'd stay up late into the night reading. Then they'd take it to the beach the next morning and sit in their lawn chairs drinking cans of grape soda.

Instead, her dad spent that evening watching football from his recliner. Next day she was dragged to a boring T-ball game for four-year-old Patrick. The promised trip to the beach? Dad spent the first hour playing catch with the little usurper. Then just as she convinced her dad to dig up some sand crabs, the kid got himself stung by a bee and *Angela* said it was time to go.

Meghan could've dealt with all that, but what she couldn't deal with was watching that presumptuous little boy crawl up into *her* dad's lap the way she used to do.

The sting behind her eyes now was the same as it was then. Was that a shadow of remorse she saw passing over Steve's features, or her own wishful thinking? She took in the sight of her husband stretched out on the couch, one arm bent under his head, pointing the remote, staring at the TV, oblivious to the pain he'd just caused his daughters.

How could she bear watching her girls head for the same fate as she'd endured? Steve seemed so blind to it. He needed to lift his head and look around before it was too late. To get involved. And she wasn't about to sit by while he put on blinders.

Meghan got up and went to the fridge, pulled out a can of soda, and approached Steve. "Thirsty?"

"Oh. Yeah, thanks, Meg." He popped open the can and drank deeply.

She cleared her throat. "So, I don't know if you know this but there's a men's workday coming up at the church on Saturday."

Steve resettled into the cushions but didn't respond.

"Brooke's husband is going—you remember Darren. They're building sets for the kids' play next month."

The silence coming off him was underscored by the tightening of his jaw but she wasn't deterred. She took her seat and continued, forcing a brightness to her tone. "I said I'd talk to you about it. They could use your expertise."

"I don't think so."

That quick? "Why not?"

"Because that's not how I want to spend my Saturday. I build stuff all week long and I want a break from it when I can get one. Is that okay?"

"But this is for the church. We said we were going to get more involved. And this is perfect for you." Her hands rose out of her lap in pleading gestures all on their own.

"I'm sure they'll get it done without me."

"Yeah but if you're there it will get done better. And maybe we'll get to know some people." Why wouldn't Steve do this?

He huffed and flipped to another TV program.

"All you do anymore is lie around on this couch. This is important to me." She hated that her climbing pitch made her sound like a child.

"And it's important to *me* to unwind on the weekends when I can. You know, like a Sabbath?"

Ouch. The verbal slap stung. "Wow, Steve. That's just—"

"Look, I'm sorry." He released a sigh that sounded more frustrated than regretful. "But this is the first Saturday I've had off in nearly two months."

She was well aware. Shaking her head, she stood and crossed the room, then stopped at the entry to the hall. "So you won't even think about it?"

"Nope." The way he stared at the screen made Meghan wonder if he even saw it. She wouldn't be surprised if he didn't. Seemed he didn't see anything anymore.

Bitter heat radiated up her neck and she spun around before the tears landed on her cheeks. She marched down the hall to their bedroom and swung the door, but slowed it before it slammed behind her. Winifred would've let it slam.

"Unbelievable." That hadn't gone well at all.

She was failing. At everything. What was she supposed to do now? Her girls were losing precious opportunities to bond with their dad, and the man she'd built a life with was no longer participating in it. Was she being selfish? Maybe she shouldn't have pushed so hard.

But should she just sit there and . . . and . . . *knit* while her family fell apart? It wasn't her fault she was the only one who seemed to notice that something had to change. It was all on her, and she was doing her best, but getting nowhere.

"What now, God?"

She plopped onto her bed, praying apologies mingled with justifications. How long she stared at the walls of that room she wasn't aware. But it was long enough to give herself a good scolding. She shouldn't have gotten emotional like that. You catch more flies with honey than vinegar, and she must smell like Easter egg dye right about now. She crossed her arms over her chest and pouted. She'd forgotten where she put the stinkin' honey.

She wanted her marriage back.

Sighing, she rose and padded across the room in her bare feet to the walk-in closet. Hanger after hanger slid from left to right. She paused, fingering leather sleeves. Leaning forward, she inhaled. Deeply. The scent of warmth and belonging and safety.

The scent of home.

Meghan slipped the varsity jacket off the hanger and rubbed the wool against her cheek. It caught the first drop of what promised to be a storm of tears.

"You promised."

The gruff man out in the living room was not the one she'd fallen in love with in high school. After three agonizing years, Steve had come home from college for her high school graduation. It began as one of the happiest days of her life. But ended in heartache when her dad didn't show up for the ceremony. Steve had been wearing this very jacket when he pulled her into his arms and dried her tears with kisses. Gentle as always. But she'd felt his anger in the tightening of his muscles as she sobbed into his chest.

He had held her face in his hands and looked into her soul. "I will *always* be there for you, Meg." He ran his thumb under her lashes. "I promise. For you and . . . and our children."

She had blinked away the moisture and stared at him then. Unsure if she was reading his meaning correctly. Hoping beyond reason. But it was ludicrous.

He nodded. "Marry me. Now. Don't make me wait to start taking care of you."

Words failed and she stood silent, unable to make her lips move. Until he covered them with his own. Then her lips, her heart, and everything else in her shouted *yes*.

They drank each other in with that kiss. His hands in her hair, her body molding to his, hungry for the promise of their wedding night.

But twelve years later he seemed to have lost his appetite. For her. For their life. And those whispered promises had slipped away.

Meghan replaced the jacket, then entered the bathroom and grabbed a handful of tissues. She sat on the toilet seat, blowing her nose. Steve wouldn't come to check on her. No doubt he had already forgotten their squabble and was cheering through the second half of the game.

1916

Tepid water poured over Winifred's hands, beading over the layers of grease and leaving a grimy film in her mother's porcelain sink. Tears dripped from the tip of her nose as she ferociously scrubbed at her one-time impeccable nails. The black embedded beneath them refused to be moved, much like the humiliation that still burned her cheeks.

"Of all the mean-spirited, thoughtless things to say . . ." An ugly little squeak twisted her words to a ragged halt. After a quick inspection nearer the dim light, she tossed the nailbrush into the sink and grabbed the bar of Fels-Naptha soap for another go-round.

She halted mid-scrub. If she was so all-fired angry at the haughty Mr. Keegan, why was she following his counsel? She should be dipping her hands in engine grease, just to spite him.

A sob caught her in the throat. "Because he's right." Her wail rose above the sound of splattering water.

"Winifred, why are you crying? Who's right?" Her mother entered the kitchen, the sash to her housecoat dragging the floor.

Winifred turned to her mother's open arms and cried against her shoulder as she hadn't done in a decade. "Mr. Keegan." Her bitter, tear-drenched accusation stiffened her mother's back.

Her mom took her by the arms and leveled mama-bear eyes on her. "And just who is Mr. Keegan?"

"An upscale bigot. He said I was dirty and not a lady."

"Seems I remember a certain little boy making a similar statement some years back."

Winifred managed a watery smile. She remembered it, too. Second grade, when it turned out Bobby Tidwell had a crush on her. Still did, despite the bad blood between their families.

"He came by for a visit this evening."

"Who? Bobby?"

Momma nodded.

Winifred had yet to hear her mother say Bobby's name. Not since the accident, anyway. Oddly enough, her mother didn't protest his frequent, unannounced visits. "Boys say those things as a way of flirting."

Winifred gave a harsh laugh. "Bobby, maybe. But no one could spin Russell Keegan's words into a romantic notion. He despises me, pure and simple."

And wasn't it just like Winifred to chase away the dashing ones?

The deep lines around her mother's mouth eased until a tiny smile took their place. "Handsome, is he, this Mr. Keegan?"

"Well . . . yes. I suppose a *lady* might think so." Winifred scrunched her brow. A cup of spiced tea would do a world of good, but it had been months since they'd been able to afford the luxury. "Did you see his photograph in the paper?"

Her mother patted her arm, then stepped across the kitchen and plucked the last lemon from the fruit bowl on the counter. "You know I don't read the paper."

At least not since the mayor had announced the races were on again this year. Winifred nodded. "Then how did you know—?"

The scrape of wood against wood drowned her out. Their fight with the utensil drawer was never-ending and more irritating by the week. Winifred might be able to fix it, if her time weren't eaten up by the shop's needs.

"I'd help, but . . . " Winifred splayed her filthy hands.

"No, no, I've got it. Just step aside in case it goes flying–and me with it." After a minute of the usual wiggle and bang, the drawer gave way with a rush, stopping short of spilling its contents onto the floor. Her mother's shoulders drooped. "If your father were alive . . . "

"I know, Momma. It never would have gotten this bad." The word *it* encompassed so much more than the drawer.

Her mother's gaze flitted about the room, looking anywhere but at the facts. The main one being that George could run the shop—*and* fix the drawer—if he ever decided to come home from wherever it was he'd gotten himself to.

Wedging her lower lip between her teeth, Winifred waited for her mother to say something—a mention of her brother, the whisper of his name, a brief acknowledgement of his existence. Anything.

Instead, she hunched over and dug in the drawer's depths until she uncovered a paring knife.

"My hands will be dirty again in a few hours. No sense wasting that lemon."

"Nonsense." Her mother's knife dug into the peel and zesty citrus filled Winifred's senses.

"We've got a grove on every corner in this town. Lemons are a dime a dozen. You've got to keep these hands conditioned for the Los Angeles Chamber Orchestra, and we have a gentleman to impress." Her mother winked and waved her knife toward the sink.

With her mother facing away, Winifred rolled her eyes. "As if either were possible," she mumbled, sticking her hands over the sink. "That dream will only ever be a dream, and even if I wanted to impress him, Russell Keegan wouldn't give me the time of day. He *is* my better. Classes above me. Heir to a millionaire, no doubt. At least he carries himself as though he is. And the way he dresses . . . "

Her mother scoured the top of her hand with a lemon wedge, cutting through the hideous, stubborn grease. Not that it mattered whether her hands were clean. She was poor and desperate enough to tarnish her complexion and her reputation doing a man's job, and that was all a well-to-do gent like Mr. Keegan would ever see when he looked at her with those disdainful eyes.

"Winifred May, you've spent the last seventeen months dodging insults from men who think themselves your better. Not a one of them has brought you to tears or made you swoon. Until this one. So either you've reached your limit, or he's a looker."

Her backbone went rigid. "I'm not swooning. I *don't* swoon, Mother."

Her mother arched an eyebrow. "You sighed."

"I didn't!" Had she?

"You did." She dropped Winifred's hand and motioned for the other.

She complied, wincing as the juice found a cut on her thumb. "If I'm swooning or *sighing* over anything, it's his car. You should see it. A Stutz. A Stutz *Bearcat*," Winifred amended, not that her mother would recognize the name. "Glossy red. So red, it glows. You've never seen such vibrant paint on a car. And, Momma, listen to this. He installed an aero engine. Or . . . Chester did. Regardless"—she waved her free hand through the air—"it's a monster of a machine just begging to hit the Boulevard. She's banged up pretty bad, but nothing I couldn't fix."

Uncontainable enthusiasm poured from her. "Did you know that before the first model even had its trial run, the Bearcat made a name for itself by coming in eleventh place at the Brickyard in Indy? Imagine that. Eleventh, and not even a proven model."

"'The car that made good in a day.'" Her mother sing-songed the slogan while opening the faucet. "Rinse. And don't look at me that way. Just because I don't have a knack for engines, doesn't mean I don't listen. Your father read that headline to me. It was a Sunday. I remember, because he made us late for church."

Her mother's chuckle sloughed tension from Winifred's body like the black water streaming from her hands and spiraling down the drain.

Her lids drifted closed at the fresh, silken feel of her hands, then popped open at her mother's sharp intake of breath.

"If Mr. Keegan owns a racecar, then he's a racer?"

Winifred nodded.

A wedge hit the bottom of the empty waste bin with a resounding *thwack*. "You could have mentioned that before I cut the lemon."

"He offered me three hundred to fix it."

"Three hundred dollars?" Her gaze went distant, as though her mind had left the room for a visit to the bank. She blinked and brought it back, along with her usual vehemence. "There isn't a purse in Corona fat enough to entice us to support those ghastly races."

"Which is why I turned him down."

"Of course you did. I didn't doubt that for a second, even though you're the only machinist in the county who could fix it." Pride beamed from her mother's voice, but she had a smidge more confidence in Winifred than she should.

The smile Winifred attempted failed to hold. "He would have gone to four."

"It makes no difference." Her mother's staccato tone punctured the air. "Mildred and Winifred Fisher are *through* with the races."

But it *did* make a difference. Winifred hated the races as much as her mother, but she also had a healthy respect for hunger, debt, and their collectors. "I know. And things aren't so bad. Mr. Shaheen will be making payment tomorrow, and—" Winifred's mind seized up.

"What is it?"

"Mr. Shaheen's Dodge. I haven't finished with it!" Her gaze tumbled to her squeaky pink hands, and she heaved a sigh.

The sooner she got over there, the sooner she'd be done.

The garage welcomed her with its usual warm memories and frigid reality. Breezing through the back door past her dusty violin case, she chose to dwell on the latter. After a quick kiss to her fingertips, she tapped the photograph reigning over the cluttered desk. "Hi, Daddy. Don't worry. I didn't forget."

She was grabbing a handful of curls to tuck beneath her cap when a clatter sounded from the bay. Her hand stilled mid-shove. Her heart lurched.

"Hello?" She palmed the nearest tool—a hefty wrench. *God, please let it be an animal.* Her thoughts zipped from the scorched rodent to the handsome face that witnessed its extraction. "Mr. Keegan, is that you? Come back to up your offer?" Her jittery laugh shot tingles of fear down her arm. She gripped the wrench and raised it to chest level, then took two steps into the inky bay.

At her presence, the clatter ceased.

Mr. Keegan would have responded by now.

"Is anyone there?" It could have been a rat. Or any one of the thousand-plus strangers already filling Corona's streets. Either way, she refused to take one step farther until she'd identified the source of the noise.

Her eyes struggled to adjust to the dark. The lamp sat across the way, its silent glass catching the moonbeams that scattered through the solitary window.

Time hobbled past in rhythm with her erratic heartbeat. Her muscles burned from holding the wrench aloft, and yet, not another sound had been heard. Relinquishing her fear, she dragged in a deep breath, spun to reenter the office, and collided with a wall of unyielding man.

Her lungs exploded in a whoosh, and the wrench tumbled from her feeble grasp.

An arm whipped around her lower back, clamping her against a soft chest. No sooner had she readied for a shriek than a hand mashed her lips against her teeth. Blood, mingling with his briny sweat, trickled down her throat in a failed attempt to swallow.

A shadowy face, not much higher than her own, lowered to within inches of her ear. "So there *are* curves under this material, after all." A Latino accent tinged his sandpaper voice. When his grip around her waist tightened, she whimpered.

One of her arms lay trapped between their torsos. The other flailed against his shoulder. "Do not worry, *muñeca.* I got orders not to do nothing to you. Yet." His sour chuckle suctioned the strength from her knees. With little effort, he took on her weight. Her ribs screamed against the vise of his grip, and she thrashed to find new footing.

When his mouth crammed against her ear, spewing hot breath down her neck, she froze. "I got a message from El Jefe. He says he been real patient, your *mamá* being a widow and all. But he is done with the waiting. You got two weeks to pay up. *Oyes?*"

Pay up?

George.

The man gave her a hard jerk. "Hear?"

"How much?" She mumbled the question against his palm.

He slipped his hand to her throat. "Any more than a whisper, and I will squeeze the life from you like juice from a grape."

"And what will El Jefe say when he finds out you ignored his orders?"

His fingers pinched the skin at her neck. "Do not tempt me to find out."

Chapter Three

Present Day

The last cookie slid onto the tray and Meghan bit her lip to keep from popping one in her mouth. Good thing they weren't oatmeal scotties or she'd be in big trouble. She yanked a length of plastic wrap from its roll, covered the treats, and glanced at the clock. Five minutes until Brooke showed up.

She dropped the spatula and baking sheet into the sink and turned the faucet to hot. Steam rose like her frustration. For days she'd kept silent, giving God room to work. But the bad vibrations still hung in the air between her and Steve. The baking sheet got the first scrubbing, then she set it on the counter to dry.

"You made cookies?" Steve's voice came from the far end of the kitchen behind her.

She hesitated, keeping her back to him. "Yep."

"Any dough left?"

She grabbed the mixing bowl, several globs still clinging to its sides, and shoved it under the running water. "No, sorry." Childish, but he deserved it.

Back straight, she continued attacking the dishes. If speed-washing dishes were a sport, she'd qualify for the Olympics.

"What are these for?" He'd moved closer, the scent of his aftershave swirling onto the scene.

She stared into the sudsy water, refusing to look at him and allow the hurt to leak through her anger. "The men at church. One of us should make an appearance." She winced, wishing she could take the words back. She pictured him nodding and biting the inside of his cheek. She hadn't meant to bait him. Her eyes closed and she exhaled through her nose.

"Hmph. Okay then." What was that in his tone? Guilt? Hurt?

Turn around. Look at him. Tell him you're sorry. Her feet were soldered to the floor like one of Steve's custom metal brackets.

As his footsteps receded into the den, she turned off the water and hung her head. She was drying her hands when her pocket vibrated, making her jump. Brooke was outside waiting.

Meghan sniffed then slung her purse over her shoulder, grabbed the tray, and headed out the front door. The path carried her through dry, crunchy grass and she groaned. The sprinklers hadn't come on this morning again? Was Steve turning them off on purpose, or was the timer broken? *Ugh.* The lawn was going to seed. It was embarrassing.

But she wouldn't bring that up today. Not with the way she'd started the morning. Blinking all the way to Brooke's car, she hoped her mascara wasn't smudged.

"Good morning, sunshine!"

Brooke sure was chipper.

Meghan lowered herself into her seat. "Morning." Hopefully, Brooke wouldn't notice that her smile was a tad forced. She arranged her purse near her feet and rested the cookies on her lap as they pulled away from the curb.

"So, what did you make?" Brooke dropped her gaze to the tray Meghan held, nodding her head of glossy, chunky curls.

"Standard. Chocolate chip. Is that new lipstick?"

"Oh. Yeah. You like it? It was my free gift with purchase when I went shopping yesterday."

"Looks good on you." Meghan flipped open the mirror in the visor and made a face at her own bland reflection. Leave it to Brooke to glam it up for a Saturday of errands.

She huffed. "Curse you, Brooke Wilder." Her and her glorious mane. Had she lacquered it this morning or what?

"Oh, stop." Brooke laughed, her pearly whites gleaming.

The shiniest lipstick in Meghan's purse was a tube of Carmex but she put it on anyway. She fluffed her bangs and pinched her cheeks, but she couldn't do anything about the dumpy T-shirt. Why hadn't Brooke texted to let her know she'd be in an adorable, figure-enhancing camisole and skinny jeans? Meghan didn't even *own* a pair of skinny jeans. Had to be skinny first.

Despair rounded her shoulders. She shouldn't have pushed Steve's buttons like that. She should have left some cookies for him. Kissed him goodbye. She wasn't helping anything. And maybe she could try a little harder to look good for him. Like Brooke did for Darren.

She shut the mirror cover and sighed. "I destroyed Steve's dough."

Brooke furrowed her brow. "What does that mean?"

Meghan slid a guilty look to Brooke. "He asked for some cookie dough. I stuck the bowl under running water and told him there wasn't any left."

"Ha! That's hilarious."

Meghan shook her head and drew in her breath. "I think I'm pushing him away, Brooke. I feel like he's losing interest. But then I get so angry . . ." She fiddled with the treats in her lap.

Brooke reached over and patted her hand. "It'll be fine, you're making too much of it. Really."

"You think so?"

"Totally. Now if you start slipping arsenic into his cookies, *then* we have a problem."

Meghan couldn't help laughing. Maybe Brooke was right and she was blowing things out of proportion. Withholding cookie dough wasn't the worst thing in the world for a wife to do.

They pulled up to the church and parked. Brooke grabbed a few bags of Subway sandwiches from the back seat, Meghan took the cookies, and they got out. A few guys headed their way, humongous grins decorating their faces.

A man in his mid-fifties was the first to greet them. "Provisions!"

"Thought you could use some." Brooke handed off the subs and the man marched in triumph toward the huddle of guys in front of the building.

Double-Dimple Tom approached. "Hey, Meghan, is Steve coming?"

Meghan's insides gurgled. "Uh, no. You know he wanted to. But . . . he's not feeling very well today." It was a small lie. A fib. A fiblet, more like.

"Ah, that's too bad. Tell him I'll be praying for him."

Meghan's conscience burned. "Of course." Her gaze shot to Brooke but her friend's face didn't betray her in the least.

Tom turned to Brooke and smiled, dimples deepening. "Darren's in the main sanctuary."

"Okay, thanks." Brooke tucked her hair behind her ear and tilted her head. "How's the project coming? You look like you're working hard."

"Yeah, you know we men can flex a little muscle for the church now and then." He curled a bicep and winked. Brooke laughed.

"Anything we can do to help?" Meghan dipped her head toward the sanctuary.

"This is all the help we need." He grinned and reached out his hands. "Here let me."

Tom took the cookie tray and they all headed to the church's small kitchen. When they got there, the subs were already half gone and several men grunted their thanks through mouthfuls of food.

Meghan chatted and made nice, but all the while she felt Steve's glaring absence. Construction, design . . . these were his specialty. Why didn't her husband want to get involved at church, serve and make friends there? That had been their plan but he wasn't even trying. Maybe she *wasn't* sorry about the dough.

Eager to get out of there, she looked to Brooke. "Should we find your hubby?"

"Okay. Good work, guys. Keep it up." Brooke flashed a bright smile at the dedicated dudes before turning to go. Meghan followed.

They wandered to the sanctuary where Darren was helping arrange heavy set pieces on the stage. He was a striking man. Brown wavy hair, five o'clock shadow, perfectly imperfect teeth. He and Brooke made the ideal "it" couple.

"Hey, Darren, food's in the kitchen. Meghan even brought homemade chocolate chip cookies."

Darren trotted down the stage steps toward them. "Thanks, babe." He kissed Brooke's cheek.

She shrugged. "Sure."

Babe. Meghan focused on the apostle's fishing boat being pushed across the stage. When had Steve last called her anything besides Meg?

Darren turned to her. "Hey, Meghan. Sorry Steve couldn't make it."

Me too. She shifted her weight and twisted her mouth to one side. "Yeah. He's not feeling good."

Brooke cleared her throat. "So anyway, you better hurry if you want something to eat. They're making short work of it."

"Don't have to tell *me* twice." He looked toward the stage. "Hey man, time for some grub!"

Electric blue eyes appeared from behind the scenery.

"Right behind ya." The eyes came with a rich, melodic voice.

Mr. Blue-eyes moved closer and smiled at Meghan with an unwavering, magnetic gaze.

She forced herself to blink. Looked down at the carpet. But her eyes were pulled back up as if against her will. Darren was introducing Brooke, and then the man extended his hand to Meghan, flustering her as he locked those luminous irises on hers. The directness of his gaze spiked her pulse.

Oh, Lord have mercy.

Shame flooded her as she released his hand. Despite the quips she exchanged with Brooke, Meghan was never one to indulge in "looking without touching." Even for a man who had such admirable features to look at.

She swallowed her . . . *appreciation* . . . and avoided further eye contact.

"Thanks, ladies." The mystery man dipped his head.

"Sure." Meghan hoped her tone was nonchalant rather than terse.

Darren lifted his hand. "Bye, hon—I'll be home in a couple hours." He pulled open the sanctuary door. "Good to see you, Meghan."

"Oh, Darren?" Brooke paused. "I have to pick out a birthday gift for a friend so you might get home before me."

"Oh okay, have fun."

"I will." She linked her arm through Meghan's and steered her out the door leading outside. "You sure you can't go shopping with me today?"

Meghan shook her head. Still in recovery mode, she forced a casual tone. "No can do. Promised the girls I'd paint their nails, and after that I've got a scene to finish."

Plus she had to try and fix the mess with Steve. The churning in her stomach told her so.

Meghan lifted a lock of light brown hair and pulled it into Faith's french braid.

"So what do you girls think?" They sat on a fluffy pink throw rug in the center of the girls' room. Meghan caught Zoey's gaze in the mirrored closet door. "What should Winifred do?"

"Hmm." Zoey tapped her chin with her purple nail and stared at the ceiling. "She should call 9-1-1. And maybe tell her mom."

Meghan stifled a laugh. "Think so?"

Faith pulled her knees up to her chest and rested her chin on them. "I think she should make up with the boy. And then he could beat up that bully."

Make up with him. Meghan's smile faded. "Well, they're pretty mad at each other. He hurt her feelings pretty bad." She blinked several times, then finished off the braid and twisted the band around the end.

"Yeah but if he knew she was in trouble, maybe he'd be nicer. And they could make up."

Meghan ran her hand over Faith's hair. "Maybe they will."

"One of them just needs to say sorry."

Meghan turned a serious smile at both her daughters. "I think you're right. When did you get so smart?" She hugged Faith and then pulled Zoey into her lap, covering her cheek in kisses. "You have got to stop growing, baby girl. I'm not ready for you to be so big."

Her chest burned. Her family meant more to her than anything in the world, but it was sagging. If she and Steve weren't careful, it would give way. She left the girls to their dress-up games and drifted down the hall in search of her husband. The *tat, tat, tat* drew her toward the back of the house.

Meghan stepped out onto the patio and closed the sliding glass door behind her. The scent of the neighbor's gardenias met her. Steve sat on the white wicker loveseat, a basketball in his hands and a faraway look in his eye.

"Hey." She swallowed and wrapped her arms around herself. "What are you up to?" *Are you thinking about us?*

"Nothing." He bounced the ball between his feet a few times, then caught it and spun it around in his hands.

Meghan perched beside him, tense. Looking for words. "So—"

"I always wanted a hoop out here."

A hoop? "Oh . . . well, maybe we can get one someday." Didn't he notice the elephant on the porch? The distance between them? She tore her eyes from the thirsty peonies hanging nearby and fixed them on Steve. "I . . . I'm sorry about this morning."

He squinted out over the withered yard, then looked her direction. "Yeah. Me too." He scanned her face, then tipped a corner of his mouth. "No biggie."

Meghan blinked. That was it? No biggie? She was stretching out her hand across a widening gulf, and he was feigning ignorance. Was he really that blind to the growing fissure in their marriage? To her feelings?

Dejected, but unwilling to give up, she studied her palms. "Are you hungry? I could make a tuna melt for lunch." Didn't they say the way to man's heart was through his stomach?

He squeezed her shoulder. "No, thanks. I had leftover chicken while you were in with the girls." The wicker squeaked and groaned as he pushed himself up. "I gotta look over some factory paperwork. Schedules and contracts and inventory type stuff."

What did that look in his eyes mean? He bounced the basketball a couple times, then let it roll across the cracked pavement to wherever it would choose to stop.

Meghan felt as though her fingers were slipping off the rope she was clinging to. She rubbed her palms on her legs and stood. "Do you want me to help you? It's been awhile but I used to know my way around the factory's paperwork."

He smiled. "Nah, that's okay. You can work on your book. I got it." He put his hand on the door handle. "Thanks for offering though."

It felt like a dismissal. A rejection disguised as kindness. "Okay." Meghan bit her lip. Her gaze flicked to his hand, the door about to open. Another about to close. Gathering her determination, she took a step forward, closing the distance. Praying it was more than a physical one. She reached for him, pressed her lips to his. They puckered in response. It was quick. Familiar. Robotic.

His eyes looked like maybe he was sorry, maybe he knew she felt rebuffed, but he just gave a closed smile, tapped her nose, then slipped into the house. The door slid closed and Meghan watched through the glass as her husband's form moved farther and farther away.

Disorientation kept her in place a full thirty seconds. She'd tried. Lord knew she'd tried. But they seemed to be speaking different languages. Would their souls ever connect again?

Her heart trembled. *Do you see me here, Father? Don't you care?*

She straightened her back and headed for her bedroom. Her book was calling, but first it was time to pull on some workout clothes, lace up her tennies, and do some sweating.

She fit her pink ear buds in and turned on her iPod. Then she took off. Alone with the sidewalk and her music, Meghan jogged through the streets of Corona. Reshaping her body. Reinventing her life.

And plotting her novel.

1916

Russell dropped to his hotel bed and let his head fall heavily onto the pillow. The feather mattress hugged his body, suffocating him. He bounced back up and resumed pacing, thoughts of the devious little mechanic chasing him around the confines of his room.

Fred. What kind of name was that for a lady, anyway? And what sort of lady dirtied herself with a man's job? Not the sort he intended to associate himself with, whether she could fix his Cat as she'd claimed or not. He considered himself a man of the times, but his tolerance ended with women who pushed for recognition in a man's world.

No, he didn't need her. In fact, tomorrow, he'd have the Cat towed to Los Angeles where he would pray to God to find a mechanic who knew aero engines. It would cost him time and money and perhaps the race, but he couldn't give up now. Not this close to Pop's dream.

That decided, he expected the nausea turning his stomach to subside, but it didn't. He groaned as he recognized the feeling—all too well.

A vandal had ruined his car, a drugstore full of people had made him the butt of a cruel joke, and a pseudo-mechanic had toyed with his mind. But his predominant emotion?

Guilt.

Over his own errant tongue.

He'd often been accused of being oblivious of a woman's delicate sensibilities, and just as often, he couldn't deny the truth of it. Clumsy he may be, but hateful? Never. Pop would have had him over a barrel.

Growling at himself and the entire maddening situation, he jammed his hands into his trouser pockets. The coins at the bottom reminded him he'd forgotten to pay Miss Fisher the ten dollars she'd required for her "professional" opinion.

"Never let the sun set on your sin, boy." It was one of Pop's favorite lines, and as Russell whispered it, he knew what he had to do, regardless of the late hour.

At the same instant that he swung the door open, Milton Silsbury, sporting a cocky smirk, reached the landing at the end of the upstairs hall. Heat ignited in Russell's chest. He fisted the coins in his pocket and told himself to keep a cool head. He had no proof Silsbury was behind his Cat's destruction. Yet.

"Having a little car trouble, Keegan?' The mockery dancing in Silsbury's eyes screamed, "guilty!" As he passed, he slammed shoulders with Russell.

Russell gritted his teeth and kept moving. "Save it for the Circle."

Silsbury's laugh pursued him down the stairs and into the street. It echoed in his brain the length of Victoria Avenue, growing more maniacal with each throbbing pulse in Russell's neck.

Longing for the Cat's twelve cylinders and an unending stretch of asphalt, Russell rounded the corner of Victoria and Sixth at a near jog. A good, stress-relieving race of any sort would come in handy, but, at the moment, the lone participant was Father Time, and he had the winning lead. Nine days and counting . . .

An engine rumbled to life and Russell looked its direction. Several blocks ahead, a car peeled out from a parking lot. The Chevrolet flashed its white paint under the beams of a streetlight. Then, tires squealing and engine roaring, it took a side road heading north.

From a nearby carriage house, a horse whinnied its protest at the racket.

Something about the whole thing made his scalp tingle . . .

Unlit headlamps.

Nighttime driving was dangerous enough on its own. Without headlamps, it was a death sentence for occupants, pedestrians, both.

Russell's squinted gaze snapped back to where the car had started. He didn't need to read the lopsided sign to recognize the place of business.

Even from where he was, he could see the bay doors were closed with no light leaking from the seams. When he arrived, he slowed and listened. Except for the wind tapping the dangling sign against the eaves, all was quiet.

Rounding the building, he found a back door swaying inward on its hinges. An unnatural scraping soundemerged from the black. He stepped to the threshold.

"Hello?"

The noise ceased. "Wh-who's there?"

He pushed the door open farther and spotted her shadowy rumpled figure. "It's Russell Keegan, Miss Fisher. Why are you in the dark? Did those—"

"Saints above, Mr. Keegan, you scared me half to death!"

"*I* scared you? What about the car just tearing out of here? If I know men, and I do, I'd say whoever was in that Chevrolet was up to no good."

"I'm fine." The scratching noise resumed as Miss Keegan dug through a mountain of who-knew-what piled on a desk. "There you are."

With the hiss of a match, light flooded the room. She neared the flame to a lantern's wick, but her trembling hand failed to make contact.

Russell relieved her of the task, then replaced the lamp's glass, not believing for a moment that nothing untoward had transpired before he arrived. "Were you robbed?"

"No. I said I'm fine."

He held the lamp up between them then frowned. "Those welts on your neck aren't from changing tires."

Her hand flew to her throat, her eyes to the door as though the intruder might return at any moment.

"We should go to the police station. They'll want you to file a report."

Her reply came quick. "No need for that."

"Who was it? What did he want?"

A scowl furrowing her brow, she took the lamp from him and headed into the bay toward the Dodge. "Forget it." After setting the lamp on the counter, she fiddled with the same wiring that had caught her attention earlier in the evening, then moved back to the toolbox and began rummaging through it. Twice, her hand skimmed the pliers she needed.

Was she still struggling to regain her composure, or did she mean to be vague?

Moving to her side, he plucked the pliers from the box and handed them to her.

"Thank you. I . . . didn't see them."

When her fingers slipped around the tool's grips, Russell trapped her wrist with his free hand. Alarm widened her eyes, but at least he had her attention. "Are you protecting him, Miss Fisher? Because a man who does *that* to a woman doesn't deserve it." He jabbed a thumb toward her throat.

"He can rot in jail for all I care." Vehemence coated her words and tilted Russell's lips into a half smile.

"Good. Then let's put him there. Who was it?"

She tipped her head to the side, casting half her face in light. A telltale trail of tears beaded over a swath of grease. "Are you still looking for a mechanic, Mr. Keegan?"

As he fought for footing in this sudden shift of conversation, she barreled ahead.

"Because if you are, I'll do it. On two conditions. One, the price goes up. Four hundred. Cash. And parts are on you."

"Whoa! Hold up there, speedy. I'm still back at the 'I'll be your mechanic' part."

"Oh." Her expression fell. "Did you find another one?"

"Well . . . no, but who says I'm willing to let a woman fix my car?"

"You were an hour ago! What changed, Mr. Desperate?" She pressed her lips into a crooked line.

"Shouldn't I be asking *you* that? What changed your high and mighty *standards*?"

"I have my reasons, none of which concern you."

Russell eyed her. Fickle women. He knew them all too well.

"I can do it, Mr. Keegan. I know I can. I'm good."

He rubbed his chin. "A racer's mechanic has got to be more than good. He's got to be quick."

"I said I could have the Stutz ready in time."

"And he's got to be hard as nails. You've seen the races. They're hot, fast, and dangerous. There are a hundred ways a man can get hurt in the pits alone, and I can't have you falling apart when I need you most."

She rolled her shoulders back and leaned toward him, her eyes shining dark and fierce. "Mr. Keegan, I told you I can do it."

Russell seized her gaze, testing her. She held it, as unwavering as any man. "Four hundred it is. Cash money." He held out his hand to shake on the deal.

With an enchanting, full-mouthed smile, she thrust her hand into his, stunning Russell with the slightness of it.

A rush of protectiveness filled his chest and clogged his throat. He swallowed against the onslaught, and blinked common sense back into his thoughts. Sweet day in the morning, what had he gotten himself into?

He dropped her hand and backed up a step. "Now *my* conditions."

"You can't make conditions once you've shaken on a deal."

"Did you forget the rules? You're playing with the boys now." He grinned and flexed the muscles in his arm.

She rolled her eyes. "Fine. What are your conditions?"

"Like I said before, every decision goes through me first. And you work solely for me. No other customers until the after the race."

She shrugged. "I can handle that. Starting first thing in the morning. Tonight, you're going to help me finish Mr. Shaheen's Dodge." She flashed him her palm, halting the protest on the tip of his tongue. "It's only fair seeing how you interrupted my work earlier and set me behind."

He harrumphed but conceded with a nod.

"Then you're going to walk me home." Her lashes dropped, along with her confident tone. "Please." She gave another slight shrug, looking every bit the timid schoolgirl.

Russell slid the cap from his head and ran a hand through his hair. What did a man do with a defenseless mechanic? Play the knight in shining armor? Tell her to buck up and be a man? Feeling as though he'd stepped into a bizarre "other" world, he stuck with the familiar.

With an understanding smile, he rubbed her upper arm a time or two, then gave it a pat. "Of course, I'll walk you home."

He half expected her to swat his hand away, but judging by the relief washing over her features, the traditional path had been the correct one. "But whenever this boyfriend of yours—or whoever he is—shows up again, I plan to give him a piece of my mind."

"I told you, it's none of your concern." She jutted her chin in the air. "The Dodge needs gas. Think you can handle that?"

He dropped a narrow-lidded gaze on her. "I reckon I can."

Besides fuel, the Dodge needed little more than fresh oil and a top-up on water, at least for his part. She messed around under the hood for a few minutes, then called it good.

Soon, they made their way down Sixth, their shoes clicking against the walk in perfect rhythm. He almost joked about it, but her sullen mood deterred him.

On a whim, he bumped shoulders with her. When her gaze swung to him in surprise, he grinned. "Say, you know what always cheers me up?"

A single brow rose in question.

"A hearty race. How 'bout it?"

An airy laugh erupted from her. "How did I not guess?"

His grin widened. "Well? First one to the corner of Ramona Avenue wins."

"I'm sure it would make *you* feel better. You'd win."

"Maybe. Either way, you're a racer's mechanic now. You need to practice working under pressure."

"Is that so?" Her voice rose in pitch. "Well, you need to practice working without getting grease on your fancy trousers."

"What?" He halted and bent to study his pants in the dim light.

In that instant, she took off.

"Hey!" He launched into pursuit, gaining ground with little effort. The wind stung his eyes, but it was his laughter that made them water. "False starts never pay, Winifred Fisher." The wind whipped away his voice as he zipped past the Ramona Avenue street sign, Miss Fisher three paces behind him.

Their laughter mingled, petering out as they walked the remaining fifty yards down Ramona and stopped in front of a modest Victorian-style home hemmed in by a white picket fence.

She dug in her pocket, then tossed him a set of keys. "Take the Lizzie back to the hotel, and let yourself into the shop in the morning. I have some business to attend to, but I'll be there by nine. Thanks for walking me home."

"Oh, sure. And may I take it as a fresh vote of confidence that you're letting me drive the Lizzie again?"

"You may, although I cast it rather hesitantly."

"Duly noted." He stopped himself short of a wisecrack about the absurdity of fearing for one's car while it was in the hands of one of the nation's top drivers. Instead, he rattled the keys in the air. "Don't you need these to get into the house?"

"This isn't New York City. We don't lock our doors." She turned to open the fence, but he caught her by the arm.

"Lock them tonight."

"Sure. I-I'll do that." She stared at him so long he began to wonder if he'd spooked her senseless, but when she spoke again, a smile graced her voice. "You were right, by the way. I feel better."

Pleasure streamed through him. He'd needed that race, too. "Told you, although if we plan on repeating, you should know that my racing manual says cheaters crash and burn every time."

A tiny gasp escaped her. Like an arctic blast, an icy wind swept over Miss Fisher, stiffening her and chilling Russell clean through. His good spirits died a hasty death.

His mind scrambled to replay their exchange. Something about a racing manual and warning her about . . . burning? He was such an idiot. "It was just a tease. No need to worry. I have yet to wipe out in a race."

Miss Fisher entered her yard, slamming the fence and making a show of latching it behind her. "Good night, Mr. Keegan."

He cleared his throat. "Good night, Miss Fisher."

Her door was closed and locked long before Russell unpeeled his eyes from where she'd last stood, interior light behind her, haloing her, bathing her features in shadow.

What had he said? More importantly, what had he *done*?

Chapter Four

Present Day

Meghan shook her hands, hanging down at her sides, and pushed away the impulse to pace the gym floor.

Brooke raised her eyebrows at her. "So. You ready for this?"

Meghan blew out a breath. "Definitely." Sorta.

She followed Brooke to the locker room . . . and the scales. Knots twisted in her stomach. For months she'd fought and clawed her way to getting in shape. She *felt* slimmer—but the scale would be the judge.

Chocolate deprivation, calorie logging, torture on the treadmill, it all came down to this. More than almost anything in the world, she wanted to cross this finish line. To reach the goal. To prove to herself she could.

And especially, to turn her husband's head the way she had back in high school. After all, guys were visual creatures, right? Physical interest came before emotional.

"Okay Brooke, this is it. Wish me luck." Staring ahead at the opposite wall, Meghan stepped onto the scale and held her breath. Her eyes squeezed shut. In slow motion, she opened one of them and peeked down. Then froze.

Brooke sidled up behind her and looked over her shoulder. "You did it!"

Meghan opened both of her eyes, which instantly filled with tears.

"I'm so proud of you!" Brooke wrapped her arm around Meghan's shoulders for a quick squeeze. "It's definitely time to party." She raised her hand for a high five.

Meghan stood on the scale a few moments staring, not wanting the numbers to disappear. Finally. Finally, she'd done it. All that weight from her two pregnancies, gone. Gone!

With more energy than she'd felt all year, she led the way out to the gym floor. For once she didn't even mind the musky smell that the AC never could quite blow out of the place.

"Meghan Townsend and Brooke Wilder?"

At the masculine voice behind her, Meghan's head snapped up. "That's us." She spun around and her breath stuck in her throat as she came face-to-chest with the sculpted trainer. Recognition sparked at the mystery man from church. Embarrassed at her widened eyes, Meghan tried to clear her throat to make room for the air her lungs required.

"I'm Curtis." He extended his hand to each of them in turn. "Hey, I know you. Met you at the church last weekend, didn't I?"

Meghan cleared her throat and stepped back. *Get a grip, woman. It's not like you've never seen a handsome man before.* Still, she couldn't help a little shiver when their gazes connected.

Brooke smiled. "Yeah, you were working with my husband, Darren. Good to meet you again."

"Darren's a cool guy. You know, it's great to meet people at Cornerstone. I've been going there a couple months now, but usually I'm at the evening service and it's a pretty small group. The men's workday was the first time I'd seen most of those people." He clapped his hands together. "So. You two are interested in strength training, is that right?"

"Um—" Meghan's brain had severed communication with her tongue.

Brooke jumped in to her rescue. "Yes. We are."

"Great. Let's head over here." He pointed and started sauntering toward the weight room, asking about their goals and experience levels as they went. He explained about muscle groups, how to build muscle without getting bulky, and what kind of results to expect in the six weeks they'd signed on for.

While Brooke started on the rowing machine, Curtis had Meghan begin with some bicep curls. Meghan's nerves made her hands shake as she reached for her five-pound weights.

Curtis stood beside her and demonstrated proper posture. "So, is this your first time attempting strength training?" His nicely defined biceps flexed as he raised and lowered a set of larger weights.

"Yeah. When I got close to my goal weight it seemed like it was time. Two kids have a way of mangling a girlish figure." She mirrored his stance and lifted her own dumbbells.

"Well, you already look great. I don't think you need to lose any more weight—we'll just get you toned up a little, that's all."

She looked great? Meghan's cheeks burned, followed by a wave of guilt. Though she hadn't heard a compliment on her looks in years, this one was harmless. Part and parcel with his trade. Besides, she had no call to be flustered in the presence of an attractive man. She was a married woman.

She stared over his shoulder and raised her dumbbells. *One. Two. Three.*

Those eyes though. Shockingly blue. They stood out from across the room, and honestly, how often could you actually tell someone's eye color when you weren't right up in their face? Eyes like his belonged on fictional heroes.

Fictional.

A jolt shot through her. Curtis was the perfect model for Russell. He *was* Russell.

That decided, Meghan allowed herself to examine his face. To memorize the details so she could put him down on paper. Proverbial chiseled jaw, dark eyebrows setting off those cerulean eyes. Perfectly balanced lips—smooth, not a peel or crack anywhere on them. They looked soft and very capable.

Their eyes met and he smiled. "So how old are your kids?"

Her cheeks flushed. Had he caught her looking at his mouth? "Uh, Faith is nine and Zoey is five."

"Oh, that's a fun age."

"Yes." Lame.

He smiled again and Meghan took note of his manicured scruff. Russell's might need to be a bit wilder, less like a GQ Magazine cover.

"Okay, keep it up. Let me check your technique."

Meghan pulled her gaze from his jawline and it landed on his chest. His flat torso must surely sport a six-pack under his shirt. *That* would work for Russell. Give Winnie something to gawk at. She gulped.

Curtis replaced his weights in the rack and stood facing her. Her skin flushed under his scrutiny as he studied her form before he moved around behind her. "Keep your posture straight like this." His voice tickled her ear and his nearness warmed the back of her neck. He placed one professional hand on the small of her back and one on her shoulder. At his touch, heat rose from her abdomen and out through her arms and she knew it had nothing to do with muscles. Not hers anyway.

It's okay. This was how Winifred would react, that's all. Good writers had to feel what their characters felt. How else could she describe it well? Harmless, harmless, harmless.

"By the way, those cookies were amazing." He moved back a step and she caught sight in her peripheral of his half-cocked smile.

"Glad you liked them." Her hands were getting sweaty.

"Do three sets. I'll be back after I check on Brooke."

"All right." She felt the goofy smile and cringed. *Come on, Meghan. Pull it together.*

She blew out a breath and composed herself. It was a good day. She'd reached a goal. Been paid a compliment.

She bit back a grin and did *four* sets with the weights, propelled by the headiness of feeling attractive and alive. As she lifted, she purged Curtis and pictured Steve's reaction. His jaw dropping, his eyebrows wagging. His hands slipping around her smaller waist. Pulling her to his chest.

Oh yeah. It was all worth it!

"Oh my gosh, Meghan. You look *so good.*" Brooke's eyes were wide and she nodded her head.

"I do?" Meghan was afraid to turn her chair around and look in the mirror. She pushed her newly styled locks behind her ears and tucked her bottom lip between her teeth.

"Yes, Meg, you *really do.*"

It was just hair. And makeup. She was still just Meghan and would never look magazine-cover perfect like Brooke.

Could she truly look that good?

Brooke spun the chair around until Meghan was staring at a very pretty woman with a bit of a resemblance to herself. She ran her fingers through the extra soft tresses framing her face, then leaned forward to study the smoky eyeliner and neutral lipstick that had transformed her from a six to an eight point five. At least.

Her eyes began to mist and she fanned them with her hands, determined not to ruin her makeup.

"I told you." Brooke spoke in a solemn whisper. Then her eyes lit up. "Ready for our next stop?" Brooke was in her element at the mall, and having even more fun than Meghan on this whirlwind makeover.

Meghan nodded. "Yes, let's go."

They paid for the new makeup and went upstairs to the department store. An hour later Meghan walked out with her first pair of skinny jeans and several new tops. None of which bore witty slogans or resembled the attire of a bag lady. Brooke's words, not Meghan's.

At home, she hurried through the kitchen, down the hall, and into her room. Steve could be home any minute. She yanked off her old ugly T-shirt and then her baggy pants. One leg and then the other slid into the new pair. The fitted denim sent a rush of exhilaration through her. She ran her hands over her hips, amazed they weren't bulging out like overstuffed sausage casings.

The new Victoria's Secret made the scoop-neck blouse more flattering than she thought possible. And the scarlet color picked up the new red highlights in her dark hair. She felt like a movie star.

She put away the rest of her purchases, then began flitting about the house. Though the wonderful silence invited her to put her feet up and enjoy an unhurried cup of chai tea, her insides bounced like she was full of Mexican jumping beans. She stood and paced the dining room floor, too keyed up to sit still. She dusted the living room, then swept the kitchen and unloaded the dishwasher, bemoaning the water spots on her glasses—no doubt a sign that Steve had turned off the "heated dry" setting again. No matter. She didn't expect either of them to be examining the tableware tonight.

The doorbell interrupted her chores.

"Hi, Mommy!" Zoey sprang into the house, followed by Faith.

"Honey, you look beautiful." Her mom looked her over with wide eyes.

Faith stared up at her. "Yeah Mom, I like your hair."

"Thanks, punkin. Did you three have a fun time?"

"Yeah, the movie was great. And Grandma let us have a big box of Butterfingers."

"Shhh. Don't get me in trouble."

Meghan laughed. "That's okay, Mom. Thanks for taking them. Do you want to come in?"

"No, thanks, sweetie. I need to stop at the grocery store on the way home, and Nancy is coming over for dinner."

Meghan relaxed. "Okay. Well, have a good time and tell her hi for me. Say goodbye, girls."

"Bye, Grandma!"

"Bye!"

Meghan waved as her mom pulled away, then looked at her girls. "Faith, Zoey, listen up. Dad should be home any minute so I want you to make sure you get your junk off the living room floor. And Faith, I want you to take out the trash. Let's make the house nice, okay?"

"Okay. Come on, Zoey."

For the next half hour, they continued finding little jobs to do around the house. Then Meghan released them from custody and allowed them to turn on the TV. Her enthusiasm was waning.

Flipping on the bathroom light, she drew in a breath and forced a smile at her reflection. She smeared a new coat of gloss on her lips and separated her bangs. Where *was* he?

She turned off the light and headed back toward the entryway to look out the window in the front door. Finally, Steve's truck pulled into the drive. Meghan sucked in a breath.

She hurried to the dining room, checking her reflection again in the mirror above the fireplace. Delicious anticipation tickled her spine when the garage door powered open then shut. She held her breath. The knob turned and Steve stepped in, head down. He tossed his keys on the counter as usual, then made a move for the refrigerator. But when Meghan passed through his field of vision, he did a double take.

"Wow. Meg. You look . . . great." He took in the full sight of her and her cheeks warmed under his perusal.

Meghan sauntered over, reached up, and wrapped her arms around him. "I hoped you'd think so." She ran a fingertip along the back of his neck, then stood on tiptoes to kiss him. He raised his hands from her waist to the back of her shoulders and pulled her closer. Satisfaction heated Meghan's insides. She felt the tremble of desire in his lips and longed to fulfill it, but then he leaned backward.

She frowned. Looking into his dark eyes, she could see plain as day the impression she'd made. So why was he pulling away? "What's wrong?"

"Nothing's wrong." But there was guilt in his expression. Her brow creased, but he brought his lips back down to hers and kissed her more deeply. Hope rose, along with Meghan's temperature. "You're beautiful." He met her gaze and Meghan tingled down to her toes. Steve smiled then gave her a safe kiss—too safe—and took her hands from around his neck, pressing her knuckles briefly to his lips. "I'm going to go change. Will dinner be ready soon?"

"Um." She glanced around the kitchen, seeking her bearings. "I've had a roast in the crock pot all day. All that's left are the rolls." She looked back up at him.

"Sounds good to me. I'm starving." He turned toward the hall, sagging under the weight of his laptop bag before depositing it on the floor against the wall.

Meghan had imagined turning her man into a pile of mush, unable to tear himself away from her. But that was a scene from a romance novel, not real life. She blinked away the sting. She had to be realistic. After all, they were in the kitchen with two daughters down the hall. She couldn't expect him to take his fill with wild abandon. So what if he didn't haul her into the bedroom and lock the door. It was obvious he was attracted to her, which was what she'd wanted to prove to herself. So why did she sense something still wasn't quite right?

She gave herself a mental shake and tried to forget it as she preheated the oven. But it gnawed at her. This wasn't how she envisioned tonight. Or her life, for that matter.

Maybe it wasn't just her looks.

A man's love language is respect. She'd read that on a blog. Maybe *that* was where she'd failed? Snatching a pen from the cup by the phone, she scripted a heart-felt message to Steve, thanking him for working so hard to provide for their family, expressing gratitude for all he did to take care of her. She folded it, glanced down the hall, then slipped it into Steve's laptop bag. When he found it, would he thank her? Hold her? Or was he hopelessly bored with her?

She arranged the rolls on the baking sheet then slid them into the oven, setting the timer for eighteen minutes. Just enough time to pull up that website she'd bookmarked.

A few mouse clicks and the Northwest Fiction Conference webpage appeared on her screen. She devoured the details. It was a couple months away, registration was open. Agents and publishers galore were slated to attend. She clicked each of their names. Most were looking for historical romances. The very idea of it made her head spin with excitement.

She needed to do something more than keep house and tinker with stories on her laptop. That was boring. But the conference was pretty pricey. Steve wouldn't be taking over the metal factory for another eight months. And her manuscript wasn't even halfway finished. What if she couldn't do it, couldn't finish in time to even pitch the story, and she wasted all that money?

Then again . . . what if *Racing Hearts* was destined for the New York Times Bestsellers list? *That* wasn't boring.

Having a book on store shelves might remind Steve—and herself—that she was an interesting woman, not just a dowdy housewife playing dress-up like her daughters.

She chewed her lip. If she was going to consider this conference, she better get real serious about finishing her novel.

The oven beeped and she closed the Internet tab. Time to heat things up—if not in real life, then in her book. Right after dinner.

1916

Winifred swung open the bakery's door and squinted when the morning sun winked at her in the glass. The bell above her head tinkled as she stepped into a wall of yeasty goodness. She inhaled, and a smile burst onto her face.

It vanished when the sudden stillness of the establishment screamed in her ear. Patrons stopped to stare her direction. Even Hattie McBride's twin toddlers became perfect, snotty-faced statuettes.

One would think she was a creature from the other side of the moon instead of a woman who defied convention. From the get-go, the town had been more than reluctant to accept her choice to step into her father's work boots, but it had been a long time since she'd garnered this much loathing in one sitting.

Her feet begged to turn and run, but eleven weeks of flavorless oatmeal kept them pointed toward the display. She would surprise Momma with a pastry if she had to wade through a sea of critical glares to do it.

Like rifle shots, her good shoes clicked against the tile floor as she moved toward the end of the line. A new smile stiffened her cheeks. "Good morning." She spoke to no one in particular.

"Good morning, Winifred. You're looking awful chipper, today."

Her gazed flicked to the front of the line and the source of the warm voice. Bobby Tidwell passed her a smile and leaned against the counter. It shifted with his weight.

He'd always been the shortest of the boys in their classes, but his brawn made up for it. If he were a stranger on a dark street, she would run the other way, but he made it a point never to be a stranger to anyone. Anyone who knew anything about Corona knew Bobby, and that he was one of Corona's friendliest faces. And today, he was proving it again.

She could have kissed him for coming to her rescue. "Thank you, Bobby."

He extended a bill to the baker, Mr. Houser, who stammered his own greeting.

Like Sleeping Beauty's castle broken of its spell, the shop sprang back to life. Mr. Houser counted back Bobby's change. The McBride twins erupted in a game of tag around their mother's skirt, and Ethel Milfort turned in line to pat Winifred on the arm. "Morning, dear. How convenient to run into you. After this, I was on my way to Danny's."

"Oh? Is something the matter with the Chevy, or does it just need a fill-up?" The Milforts hadn't spoken to them since Winifred first donned her brother's coveralls, much less come by the shop. Maybe people *were* starting to accept her choice to keep the garage open.

Ethel chuckled. "Heavens, no. We've been going to Mitch and Clarence's for years. It would feel disloyal to seek service elsewhere." She patted Winifred again. "You understand."

Winifred's smile felt sickly sweet, as she bit back the reminder that those "years" had been those since her father passed.

"No, I was coming for a different reason. My—"

"It's all over town about your work on Shaheen's Dodge." Bobby lifted his voice as he approached from finishing his business at the counter. Several patrons made way for his solid frame.

Ethel's brow puckered. "Oh, no, Winifred. Don't tell me you ruined his Dodge."

Bobby chuckled, his soft, brown eyes never leaving Winifred. "Hardly. My neighbor, Earl Gibbons, stopped me when I went out to collect the paper. He heard from Lou Richards that you pulled a dead rat from Shaheen's engine. Quite impressive."

A few customers nodded, but Ethel looked near to fainting. "My stars, girl, you didn't!"

Winifred's hand flew to her chest. "Mr. Shaheen collected the Dodge not more than an hour ago. The Corona telegraph is at its finest this morning, I see." A small laugh bubbled up her throat. "It wasn't a big deal. I just followed my nose to the stench."

Ethel fanned her flushed face while Bobby quirked his lips. "If that's true, Mitch and Clarence must have broken whiffers."

Winifred cocked her head. "Clarence looked at it first but didn't figure it out?" Was he drinking again?

Bobby crossed thick arms. "That's the story."

"A part of the story I hadn't heard."

"Well, Shaheen's telling everyone now. I ran into him myself at the dry grocer not fifteen minutes ago. When I saw him, I decided to ask, but he beat me to it. Says the engine's purring like a fat cat. His words, not mine."

Great. The last thing Winifred needed was for Mitch and Clarence to get worked up over this and spread more nasty rumors. There was no telling what those two would cook up when they heard they'd been bested by a rat. Or worse . . .

A woman.

"Now, now, Winifred, don't let it rock your boat. It'll do 'em good to have a little competition." Bobby tugged at his collar. "Next time I have engine trouble, I just might head your way."

Ethel gave a small snort, then dabbed her nose with a hanky.

A wave of red crept up Bobby's throat.

Winifred kept her reply to a smile. He'd given good effort to mend old bridges, but they both knew his car would never enter her shop, and if it did, she could never touch it. Some hurts, time could not mend no matter how amiable the relationship.

Winifred clasped her hands in front of her. "Still planning to enter the Sunbeam in the race?"

Bobby shrugged. "If she can hit a hundred miles per hour during the qualifying rounds. Her eight cylinders might not be able to hack it, though."

Winifred nodded. Plus, the Sunbeam was too heavy. Bobby needed to lighten her up, remove the running boards for starters.

But Winifred wouldn't be the one accused of telling him. The more weight, the less chance of him racing—and dying.

"Pleasure chatting with you, ladies." He shoved a thick finger under the brim of his cap, nudging it upward.

Ethel turned to her the instant Bobby stepped away. "I simply can't believe you wrangled with that beast. It must have been dreadful! You're a brave girl, Winifred, and I daresay"—she dropped her voice to a whisper—"God has His hand on you."

Winifred's brow arched.

"Indeed He does. You just wait and see. He'll make everything right." She moved forward with the line and continued at her normal volume. "As I was saying, my Berta got a violin from her grandparents last Christmas, and she's been hounding me for lessons. Now that the Red Line is open, we could make it to Riverside easy enough, but I told myself, 'Now why would I do that when our very own Winifred Fisher might appreciate the income?'"

The woman ahead of Ethel turned pity-eyes on Winifred, whose pulse quickened with concealed irritation. "But I'm not trained to teach."

"Fiddle sticks! You're all my Berta needs. Just teach her the basics. Maybe she'll realize she hasn't got any talent to speak of and will let go of this foolhardy notion to play. I'll pay you well. As much as I would at the academy. You'd be doing us a favor by not obliging us to take the trolley all the way to Riverside. What do you say? Shall I send her by next week?"

Although she couldn't see the housewives behind her, Winifred had a strong suspicion they were all perched on the edges of their chairs waiting for her answer. She sighed. "I suppose we can give it a try . . . assess Berta's progress after a few lessons and decide *then* if it's something we're both happy to continue."

Ethel clapped her gloved hands. "Excellent! You'll be a fine teacher. In fact, you might find you enjoy it so much, you'll take on more students. Don't you play the piano, too?"

Winifred gave a slight nod.

"There you have it. The perfect solution to get you out of that filthy garage. Well, then. Berta and I will see you next Wednesday at four, sharp? I'll warn you, I'm never late."

"What'll it be this morning, Mrs. Milfort?" the baker asked.

Ethel swiveled to place her order, and Winifred breathed in relief.

This celebratory pastry excursion had turned into more of an ordeal that she'd bargained for, but she refused to let snickering biddies get her spirits down. She had a fine paying job. More than fine, and she didn't feel the slightest bit guilty about demanding such an exorbitant price to fix the Stutz, either. Well . . . maybe a little. Regardless, she intended to savor every bite of her bear claw and every sip of her precious spiced tea, guilt-free.

It would go on their lengthy tab today, but soon, she'd eliminate that beast and tick her first debt off the list.

Five minutes later, with her mother's favorite chocolate muffins and other treats bagged, Winifred made a beeline for the door. She could already hear Momma's squeal of delight, and chocolate would be the perfect distraction from the news that Winifred had taken the Stutz job. In a town like Corona, there would be no hiding it—may as well confess before one of the neighbors did it for her.

Three paces from the door, the bell jingled and Russell Keegan crossed the threshold, shoulders squared, head held high, taking in the arena as though he owned it. His typical cocky air was even more blatant in daylight . . . as were his striking blue eyes set against a backdrop of olive-toned beauty.

Winifred felt her eyes expand before she regained composure. She could admire a fine specimen without looking the awestruck idiot. Glad rags aside, Mr. Keegan had every reason to step with confidence. He had it all.

He looked like the million bucks she imagined he owned, some of which would be in her pocket before long. Four hundred of them, to be exact. More than enough to cover her brother's debt as well as a small pile of her own.

At the thought, a smile slid up one side of her face.

Mr. Keegan's wandering baby blues finally settled. On her. He tipped his hat, matched her half-smile, and took in the length of her. "Well, good morning." His voice was low and . . . seductive?

Winifred stared, tongue-tied and more than a bit uncomfortable with his perusal.

"Lucky thing I chose to skip breakfast at the Del Rey. Otherwise, I might have missed out on this rare beauty. What a shame that would have been."

Winifred's jaw clenched. How dare he razz her! His "lady" comment from the night before stung all over again. Wasn't it just like a man to retrample a woman's feelings?

Ignoring his extended hand, she tipped her chin up, and moved to leave the building. He grabbed the door handle and froze, forcing Winifred to stop beneath his voice—and to smell his profession clinging to him.

"Have I offended you? I've been known to do that. Please, let me apologize, Miss . . . Miss . . . ?" His soft words drew Winifred's gaze from beneath her narrow-brimmed hat.

His open expression was beseeching, with a touch of regret drawing his brows. Which meant, he truly didn't recognize her. Which meant his earlier perusal had been a sincere appreciation.

Her heart backfired, and the bag of muffins plopped to the ground.

They both squatted, but when Winifred reached for the bag, Mr. Keegan plucked her hand from the air and drew it to his face.

For half of a breath, she thought he would kiss it, until he bent her fingers to study her nails—her grease-embedded nails.

He dropped it like a hot radiator cap, his gaze popping to her face. "F-Fred?" Confusion, embarrassment, wounded pride—all three transformed his features in rapid succession.

She straightened and brushed a hand down her dress. "Mr. Keegan, a *lady* always appreciates a man's admiration, but I must insist that we keep our relationship strictly business."

He rose midway before squatting again to pick up her bag. "Of-of course. I wouldn't have dreamed. It's just that, you're stunning. I mean, you stunned me. I didn't recognize-realize . . . You're the mechanic. *My* mechanic." He stuttered a chuckle and extended the muffins.

Winifred took them and raised an eyebrow, wondering how far he'd bury himself before he stopped. Watching the roadster go down in flames was far too enjoyable to advise him to shut his mouth.

She was almost disappointed when he flung the door wide. Had a man ever been so eager to help her out?

"A fine morning to you, Miss Fisher." A cheery voice rose above the steady clop of hooves. From the shadow of a parasol-topped surrey, Mrs. Hastings smiled and lifted a gloved hand.

Winifred's mouth fell open. The city's most influential lady greeting the city's most disdained? An instant before Mrs. Hastings broke eye contact, Winifred remembered her manners and returned the greeting.

Beside her, Mr. Keegan cleared his throat, breaking her fixation on the shrinking back of Mrs. Hastings' oversized, plumed hat.

She regrouped and stepped onto the street. "Have you arranged for the Stutz to be towed to the shop?"

At the mention of his car, he regained a bit of stature. "Already there. Waiting for you."

"Nine o'clock is still forty minutes away. I'll see you then."

Present Day

"Captain. C-A-P-T-A-I-N. Captain."

A woman with dark corkscrew curls clapped madly as her mini-me returned to her seat with a smirk. Meghan rolled her eyes. Big whoop, easy word.

Sunshine streamed down through the smattering of leaves hanging overhead and Meghan swatted at something buzzing around her face. School assemblies on the front lawn were a new thing, but it beat cramming everyone into the multipurpose room. She re-crossed her legs, stepping on an acorn. The Bee was moving along at a rapid pace, but still she found it hard to stay focused on the event when all around her fiction fodder waited to be noticed. The demure young mother in the middle of the second row wearing a sari could be a beautiful princess forced into an unwanted marriage for political reasons. The dad wearing sunglasses and Birkenstocks was a rich business mogul on vacation in Tahiti. And the elderly grandfather in the front? Obviously a war hero.

Her attention snapped to the mic when Faith stepped up.

The redheaded teacher, who was acting as one of three judges, pushed her glasses higher on her nose, then flipped to the next page of words. "Your word is . . . Encyclopedia. The Encyclopedia is the best place to find information. Encyclopedia."

Were they kidding? Mini Corkscrew Curls got *captain*, and Faith got *encyclopedia*? Meghan scooted forward in her chair. Faith cleared her throat.

"Encyclopedia. E-N-C . . . Y . . . C-L-O . . . P-E-D-I-A. Encyclopedia."

"Correct."

Now it was Meghan's turn to let loose. Or to at least give two thumbs up and a Cheshire Cat smile to her daughter. They'd been instructed to hold their applause, after all.

The number of remaining students dwindled. Faith was 'in it to win it.' One contender—a ruddy boy, descended from Vikings, Meghan imagined—stood in her way. Meghan noted the slight tremble of her daughter's hands as Faith stood for what could be the last turn.

"Your word is . . . Metamorphosis. We observed the metamorphosis of the caterpillar into a butterfly. Metamorphosis."

"Metamorphosis. M-E-T-A . . . M-O-R-P-H . . . E-S-I-S. Metamorphosis."

"I'm sorry, that is incorrect."

Ouch. Her daughter's face fell but there wasn't much time for disappointment. She'd come in second and beat out many kids older than her.

Meghan's palms smarted from clapping so hard. She let out a "whoop," then snapped a dozen pictures. Faith beamed at the camera as she posed with her medal.

"You were uh-mazing." Meghan ran her hand over Faith's hair. "Can't wait to tell dad all about it."

"Thanks." Faith's subdued response didn't fool Meghan. She saw the thrill in her daughter's eyes and the flush of her cheeks.

After hugging Faith and kissing the top of her brilliant little head, Meghan watched as she and her friends carried their chairs back down the cement path to their classroom. Meghan's smile refused to fade. She was one blessed mama.

She checked the time on her cell, then twisted her mouth to the side. With an hour left before she had to pick up Zoey from her half-day of Kindergarten, Meghan had just enough time to run to the grocery store. Steve had missed dinner the last three nights but had promised to be home on time tonight to share a family meal with the kids.

Tossing her bag on the passenger seat, she sat and pulled her seatbelt on. Eighties classics filled the air when she turned the key. As she pulled into the left turn lane, her phone rang. With the phone on her lap, she hit the speakerphone button and moved through the intersection. "Wassup?"

"Is . . . this Meghan?"

She almost swerved into the next lane. "Dad?" How long since she'd heard his voice? Three years? Longer?

"Yeah, it's your old man. How ya been?"

How's she been? How's she *been*? "Just fine, Dad. You?"

"Oh, you know, life keeps me busy."

She rolled her eyes. Yeah, she knew.

"Listen, Patrick's birthday slash graduation is coming up. Just turning twenty-five and that savant kid's already got his PhD if you can believe that. So I'm throwing a big party for him. It would mean a lot if you could come."

Pfft. Her dad had never done more than a card on her birthday, and many times not even that. She twisted her lips to one side "Uh . . ." It was the last thing she wanted to do but she didn't particularly enjoy looking like a jerk. "I don't know. When is it?" She slowed as she approached the red light.

"July fifteenth."

The weekend of the conference. He used to tell her she'd make a great author someday. Maybe . . . maybe he'd be impressed. Proud. A spark of hope dared to flicker in her heart. "Actually, I'm writing a novel and was planning to go to a writer's conference that weekend." Or at least dreaming of going.

"That does sound like fun, but . . . do you think that should come before family?"

Family? They hadn't been a family since she was five years old! "What's that mean?"

"Meghan, be realistic."

"Realistic." She pulled into the grocery store parking lot and cut the engine.

"Yeah. You know it's almost impossible to make it as an author. I'm surprised you didn't give up that dream a long time ago."

The vein in her neck pulsed and she gritted her teeth. *Give up that dream.* Like it was a childish fantasy ranking up there with owning a unicorn or capturing a leprechaun. How had she found herself back in this place with him?

"Meghan?"

"Goodbye, Dad." She pressed the End Call button, feeling the tiniest bit of satisfaction for hanging up on the man. How dare he try to pluck away the dream he'd help plant all those years ago? It was one of the very few good memories she had of him. Realistic? She *was* being realistic. She was a *good* writer. And she'd prove it.

Her angry fingers moved over the smartphone's keys until she had the Northwest Fiction Conference registration page up on the tiny screen. Muttering under her breath, she keyed in all her information. Determination fired in her blood, followed by exhilaration the moment she hit Process. She was going. Done deal.

On the inside, she did a giddy Snoopy dance.

Until the confirmation page displaying her order number sobered her up. She gulped down the lump of fear blocking her throat. Had she just approved a non-refundable deposit without talking to Steve? On a whim?

Yeah, but . . . he'd understand. She hoped.

She marched across the asphalt to the store entrance, grabbed a cart by the door, then shoved it ahead of her as she stormed through the aisles. What a piece of work her father was. Why had she thought for one instant he'd be impressed?

She tried to relax and concentrate on the good stuff. Faith's outstanding performance deserved a special dinner and dessert. Brownies sounded good. The fudgiest ones on the shelf, please. A side of macaroni would go over well with the girls. And for the main course? She was in the mood for big, greasy bacon burgers.

She meandered over to the meat counter and tossed in a pack of bacon then reached for a thing of ground beef.

"Meghan?"

The voice cut into her pity party and she swiveled toward it. Russell—er, Curtis—cast a turquoise gaze her way, and then smiled. "Hey, I thought that was you."

She fought for breath control. "Oh, hi. How are you?"

"Not bad. Been keeping up with the weights this week?" His thick eyebrows rose.

"Yeah, trying."

"Good." He tipped his mouth then pointed to the package of meat in her hands. "If I may, I'd suggest some lean ground turkey instead of that hamburger you got there. To get the most out of your training."

Meghan's cheeks burned as she glanced into her cart at the bacon, brownies, soda, and other junk she'd tossed in. *What a pig.* His handheld basket carried some nonfat milk, Greek yogurt, brown bread with that cracked grain stuff on top of it, and a box of protein bars.

She knew her grin was sheepish. "My daughter just got second place in a spelling bee. We're celebrating with junk food. I don't always buy this stuff. Really."

"No need to apologize for it. I'm your personal trainer, not your personal health Nazi."

"Are you sure? Heil health food."

His throaty chuckle evaporated the cloud hanging over her and lifted her cheeks.

"Yeah I'm sure. And hey, congrats to your daughter."

"Oh, thanks. I'm very proud." She glanced at her cart again. "I suppose I could still make a few healthy swaps."

"That's the spirit."

She put down the beef and took a step closer to the turkey—and Curtis. Man, he smelled good. She hesitated in front of the selection, running her fingers across her bottom lip. She'd always been a Hamburger Helper kind of gal.

"Here. This one's good." Curtis came to her rescue and pointed to a package of Jenni-O. "If you're trying to build muscle you want to have the right kind of protein. Nice lean cuts of meat are best." He singled out the best options while Meghan took mental notes.

She slid the turkey into a plastic bag from overhead and dipped her chin. "Thanks."

"Sure."

She exhaled. "Don't want to sabotage my fitness. It's the one thing I haven't messed up yet." Unlike the rest of her life.

Curtis squinted at her. "You okay?"

"Yeah, sorry." Pressing her lips together, she rubbed the creases on her forehead. "I just um . . . well, I just heard from my absentee father, who pretty much told me I had no future as an author. And if that wasn't bad enough, I hung up and on impulse registered for a writing conference I'm not sure I can even afford."

He gave a thoughtful tilt of his head. "Hmm. Tough one. Well ask yourself this. . . do you feel writing is what you're meant to do?"

She paused, shifting her eyes as she considered. "Yes." She nodded to herself. "I do. I've always thought so."

He beamed at her, blue eyes wide and sparkling. "Then go after your dream. You'll find a way to cover it. Maybe you can do a fundraiser or something. Take a step of faith."

A spark of confidence expanded her chest. She nodded. "You know, you're right. Thank you."

He shrugged. "Sure. Incidentally, I once fantasized about writing a courtroom drama, but then decided it was easier to just go to law school. I love to read, but can't write a lick!"

They shared a laugh, raising Meghan's spirits further. "Well, you give wise counsel. I bet everyone comes to you for advice with their problems."

His eyes went distant and his smile fell a notch. "I wish they did. My sister wouldn't listen to me even if her life depended on it. But, like with your dad, all we can do in these situations is pray, right?"

"Right." With a slight shudder, goose bumps rose on her arms, signaling it was time to step away from the chilled meat. "Glad I ran into you, but I better get going. Kindergarten gets out soon."

"Take care." He nodded his goodbye and moved on toward the produce end of the store.

Meghan shivered before starting down the next aisle—one wheel of her cart rattling and squeaking. Her anger had simmered, but as she approached the bread display for some hamburger buns, worry bubbled in her gut.

She still had to break the news to Steve.

What would he say? She chewed on her thumbnail as she scanned for sales. He *might* be glad. Take it as a sign she indeed was serious after all these years. Maybe that's all it would take to make him sit up and take notice of the woman he was married to. A real go-getter. The kind of wife you brag about to your buddies during the day, and can't wait to get home to at night.

It could happen.

She rounded into the cereal aisle and found herself face to face again with Curtis.

He jerked his chin. "Hey, long time no see."

"Hi again." She moved her eyes from the sugary stuff she usually bought the girls, and grabbed a box of Kashi as if she'd done so a thousand times before. They'd just have to deal with it. Man, shopping in front of a personal trainer was hard! "Well, bye again."

"See ya."

Phew. She hurried away to the safety of the coffee aisle and loaded Steve's favorite brand into the cart. As she stood in front of the wall of tea boxes, trying to decide between Spiced Vanilla and Caramel Chai, someone cleared his throat.

"Quit stalking me," Curtis teased.

"Uh, I was here first so it's the other way around. Are you making sure I don't buy more junk food?"

"Course not." He peered into her cart with exaggerated flourish. "Yep. Everything appears to be in order here. Good coffee choice, I drink that too."

Her nose wrinkled. "Not mine." She pulled the vanilla tea off the shelf and waved it. "*This* is for me."

"Oh, my mistake. The lady drinks tea."

"Like a Brit."

"You even pour your milk in first?"

"Uh, no."

"Then you're all American."

"Okay, well, God bless the USA."

He chuckled. "I second that. All righty then. Enjoy your day." He grabbed the coffee and nodded to her as he walked away.

"You, too."

It was getting late. Meghan made short work of picking up the last few items needed, then hurried toward the checkout. When she pulled her cart into line and found Curtis was in front of her, she almost laughed out loud.

He must have heard her snort because he glanced over his shoulder and did a double take.

Meghan held up her hands. "Not my fault."

Curtis turned around and smirked. "We have to stop meeting this way."

"Ugh! Cheesy!" She laughed. "Seriously, that's the best you've got?"

He flipped his palms up and shrugged. "This time."

She shook her head at him, then checked the time.

"Here, why don't you go ahead of me." Curtis backed his cart up and waved her ahead.

"Oh, you don't have to do that."

"No, it's fine. You've got kids to pick up and ice cream melting in your cart. That would ruin the celebration tonight and I can't have that on my conscience."

"No, I guess you can't." She hesitated. "I *am* running short on time . . . are you sure?"

"Positive."

"Well . . . okay then, thanks." She moved forward and began unloading her cart.

After paying, she waved goodbye. "Hey, if you see me at the gym, it's not stalking, it's paying for torture. So no restraining orders."

He chuckled freely. "Okay, I promise."

Meghan crossed the parking lot to her car feeling a thousand times lighter than when she'd arrived. Seemed a little bit of kindness was all she'd needed to break out of her funk.

See? She wasn't so hard to please.

.

Chapter Five

Present Day

"Wow these are yummy, Momma." Zoey licked ketchup from the corner of her mouth.

Meghan smiled. The turkey burgers had gone over well. Even Steve liked them. Sipping her soda, she watched his russet eyes dance as he listened to the girls. Just like the good ol' days. He seemed in a good mood and the family was enjoying an evening of board games in honor of Faith's achievement in the spelling bee.

"And then Whitney got out in round three on the word *prejudice*. Duh, there's no *d* before the *j*. I couldn't believe she missed that one. I told her it was a tough word to make her feel better but it really wasn't. After that I was nervous because I was the last fourth grader left! So even though I didn't win, I still kinda did." Her cheeks lifted under sparkling eyes and Steve patted her head.

"Good job, sweet pea." He winked and kept chewing.

Zoey swung her dangling legs back and forth. "Can we watch a movie? Pleeeease." She batted her lashes and oozed charm all over the place. Resistance was futile.

Meghan fought a grin as she raised questioning brows at Steve. He rubbed his chin. "Hmm. I don't know. What do you think,

Meg?" He lifted his mischievous warm gaze to her, filling her with joy.

She twisted her lips to one side. "Hmm. It's getting pretty late."

"It's only 6:18!" Zoey pointed to the digital clock on the oven behind them.

Meghan giggled. "All right. As long as it's not a long one."

"Yippee!" Zoey sprinted out of the room and returned with her favorite princess DVD, *Sleeping Beauty*.

Meghan released four warm brownies from their nonstick holding cell and carried them on paper towels to the living room. It had been *months* since she'd tasted anything so decadent and her eyes fluttered closed as she bit into gooey bliss.

She sank further into the black, faux-leather couch cushion next to Steve, who put an arm around her shoulders and grinned. Her world was being flipped back around. This was heaven. With an exhale, Meghan answered the beckoning call of the lift-top coffee table and propped up her tired feet. Faith parked on the other side of Steve, and Zoey curled up in the beanbag nearby.

"This is nice. I'm glad you're here." She leaned into her husband.

"Me, too," he replied, and seemed to mean it.

"Shhh! It's starting!" Zoey shushed everybody as the Disney castle lit up the screen.

Faith linked her arm through Steve's and rested her head on his shoulder. Meghan's nose stung and she wished she could put the moment right into her pocket. Her undisclosed news about the conference sat like a boulder in her conscience, but she wouldn't spoil the mood tonight for a million dollars. How long it had been since they'd had a night like this, she couldn't remember.

By the time Prince Phillip slew the dragon, Zoey's head had lolled to the side at an uncomfortable angle, accompanied by the light, rhythmic sounds of her breathing.

"She always does that." Faith shook her head. "Poor thing."

Chuckling, Steve tousled Faith's hair. "Go on and brush your teeth. Meghan, you wanna take Zoey?"

Most of the time, she preferred Steve scoop up their sleeping offspring, but tonight she was eager to feel the silky hair beneath her chin. She padded down the hall to her daughters' bedroom and lowered her sweet bundle onto the mattress. After tucking Mr. Bear under one arm and pulling the blanket to Zoey's shoulders, Meghan pressed her lips to the soft, round cheek.

"'Night, Momma," Zoey muttered.

"Goodnight, punkin." She straightened and turned. "And goodnight to you too, sweetie." Faith had finished brushing and was climbing into her own bed next to Zoey's.

"Goodnight, Mom. I love you."

"I love you, too. I'm so proud of you, Faith." Meghan stroked her cheek, gave her forehead a kiss, then gently closed their door on her way out.

She found Steve in the bedroom, changing into his ratty old sweats for the night. He adjusted the waistband then looked at her. "They down for the night?"

With her head against his chest and arms around his waist, Meghan inhaled his scent—hot metal and toner mixed with Irish Spring soap. "Mm hmm."

He patted her back. "I found your note in my laptop bag today . . . thanks. It meant a lot to me." He kissed the top of her head.

Cheek still resting on his chest, she smiled to herself. She'd gotten through. "You're welcome."

"It's still early. Why don't you head to the coffee shop and write?"

Her eyebrows rose. She tilted her head back to see his face. "You mean it?"

"Sure. Why not?"

She pulled in her head and furrowed her brow. "You wouldn't feel like I was ditching you on a Friday night?"

"Nah. I'll find a game to watch on TV. You go, I'll be fine."

Wow, first a fabulous family night and then a visit to her most inspiring and cozy place to write? This really was heaven on earth.

"Go, go." He turned her around and playfully eased her toward the door.

She felt her eyes crinkle. "Okay, okay." With the conference looming, she did need to pound out the story. She looked back over her shoulder. "Thank you."

Maybe he was starting to come around. He sure seemed to be. If this kept up she had no reason to worry about her marriage, or that registration. Whenever she got around to bringing it up.

She gathered her things and scurried out to the driveway. The night was clear, the moon bright. Driving down Grand Boulevard brought a dreamy smile to her face. Cheering crowds echoed through time. *Russell Keegan speeds past Silsbury and they go into the second lap.*

She made a turn onto Ramona Avenue and passed First Congregational Church—the first church to be erected when the town was built, and still standing today. In her mind's eye, a rush of lace and suits emerged from the front doors, Winifred and Mildred among them.

Five minutes later, she pulled into a parking space at It's A Grind and turned off the car. The shop would stay open until eleven, so her goal was to write a full chapter before leaving.

The sugar rush from the brownies was wearing off and she was crashing. Nothing a double foam chai latte couldn't fix, right? She admitted it was a bit hoity-toity, but she loved the stuff.

Curtis's disapproving expression flashed in her mind. No, no, after how bad she ate at dinner she better stick with the plain tea.

She blew a wisp of hair from her face as she opened the glass door. The sound of milk steaming and the warmth of the inside air replaced the chilled stillness of the April evening. A few other patrons lingered in armchairs. To her delight, her favorite spot by the fireplace was available. She set her laptop on the table and stepped to the counter to order. But she was only half present and accounted for.

The rest of her was already at the Hotel Del Rey, in 1916.

1916

"I don't know if it'll get done in time, Cooper. I just don't know." Russell shoveled in another heaping forkful of scrambled eggs and chased it with a swig of pulpy orange juice. Hotel Del Rey meals were nothing to be squandered, but Russell didn't have the time to pay breakfast its proper respect.

"That bad, huh?" Earl Cooper, driver for the Stutz racing team and winner of the 1913 Corona race, scraped butter over a piece of toast.

Russell gulped his food and leveled a heavy-lidded gaze on his friend. "Worse than you can possibly imagine."

With a shake of his head, Earl clicked his tongue. "Any idea who did it?"

"I got a pretty good one."

"Does the name start with *Sils* and end with *bury*?"

Russell poked at the air with his fork. "That's why I like you, Cooper. Your mind turns as fast as your wheels."

Cooper chuckled around the toast crammed into his mouth. His Adam's apple bobbed as he swallowed. "Nah, I just got eyes in my head." He wiped his mouth, then dropped the linen onto his empty plate. "Speaking of wheels. Who'd you find to fix yours?"

"Aw, come on. You haven't heard?"

Cooper crossed scrawny arms over his chest. "Heard? Sure, I heard. It's the believin' that's the problem."

"Believe it."

"So, Miss Fisher, huh? Thought that family was done for."

Russell's eyebrows perked up. Seemed he was the *one* person in Corona in the dark about the Fisher family's history.

Cooper held up a hand. "Not speaking ill of the dead, mind you. Just saying, by the end of the whole thing, half the town expected the Fishers to move on. If given the chance, some would have personally packed 'em up and ushered them onto the train. Almost soured the race for everyone. It was that bad. 'Course, it was a broken timing chain on lap fifteen that did it for me."

The timing chain was old news. It happened a year and a half ago. Three months before Russell met the man. The rest was fresh. "What happened in fourteen? Who died?" He leaned forward, eager to know the story, to know what had sprouted Miss Fisher's prickles.

"Danny Fisher, that's who."

Bits of information began to click together in Russell's mind. "Danny was . . . her pop?"

Cooper nodded. "Some amateur had grand illusions of racing that year. Fisher was his mechanic. Three days before the race, he took the guy's car out onto the Boulevard for a test drive. It was dark. There was a kid in the street. Fisher swerved to miss the boy." Cooper bumped his fists together. "Hit a palm and never woke up."

Russell sat back hard in his chair. "Why didn't I hear about this?"

"The Fishers' saving grace was it never made more than a byline in the papers. Townsfolk were smart enough to keep it buried. Bad publicity and all that." Silence settled between them until Cooper lifted a compassionate gaze. "And you had your own grief to deal with."

Russell did a quick mental calculation. *Pop*. It appeared he and Miss Fisher had something in common, after all—autumn of 1914 had been heart-rending for both of them.

It explained a lot about her, but not everything. "Did the owner die too? Why'd the town expect them to clear out?"

"The racer wasn't even in town that night. Fisher took the car out against his say-so." Cooper leaned over the table and lowered his voice. "I heard tell, Fisher was double-crossing the guy and planned to rig the race in order to make good on a high stakes bet."

Russell's fork clattered to his plate. He was in business with known cheaters? No wonder Coóper had a hard time believing Russell would let Miss Fisher work on the Bearcat.

His lids drifted closed. He'd thought it was because she was female, but his problems went much deeper. Regret seeped into his bones.

"Don't sweat it. Some say she's worth her salt. Besides, better a cheating, rag-a-muffin female mechanic, than no mechanic at all. But next time you get it into your head to make a hair-brained business deal"—he jabbed a thumb at his chest—"talk to me first."

Appetite gone, Russell got to his feet, but before he'd finished brushing crumbs off his trousers, he'd regrouped and found bravado. "Ha! I can handle my own business. In fact, I'll make you a bet. If I don't pull up to the starting line next Saturday, I'll hire you as my personal advisor. If I do, you give me half your winnings."

Cooper broke into a fit of laughter and smacked the table top. "Keegan, that's the first halfway decent bet anyone's offered me in months." He pushed away from the table. "The Stutz team isn't the same without ya, buddy. What's an aero engine got that a Stutz don't, anyway?"

"Give me time to get her fixed, and I'll show you." Russell grinned.

Cooper popped him on the arm with his cap. "Best get working on it then." His focus shifted to somewhere behind Russell. "Speak of the devil . . ."

Russell looked over his shoulder then wished he hadn't.

Milton Silsbury strutted into the dining room like the peacock he was. All eyes turned to him, most of them round with awe. The man ignored the diners who rose to greet him. Instead, he swung a hard gaze at Russell, who refused to duck. Their eyes held, and Silsbury's grew bright with the perceived challenge.

Sensing an impending confrontation, Russell determined to meet it head-on. He stepped toward Silsbury, who adjusted his path to intercept him. "How's the little mechanic holding up, Keegan? Saw her over at the salvage yard yesterday. She's got a hot chassis . . . if you like a manly figure on a woman." Silsbury's laugh scrambled up Russell's spine like an enraged cat.

Gasps came from the three ladies seated in the corner.

"Holding up just swell." Russell ground the half-truth between clenched teeth.

After half a day with her in the garage, he wasn't convinced Miss Fisher was capable of finishing on time, but she did seem to know what she was about. At least in theory. She'd made a thorough list, then spent most of yesterday's remaining daylight searching other shops—ending at the salvage yard—for parts Danny's lacked.

He'd taken the train to LA for a radiator intake hose she'd insisted could only find at a particular shop. She'd been correct, but he was still chomping at the bit, eager to get going on repairs. They had yet to make a single one. The Circle was opening this morning for a week of practice rounds, and he was missing it.

"Better tighten your goggle straps, because my aero engine's as good as fixed." Russell stepped around a chair and into Silsbury's personal space. "It's pretty sad that a *woman* can put your mess back together. What happened? Crowbar too heavy?"

Silsbury snorted. "You're bluffing. That dumb Dora couldn't fill her own gas tank if her life depended on it. You're dead on the track, Keegan."

Bluffing? Absolutely. Russell cocked an eyebrow, one side of his mouth sliding upward. "You sure 'bout that?"

"Yeah, I'm sure." He tossed out the words like a challenge. He did seem sure. More sure than Russell that she was worth the four hundred he'd shaken on.

Doubt must have flickered across his face, because Silsbury's confidence took on a new level. "I imagine under that monkey suit, she's got the same wares as any dame. Is it the familiar smell of grease that draws you to her? Or because there isn't another who'll give you the time of day?"

Russell's ears rang with a surge of anger. "You're a schmuck, Silsbury! A lowdown, rotten—"

Chairs squealed against the floor as the women rushed to exit the room.

Cooper stepped around Russell, nudging his chest with an elbow. "Ease off. He's not worth it." He jabbed a finger toward Silsbury. "Watch it, Silsbury. Don't matter what she looks like. Miss Fisher is still a lady."

Russell blinked. Why hadn't *he* thought to come to her rescue?

"Now, which is she?" Silsbury asked. "A lady or a mechanic? You can't have it both ways." He sneered at Russell's gaping mouth.

It should be a simple question . . . right? Was she a lady?

His mind skittered over yesterday's memories and came to a screeching halt on the soft curve of the calf peaking at him from beneath the lace trim of her dress. The creamy white of her throat, the delicate pulse at its base, and that blood-sizzling smile . . . She'd dazzled him senseless.

"Yeah, she is."

"She's what?" Silsbury stepped closer.

"A lady." Whether or not she was a mechanic—a *genuine* mechanic—was yet to be seen.

"Prove it."

Russell shrugged. "That's easy." Silsbury just needed to see her wearing a dress that hung on her figure like a caress.

Cooper wedged himself between them. "Now hold on, boys. You can't treat her like—"

"Relax, Cooper. I'm not going to do anything—"

"Am I hearing right?" Silsbury shoved the smaller Cooper out from between them. "Russell Keegan backing down from a challenge? First your car goes, then your courage."

"I *never* back down."

"Good, because I was looking forward to watching you kiss her."

Russell laughed. "What is this? Middle school?"

"You say she's a lady, so kiss her like you mean it."

"It would be a pleasure!"

Cooper grabbed his sleeve. "Russell, you can't."

"I agree, Cooper. I *bet,*" Silsbury plunked down the word-of-no-return, "Russell Keegan can't bring himself to kiss Miss Winifred Fisher's greasy lips."

Russell shrugged out of Cooper's grip. "How much?"

"Two dimes and a nickel."

Twenty-five bucks was an insane amount for such a bet, but he had no qualms about kissing the lovely Miss Fisher and pocketing Silsbury's money. "You're on."

"You know the ice cream parlor on Eighth and Main?"

Russell's voice dropped to a graveled whisper. "Nothing doin'. I won't kiss her in public like she's some . . . some . . . *tramp*."

"How else do you expect me to believe that you've done it?"

"You take my word as a gentleman!"

Silsbury sneered. "Just as I thought. A coward."

Heat exploded from Russell's every pore. "Fine. I'll do it." He spit the word from between clamped teeth. Surely, he could manage to stumble into a quick peck on the lips.

"Now you're on the trolley. Three thirty, sharp. Be there."

Winifred made her way toward the Stutz, jamming her hands into work gloves as she went. Never again would greasy nails betray her.

On her way past the counter, she snatched the toolbox then set it down next to the driver's side door. Wrench in hand, she inspected the broken monocle. It needed to come off, but one of the bolts had been bent during the vandalism. It would be a doozy, but not impossible.

She fit the wrench to the nut and tugged. It glided for two rotations then jammed. Putting her weight into it, she grunted with fruitless effort.

"Blast my woman arms." Her gaze flicked to the clock on the wall—9:05. He was late.

"I'm not late."

Winifred spun to look over her shoulder.

Hands in his pockets and ankles crossed, Mr. Keegan leaned a shoulder against the frame of the open bay door. She never knew a man could be irritating and delicious in the same instant.

"Your clock is fast."

"Whatever floats your boat. Are you going to stand there all day, or are you going to offer to help me out? This bolt is warped and won't release the nut."

"What am I paying you for?"

"You haven't paid me a cent yet, and I bet you can't resist the offer to show off your virile strength."

He pushed off the door and walked toward her, his broad shoulders rocking with each step. "How much?"

"What do you mean, how much?"

"How much do you bet?"

"Nothing. It's just a saying."

"Not to everyone, it isn't. For example, if I said, 'I *bet* your visitor from the other night wasn't a beau,' you'd interpret that to mean, 'I *think*.' But to most others, 'I bet,' means 'I'm so confident, I'd be willing to lay down cheddar on it.'"

"Are you done? Because I have work to do."

When he made no move to help her, Winifred huffed and grabbed the wrench with both hands. "Oh, never mind." She strained for a few seconds before Russell stepped up behind her, reached over her shoulder, and rested his hand on top of hers, stilling them. And her heart.

"Don't get used to being right." His voice hummed low in her ear, and his heat warmed the back of her neck, or was that her own bearcat instincts kicking in?

Trapped between him and the side of the car, she tilted her head toward him as much as she could without colliding with his face. The side of her eye caught his baby blues, which had zeroed in on her lips.

She licked them as her gaze jumped to his half-cocked smile.

"Do you?"

"Do I what?" Her voice was little more than a whisper.

"Have a beau."

Had he asked her that? A single breathy snort blew a dangling strand of hair off her forehead. "Do I look like the sort of woman a man would find attractive?" In her flustered state, she neglected to tack a sarcastic tone onto the question. Instead, it came out like an invitation. Her mind cringed.

"Absolutely."

Her breath caught. If she moved another four inches, she'd taste a man for the first time in . . . All coherent thought ran dry as her pulsed revved.

His face moved almost imperceptibly toward her. "Winnie?" His moist lips formed the nickname she'd always begged friends to use. It was a thing of beauty coming from his throat.

"Yes?" Her dreamy voice startled a gasp from her.

What, in the name of common sense, was she doing? Her spine stiffened. Her gaze snapped back to his.

Brows raised, he eyed her with sarcastic patience. "Do you want help or not?"

She released the tool to him and ducked under his arm. In her scramble, the hammer loop of her coveralls caught on the car's door handle, lurching her to a stop. Flushing, she unhooked herself then leaned against the car and crossed her arms in an attempt at nonchalance.

Good heavens, she'd made a fool of herself. Or had she? Surely, she hadn't misinterpreted the desire in his eyes. She wasn't *that* out of practice, was she?

He glanced at her then refitted the wrench to the base of the nut and applied pressure. With a little coaxing, it gave a resounding *pop*. He pointed at her midsection with the tool. "Kinda big for you, aren't they? Were they your dad's?"

So, he'd been snooping around town, learning about her family? She fingered the rough fabric of her sleeve. "My brother's."

"Right. Your brother." Using his fingers, he spun the nut loose of the bolt, then started on the next.

"I can do that." She reached for the wrench, but he waved her hand off.

"I heard he's missing. Where do you think he took off to?"

If Mr. Keegan was anything, he was thorough with his research. She scowled. "I liked you better when you didn't know a thing about me."

He grinned and handed her the two nuts he'd removed. "You haven't answered my question."

"Only George knows where George is."

"So, does George at least write, from . . . wherever it is he's gotten himself to?"

"Getting a little too personal, aren't we?" she snapped and spun to locate the three-quarter inch wrench. Wasn't there a tire that needed changing?

"I'll take that as a no." The scent of the racetrack rose off him. Was it embedded in every blasted article of clothing he owned?

"You're obnoxious." She crossed the shop in search of the wrench.

"You should hire someone to find him for you," he hollered after her.

"What are you talking about?" She slipped the tool into a pocket, then hefted a tire off the pile and began rolling it back toward the Stutz.

"You know, a private eye. Want me to find one for you?" His voice tightened as he took on the weight of the busted monocle and lowered it to the ground.

Laughing, she laid the tire on its side and went back for another. "And how do you plan to do that? Ring the Pinkerton Agency?"

His footsteps followed her. "Maybe. I know a guy."

"A guy?" She passed him a tire, then took another down for herself. "My brother will be found when he's good and ready."

He stared at her, blocking her path back to the car. "You sure? I'd be happy to help."

She cocked her head at the genuine concern and kindness in his voice. Maybe he wouldn't be so bad to work with, after all. "Of course I'm sure. There's nothing you can do to help, but . . . " She dropped her volume. "It's very kind of you to offer."

"You were right, remember?"

Her gaze popped up.

A brilliant smile lit his face. "I can't resist helping a damsel in distress."

She scrunched her brow. "That's not what I s—"

"How about, after we're done working today, we grab some ice cream?"

"Ice cream?" Ice cream with Russell Keegan sounded so good, it had to be sin.

"My treat. To seal the deal on our little arrangement here."

She gave a breathy laugh. "That's not necessary."

"Which is precisely why we should do it."

"What are you talking about?"

He laughed. "Just say yes."

With *those* eyes begging, how could she say otherwise?

Present Day

Meghan yawned and pulled her eyes away from the screen. Around her, all was still. She blinked then scanned the room. Was she the sole customer left in the shop?

Closing her laptop, she pushed her chair away from the table and stretched out her stiff legs. She smiled at the barista on her way out. "Thank you."

As she wound her way through the twists and turns of the familiar neighborhood, Meghan saw Corona the way it had been a century earlier. The lit gas station sign stood out of place in what otherwise felt to her like 1916. Winifred herself might have walked these sidewalks. Had she not been fictional. Meghan's story world was becoming more real to her every day, her characters like good friends. Friends who had kept her out way late tonight.

By the time Meghan closed the garage door and stepped into the kitchen, she could barely keep her eyes open. She wrapped the leftover brownies and put away the board game, then picked up Steve's shoes and socks from in front of the couch with a sigh.

Faint snoring rumbled from the other side of the bedroom door. Creeping in, she stepped on the back of her shoe and wriggled one foot out, then repeated with the other. Once she changed and brushed her teeth, she tiptoed over to the bed.

Sliding in next to her husband, she kissed his cheek and laid her head on the pillow. It had been a wonderful night. With a contented smile on her lips, she listened to the air going in and out of her lungs and waited for sleep to find her.

But it didn't.

She tried harder to drift into that delightful floaty place, but Steve's noises anchored her in place. Her jaw tensed and she rolled toward him. "You're snoring," she whispered, and nudged him. The rattling continued so she pushed him harder and tried again. "You're snoring, honey, can you roll over please?" She really did not want this night to end in irritation, but after half an hour she was going to lose her mind.

The sound stopped mid-grunt and Steve turned on his side facing away from Meghan. She listened, relieved when the room stayed quiet. Sleep inched closer.

But the sound started again two minutes later. Meghan grabbed a fistful of hair and groaned. Had his snoring always been this bad? Facing the other way, she closed her eyes and pulled the covers over her head as an unbidden thought sprang to mind before she could stop it.

Curtis probably didn't snore.

Chapter Six

Present Day

Spongebob's cackle scratched Meghan's eardrums as she folded a rust-colored towel and piled it on the coffee table. "Girls, change the channel." If the giggle wasn't bad enough, the potty humor pushed her over the edge.

"Aww, why, Mom?" Faith whined.

Meghan ignored the question. "Put on Franklin or Strawberry Shortcake or something."

Zoey's eyes widened. "Ooh, how 'bout Backyardigans?"

"Ew, no way. That's a baby show. Mom said Franklin."

"But I don't like Franklin."

"Girls, I don't want any fighting today. You have about ten seconds to agree on a show before I turn it off. Daddy's home today. Let's be kind so we can enjoy the day together, all right?"

Faith picked up the remote. "How about Arthur?"

Zoey tapped her chin and looked up at the ceiling. "Um . . . okay."

Meghan released a breath, praising God they were able to come to an agreement.

And for DVR.

She needed today to be good. The aroma of coffee blew through the house—Meghan's gift to Steve after the pleasant night last night. He'd slept in, but when Meghan heard the shower go on, she'd started the pot. Now the thing sputtered out the last of its tarry nectar. She was on a mission to find more "little things" to show she appreciated her husband, and hopefully incline him to be home with the family more often.

Finding a pair of Steve's socks full of holes, she tossed them into the discard pile and made a mental note to pick up a package of new ones for him later that day. She reached for a pair of purple jeans with butterflies on the pocket and folded them lengthwise. Steve's footsteps announced his arrival and she looked up to see him following his nose into the kitchen.

"Good morning." His greeting was cheerful and made her heart glad. "Thanks for the coffee."

"You're welcome." Meghan grinned while Steve opened the cupboard door and pulled out a mug. The perfect start to a lazy Saturday morning at home.

Rattling sounded as he filled his cup, dug out a spoon, and dumped in some sugar. "So, uh . . . you don't mind if I go out today, do you?" He peered into the fridge and retrieved the vanilla creamer.

"Go out? Where?" She'd so hoped they'd all be home today. Maybe throw some steaks on the grill or go down to the community pool.

She grabbed a pink turtleneck and pulled the sleeves right-side in. With the warming weather, it wouldn't be worn again for months. She set it aside to be packed up in the garage, then glanced up at Steve.

Steve's eyes were on his coffee as he stirred in the cream. "Paul invited me to a ball game and we thought we'd stop off at Perry's Pizza on the way. Haven't seen him in ages."

Meghan's shoulders slumped. Was their new chapter over so quickly? She wasn't ready to share him. Not yet. "When did this come up?"

"I dunno. Couple days ago."

She jerked her head back. This had been planned for days? She and the girls had seen little of Steve for weeks, but he'd made plans for a guys' day out? And hadn't told her until now? She swallowed against the tightening in her throat, feeling about as interesting as the laundry she folded.

He tossed his spoon in the sink and took a sip of her love offering. She sorta hoped it would scald his tongue.

Meghan rubbed the corners of her eyes and shook her head. Quit it. He didn't mean anything by it, he was just . . . a guy. Last night he'd been so sweet. She was going to ruin it by taking everything so personally. She had to be a better wife than that.

But, she felt like his old socks. Faded, old. Discarded.

She laid another shirt in the stack and chanced a look up at him. He was leaning against the counter, holding his mug, casually observing her. He cocked his head. "What?"

She brightened a smile for him. "I was hoping for some family time today. We miss you."

"We just had family time last night."

Her lips parted as the fog lifted in a moment of stinging clarity. Was this why he'd been so attentive last night? Why he waited until this morning to mention these plans? Her nose tingled and she blinked rapidly. The nice family night, the writing time. The arm around her shoulders, even. Was it all prep work for a hall pass out of town today?

The mingling of guilt and hope in his eyes undid her. Meghan felt sucker-punched. He'd been buttering her up. And she was so desperate for his attention she'd bought right into it.

Meghan's eyes smarted but her jaw clenched. She didn't know whether to break down crying or tell him off. She thought they'd turned a corner, but he'd played her. She was so stupid.

She worked her throat.

"So, it's fine, right?"

She busied herself matching up socks so he wouldn't see her pain. "Sure." What would it help to lay into him now? It wouldn't. Tears would only drive him further away. And once she started, she feared she wouldn't be able to stop.

"What a wonderful kind of day. What a wonderful kind of day—hey!"

The cartoon came to an end as Meghan attacked another pile of towels. In a return to the land of the living, the girls looked around them and Meghan forced the dial of her emotions down from a hard boil to a simmer.

"Mommy, can I have more apple juice?"

"Of course, punkin." She untwisted the top of Zoey's elephant cup from last year's trip to the zoo—the one Steve had missed—and poured in the juice along with a covert splash of water.

The next show began and Meghan finished terrorizing the towels as Steve gathered his wallet and keys and opened the garage door. "Okay, I'll be back later."

She scooped up the linens and headed for the hall closet, calling over her shoulder, "We'll be here." As always. Like the rest of the furniture.

She groaned as she deposited the towels into the linen closet. Every muscle in her body was tense. She should schedule a massage.

Her nostrils flared. Or maybe an extra trip to the gym would work off the anger.

After dumping everyone's socks in the appropriate drawers, and sorting everyone's shirts from pants from pj's, Meghan ushered the girls out into the yard for some fresh air and plopped into her favorite writing spot in front of the window. No use wasting these fumes when they'd be put to much better use by Winifred.

1916

"You're sure you don't want to change first?" Russell's hand hesitated on the Lizzie's door latch.

Winnie cut the engine and bounced out. "We're going right back to work again. Besides, almost everyone around here's gotten over their envy of my exquisite fashion sense." She patted the fabric of her oversized trousers then took off across the street, the sway of her hips barely discernible beneath the distraction of her bulbous, lumpy backside. A man's shirt jammed under a cinched belt wasn't her most attractive look.

Russell suppressed a groan. He'd so hoped Silsbury would feel the full effect of his loss. As it was, he'd get yet another eye-full of Miss Fisher bedecked in a man's baggy clothing and wearing engine grease for rouge.

She stepped onto the sidewalk three stores down from Thomas Drug. Russell plodded behind her. Heat radiated off the asphalt in waves. The soles of his shoes grew tackier with each step. If the thermometer didn't back off, the race would be a tire-changing circus.

Winnie swiveled on the ball of her foot and took several long steps backwards. "Get a wiggle on, slow poke. There's ice cream in that building!" Her giggle ignited a chuckle in his throat.

"All right." He jogged to catch up, then passed her and opened the door for her.

A suited man emerged. "Why, thank you, Mr. Keegan."

"My pleasure." Russell squinted at the distinguished gentleman. "Have we met?"

"We haven't." The man tipped his bowler hat. "The name's Raymond Laurent Hastings the Third, of the Corona Land and Water Company." He tucked a parcel under his arm and extended a hand. "I'd hoped for a chance to meet you before the big day."

Russell shook it, surprised at the fierce grip and narrowed eye. If Hastings had been a younger man, Russell would have taken it as a challenge. "I'd introduce myself, but it seems you already know me."

Hastings' mustache twitched. "Who doesn't?" He tipped his head to look behind Russell. "Good to see you, Miss Fisher."

Russell stepped aside. What was she doing back there? Hiding?

She emerged with a timid smile. "How is Mrs. Hastings today?"

Hastings patted the brown package under his arm. "Poorly, but you're kind to ask. We're hoping by this evening's social, her headache will have abated. We'll see you there, won't we? I don't believe we got your R.S.V.P."

"No, I . . . never replied. I didn't think . . . " Her gaze flicked to Russell then the ground. Afraid? Uncomfortable?

Either way, it seemed Russell had found a weakness in the armor of hard-as-nails Winifred Fisher, and its name was Raymond Laurent Hastings the Third.

"Now, now. Never mind what you thought, or what the town might think, for that matter. It's high time you stepped out again."

Winnie's gaze leapt off the sidewalk and landed on Hastings. A solitary curl slipped from beneath her hat. The wind shivered it against the cream of her neck.

Russell moistened his lips. Maybe he could kiss her on the neck, instead? No, no, the bet had been specific. Her lips, Silsbury had said. Although, at the moment, they were anything but greasy.

"You're a charming young lady," Hastings continued. "It's a shame you hide yourself away like you do. It appears Mr. Keegan agrees."

Russell unglued his gaze from the dark lashes framing Winnie's saucer-eyes long enough to nod at Hastings. "I—yes. Of course." What had he just agreed to?

"You'll escort her then."

"Excuse me?"

Winnie took a small, quick step forward. "Oh, but—"

"I'm considering a Twin Six," Hastings said, his gaze on Russell. "I'd value your opinion on it."

The man had dough. "I never miss a chance to talk engines."

"Excellent. Seven p.m. North Richards Street. Miss Fisher will show the way, won't you, dear? Oh, and Mrs. Hastings would have me tarred if I didn't insist you bring your instrument. It's been far too long since you've graced us with your talent."

"And it's been far too long since I've practiced. I'm afraid, I won't—"

"Not another word about it. Bring your fiddle and your smile, and wear that pretty blue number you wore to George's graduation. We'll charm them all, won't we?"

Winnie blinked in rapid succession, her jaw slack.

He lowered his voice to a harsh whisper. "In my house and under the blanket of my approval, not a one of them will dare say a word against you." He winked then slipped his hand out of sight down her back to . . . do what?

Alarm bells clanged in Russell's head, but when Winnie's weak smile didn't waver, he shut them off.

He reopened the door. "We'll see you at seven, sir."

Without another word, Winnie slipped into the store. She stopped, took a deep breath, and let it out with a drop of her shoulders. The hand that tucked the curl back under her hat trembled.

He frowned. A man that caused a woman such distress hid an untold story. Or was it just the notion of going to the social event that disturbed her?

"Howdy, Fred. Mr. Keegan, it's an honor. Make yourself at home."

Russell nodded at the stick of a man behind the counter. "Appreciate it."

Winnie waved. "I need ice cream, Boris. Vanilla with extra chocolate fudge. And a cherry, if you have any today."

"Extra chocolate and a cherry? Someone needs a pick-me-up." Boris's wink shifted the wrinkles on his face.

Remembering why they'd come, Russell swept his gaze over the empty stools at the counter then to the tables across the aisle from it. Big Belly and Railroad Cap, the tricksters who'd sent him to Winnie's shop, occupied the same table, a checkerboard spread between them.

Silsbury and two of his pit crew filled the last booth in the row. He met Russell's gaze then puckered his lips into smooch.

Russell leveled a glare at him then directed Winnie to the stool farthest away.

Railroad Cap half rose, removing the cap and squishing it against his chest in a sort of salute. "Mr. Keegan, good to see you again, sir. Found yourself a mechanic, I see. How's Chester holdin' up?"

How did this stranger know Russell's old mechanic's name? Small town gossip was a wonder to behold. "He'll mend."

"Shut up, Mitch." Big Belly twisted his thick neck to watch them pass. "Oh rats, Miss Freddy! Bad business got you down?" His wheezing laugh filled the place. "Get it? Rats." His chortle redoubled.

She gave the man her back and continued toward the end of the counter. "I'll tell you what's bad around here. That move you just made. Better get your mind back in the game, Clarence."

The game pieces rattled as Clarence Big Belly jerked back toward Railroad Mitch who executed a double jump and flashed a triumphant grin. "King me."

"What? Ah, come on now, Mitch. You was the one who told me to poke fun! That was intentional distraction." The two launched into a dispute, which Russell tuned out in favor of Winnie's silky voice.

"Ignore them, Mr. Keegan. They're just sore over losing a customer to me."

"Those are the two who couldn't find the rat?" The two who, according to Cooper, were suspected of spreading lies about the Fisher women in order to hurt their already failing business.

She nodded then flushed pink. "Who's that?" she whispered, mounting a tall stool.

Russell took the one next to her, placing her in a visual path between himself and Silsbury. "Who's who?"

"The tin of pomade who just blew a kiss at me. He a racer?"

"Never mind him."

She looked back over her shoulder, then gasped and swung back to face Russell. "Now he's winking at me," she hissed. "You racers have some nerve!"

He plopped his arms on the bar and smoothed out his napkin. "Hardly. Come here. I'll let you in on a little industry gossip." He shifted toward her, narrowing his lids.

Eyes softening with intrigue, she met him halfway, stopping when their elbows touched.

Not much more than a foot separated them. He could lay one on her before she knew what hit her, but where was the honor in that? He wanted her to want it.

She gazed at him expectantly.

Do you want your kisser warmed, Miss Winnie?

In all likelihood, he'd get slapped. Any decent woman would.

Boris appeared out of nowhere and wedged a dish of ice cream between them. "One vanilla ice cream. Extra fudge, topped with a cherry."

"Thank you, Boris. It looks delicious." Winnie wrapped a stained hand around the frosty glass.

"If there's anything else you need, just say the word." Boris' tone matched the sidelong glance he nailed to Russell.

"I'll take the same." He returned the man an overgrown smile until he moved to fill the order. Russell picked back up. "That tin of pomade winked because he thinks he's going to beat me."

Her eyes widened as she mouthed, "That's Milton Silsbury?"

A wry smile twisted Russell's lips. "The one and only. And the man who took a tire iron to my Cat."

She gasped. "Why isn't he in the clink?"

"Can't prove it."

"Rev her up, Keegan!" Silsbury's pit crew hooted at his taunt.

"Take it to the track," Russell shot back at him. The pig-headed jerk better keep his mouth shut.

"Well, we'll just show him what we're made of, won't we, Mr. Keegan?" With a single crisp nod, she dug into her fudge.

A smile crept up Russell's face. The longer he knew the woman, the more he liked her.

The door banged open. A freckle-faced kid entered and clambered up the barstool nearest the door. He slapped a nickel on the counter. "Cherry soda, please, Mr. Thomas."

"You got it." Boris chucked the kid under the chin.

"Hey!" The boy's eyes grew huge. "You're Russell Keegan, right?" He jumped down and darted to Russell's stool.

"That's right. What's your name?" Russell grinned and held out his hand.

The boy grabbed it with both of his and shook Russell's arm. "Ronald Moore, sir. Nice to meet ya!" His red freckles blended into his flushed skin.

"Same to you."

"I'm rootin' for you to win, sir."

"I'll take all the rootin' I can get. Mr. Thomas, Ronald's soda is on me. Add an ice cream cone to his order, too."

Boris waved his bar mop in their direction. "Sure thing, Mr. Keegan."

"Gee, thanks!" Ronald displayed the gap in his front teeth.

Russell tousled the kid's hair. "You bet. Save that nickel for the races and buy yourself a pickle."

A silly grin on his face, Ronald went back to his stool, and Russell returned his attention to Winifred.

Winnie tipped her head, appraising him. "That was very sweet. No wonder everyone adores you."

"Everyone? Do you adore me, Miss Fisher?"

Splotches of red broke out on her throat, but she donned a saucy smile. "I adore the four-ten you owe me."

He drew his chin back a fraction. "Four ten?"

"That's right. There's still a balance due from my initial assessment."

Dad blast it, she was right.

"And"—she pointed her spoon at him—"the half upfront you promised."

"Yeah, yeah. I hear you loud and clear." He laughed.

They spent the next ten minutes savoring their treats and planning the last couple hours of their workday. Soon, their to-do list grew overwhelming.

Pop's dream was slipping between Russell's fingers. Corona citizens had almost succeeded in preventing this race, and there was already talk of never repeating it. It was now or never. Fix the Cat and race, or forever live with the knowledge that he'd let Pop down.

"It isn't looking good. Even with me lending a hand, I got this feeling the Cat won't be ready for the qualifying rounds." He let out a rush of breath and ran a hand over his face.

Cool fingers slid over his wrist and gave it a little shake. "Hey, snap out of it, roadster. Where'd your fight go? I thought all racers were born with superhuman quantities of it." Her eyes twinkled.

Irresistible. He stood, then crooked a finger and tipped her chin up. "Are you, hater of all things racetrack, cheering me on?"

Her chest rose and plummeted then rose again, but held when his gaze traveled to her mouth. That was a good sign, right?

His pulse shifted to a higher gear. Just one small taste. Enough to fulfill the bet. But would it be enough?

"I—I suppose I am. It's what you want, isn't it? To win? To beat the socks off that cheating Silsbury?" Her hushed words carried the scent of chocolate and goodness. In her core, under the prickles and coveralls, that's what Winifred Fisher was. Good.

And Russell? All he wanted was to score a bet. No, that was a lie. He wanted to test drive those lips just as bad.

He scanned the room.

His back to them, Boris mixed a soda for Ronald who chattered to him about school being out for the races.

Mitch and Clarence argued over whether or not Clarence had lifted his finger off a checker piece.

Accidental "bump" be hanged. Russell clamped her chin between his thumb and forefinger and moved in. But just shy of contact, his conscience slammed on the brakes. A kiss with this woman was too valuable to be wasted on a bet.

In the half breath he hesitated, she completed the meager distance and settled her lips on his. Passion trembled through her jaw into his own.

Need gripped him. Terrified by the power of it, he lurched away.

She stared at him, wide-eyed. Had she felt the draw, too?

Moisture shimmered on her mouth. He wiped it clean then looked around.

Ronald stared at them, his tongue frozen mid-lick on the ice cream. Luckily, no one else had noticed Russell's moment of weakness.

Except Silsbury. He stood.

Having no desire to collect on the man's debt, Russell dropped a couple dollars on the counter and hooked Winnie under the arm. "Let's get out of here."

She stepped down as Silsbury spoke. "I didn't think you had it in you to pucker up to the man-girl, here."

One of his buddies guffawed and slapped Silsbury on the back.

Winnie's arm tensed beneath Russell's grasp.

He took a menacing step toward Silsbury. "I'm warning you—"

Silsbury dropped a handful of bills next to Russell's napkin. "You win the bet this time, but don't get used to it."

"The . . . bet?" Winnie's soft question pierced Russell clean through.

Unable to face her, he kept his glare on Silsbury, who returned it with a smirk.

"This was a bet?" She yanked free.

"Hell hath no fury like a woman used." Silsbury laughed as he brushed past. "Good luck with the repairs."

Winnie's accusing voice faded into the background. Russell's lids slid shut as the full implications of what he'd done sank in. Idiot. Russell Keegan, you're a complete idiot! He'd walked straight into this one.

"Why won't you look at me?" Her shrill words drew his eyes open just in time to see green bills tossed into his face. "Take it! Isn't that what you wanted? Or was it my complete humiliation you were after? Well, congratulations. Now you have both!" Tears swam in her eyes. She blinked frantically, then shoved past him and left the store at a run.

"Don't look at us to fix that beast of yours." Clarence wagged his head.

Boris pointed a bony finger at the door. "You'll kindly leave now."

On wooden legs, Russell obeyed, giving Ronald a nod as he passed. "Money's yours, kid."

God knew Russell didn't deserve it.

Present Day

Meghan's humiliation was less public than Winnie's, but she burned just the same. At least Winnie's hero felt remorse. Did Steve? She wasn't sure.

He'd come to bed late and traced his finger along Meghan's jaw, no doubt thinking her asleep. She felt his hand find her waist under the covers, dissolving the distance between them. Longing awakened. How could she be so mad and so desperate for him at the same time? She was tempted to stir and tuck herself closer, but she didn't want to break the spell. He might roll away, as so often he did. So she remained still and let herself drift to sleep under the comfort of his touch, praying for things between them to right themselves. And confused about what her husband wanted from her.

The alarm woke her to an empty bed. No Sunday morning snuggles today. She pulled in a deep breath, shoving aside her throbbing loneliness.

Meghan moved through her morning rituals with the speed of a sloth. Stress plus long hours of writing always sapped her. After a quick coat of mascara, she turned off the bathroom light, then found Steve at the kitchen table reading his iPad over a bowl of Cheerios. Faith and Zoey shoveled Lucky Charms into their faces. Her stomach rumbled in response.

With an iron will, Meghan grabbed a banana. "Everyone ready for church?"

Zoey hopped down from her chair, milk clinging to her chin. "I am!"

Meghan filled her lungs and shook her head. "Uh, no. You're not. Go wipe your face and put your bowl in the sink and then you'll be ready."

Zoey bounced off to do as she was told as Faith knelt and squinted into the darkness beneath the couch. "Has anyone seen my shoes? Mom! I can't find my shoes!"

Meghan fought the growl rising up into her throat. Peeling open her banana, she caught sight of one glittered sandal right there in the middle of the kitchen floor. Its twin was three tile squares away. "They're in here, Faith."

"Oh yeah." She flashed a sweet smile. "Thanks, Mom."

"Mmhmm." Meghan mumbled around the banana filling her mouth.

At last, they gathered their stuff to go. The troop filed out through the garage door, then a short time later, filed in through the double doors of Cornerstone. The quartet scurried across the foyer.

Steve reached for the Bible in Meghan's arms. "Here. I'll save you a seat inside while you check in the girls."

"Thanks. I won't be long."

He made for the sanctuary while Meghan and the girls headed around to the classrooms on the other side of the building. Guitar music filtered through the speakers in the foyer signaling the first song had begun. Uh oh.

Meghan lengthened her stride, then looked back at her girls. "Let's hurry it up, please." Didn't they understand what it was like to squeeze past the knees of already-seated parishioners when arriving after the first praise song was finished?

They reached the five-and-six-year-old Sunday School classroom first and Meghan scrawled her name on the sign-in sheet in penmanship befitting a doctor.

She blew a kiss. "Okay, have fun."

"Bye, Momma." Zoey plunked down in front of a coloring page and crayons laid out on the long, low, table. Thank you, Jesus, for an easy drop-off this week.

Faith's class stood two doors down. They lined up behind another latecomer and waited for the clipboard to be handed over. Meghan snatched it and started scribbling her name for the second time while Faith headed toward one of her friends.

"Meghan?"

She raised her head as she held out the sign-in sheet, and locked eyes with a familiar face. Curtis. A little gasp escaped before the board and pen clattered to the floor. His gaze always perforated her lungs.

She blinked. "Sorry."

"It's okay." They both knelt and he reached for the clipboard.

Meghan caught the pen before it rolled out the door, then stood and handed it over. "Hey, there. Wow, what a surprise."

He shrugged a shoulder. "Yeah, my workload shifted and I can get here on Sundays now." A snazzy, electric-blue dress shirt concealed his muscles, but she'd seen them enough at the gym to imagine their shape anyway. "I've always had a soft spot for children's ministry, so I signed up and got fingerprinted last week. And here I am." He rocked up on the balls of his feet.

Soft spot for children? Ministry? Her belly flipped. She shook her head and smiled. "That's . . . great. You have a lesson plan or games or something?"

His eyes lit up. "Oh, yeah. Songs, story, memory verse, the whole shebang."

Her mouth went dry. "Huh." She nodded. "You do a little bit of everything, don't you?"

"Nah. It's no big deal. Not like writing a novel. You getting ready for that conference?"

Meghan swallowed, dropping her smile, and snapped her gaze across the room to Faith, then scanned for anybody else who might have heard. "Uh, yeah." Her elbow itched. And her earlobe.

"Let me know if you're going to do a fundraiser and I'll toss in a few pennies."

Heat crawled into her cheeks. "Well, thank you. That's nice of you. I, uh . . . I better scoot or I won't be able to sneak in during the stand-and-greet." Rolling her eyes, she took a step back.

Curtis chuckled and hung the clipboard back onto its hook. "Right. Enjoy the service."

"Will do." Meghan turned and headed back to the sanctuary. Had Faith been listening, that could've been bad.

Time to talk to Steve about the Northwest Fiction Conference.

After service, Steve went to start up the car while Meghan rushed to be the first in line to check out the girls. Zoey crammed half a dozen papers into her hands—coloring pages, story lessons, and who knew what else. Together, they got in line third from the front at Faith's class. Why on earth were her palms sweating?

Curtis stood, waiting for her to step closer and take the infamous clipboard. She tucked her hair behind her ear and grinned. "Thanks. So, how was it? They tire you out?"

His eyes sparkled. "We had a blast. Your daughter is very smart. Only one in the class who could spell Deuteronomy."

Her cheeks lifted. "Yeah, she's our spelling guru."

Faith slipped through the doorway into the hall, then took off with Zoey toward the donut table. Meghan winced. "Just one, girls! And hurry—Dad's already in the car!" She handed the clipboard to the lady behind her in line, then tossed a goodbye glance to Curtis. "Enjoy your day."

"You, too." A quick nod and his attention shifted to the next parent.

Meghan strolled toward the parking lot, seeing Faith and Zoey walking away from the table with hands full of pastries.

The girls knew how to get in Steve's good graces and handed him his own jelly-filled. Savvy. Maybe a favorite food would help her break her news, too. As she climbed into the car, Meghan chewed her lip. Partly because she was fighting the urge to bite into a donut herself, and partly because of the conversation looming before her.

She cleared her throat. "So, how about a burger from In-N-Out?"

Steve raised his eyebrows. "You sure?"

"Yeah. Haven't had it in a while and it sounds good. Doesn't it?"

"I always think it sounds good, but you've been on this health kick since spring."

She shrugged. "I want to live a little." Meghan flashed what she hoped was a convincing smile.

Steve smiled back then put the car in gear. "Well, okay then."

"Mom, my new teacher is so cool! He was super funny and I think he must have the whole Bible memorized."

"Hmm." Meghan drew in a breath, clamping down the tingling in her belly. "I doubt that."

"Okay, maybe not the entire thing, but he knows a lot of verses and he's super nice."

"Well . . . that's good." She forced a grin at Steve as he pulled out of the parking lot and headed toward the burger place.

When they got there, a long line of cars stretched out from the drive-thru line, but Steve found a parking spot and cut the engine so they could eat inside.

Once seated with their fries, shakes, and burgers-with-grilled-onions, Meghan's stomach fluttered. "So . . . " She popped the lid off her chocolate shake and picked up a french fry. Brooke would never have to know. "I have something to tell you." Busying herself swirling the fry around in the shake, she kept her lashes lowered.

"Okay, shoot." Steve opened his mouth wide and took a monster bite of his Double Double.

When Meghan looked up, a blob of ketchup had collected at the corner of his mouth. "You've got a little . . . " She touched the corner of her lips and wrinkled her nose as Steve wiped a napkin across his mouth. "My dad called the other day."

Steve's brows hiked up. "Can't be good."

Meghan ran her tongue along her bottom lip. "I guess Patrick is graduating and having a birthday. My dad is throwing him some fancy party."

"Never did that for you."

"Nope. He surely did not." She puffed out her cheeks. "But he wants me to come."

He gave a slow, thoughtful nod. "And what do you want to do?" His understanding regarding her father warmed her, but she didn't have time to savor it because now came the hard part.

She bit into her burger to buy a moment's time. "Well, see, there's a writing conference I wanted to go to that same weekend. And when I mentioned that to him, he ripped into me. Pretty much said I should quit writing, that it was a waste of time, I'd never succeed at it anyway." She squeezed her eyes shut against the sting.

Steve propped his elbows on the table and shook his head. "That man's a . . . " Jaw sliding to one side, he inhaled through his nostrils and glanced at their girls "A real jerk."

Meghan pulled her shoulders back, comforted that he still rose to her defense. Maybe this would be easier than she thought.

Steve took a drink from his soda, then set down the palm tree - printed cup. "But I don't think we can afford a conference like that this year, so maybe you should leave your father out of the decision and focus on Patrick. Do you want to see your brother?"

Meghan swallowed against the sand coating her tongue. Her heart thumped against her ribs. "Well. The thing is . . . She chewed her lip, then looked at him. "I kind of already registered for the conference." When Steve's shocked expression stared back at her, she rushed on. "I was so angry and so hurt when I hung up with him that I . . . I just did it. I registered and put down a deposit without even thinking."

Steve's lips pressed into a thin line and the muscle around his left eye twitched. "Excuse me?" His eyes narrowed, and Meghan dropped her gaze to the food in front of her, then forced herself to face him.

He shook his head. "I can't believe you'd commit to something like this without discussing it with me first. How much is it? When is it?" He wadded up his napkin and threw it onto the tray.

Meghan scratched with her thumbnail at something stuck on the table. "Mid-July. And it's seven hundred dollars." She'd hoped he couldn't hear her quiet voice, but he did.

His eyes widened and the muscle in his jaw jerked again. He shot a glance at the kids before cutting his gaze back to her. His voice cut even deeper. "Seven hundred dollars? And that doesn't even count airfare and hotel, I'd bet. I don't have that kind of money right now. How could you make this decision on your own?

Obligate us this way? Doesn't it mean anything to you that we're married—major expenditures should be decided together."

Meghan shrank inside—until he shook his head like he was disgusted with her. Yes, they were married. Maybe he should remember that more often. Maybe even act like it in the bedroom. Maybe he should get up from the couch and turn off the TV once in a while.

Her chest rose and fell as he continued. "Do you have to go to this particular conference?" He jabbed a finger on the tabletop with each of the last three words.

She straightened. "Yes. I can't believe your reaction. I knew you'd be irritated that I hadn't talked to you first, but nothing like this. I mean, you know how my father makes me get. You used to say not to let his words discourage me. Well, they were. That's why I took action. It's not that big a deal. You'll be taking over the factory soon. We can put this on the Visa for a few months. Or I'll do a fundraiser or something if you're so worried. I already have friends willing to pitch in." She leaned back in her chair and evened her tone. "This is my dream. You know that."

Three heartbeats passed before he responded. "Then I guess you're going. You gotta do what you gotta do."

The words were relenting, but his tone was not. Steve gripped the food tray and marched it to the trashcan without a word. He dumped the scraps and walked past her toward the door.

"Let's go."

Her chest expanded and contracted in rapid succession. Feeling like a child put into time out, Meghan shot a glance around the establishment. Keeping her head down, she blinked back burning tears and stood to follow, gripping her purse strap like a security blanket.

Would she ever feel worth something again?

Chapter Seven

1916

Winifred tossed the hanger on the bed and lifted the dress to slip it over her head. As periwinkle chiffon slid past her eyes, Mr. Hastings' voice replayed in her mind. *. . . Wear that pretty blue number . . . George's graduation . . .*

"That was almost two years ago," she groused into the fabric. How did the man remember what dress she wore to what event? Chills radiated from the spot on her lower back where his hand had landed. Even in the heat, she shivered.

One arm already through a sleeve, she stopped and began wiggling back out of it, then stopped again and, with a huff, finished putting it on. Not even the daring Winifred Fisher was brave enough to press her luck going against Hastings' wishes. Rumors abounded about the odd things that happened to those who crossed him, and there had been something in his tone today that told her she better toe the line.

She might end up hating every moment of it, but she'd obey—in all things, except the last.

Mr. Keegan would *not* be escorting her. She'd be a monkey wrench before she was found in his company again. If he wanted to go, he could find his own way and another girl to use.

All day he'd been helpful, charming, alluring. But the whole time he'd had the bet with Silsbury in his sights.

She scowled at herself in the mirror. "As if such a man would find you attractive. Should have known better, *Fred*." Her voice thickened and the room blurred. *No more crying!* A quick dab with her hanky set her face to rights. Ten minutes flung out on the bed had been all she'd allowed herself. With four hundred and twenty-five smackeroos to come up with, and fast, she needed a clear head.

She plucked pins from her upswept hair and threw them onto the vanity. "Arrogant roadster." *Ping*. "Selfish, selfish man." *Ping. Ping.* Her cheeks tingled at the memory of his beautiful, turquoise eyes inches from her own, lying to her. "Infuriatingly handsome—"

"Are you going out?"

Winifred spun and stared at her mother through a wall of red curls.

Momma stood in the doorway of Winifred's room, folding an empty shopping bag, censure darkening her eyes.

She'd heard something. Gossip. About her and Mr. Keegan. But how much did she know? If that cheating snake who put Russell up to the kiss understood small towns and how devastating gossip could be—and if he was smart—he would have started the chain immediately.

Winifred dropped her arms to her sides and blurted the confession she'd been avoiding. "Momma, I've been repairing Keegan's Bearcat. Getting it ready for the race, but I'm not doing it anymore. I'm sorry. I should have told you sooner."

Her mother cocked her jaw to the side. "You decided to let him kiss and court you instead?" With a sweep of her arm, she indicated Winifred's form.

"I'm not courting him!" Just kissing. Publically. She rushed on before her mother could put those dots together. "I bumped into Mr. Hastings at the drugstore. He insisted I go tonight."

Momma's lips formed a silent "oh."

They'd talked about the unexpected invitation in the mailbox and whether they should accept. Mr. Hastings may welcome their presence, but he'd be flying solo. They'd also considered the consequences of turning down the county's most powerful man. Neither of the Fisher women had stepped out in society since the 1914 race. And for good reason. Attending the Hastings' soirée was bound to be more than a little uncomfortable.

Her mother dropped her bag and coin purse onto Winifred's bed and marched toward her. "Then we'd better get you ready."

Soon, they stood side by side in front of the freestanding mirror. "Oh my, you're . . . dazzling." Momma sniffed and touched a finger to the corner of her eye.

Hardly. Under the luscious fabric and silk stockings, Winifred was still a bedraggled grease monkey, the rebel, the woman no man would kiss unless a few greenbacks were on the table. But the feel of chiffon against her skin did wonders to revive the long-dead girlish side of her. How long had it been since she'd felt like her daddy's princess?

The small porcelain coffer on her vanity beckoned. Its tiny hinge creaked as she lifted the top. At the sight of the box's contents, treasured memories swarmed and blurred her vision, but even through the damp, Grandmother Fisher's ring glistened. Its medley of rubies and diamonds captivated Winifred just as it had the day her daddy first slipped it on her finger.

She stretched out her free hand and frowned at the black rimming every nail. Hideous.

With a resounding clank, the top fell back into place.

"I wonder if some won't recognize me in a dress." Mr. Keegan hadn't.

She fingered the smooth spot under her jaw where the chinrest of her violin, at one time, had toughened the skin. "I've changed so much."

Momma rearranged one of Winifred's curls. "Such beauty wasted on a town that sees—Winifred, your hands!"

The clock read 5:35. Winifred shook her head. "No time. I've got to swing by the shop to get the violin. They'll judge me anyway, clean nails or not."

"No, wait." Her mother whisked the ring from its velvety nest, took Winifred's hand, and pushed the ring onto her middle finger. "Remember who you are, dear."

Winifred gave a crisp nod. "A Fisher."

Cupping her palm to Winifred's cheek, her mother donned a bittersweet smile. "A *woman* and a lady. Beautiful and talented in so many ways."

"Thank you." She stamped a grateful smile on her face, then pecked her mother on the cheek and snatched the Lizzie's keys from her nightstand.

"Winifred." Her mother's voice stopped her on stairs. "Later, we'll talk about that racer and his car." And that kiss, no doubt.

Winifred should have known better than to think that topic dead. Her shoulders sagged. "Yes, Momma. If he should, for some reason, swing by thinking he's still escorting me to the Hastings', you can tell him . . . tell him . . . he's on his own."

Twenty minutes later, violin at her side, Winifred handed her keys to the valet outside the Hastings' estate. Champaign flutes in hand, a smattering of guests mingled on the lawn and under the awning that covered tables of hors d'oeuvres and a pyramid of oranges—fresh from Hastings' groves, she guessed.

Despite the luxurious spread, the heat seemed to have sent most indoors. Winifred followed the sound of the crowd through the massive front door and into the foyer. Blessedly, no one noticed her entry.

Breathe, Winifred. They're just people, and Mr. Keegan won't even make it. She scanned the room, hoping she was right. He hadn't yet, anyway. Unaccompanied men that she didn't recognize filled the home. Racers, most. A group of them gawked at her, grinning and talking amongst themselves. No doubt betting which she would kiss next.

She spun away, desperate for a friendly face. Not finding any, she lifted her chin, pulled her shoulders back, and decided to search for Mrs. Hastings. But with the first step, she lost her footing on the slick marble. The world tipped for half an instant before a steadying hand gripped her elbow.

"Don't get ahead of yourself, Miss Fisher. The quickstep is *after* dinner." Bobby Tidwell's teasing voice coated her anxiety like warmed oil. That, combined with his perfect timing and black evening jacket, made him the hero of the day.

"Bobby! How nice to see you."

He cocked his head, his smile growing. "And how nice that I find you alone and in need of saving." He drew her hand under his elbow and brought it to rest on his forearm.

She tucked her stained fingers into her palm. "Yes, well, this afternoon Mr. Hastings extended a personal invitation, and I couldn't refuse. Mother didn't have time to prepare." *And my escort confused me for a derby mare he could make a winning on.*

Bobby's eyes twinkled. "Then I have him to thank for my good fortune. I see you're playing for us." He took the case from her.

Her laugh, meant to be airy, came out shrill. "I'm more apt to fall on my face."

Bobby set down her case then angled himself so that he looked her full on. "Winifred Fisher, I've never known you not to succeed at anything you set your mind to." Gently, he uncurled her fingers, then studied them.

Shame filling her, Winifred fought the urge to make a fist again. She ducked her head instead.

With a finger, he tipped her chin back up, forcing her to meet his softened gaze. "Whether or not they know it, Miss Fisher, you're the very woman this town needs. You can play believing that."

Could she?

From atop Bobby's arm, the ring on her finger sparkled.

Yes, she could.

She'd have to.

Present Day

"Meghan . . ." Steve plunked down into the armchair beside her. Meghan closed her eyes and struggled not to lose the movie playing out in her head. What was Winifred about to say?

"I think you should consider getting a job when the girls go back to school in the fall."

Her eyes sprang open and the reel went dark. She spun her head toward her husband. "What are you talking about?"

He ran his hand through his hair then rubbed his head. "Just something I've been thinking about."

She flipped both palms up. "With Zoey starting first grade and moving to a full-day schedule, I'm finally going to have time for my writing career. We've talked about this since the girls were babies." She stared at him, unblinking. Was this some sort of payback? Because of the conference?

"Well . . ." Steve pushed himself up. "In case that doesn't work out, it might be a good idea to consider a backup plan. That's all." He looked down at her, shifted his eyes, then left the room.

Backup plan? *Backup plan?* Meghan wasn't anywhere near ready to give herself a backup plan. She hadn't even tried yet and he already assumed she'd fail. When had he taken up her father's mantle?

Her only option was to finish this story and sell the manuscript at the conference. No excuses. She had to prove that writing was a viable career for her. Bottling her anger, she tensed her muscles and turned back to her keyboard.

This chapter was gonna sing..

Chapter Eight

Present Day

Meghan lifted her eyelids, then lowered them again with a groan. Brows drawn together, she tried to swallow what little moisture was on her tongue. What day was it?

Oh yeah. . . Monday.

She rubbed her face, then ran her fingers over her scalp, smoothing away the mess of hair in her eyes.

Her shuffle into the kitchen was a strained effort. These days, she was running on fumes. Thin ones. She felt drained, as though she'd donated a pint of blood. Cut open and bled dry of emotion and energy. All that was missing was a cookie and an "I donated" sticker.

It wasn't the same as a cookie, but she popped a low-calorie Alternative Bagel into the toaster and turned on the flame under the teapot. After pulling out a wedge of Laughing Cow cheese, she leaned a hip against the counter and waited.

Steve's scowl flashed across her memory, along with his angry words . . .*Excuse me?*

When the teapot hissed, she wrinkled her forehead and peered at the toaster where her breakfast should have sprung up by now. The cord lay below the outlet like a sleeping reptile.

Oh, for the love—

Enough already with Steve's new unplugging-everything-at-night habit. She plugged it in and started her bagel-watch all over again.

Doesn't it mean anything to you that we're married?

Consider a backup plan . . .

Her mood soured a notch more but she gave herself a mental shake, stretching out the tight muscles in her neck and shoulders. Maybe she shouldn't have become used to leaning on Steve as much as she did, but he'd been taking care of her since high school. It was all she knew. She assumed it would be all her daughters knew. Instead, they'd been left floundering. And Meghan had never felt so alone.

Slathering the cheese on her bagel, Meghan felt her body sag. But she had no time for self-pity. She had exactly twelve minutes to get the girls up, dressed, and seated at the table with their cereal bowls. Was there time for a morning devotion? Didn't look like it. One of these days she'd get in the habit.

She licked the crumbs and soft cheese from the corner of her mouth and headed down the hall. The morning routine went in the usual practiced manner. First the pleasant "rise and shine, girls!" Then the "come on, don't make me say it again." And last, the bed-bounce that meant she was serious. Why couldn't she convince them she was serious the first time?

After smoothing Zoey's wispy blond hair back into pigtails, she contained Faith's brown tresses beneath a sparkly headband, then ushered them toward the kitchen. Meghan poured their cereal as they finished rubbing the sleep from their eyes. They looked like she felt. They must all have been thinking the same thing: *How much longer until summer?*

"Mom," Faith formed her words around a mouthful of cereal, "you're signing us up for choir, right?"

Meghan took a breath and nodded. "Yes. Choir. Right." She'd almost forgotten.

Zoey kicked her dangling feet back and forth and made a silly face. "Yay!"

Stifling a giggle, Meghan smiled behind the teacup she held to her lips. Looked like the Sugar Smacks were already working. Maybe someday she'd get them onto egg whites or that box of Kashi that was accumulating dust in the pantry.

They made it out of the house alive, and nobody was even late to class. Small miracles.

Now to fight through the sadness following her.

She pulled the car away from Lincoln Alternative Elementary's curb, trying to figure out how this gulf had grown between her and Steve. The outraged memories morphed into bittersweet ones. Post-honeymoon mornings of being wakened by kisses warming the back of her neck. Evenings when Steve came home and asked how her stories were coming along, or told her about local writing classes she might be interested in.

What had changed? Had she stopped doing something right . . . or started doing something wrong? Huffing, she stared at the red light. "What happened to us?" They'd stuck together through so much.

Losing Steve's job at the up-and-coming software company, an IT stock crash that wiped out their finances, none of that had pulled them apart. They'd tackled the challenge as a team and he'd scored this custom designing job at the sheet metal factory a short time later.

A quick honk from behind alerted her to the green arrow. She raised a hand in front of the rearview mirror as apology, then turned left onto Valencia Avenue and then into the gym parking lot.

Brooke met her at the entrance. "Hey, good lookin'." Her grin burned away a small measure of the dreariness clinging to Meghan.

Meghan gave her a quick hug. "Hey, you." Brooke would sympathize, she knew, but Meghan didn't feel like opening a vein right now. So she arranged her features and reached for funny. "Time to torture ourselves for whatever we shouldn't have eaten over the weekend." She swept her hand out in front of her. "Shall we?"

"We shall." Brooke took bouncing steps down the corridor and Meghan followed.

The workout began with a stint on the treadmill. Brooke put in her earbuds and both women fell into a silent, steady rhythm that Meghan was grateful for. But she couldn't stave off the melancholy for long and as they moved onto their assigned weight circuits, her thoughts drifted back to Steve. Even Curtis's usually distracting presence as he entered the room barely registered.

"Good morning, ladies. Good job on your circuits this morning. Brooke, I'm going to have you do some tricep extensions today. Meghan, leg presses. Let's go."

He adjusted the back rest and sled, then set the weights. Meghan positioned her feet on the foot plate, knees at a ninety degree angle, then pushed against the weights to straighten her legs.

"Exhale as you straighten, and don't lock your knees." Curtis stood, arms crossed over his chest, and studied her as she completed a couple reps. "Exhale on the extension, inhale as you return to starting position. Remember it's a slow, fluid motion. No stopping."

Meghan nodded and focused on the smooth movement. Bend in, press out, bend in, press out.

"Okay, good. Keep going, I'll be right back."

He crossed over to Brooke on the tricep machine, though from Meghan's perspective she already worked it like a pro. Back straight, head held high above a long, slender neck. No doubt *her* husband still found her desirable.

Curtis had given her a low weight burden, but the exercise proved difficult to get into. Sweat trickled across her temple. She blew out a breath and continued sorting through the pieces of her life, looking for the source of the break.

Maybe they'd made some foolish mistakes, gotten married too young, but they'd defied the statistics. Bounced back from financial ruin when Steve became second-in-command at a profitable company. Soon to be full owner, no less. They'd made it. Together.

Or so she thought. Her chin dropped to her chest.

"You okay?"

Curtis's voice startled her. She glanced at him from the corner of her eye. "Yeah. Fine," she grunted.

Lines appeared on his forehead and he reached out a hand and tapped her knee. "Stop."

She did, allowing her thighs some blessed rest. Her breathing was deep, measured.

"Don't overdo it. Last thing you want is an injury."

"You don't have to worry. It's not the workout."

"Then what is it? What's on your mind?"

Meghan let out her breath through pursed lips. She shouldn't have let her armor crack. Her shoulders rose. "Just a rough patch, I guess. I've had a discouraging couple of days is all. But I'll be fine."

He moved an inch closer. "Your book?"

Brushing her bangs off of her face, she lifted one side of her mouth and shrugged. "That's part of it. I'm not sure my writing career's going to get anywhere." She tucked a lock of hair behind her ear. "Especially when people I thought believed in me, instead think I'm wasting time and money on this conference. That I should get a regular job instead, even though I've been writing for years. Have sold articles and a couple short stories back in college. So it's not like I haven't paid my dues." She looked into his bright, attentive eyes. "I just don't have any support. And I'm not sure I can do this on my own."

The lines on his brow smoothed away. "Don't let negative people like your dad stop you. Go to the conference and succeed despite him. You can do anything you put your mind to, if God is in it."

She dropped her gaze and shook her head. If only that were true. But right now she felt like a miserable failure. "I don't know. I'm feeling pretty disheartened right now to be honest. Maybe I should give up the dream. Join the PTA."

He bent his head down to her eye level and lifted her chin. "Meghan, Look what you've accomplished here at the gym. You're curling the ten pound dumbbells now. Because you kept at it even when it hurt. Resistance makes you stronger. In the weight room and in life. Don't give up just because it isn't easy. Believe in yourself. I do."

Meghan studied his eyes, her gaze darting back and forth from one to the other, and her heart tripped.

"Come here." He motioned for her to follow then made his way to the mirrored wall, flagging down Brooke along the way.

"I've got your next challenge."

The girls exchanged a look and Meghan shrugged.

"A little competition between friends. Ladies, we're going to see what you're made of." He clapped his hands and rubbed them together, then pointed to the dumbbell rack. "Go grab the twelves."

"Twelves? Are you crazy? I'm lucky to do the tens, I'm not ready for twelves yet."

He wiggled his eyebrows. "You scared?"

Yes.

She cocked her head and shot him a deadpan stare.

"Okay fine, we'll stick with the tens then."

Brooke complied, a giggle on her lips, but Meghan's feet remained glued to the mat.

Curtis, hands on hips, tipped his head at her. "Come on, Meghan. Trust me." He went to the rack and grabbed the weights then returned to stand in front of her. "Here."

Quirking her lips, she regarded him with a half-lidded gaze. "Well, I *have* heard a hearty race is the best way to cheer up. I guess this is sort of similar." She took the offered weights, shaking her head at this crazy notion.

"Atta girl. Okay, here's how it's gonna work. When I say go, you're each going to start curling those weights while I count it out. We'll see who can last the longest."

"This won't take long," Meghan muttered, but a smile curved her mouth.

"Ready, and go. One . . . two . . . "

Meghan lifted the weights, watching her face contort in the mirror with each rep. Somehow, despite how impossible it felt to raise her arms, she did just that. Her muscles screamed but obeyed as she curled the dumbbells once, twice, three times.

"Seven . . . "

"I . . . can't—" Brooke squawked her version of a growl and dropped her weights, then stretched her arms behind her.

Meghan watched her from the corner of her eye, hardly believing she'd won this insane contest, and surprised to find she had the strength for another rep. She'd always done sets of five; she'd never attempted more.

Curtis' voice pitched up with excitement as he continued his count. "Eight . . . nine . . . "

She suddenly felt like superwoman as she set her mind at hitting ten reps. Her arms shook as she hit her goal, but she wanted to go until her muscles absolutely refused. Could she do one more?

Curtis called out *twelve,* a smile in his voice. Meghan's muscles maxed out, her biceps no longer responding to her demands. She deposited the weights on the floor and dragged in air, exhilaration filling her chest.

"I won."

"Congratulations, Meg." Curtis gave her shoulder a squeeze. "You just did twelve reps . . . with the twelve pound weights."

"Ten."

A mischievous gleam in his eye made her blink. She examined the weights at her feet, then snapped her gaze back to him. "Twelves?"

He nodded. "Twelves."

"Wow, Meghan!" Brooke looked at her wide-eyed. "I had no idea you were that strong."

"Neither did I."

"I did," Curtis returned the weights to the rack. "She just needed to realize it herself." He smiled at her, making her throat go dry. "Don't quit too soon. Press on and see what you're made of."

She swallowed and gave a single nod. "You're right, Curtis. You are." She grinned. "I just needed someone to remind me. Thank you."

"Anytime." Curtis's mouth curved into a smile that made Meghan squirm inside. "Brooke, back to your triceps. Meghan, back to leg presses; let's go." She followed him back to the machine, wonderstruck.

"And here's my donation to a very worthy cause." He reached into the pocket of his charcoal-gray workout shorts, and pulled out a twenty dollar bill.

Meghan blinked. "I can't . . . " She looked from him to the money and back again, shaking her head.

"Yes, you can. I won't take *no* for an answer." He grinned and she crumbled. There was that stubborn determination that made Russell famous.

She held his arctic blue gaze a moment longer before accepting it. "Thank you."

"You're welcome. Now let's get back to business." He patted her shoulder then took a step backward. "I need three more sets of ten before we move you to the rower."

"I think I can do that."

"I know you can."

New strength spread into her quads and steeled her resolve. Curtis's confidence was contagious. Heady. Exactly what she needed. She embraced the burning in her legs, pushing herself. Man, how she'd love to box up his encouragement and take it home, where she needed it most.

1916

By the time Russell stepped from the cab, the moon had already made its appearance over the top of the Hastings' grand home. For the past two hours, he'd waffled between giving Winnie time to cool off, and hitting on all sixes to hunt her down and kiss some sense into her.

He'd been a fool to not run after her. The more he thought on it, the more he realized what a complete boor he'd been, but everything would have been fine—more than fine—if she hadn't found out about the bet. Russell had been double the fool to think Silsbury wouldn't publicize it.

The easy win had blinded Russell . . . as had the opportunity to kiss the pretty lady he'd bumped into at the bakery. Now, he'd not only risked the seedling of a friendship they'd developed, but he'd squandered his last resort to make it to the race.

Few men were more clueless about the female gender than he, but the sparks between them earlier today weren't difficult to interpret. That kiss had meant something to both of them. He'd seen it in her eyes, felt it travel through her lips. Of that he was certain. She needed to be told there'd been more to it than a bet. A lot more.

And doing so couldn't wait until morning. If he was on the money about her—and he was—then she was as sick over this whole thing as he was. And that just wouldn't do.

Her mother had been no help at all. "You're on your own." She'd punctuated her words by grazing his nose with the screen door and slamming it so hard, it rattled the porch floorboards. If Winnie shared the same sentiment, he had his work cut out for him.

He was about to find out. Straightening his bowtie, he filled his chest with air then took the broad steps to the front door two at a time. Soft light from the massive windows on either side of the arched entry set the shrubs aglow, but the night was absent of the hum of conversation. The event couldn't be over already.

Then, music penetrated the glass—a single sweet strain.

Before the knocker left his fingers, the door swung wide. A sober-faced majordomo bowed then ushered Russell into the empty foyer.

The song, a hypnotic plaintive tune, burrowed itself into Russell's already raw emotions. If ever an instrument could make a man weep, this was it.

"May I relieve you of your hat, sir?"

Russell swiped it from his head and passed it over without a glance the man's direction. Uttering his thanks, he moved toward the music.

He entered the back of a grand salon, spotting Hastings in intimate conversation with a man of obvious Hispanic descent. The man's nose belonged in the ring, his attire in the orchards. When their attention turned to the front, Russell followed it.

Through the crowd of racers and Corona elite, Russell's gaze came to rest on . . . Winnie?

Eyes closed, she swayed with the music pouring from her bow. Her slender fingers graced the fingerboard in a seductive caress. Jewels glittered on her hand, adding to the glow radiating from her entire being.

He jumpstarted his heart and weaved his way toward the front for a better view.

Copper curls shimmering in the gasolier light, she took his breath away. Even in the bakery, she hadn't been this—

"Stunning, isn't she?"

Russell didn't turn at the sound of Cooper's voice. "My thoughts exactly."

"I hear you laid a good one on her." Cooper failed at an attempted whisper.

Several heads turned their way, including Silsbury's.

Russell's pulse jolted at the sight of him. He raised his voice. "Aren't I the lucky one?"

The man gave an appreciative raise of his brow, lifted his glass, then put it to his lips before turning a narrowed, lustful eye on Winnie.

A growl began deep in Russell's throat, but Cooper's sudden grip on his arm squelched it. "Easy tiger. Not the time. She still gonna fix the Cat?"

"I can hope. Now shut up so I can listen."

Cooper chuckled and gave Russell some space.

Time flew as Winnie's talent and loveliness mesmerized him. A pearl in an oyster shell. That's what she was. He thought he'd seen beneath her rough exterior, but the vision in the bakery had been no more than a glimpse. Tonight, he—along with the rest of the town, judging by their adoring faces—had been given a lesson in true beauty and elegance.

One song led into another until she drew the bow to a slow, heart-wrenching stop.

The crowd erupted in applause. She gave a shallow curtsy, then, as if it were the most ordinary thing in the world to captivate a hundred people at once, she opened her case and stowed her instrument. When she straightened, her gaze searched the room. It passed him without a flicker, then returned. A smile lit her face, and hope ignited within him.

Russell returned the smile and lifted a hand before he realized she wasn't looking at him. Three feet to his right, another man—twice Russell's brawn—stepped forward. Who was *he*?

Cooper nudged Russell hard in the back. "What are you waiting for? You're gonna lose her to that muscle."

Russell lurched forward, intercepting the competition and beating him to her by four strides.

Winnie's gaze realigned to Russell, and her peaceful expression turned stormy. "I was just thinking what a pleasant evening I've had, but I see my luck has run out."

Determined not to let it affect him, Russell laughed. "Au contraire. That was beautiful. You charmed us all. Just as Hastings promised."

"No thanks to a certain blood-sucker I know." Her face maintained perfect, sweet composure, but her words bit deep.

"Well done, Winifred." The other guy sidled up, casting a sidelong glance at Russell, who noted that the arm seams of his opponent's suit strained against the bulk beneath.

"Would you like me to escort Mr. Keegan out?" The man's voice was quieter than Russell expected.

"No, thank you, Bobby. I can handle this one."

Bobby said nothing for long moments before nodding. "Let me know if I can help you with anything." Then he took a hesitant step back and walked way.

Winnie's eyes grew wide as she stared after him. Hurt flickered across her features before she squelched it and lifted her chin.

Whoever Bobby was, he was a dunderhead to let Winnie slip through his fingers without a fight that was as good as won. Russell held back a smirk. All the better for him.

"May I speak with you? Outside?" He motioned toward a set of open doors.

She snapped her case closed and moved to set it on the ground in a quiet corner. He followed her through the room, waiting by her side as person after person stopped her to gush over her performance. At last, she made her way out of the salon and into the garden beyond.

Without a word, he trailed her. When they'd reached a considerable distance from the house, she spun and gave him a resounding smack.

His cheek smarted, but he ground his teeth and took what he deserved. He let her rant, knowing she needed to purge every hateful thought she must have had of him over the last hours.

"And finally, there's more to life than winning a bet, than racing, than crossing the finish line first!" Like a leaky tire, she expelled a long, slow breath. "If Daddy had realized that, he might still be here."

At the crack in her voice, Russell nodded. She had a point, and it applied to Pop, too.

"Is that what you want?" Her tone softened, and he dared hope she'd expended her anger. She stepped toward him. "To end up wrapped around a hunk of metal? Dead?"

"Of course not." But would he? All because he couldn't walk away from the chance to compete, to bask in the glory of victory?

Then again, what alternative was there? Settle down? Raise a family? Looking at Winnie—the full moon's glow framing her hair, kissing her skin—for the first time in his life, he could almost imagine allowing the word *marriage* into his vocabulary. Almost.

"I know it's been rough for you. Real rough. But you're not the only one who's lost a dad to the sport. I've learned that when life throws flats at you, you change them out and keep driving. Look, I'm sorry I hurt you, Winnie, but I won't say I'm sorry I kissed you." He moved closer. So close the toe of his shoe bumped hers.

When she lifted her head to look at him, the scent of baby powder wafted up. He drank it in. "Yeah, it was stupid to take that bet, but all I could think about was a good excuse to . . . to . . . " He eyed her neck, certain it was the source of the delicate scent. If he just got a little closer . . .

Her breath hitched and rode from her mouth on a tiny gasp.

"Keep looking at me that way, and I might do it again."

"I don't doubt it for a moment." Her voice was silky smooth—an invitation if ever he heard one. He should have known she was too good a person to hold his mistake against him for long.

He reached around her and found the curve in the small of her back. With the other hand, he shifted a lock of curls off her shoulder, exposing the gentle slope of her neck. He could taste her already. Boris's ice cream had nothing on this woman.

"You're good, Russell." She pressed a warm palm against his heart, holding him off yet still sending his heart on the race of its life. "At humiliating a woman. In *public*. For a bet. A measly ten bucks."

He halted. The invitation had clearly been retracted.

"Here's a wager for you." Her voice was pure ice now. "I bet you can't swear off betting between now and the race. Not even at the risk of my refusal to keep working on the Stutz."

Not bet? Whyever would he want to do that? He faltered, hovering between speaking the truth—that she was being ridiculous—and the promise she wanted to hear. His jaw hung, as air passed in and out of his mouth.

"That's what I thought. Beat it, roadster." She shoved him hard in the chest and spun, but she didn't get far before he gathered his wits, lunged after her, and grabbed her by the arm.

"I'll do it!"

She laughed. "And you expect me to believe you? I don't think so. No deal. Find another mechanic who can put up with your repulsive habits."

"You don't understand. I have half your money. Just like I promised." He dug in his pocket for the wad of cash he'd rolled together just for this moment—to entice her. When he shoved it into her hand, she didn't look at it—but neither did she refuse it.

"I'll give you the rest later, as we agreed. Or I can give it to you now. Just ask. I need to race. I need you." Had he resorted to begging? Was he that desperate?

Yes. Absolutely.

"Please, Winnie."

Fire flashed in her eyes. "No one gave you permission to call me that!"

He took a deep breath. "I'll call you whatever you want. Just give me another chance? Please. It was Pop's dream, to be here. To race. Would you deny me the chance to do this? For him?"

The tension in her arm eased. He *knew* she had a heart of gold. As he waited for his words to sink in, he worked up his most dashing smile, then winked. "Besides, you can't blame a man for falling for a pretty doll *and* a good bet."

Her nostrils flared.

He swallowed. Perhaps the wink had been a bit much?

She yanked her arm free. "Yes. Yes, I can. Never fear, Mr. Russell. You and your ego will be just fine without me."

Ego? Against his better judgment, a snort escaped him. "Don't be ridiculous. It's not that simple, and you know it."

Her eyes narrowed. "What are you talking about?"

Fine. If she insisted, he could pull out all the stops. He leaned in and lowered his voice to a gruff whisper. "You can't afford to lose my business."

She sputtered for a full three seconds before finding her tongue. "I can do anything I set my mind to! And just this moment, I've decided to succeed. Despite you! I'll lose good business a hundred times over before I make the mistake again of losing my better judgment to an egotistical racer."

He flinched. Crickets chirped as the dry night air baked the inside of his gaping mouth.

Unaffected by his inability to process a rebuttal, she shoved the bills back into his hand, rearranged her hair over her shoulder with painstaking care then looked him dead in the eye.

"Get out of my life, Mr. Keegan."

Nineteen hours had passed since Winifred told Mr. Keegan to exit stage right. Nineteen miserable hours. She'd spent half of them tossing in her bed; the other half, in the garage twiddling her thumbs and waiting for him to relieve her of the Stutz. And the whole time, she'd wracked her brain over how to come up with a mountain of dough in twelve days.

Before her, on the shop counter, sat a wrapped package—the circulating pump Russell had ordered while in Los Angeles. With ringless fingers, she picked at the twine enwrapping it.

A lady didn't belong in an auto shop and neither did her jewelry, which was why she'd left both at home. The stiff fabric of George's coveralls rustled as she reached for the utility blade in a nearby toolbox.

"Good afternoon, Winifred."

She spun toward the open bay door. "Bobby. I didn't hear you."

Hands in his pockets and wearing a shy smile, he entered the shop—for the first time in almost two years. "Little wonder. You look like a kid at Christmas itching to open a gift." He rolled a burly shoulder toward the counter.

With a grunt, she shoved the package away. "It's a part for the Stutz, and it's no longer my business."

Grabbing an old rag, she jumped off the stool to meet Bobby in the middle of the floor. On her way, she stretched out her hand and glided it along the Bearcat's side.

He quirked an eyebrow, his gaze on her hand. "Are you sure? You seem pretty attached to it."

Winifred took the rag with both hands and twisted it, annoyed with her transparency. "It's a beautiful piece of machinery. I'll miss working on it. If Mr. Keegan ever finds the time to bring a tow truck by for it."

She continued to the door, stuck her head outside, and looked both ways down the street. Just as every other time she'd checked today, no Mr. Keegan.

Disappointment tugged at her lips. "Come on, already," she muttered and slapped the rag against her thigh. She couldn't move on with her life until he stepped out of it.

Bobby cleared his throat, regaining Winifred's attention. "You seem sorta attached to its owner, too."

She laughed. "Hardly."

With slow steps, Bobby joined her at the threshold. He cocked his head to the side and studied her. "We've been friends since grade school. I don't need town prattle about a kiss to see that you're stuck on him." His voice held a trace of disproval.

Heat rose in her chest and made its way clear to the tips of her ears. "I'll admit he's grown on me." She worked double time on the rag. "You know how . . . difficult things have been since the accident." Blasted tears. She glanced away.

"The last days with Mr. Keegan have been some of the most pleasant in . . . well, never mind how long. You know how I keep to myself in here. I've grown accustomed to being lonesome and didn't realize I'd forgotten what it feels like to be accepted, needed. He did that. Reminded me."

He'd also reminded her she was a woman, with all the natural desires that came with the role.

Desires . . .

Her heart skipped at the memory of his fingers on her back pressing through the flimsy chiffon, tugging her closer. She quirked her lips. Too bad he was a conceited rake. So why on earth didn't that knowledge stop her from wishing he'd walk back through her doors?

She was pathetic. Desperate.

Lonely.

"He was a friend," Bobby said.

A great breath raised her shoulders. It rode out on a slow, rueful sigh. "Yes, and you know I don't have friends, Bobby."

He took the rag from her, then enveloped her hand in his. It was warm, strong, and sure. "You have me."

A smile curved her mouth. "Yes, I do." Despite his personal involvement in the Fisher family calamity, despite goading from others for him to shun Winnie and her mother, he'd continued to show support, meager though it had been.

"Well, I told the man to take a hike, and the sooner he complies, the better."

Bobby grinned. "Good."

In her peripheral vision, the Stutz's coat glowed fiery red, mocking her, summoning her to its crippled engine. She locked her knees, refusing to give one more moment's aid to the arrogant racer—even at the expense of her own enjoyment. "Although after his car leaves, I'll have no business to speak of."

"I told you I planned to bring the Sunbeam by next time I had trouble. And you played like an angel last night. Gave the town a good wake-up call. Maybe that'll bring a few customers around."

She ducked her head. "You're too kind and a shade too optimistic."

"I disagree. After you left, I heard a couple of men grumbling about the service they're getting over at Mitch and Clarence's. Your name came up and not in a bad way."

She pursed her lips. Really? She couldn't imagine it.

Bobby laughed. "But until they walk through these doors, there'll be no convincing you."

She glanced at her hand tucked inside his. Besides her mother, he was all she had left. "Speaking of convincing. Is there any way I can talk you out of racing?"

He squeezed her hand then let it drop. "Why would you want to do a thing like that?"

"I'd hate to see you get hurt."

"Care for me that much, eh?" He gave a light-hearted laugh.

She returned him a dead-level stare. "You know what I think of racing."

"And yet, you were willing to fix a racer's car. Is money that tight?"

Her gaze fell.

He grasped her chin and coaxed her to look at him. "How many times will I have to offer to help you out before you accept?"

Accept a handout from the man her family had wronged? Preposterous. "I'll make my own way." She tilted her head to the side, releasing his hold.

He heaved a sigh. "I'm heading past your house. Want me to tell your mother anything?"

"Let her know I'll be here until Mr. Keegan comes to collect his car."

"Sure thing." He returned the rag to her then made his way out.

"Bobby?"

Hands back in his pockets, he twisted to look back at her.

"Thanks."

"My pleasure."

She took several steps toward him. "I meant for stopping by my house. And for coming by. Here."

"I . . ." Expressionless, he held her gaze, then turned to face her full on. "I should have been by the shop a long time ago. No excuses, it was wrong of me to stay away. I'd like . . . I'd like a fresh start, Winifred. For us. Like the past never happened. Will you give it a chance?"

She blinked at him. "That was quite a speech."

He chuckled and shrugged. "It's been a long time coming."

Could they do it? Pretend it was water under the bridge? It was worth a try. "All right, Mr. Tidwell. It's a deal." She smiled and held out her hand, loathing herself for taking up Mr. Keegan's habit. Before she could withdraw it, Bobby clasped it and shook, then winked.

"See you soon."

She smiled back and continued smiling until the click of his heels faded. He was a good man. Insecure at times, but that seemed to be fading with his increasing optimism, unrealistic though it was.

Even if Bobby's miracle happened, what she earned between now and next Monday wouldn't put a dent in George's debt. She'd still be broke and that thug would throttle her, for sure. She rolled the rag into a tight ball and hurtled it toward the Cat.

Fear gripped her gut, setting off a core tremble. To shake it off, she began pacing and soon found herself standing in the office, hugging her father's picture frame to her chest. "What do I do, daddy?" she whispered, then took several deep, steadying breaths. There was a way, and she'd find it.

Sell.

The thought cut off her breath. No, she couldn't! She leaned the frame away from herself and studied her father's face. His eyes crinkled with a smile hidden by a long mustache. "You wouldn't want me to sell, would you? Not the shop. But maybe . . . something else?" Her heart twisted at the thought of her precious violin.

A dull clunk emanated from the garage. She gasped and spun toward the sound.

"Miss Fisher?" a small voice called. "Are you here?"

Winifred laid the frame down and rushed back into the bay. "Berta Milfort, what are you doing here?"

"It's Wednesday." The girl stood in the center of the garage, hunched in on herself as though afraid to breathe lest the air stain her. She clutched the hem of her skirt in one hand and a violin case in the other.

"Your lesson!" Winifred's gaze darted to the clock. The short hand sat a smidge beyond the four.

"I went by your house. Mrs. Fisher said I'd find you here." Berta studied the garage floor then scooted her feet closer together.

"You don't mind having the lesson here, do you? I'm expecting someone, and it's important that I not miss him."

Berta's gray eyes lit up. "Your racer beau?"

"Excuse me? No, he's not my beau."

Her face fell. "Oh, that's too bad. Is this his auto?" She picked her way to it, rose up on her toes, and leaned over the door. "It's beautiful." Her whisper teemed with awe.

Winifred joined her and ran a hand over the sleek, wooden steering wheel. Berta replicated her motion then turned wide eyes on Winifred.

She smiled, recalling the moment she first took in the Bearcat. "I know the feeling." Russell's words. *Russell.* Why *not* call him by his first name? When a woman lets a man kiss her, first name status should be a given.

"How long until you finish fixing her?"

Winifred patted the leather seat, working to keep the sorrow from her voice. "I'm not going to work on her anymore."

"Then who is?"

"No one, I suppose. Not in Corona, at least."

Berta shook her head wide and slow. "No, Miss Fisher. You *have* to make her run again. She's too beautiful not to race."

"It's not that simple." Her thoughts jolted. She hadn't meant to quote Russell.

Don't be ridiculous. It's not that simple and you know it.

A forlorn sigh escaped her. Debt was a cruel taskmaster.

Berta hopped away from the car and tiptoed across an oil stain on the floor to one of the cleaner patches. "I'm just eleven. I don't understand about love, but Mr. Danny Fisher wouldn't have quit a job halfway through. That's what Momma said."

"Did she, now?" Winifred propped a hand on her hip. "And how did your momma know I planned on quitting?"

"Everybody expects it. You'll quit to teach your beau a lesson."

Winifred rolled her eyes. "He's not my beau."

"Whatever you say, Miss Fisher." Berta grinned. "Can you teach me to play now?"

Gladly.

Their first lesson went smoother than Winifred had anticipated. Most children were clumsy their first weeks holding a bow, but Berta's fingers seemed created for the task. *No talent to speak of, eh Mrs. Milfort?*

An hour later, the shop was quiet again, the Cat Winifred's sole companion. Her stomach rumbled, but she wouldn't leave to find dinner and risk missing Russell.

She stared at the package on the counter, feeling much like a dog drooling over a bone. She threw her arms up in the air. "Oh, what could it hurt? It's not like he'll hold it against you." After all, she was angry at Russell, not his handsome car. Why deny herself a little fun?

She lit the lamp, snatched the package, and carried both to the Stutz.

Hours later, the circulating pump was installed and Winifred climbed into the driver's seat, exhausted. She propped her arms on the wheel. "Where are you, Russell?"

He wouldn't abandon his pride and joy. She'd just have to wait him out. With a yawn, she let her head drop onto her forearms.

Tidbits of dreams swirled through her mind as sleep took hold.

Heavy footfalls yanked her upright. "Russell?" The lamp had all but gone out, leaving the shop awash in late evening shadows.

A strange man sauntered toward her from the right.

With a squeal, she scrambled to climb over the gear shift.

Another stepped out of the shadows on her left. He opened the passenger's side door and draped an arm over it.

"What do you want?"

"Hola, señorita." No mistaking that slimy voice.

"Wh-who are you?" She dug for bravado but came up empty.

"I can be Señor Keegan. You like? Would be better to get money for kissing a lady instead of breaking her. No?"

Blood whooshed in her ears. "Break? But I have until Saturday! I'll get your boss his money. I-I promise."

The man *tsk*ed and shook his head, casting a crooked nose in the faint lamplight. "Things was looking good with the racer, his car needing fixed. But now . . . " He spread his hands wide. "El Jefe seen him in Los Angeles. Looking for another mechanic. So you see? He is gone." The man clamped a meaty hand on her wrist. "And you, *bonita*, are mine."

Chapter Nine

Present Day

"Hurry, Mom. It's almost time to go." Faith finished tying her shoe and sprang to her feet.

Zoey jumped up and down. "Let's go, let's go, let's go!" Her blonde waves bounced with her.

Meghan pressed her lips together to camouflage the grin struggling to get out. "Relax. We don't need to leave for fifteen minutes."

"But Miss Baber and Sarah are already there, and we want to be early for choir. Please can we leave now?"

Meghan wiped down the kitchen counter, then angled her head and looked from one girl to the other. "I'll call to see if Dad's almost home." She grabbed the cordless and dialed.

"Hey, Meg." His voice was strained. As usual.

She crossed her free arm over her chest, hand under her elbow. "Hey." Thick silence stretched between them as she turned and paced the hall. "How was your day?"

"Stressful," he bit out.

Okay then. So he was impatient. She scratched the back of her head. "I was just calling to find out—"

"I've still got some work to finish up. I'll need a couple more hours."

Her shoulders slumped. He'd be missing church and working late. Again. That was three days in a row, even though he'd wrapped up the Johnson project and she knew there were no big jobs on the docket this week.

She shoved her feet into her shoes.

He must have other reasons for staying away. Namely, *her*. He was still mad about the conference. About their budget. Lord knew he wasn't taking any pleasure from her, so what was left to come home for?

Her shoulders tensed. "Fine. We're going to church. There's leftover spaghetti in the fridge."

His exhale whooshed through the phone line. "'Kay. Thanks."

At the staccato answer, Meghan stomped toward the living room. *Fine. Be that way.* "I guess we'll see you later then."

"Yep. Later."

She threw the phone onto the couch, then buried her hands in her hair.

Resistance makes you stronger. Succeed despite him. Succeed despite him. Succeed despite him.

She released her upper lip from between her teeth, unsure how long it had been there. With a strengthening sniff, she pulled her shoulders back and lifted her face. She wouldn't be invisible forever.

"Okay girls, time to leave." She hustled everyone into the car and pulled out of the driveway toward church, but anger burned in her veins as she drove.

She parked and before she'd even cut the engine, both girls were unbuckled and opening their car doors.

Meghan watched them take off across the small parking lot in a foot race toward the choir room. "Be careful!"

"Okay, Momma!" Zoey yelled. But neither girl slowed down until they reached the door.

Meghan grabbed her purse and Bible, and headed inside, feeling far from holy. *Forgive me, Lord. I know my attitude stinks, but I'm just so angry.* She swung open the sanctuary door with a little more gusto than necessary.

Trying not to stomp down the aisle, she scanned the room for a place to sit.

"Meghan! Over here."

To her left, Curtis waved, then beckoned her over. "Hey, how are you? Is your husband here? I'd like to meet him."

Behind her plastic smile, Meghan ground her teeth. "No. No, he is not."

"Oh well, I'll meet him next time. Want to sit with us?"

She scanned the other faces in the row. "Sure. Thanks." She took a seat between Curtis and a woman she recognized as a nursery worker.

The worship team started in on the first song. A hymn she didn't recognize, but whose lyrics brought an ache to her soul. By the second verse, the song seemed to rip her wide open.

Are you disappointed, wandering here and there,
Dragging chains of doubt and loaded down with care,
Do unholy feelings struggle in your breast?
Bring your case to Jesus, He will give you rest.

Meghan's bottom lip trembled. She swallowed hard, closed her eyes, and gripped the leather edge of her Bible.

She would *not* cry.

As the pastor began his sermon, her anger melted into grief. What was happening to her marriage? She fought her distraction and opened her Bible.

"Turn to Nehemiah, but keep a finger in Acts," Pastor Mike directed.

She opened to the right passages but the words blurred on the page.

Her shoulders sank.

Beside her, Curtis leaned forward, resting his arms on his knees as he focused on the pulpit. Meghan shifted her own attention back to the pastor.

"Nehemiah was a restorer. The walls of Jerusalem were in ruins, and he was the one God commanded to take the lead in getting them rebuilt. Are there walls in your life that God is calling you to rebuild and restore?"

Yes. Meghan swallowed. She'd been watching the walls of her marriage crumble, trying to deny it, for a long time now.

Pointing her face down to the Bible in her lap, she squeezed her eyes shut and let her heart carry her back again to the days following her high school graduation.

She saw the beach. Sand, gulls, long serpentine lengths of seaweed crawling up onto the shore. Salty air whipping her then highlighted locks off of her face. Surrounded by other friends newly released from the prison of high school, Meghan and Steve spent hours throwing Frisbees, burying each other in the sand, then best of all . . . sitting close in front of a fire pit once the sun went down. While those around laughed or made out, she and Steve had grown solemn, sharing glances that underscored the significance of the plans they'd been making.

Pulling a marshmallow off the skewer and pressing it between two crackers, Meghan whispered, "What about school? You're supposed to go back in the fall."

"I can go back and finish any time. I want you with me when I do. I'm not going to leave you here again."

Her heart melted, then coursed into her veins, warming her more than the fire that crackled in front of them. She scooted closer to him, watched the light dance and reflect off his tanned face. Her lips parted, but no words came.

He looked out toward the horizon. "I love you, Meghan Campbell. That's not gonna change. So unless you say *you* aren't ready, I'm not going back to school this year." His chestnut eyes met hers again. "Are you? Ready, I mean. To let me take care of you forever?" He reached his hand up and trailed her cheek with his thumb.

Her eyes had stung, then pooled, and with a hard swallow she nodded. Oh, yes. She was so ready. Forever wasn't long enough to spend with this man.

He moved his face closer until she felt his breath on her skin. "Good." Then his thumb moved to her mouth, caressing her lower lip.

His kiss seemed to mark history, to separate two versions of herself—the Meghan who sat in Mrs. Pearson's Language Arts class a week before, and the one kissing the father of her future children.

Lost in the memory, Meghan wiped a tear from her cheek and sniffed.

"You all right?"

She started at Curtis's quiet question. She managed a nod, but her heart lurched as the tender memory shattered, then was buried under the weight of Steve's absence. She lifted her eyes to the front of the church. Beside her, Curtis closed his Bible and zipped up the cover, then laid it on the floor beneath his chair. She did the same, then straightened.

Heads bowed around the room as Pastor Mike closed the sermon and the musicians took the stage. She'd tried not to be distracted during his message, but couldn't escape the hopelessness. Tears slipped down her cheeks during the last song.

The minister's voice carried over the final chords of the guitar. "If anyone needs prayer tonight, please stand."

A spiritual cattle prod jabbed her soul. If she really cared about her marriage, was she willing to stand up for it? Throat aching from effort, Meghan gripped the back of the seat in front of her. She'd never done something like this. In front of everyone? A game of tug-of-war raged inside until, arms and legs shaking, she rose.

"Now I'd like the rest of you to pray for those who are standing."

Meghan kept her eyes squeezed shut, but felt a firm, strong hand come to rest on her shoulder.

Curtis.

Another hand rested on her arm—the woman seated on her other side.

When the final "amen" was spoken, Curtis squeezed her shoulder and rubbed her back before his hand fell away. The prayer felt good, but she doubted it would carry her farther than the church doors. Meghan ran her fingertips under her eyes and looked up at those who had surrounded her. Gaze settling on Curtis, she blinked and nodded her thanks, unable to form the words.

With concern in his eyes, Curtis wrapped an arm around her back and drew her to his side for an embrace. His warmth seeped into her, a brief comfort.

He picked up his Bible and tucked it under his arm. "Hey." His voice was gentle. "A couple friends are going out for pie and coffee, if you and your daughters would like to join us."

A soothing gratitude curved her lips. "No, I better get the girls home. It's a school night. But . . . thank you." She drew her brows together and chewed her lip, hoping he realized the appreciation wasn't just for the invite.

"Sure."

When he shifted his weight as if to turn away, she inhaled and rushed to speak. "How's your sister doing? The one you mentioned." She wasn't ready for the conversation to end just yet.

Releasing a sigh, he propped a foot up on the seat and leaned onto his knee. "I don't know. I'm worried about her." He shook his head and looked out across the room. "But she won't listen to me." He rubbed the back of his neck. "I'm still praying over that one."

"Then I'll be praying, too."

He paused and looked into her eyes. "That means a lot to me. Thank you." He gave a crooked smiled, awakening that tingle inside her again.

"Mommy!" Zoey ran down the aisle, Faith right on her heels.

Meghan cleared her throat. "Hey girls."

Faith smiled at Curtis. "Hi, Mr. Curtis."

"Hey, how's my spelling whiz?"

Faith blushed. "Good."

He gave each of the girls a high five, holding his hand just high enough to make them jump for it. They laughed and Meghan's chest tightened. She coughed then wrapped her arms around herself. "Well, we should get going now."

"I'll walk you out."

Her gaze flicked over his features, buoying her spirits all over again. She smiled. "Okay."

She and Curtis followed behind the girls as they skipped out to the car beneath the moonlit sky.

"Meghan, I don't know what you're going through, and I don't need to know. But, if you ever need to talk, or pray . . . I'm here, okay?" Hands in his pockets, he shot her a sidelong glance.

Tears pricked Meghan's eyes again and she blinked until they were under control. "Thank you. I" —she hesitated— "I'll keep that in mind."

Everyone said goodbye, then Meghan started the engine and headed home, little-girl voices singing in the back seat.

"You two sound wonderful. I'm glad you had fun."

Though she offered the encouragement and flashed a smile in the rearview, her focus was still turned inward. Tending to her injured heart. Life had been giving her such a beating. Prayer had helped, but she was so worn out. "I can't do this, Lord," she muttered under the girls' singing. "I can't. I'm unequipped for this." Like some vital part of her was broken. And therefore, so were her dreams.

Driving on autopilot, her thoughts detoured past the life she had always imagined, to the reality she was headed toward—one absent of her hero.

Sometimes even the best-laid plans . . .

But she wasn't ready to pull the brake just yet; no matter how hard it was to keep going.

When she pulled into the driveway, a knot cinched deep inside her.

Steve's car was still gone.

1916

Russell stepped off the passenger car onto the Corona Station platform. Except for getting Chester out of the hospital and onto a train toward home and full recovery, it had been a tiring, unproductive day.

A couple of Los Angeles mechanics had been fascinated by his Stutz, his aero engine, and his dilemma. None, unfortunately, believed it could be repaired in time for the qualifying rounds. Russell had assumed they didn't want to admit they were clueless about aero engines. That is, until he sniffed out the local crop duster mechanic who had parroted the others—too much damage, too little time.

The platform was empty. Steam enveloped him as the last train of the day lumbered past. Russell dragged his weary feet toward the exit and longed for a bed to put an end to this miserable day.

Where had he gone wrong? Maybe his mistake had been not renting a tow truck for the day and hauling the Cat with him to Los Angeles. If they'd seen his baby, they wouldn't have been able to decline. On second thought, Winnie *had* seen it and still rebuffed him, at first. He stopped and stared down a dark street. What had changed her mind?

Desperation. That's what. She was just as desperate as he was. But for what? He rubbed the stubble on his chin while his mind replayed the fear that flashed across her face when he'd encountered her alone in the dark shop. If the man who'd been there hadn't been her beau, then . . .

Money. He'd wanted money. Was Winnie in debt? She'd changed her mind and upped her fees right after her encounter with the slug. Debt created desperation, sometimes enough for a person to go back on her principles—like having nothing to do with racing.

He resumed walking. The humiliation of one perfect—albeit public—kissing bet couldn't be enough to cancel that out. He'd just have to offer her more dough.

"Now or never." He adjusted his path to intercept the shop. She might be pulling another late night. When he rounded the corner, he smiled at his own good thinking.

Bathed in shadows, Winnie stood outside the closed back door of the garage, facing away from him. The faint sound of jingling keys reached his ears. He stopped to gather his thoughts and plan his approach. *Apologize again. Lots of apologizing. Agree she has every reason to hate you, sock you one. Bring up Pop's dream—that got her attention last time. Offer more cash. A bunch. An amount she can't resist.*

"Here goes nothing." He rubbed his palms together, but hadn't gone five steps when she spun and dropped her keys.

Like a cornered rabbit, she backed against the door then leaned forward, as though straining to see in the dark. "Russell? Is that you?"

The tremble in her voice set him on edge. "What happened? Did that weasel come back?" He scanned the area, jogging toward her.

With a cry, she launched into a run and didn't stop until she'd plastered herself against him.

He wrapped his arms around her and tried to absorb the violent shakes wracking her body. "When did he leave? Is he still around?"

"I don't think so. There were two this time." Her ragged breath heated his chest—and it was all he could do not to growl.

With his next breath, guilt joined the anger. He should have been here.

He pulled her closer, and she cried out. Like an encounter with hot lead, he released her. "Are you hurt?"

"My hand." She cradled it against her stomach. "He took the pliers, and-and—" Several quick intakes of breath crippled her speech.

"Pliers? They took *pliers* to your hand?"

Tears dripped from her chin, as her mouth opened to drag in another jagged breath.

His hands spasmed into fists. *Not now, Keegan.* He took a moment to calm himself then reached for her. "Let's have a look." With great care, he flipped her hand over, then angled her so that she faced the street lamp on the corner.

The light revealed a pinky bent where it shouldn't be, pointing a direction God did not intend.

She gasped then threw her good hand up to her mouth. "I think I'm gonna be sick." She spun and ran back toward the garage.

He followed and arrived in time to catch her hat before it tumbled into the rubbish barrel she flung herself over. Patting her back, he spun mental wheels trying to decide what to do next.

"I feel better now," she mumbled through the quaking hand that wiped her mouth.

"Good." Not that she looked any better. "Now, let's get you out of these coveralls before you leave. With swift fingers, he freed the first three large buttons, revealing the shirt beneath. He was moving onto the fourth before her head tipped toward his hands.

He was undressing her on the street, and she had nothing to say? Was she in shock? Her trembles had yet to slow.

What did a person do in a situation like this? Should he keep her warm? He grasped her right hand. It was icy cold. "You know what, never mind the coveralls. I'm taking you home. Did you bring the Lizzie?"

"Umm." Her gaze swept the small rear lot. "My keys. What did I do with my keys?"

He snatched them off the ground where they had fallen earlier. "I've got them."

"Maybe the car's around the front?" On unsteady legs, she moved to go around him.

"Hold up. I'll check." He reached for her, but she stopped, bumping her finger against his arm.

Fresh tears spilled. "I want to go home, Russell." Sniffles garbled her voice. "Will you take me home?"

His heart squeezed. "That's it. Enough talk." He swept his arm under her knees and plucked her off her feet. The air left her mouth in a whoosh, but she dissolved against him without a peep of protest. The scent of baby powder with a touch of gasoline reached his nose, and he fought the distraction. Winnie truly was a man's favorite things—women and motor cars—mixed into one bewitching package.

A walk around the building answered their question. No Model T. "It's just a few blocks. I'll walk it." He readjusted his hold on her, and she settled in.

Her silence worked for him since he wasn't sure he'd be able to speak without either cursing the piker who did this or begging her forgiveness for not being there to protect her.

The cursing she could do without hearing, being a lady and all—although he had a sneaking suspicion she would agree with his sentiment. The begging, he'd spare her, because Winifred Fisher was a woman of action. To reach her, he would have to speak her language.

They passed Ramona Street—the halfway point to her house, and the spot they'd first raced.

Say, you know what always cheers me up? A hearty race. How 'bout it? He cringed at the memory of his own words.

A race, a bet, the thrill of a win—they'd always cheered him up. This time, they'd driven him down a dark road, and for the life of him, he couldn't light the headlamps to find his way home. Shoot, he couldn't even *find* the headlamps. Even worse, in his mad scramble in the dark, he'd taken down the one person in town who'd already had her fill of tragedy, and then some.

A cramp took up permanent residence in his shoulder. It burned like the dickens but he would welcome ten more just like it if it would undo the results of his selfishness.

A glance down at her brushed a curl against his chin. Her left hand lay against her stomach at an awkward angle that kept her crooked pinky in the air.

She dug her good fingers into his shirt and pressed her face into his shoulder, but he heard her small squeak of a cry anyway. He winced and did his best to even his strides.

By the time he reached her picket gate, sweat dripped down his back. He fumbled with the latch while trying not to drop her.

"I can walk now." Her shivers had subsided a bit, but there was still a catch in her voice.

He tipped his head to get a look at her face, illuminated by the faint light from the house windows. Pale. "I don't think so."

She narrowed her lids. "Put me down, gamester."

"Ah, there's my cranky girl. I've missed you." He set her on her feet, taking care not to disturb her hand.

"I'm not your girl, and I'm not cranky." The bite dropped from her tone. "I just can't have Momma seeing me like that. She's been through enough." Her arm shook as she fiddled with her hair. "How do I look?" She dragged the back of her hand across a drippy nose and smeared grease across her cheek.

"Like a million bucks. You're not going to hide this from your mother, are you?"

"I don't see how it's your business what I say and don't." The words were tough, but the accompanying hiccup dissolved the bluster.

"It's safe to say your judgment's a little blurry at the moment. That's what I'm here for." *Partly, anyway.*

He'd find the thugs and deal with them in his own way. But what about in the meantime? Could he risk letting her out of his sight . . . for even an hour?

Present Day

Meghan hit *save* and leaned back in her chair. Her shoulders were stiff from hours bent over the keyboard, but for the scene she'd just written, it was worth it. She stretched her neck toward each shoulder and rotated her hands in circles, then sighed.

Oh, to have her husband come to *her* rescue. To fight for her, carry her. But these days Steve felt more like the enemy. The one taking the proverbial pliers to her heart. It felt good to focus on a relationship she could actually do something about. Even if it was fictional.

Her chest expanded, thinking about what was coming up for Winnie and Russell in the next scene. Winnie would be shell-shocked. Meghan could relate. And her dreams of the symphony dashed. She could relate to that, too. How would the handsome new man in her life fit in? Meghan ran her finger across her bottom lip, thinking through all the delicious possibilities.

A horn honked outside Meghan's living room window. Brooke was already there. Meghan picked up her cell phone.

Sorry. Give me five.

Her tingling middle somersaulted. Hurrying to her bedroom, Meghan pulled on the cute new track suit she'd purchased, then applied a coat of mascara and some lip gloss. Red Berry. Maybe a dusting of loose powder would keep her face from getting too shiny.

She stopped at the mirror by the entryway and separated the strands of hair resting on her forehead. She smiled at her reflection, so much improved from a few months earlier, then slipped out the door.

Meghan climbed into Brooke's car. "Hey there, gorgeous."

"Hi, beautiful!" Brooke grinned as she put the car in gear. "You're in a good mood."

"For the most part. Writing time and prayer will do that for a girl."

"And a bit of mascara always lifts my mood, too." She winked.

So she noticed? Meghan shrugged. "After the trauma of running into Tom that day, I'm afraid to work out with a nude face anymore."

"I'm glad you're feeling confident today."

Confident. Yeah. "I do have one thing still nagging at the back of my mind . . . " She wagged her head side to side. Should she even bring this up?

"What?" Brooke twitched her brow as she looped through the neighborhood, following the latest detour signs.

Meghan lifted one shoulder. "It's nothing. Just . . . Steve worked so late I'm not even sure what time he got in last night, and he left again real early this morning. I didn't even get to say hi. So of course I think he's upset. But I know . . . I need to let it go."

One of Brooke's waxed eyebrows arched high, and she cocked her head. Something about the uneasy gestured chilled Meghan's blood.

"Right?"

They stopped at a light and Brooke turned toward her. "Well . . . I know what *I* would think if my husband was staying out late and leaving real early."

Meghan's face went slack. She took a deep breath and swallowed, heart pounding against her ribs.

Brooke shook her head. "But I can't imagine Steve being anything but honorable."

Meghan blinked. Right. Of course he was honorable. Things had been tense, but . . . "He would never . . . " She shook her head emphatically, then shifted her gaze out her window.

Would he?

"No. He wouldn't. So let's not go there. Next subject. Are you still planning that Tara May party? You know I turned down a facial yesterday so I could try out their stuff."

Meghan stared out the window and ran a finger along her bottom lip.

"Meg, did you hear me?"

Meghan nodded. "Yeah, I'll give you the flyer. I still need to do the email invitations."

"You know I'll be there. And I'll help you round up more church girls, too." Brooke shook Meghan's knee. "Come on, buck up, soldier. We're here."

"I'm good." Meghan shook off the chill hiding in her bones as she unclasped her seatbelt.

Inside, Curtis was sending off another client. He approached and greeted them. He and Meghan exchanged a wordless dialogue, the subtle question in his eyes asking how Meghan was doing. Basking in his concern, she smiled her reassurance.

While Brooke sat to do leg presses, Curtis led Meghan to a scary new contraption that made her want to run: The cable crossover machine. She stood in the middle of what felt like a stage, wishing she had a bench to recline onto so she'd be somewhat obscured. But no. Today she had to stand boldly in front of anyone who might walk by and watch her struggle. Well, maybe not boldly.

"I don't know about this." She hugged herself as Curtis set the weights.

He laughed without looking up. "Don't be such a worry wart. What are you afraid of?"

"People watching. Me, looking like an idiot. I don't know how to work this thing." It was huge.

"That's what I'm here for." He motioned for her to take her place in the very center of the arched machine. "Come on. Stand right here."

She stood where told and chewed her lip.

"You can do this, I promise. Okay, grab these two handles." He pulled the first one down and placed it in her right hand, meeting her eyes as she adjusted her grip.

Meghan had to stretch both her arms up and out wide to reach the other handle, then Curtis showed her how to stand. "Now step one foot forward, in front of an imaginary line stretching between both pulleys, and pull the cables down in front of your navel. This is your starting position."

With a grumble, Meghan complied. The tension in the cables surprised her; Curtis hadn't gone easy on her today.

He gave a light touch to the small of her back, tingling her spine. "Slight bend forward at the waist, and bend that front knee. Good. Now breathe in, and extend your arms out to the side in a wide arc until you feel a stretch on your chest. Then use your chest muscles to return to the starting position as you breathe out."

She tried the motion and her arms whipped outward.

"Whoa, whoa. Don't let it snap your arms back. Control."

"Sorry. It's just . . . everyone is watching."

His mouth quirked to one side. "Tune everything else out. Just focus on what I'm telling you. Okay?" His soft smile drew one out of her and she nodded. "Keep a slight bend in your elbows and try again."

After a few jerky attempts, she got the simple movement down to a smooth science. Well . . . almost.

Curtis raised his brows. "Better!"

She glowed and peered up at him through her lashes. "Thanks." They both glanced at Brooke on her machine, then back to each other. Meghan exhaled with the descent of her weights and searched for conversation. "So, how are you today?" She pulled her arms in. "You ready for this heat coming our way?"

"I'm . . . good." He ran a hand over his clean-shaven jaw. She kind of missed the stubble. "Ready for summer. Just not as prepared for seeing my sister today at lunch." His eyebrows shot up and he pressed his lips together. "She called this morning, so if you want to pray for me, that'd be great. It's not an easy subject, but . . . I have to talk to her about her health."

"Her health?" She cast a worried look at him and took the opportunity to catch her breath between sets.

"Yeah." He rubbed the back of his neck, showing off his well-defined arm. "Our mom died of diabetes about five years ago, and since then Tanya's health has suffered and her weight has climbed at a steady clip. You'd think seeing our mother's ordeal would've set her straight, but . . . " He shook his head.

"Oh, I'm so sorry." She stopped herself from reaching out to touch his arm.

"Me, too. It's so frustrating that I can help other people get in shape, but not my own sister. Every time I try to go over the data—talk to her about eating better, exercising, or losing weight, she gets angry."

Data? Oy.

"I've even offered to work out with her, take her for bike rides. Start a weight circuit. She's not only uninterested, she's offended. But this is my sister. She's at risk. I have to convince her to do something before she ends up like our mom." His eyes met hers. "I don't want to lose her, too."

Meghan's heart twisted. "That's what you need to tell her, Curtis. Not the data. Don't talk to her as a professional trainer, talk to her as her brother. Guide her back to the days when you were kids together and build on that emotional foundation."

He puckered his mouth and exhaled, eyebrows raised. "Yeah. You're right. I never thought about it like that, but you're exactly right." His cheeks puffed out. "I've been trying to convince her with logic when I should've just loved her." Crossing his arms over his expansive chest, he looked down at the floor. "I guess I have some praying to do. Thanks." He coughed, and when he looked back up, he was back to business. "Start your next set, woman."

Meghan gave an exasperated groan. "I thought I was done."

"No way. We're just getting started." He flashed a wicked grin that seemed to say he couldn't wait to torture her. "Let me check in with Brooke while you keep doing these, and don't stop until I say. You can take a thirty second rest between sets of five and that's it." He winked. "You can do it."

When he returned a few minutes later, Meghan's loose powder had surrendered to the sweat gathering on her forehead.

"One more set and then we're moving to leg lifts."

She narrowed her eyes and glared at him. "Is torturing people all you do for fun?"

"No. Just when I'm hired to." The broad smile made it hard to believe him. "I also watch TV, play games on my phone, and I love trips to Best Buy." His smirk drew a chuckle from her throat as she extended her arms out again. They shook as she used every drop of determination she had to pull them down again. Last rep.

She let the handles go and massaged her poor muscles. "Didn't realize you were such a techy. I thought you were more granola than that."

"Pfft. Granola? No. But health and technology are not mutually exclusive."

"Well, maybe *granola* is the wrong word. But I somehow pictured you using all your spare time outdoors exercising. You know, when you aren't putting together stage sets, teaching Bible songs to little kids, or praying with distraught women at church."

Her assessment drew a deep laugh from Curtis. "No, not at all. I'm pretty attached to my phone. Kinda sad, really. I just discovered a new word game last week that has me totally addicted. Lex Linx. Heard of it?"

"Uh, yeah! I love that game." The lexicon linkup had never interested Brooke or Steve, but she'd spent weeks playing with random strangers.

His eyes sparked like summer sunlight reflecting off the bluest lake. "You do? We should play sometime." He directed her to the bench where her next round of agony would take place. "Although it wouldn't be fair. You have an advantage being a fancy author. Words are your forte."

"What are you talking about? You must know a bunch of legal jargon I'd have no idea of." Back against the rest, she slid her feet behind the cushy foam, ready to light her legs on fire.

He pulled his head back. "You knew I went to law school?"

Her cheeks warmed. "You mentioned it in passing once. At the grocery store."

"Oh, that's right. Very *astute* of you. I'm interning now. Working toward my dream same as you are. Slow but sure. Someday I hope to have my own practice. To see *Jameson Law* engraved on the side of a fancy office building. Hey, when you get your first publishing contract I'll review it for free."

Jameson? Like one of the city's oldest families?

"Your last name is Jameson?"

"Yeah."

"As in . . . " She squinted. "You're not by any chance be related to W.H. Jameson, are you?"

His eyes rounded. "Yes, I am! You're a Corona history buff?"

"Well, in a manner of speaking. My book revolves around the Corona Road Race of nineteen sixteen."

"Are you serious? Oh, I have a ton of stories I could share if you're interested. I grew up hearing them told over and over again. The original Jameson house isn't in the family anymore but I'm friends with the owner, and could probably get you a tour. You know, my great-great grandparents were one of the few avocado ranchers around and I've got a killer secret recipe for guacamole." He gave a low whistle. "This is so cool. You've got to let me read your story."

The heat spread from her cheeks toward her ears. "You're the first one to ask. Um . . . Sure, you can read it." Oh, what did she just say? "I'd love to hear any stories about the prominent families, business owners from back then. What was the local watering hole? Do you have any insight on the races? My character has musical aspirations— do you happen to know who might have taught her music back then?"

"Not sure, but I do have a lot of anecdotes from my grandparents, and their parents. Old love letters. Journal entries that talk about my great-great grandfather's first job working at the grocery. Courting my great-great grandmother. Plenty of names.

And I think they might have been at that last race, too. The one in 1916."

Meghan's heart thumped. Just imagine the details she could add to her book. Make it come to life. This was huge. Something wound its way from her gut to her nerves, making them prickle. Maybe *Racing Hearts* would be more than just another romance novel. It really *could* be a New York Times best seller.

Now she *had* to pitch it at the conference!

As she told Curtis about her plot, he asked questions and nodded at her answers. He became so animated, his smile wide and genuine. No one but Meghan had ever gotten this excited about her story. It felt so good to share her enthusiasm with someone.

"It's a great idea for a story. I love it. And I gotta say, I'm pretty stoked to share some family history and see it in a book."

Meghan bit her lip to hide the smile lighting up her insides. "Well, I'd be so grateful for it, I'll thank you in the book for your research help." Tickled pink, that's what she was. "The house you mentioned . . . do you know when it was built? Do you have any pictures of it from back then?"

"Hmm." He pressed his lips together and shook his head. "I don't know off the top of my head, but I'm sure my aunt or somebody will."

"Okay, I'll give you my cell number so you can contact me when you find out."

He pulled out his phone and handed it to her so she could type it in. She handed it back. "Here ya go."

"Hey, now we can play Lex Linx."

She laughed. "I have to play late at night after the girls are asleep and the house is picked up. And lately I've used that time to write. But I'll look for your handle next time I log on."

A warning bell rang in her spirit, but she silenced it. What was the big deal? They weren't doing anything wrong. Curtis was just a friend.

A very good friend.

One who was actually interested in what she was doing and thought she was talented. Who was a spiritual leader, a prayer warrior.

And whose piercing eyes saw her more clearly than anyone had in a long time.

Chapter Ten

1916

Orchards zipped by on both sides of Magnolia Avenue, the long stretch of road between Riverside Hospital and Corona. The headlamps led the way, their light bobbing and weaving with every bump and pit in the dirt road.

Bracing her bandaged hand against her chest, Winifred fought to keep herself from sliding into Russell on the next turn. Their hips collided, and she pushed her feet against the floorboard to put distance between them. "Land sakes, Russell, this isn't the speedway," she hollered above the whipping wind.

His foot came off the gas. "Sorry. Habit. Is it making your hand hurt?" A grimace roughened his voice.

"Sorta." And her hip was on fire.

Her hair settled back against her forehead, but she still gripped the bench with her legs, uncomfortable with his speed—and her inability to stay out of his lap.

He took another curve, and she braced herself, determined not to slide again. She opened her mouth to protest then snapped it shut. He'd been more than generous with his time the last few hours.

Exhaustion weighted her lids. She rubbed her eyes with her thumb and forefinger. "Why don't you use the car to get back to the hotel tonight? I won't be driving for a while." Not driving, not working, not playing the violin. Would she ever be able to play again? Doctor Rosenthol had said it was a clean break and should heal well, but she'd also been promised there were more breaks where that one had come from.

Nausea churned her insides. The car's bouncing didn't help, and Russell seemed to be finding every rut.

"No need for the loan. But thanks," Russell said.

She puffed her cheeks and wished for her bed.

His head turned, and her face burned with the awareness that he studied her profile. "I know you're tired. I'll have you home in a jiffy. Promise."

"Promise." She choked on the word—and the memory of a commanding hand around her wrist, another clamped over her mouth, squelching her scream. The cold pliers, the crack of bone, and the searing pain.

"Say something?"

"Mumbling about promises."

"What about them?"

"Just that tonight seems to be the night for men and promises."

His head snapped toward her. "How about you elaborate."

Her throat constricted. She didn't want to elaborate. She wanted to bury her head in an engine block and forget there was a world outside the shop. She wanted to curl her fingers around her bow and lose herself in Haydn. These things were her life. They defined Winifred Fisher, made her who she was—and both were about to be yanked away from her forever.

Desperation loosed her voice. "That man . . . he promised . . ." Her mouth went bone-dry, but she forced a swallow, hoping to down the fear scorching her tongue. "He promised a new broken finger. Every time he has to pay me a visit."

Russell's leg jerked. Three second later, amid squealing tires and swirling dust, they came to a dead stop.

Mouth gaping, Winifred found herself on the edge of her seat, her knees less than an inch from the dash, her good hand before her, pressed against the half-windshield. Her shirt stretched taut against her front. She spun to see what had snagged it.

Russell had a solid grip on the back of her clothes. "Close your mouth. I had you. You weren't going anywhere."

"A little warning would have been nice."

He dragged her backward until she sat full on the bench; then he killed the engine and angled himself to face her. "Who is he and how much do you owe him?"

Shame washed over her, suffocating her in its heat. "This town is the worst for gossip!"

"Winnie . . ." He spoke her name with such tenderness, she couldn't conjure anger. And she couldn't fool him. He'd seen too much.

Her shoulders drooped. "Four hundred and twenty-five."

"Who is he?"

That was it? No exclamations of horror at learning how deep her hole went? No gloating in the knowledge that her cocky confidence had been nothing but hot air?

"I . . . don't know." She picked at the splint between her last two fingers. Her entire hand throbbed. Her body dripped with fatigue. Why was he pestering her about this?

Tension filled the air between them. "How can you not know?" At last, a touch of impatience.

She shrugged. "Can we go now?"

Silence cloaked the car. Moths darted about the car's lights, and the scent of orange blossoms tickled her nose.

Russell leaned toward her, his voice quiet but hard as iron. "It's George's debt, isn't it?"

Her gaze popped up to meet his. The moonlight caught in the baby blue of his eyes and reflected unmistakable anger. "He left you with his debt. And now, you can't find him."

"I don't mind helping him," she lied.

"Well, I do," he snapped. "He doesn't deserve your help."

"He's family, Russell." Why did she feel compelled to defend George? Russell was right, but she only had one brother.

"Which is why I'm not calling him a few choice names. And let me guess. The one who did this"—he pointed at her bandage—"isn't the man your brother owes. Some lackey?"

She expelled air through pursed lips. May as well spill it all. "Right. He calls his boss El Jefe. It's all I know."

"It's a start. Any other debt? Mortgage? Rent?"

He was pushing it. She sat up straight. "Who are you to ask such a—?"

His hand slid over her knee. "I'm trying to help you. Just answer the question."

Her muscles tightened beneath the weight of his hand. He sat too close, spoke too tenderly. Her resolve turned to mush. "The house is paid for. We're two months in arrears on the shop."

"I'm so sorry, Winnie." The sound of her pet name on his tongue made her wish for another curve to deposit her in his lap.

She patted the hand still on her knee. "I can assure you, my near financial ruin is *not* your fault."

"No, it isn't. But your broken finger is. I should have been there." He growled and swung the door open. The car shook when he leapt out. Hands on hips, he stopped and stared up at the nearly full moon.

Winifred leaned across the bench and admired the excellent view. But it was more than broad, muscular shoulders, and a chest tapering to narrow hips that made her breath come ragged. It was the uncontained energy that flowed around him, the raw virility of his every move, the cocksure stance that emphasized his lean form.

She stepped out and leaned against the open door. "You're being awful hard on yourself, aren't you?"

He didn't answer right away, and when he did, she had to tip her head to hear. "Am I? If I hadn't made you so angry that you kicked me out . . . If I hadn't taken that stupid bet. I would have been there tonight."

"Not necessarily. It was late. You would have already been back at the hotel."

"Pop said betting's my greatest weakness, but I never saw it as a weakness at all. It never affected anyone but me. Until now. And when I think about you in that dark shop alone with those criminals . . . " His voice went dark. "Men who hurt a lady in such a way deserve to be beaten to within an inch of their lives. I'll volunteer, and thank you for the privilege, too."

His anger scared her. She approached and stood behind him. "Noble sentiment, but you would be stooping to their level."

He snorted. "Almost there as it is."

"Nonsense. You're a good man, Russell Keegan." She rested a hesitant palm against his shoulder. His muscles stiffened. "Easily distracted by refined ladies of class, such as myself, but good nonetheless."

He chuckled, and she smiled.

"Come on, speedy. Take me home." After a couple of firm pats to his shoulder, she made her way back to the car.

"Winnie." His husky voice raised gooseflesh on her neck and stopped her a few steps from the Lizzie.

She peered over her shoulder. He stood where she'd left him, facing her, hands dangling at his sides. "I'm done with Corona. The race. I couldn't find a mechanic in Los Angeles, and I'd never ask you to work on the Cat. Not now."

"No more race?" Her voice rose on a squeak. He didn't mean it.

"I'm through."

She'd known she wouldn't be the one to put him on the track, but she'd still planned to cheer him on in secret. She never believed that her backing out of the deal would keep the Stutz off the Circle. "There's got to be someone . . . There's a crop duster I know on the north side of Los Angeles. His mechanic, Rob Henson, might be able to—"

"Talked to him. He's a no-go." He walked toward her.

"Oh." Disappointment tugged at her—an unpleasant sensation. And unexpected. Racing would never make it to her approved sports list, but she'd grown fond of the car. Or was it the man behind the wheel . . . ?

"It's a shame we won't see the Cat on the speedway. She was built for Corona." She looked up through a misplaced curl. "If my finger wasn't broken, I'd change my mind about helping you. Honest, I would. A real shame."

"It's nothing. Just another race, and I didn't mention it to make you frown. Refined ladies of class, such as yourself, should never have to frown." A crooked smile bunched his cheek and stole her breath. With a single finger, he brushed the curl away, and Winifred found herself wishing he would succumb to another bet.

She ran her tongue along her lower lip. "Mr. Keegan, I've decided I like you, after all." Doggone her shaky voice.

He shifted, hovered above her. His rapid breath blew the curl back into her eye.

Her finger shrieked, but the pain was dull compared to the longing tightening her body.

With a grunt, he pulled back, and she blinked in confusion. "You're tired and your mother's gotta be worried. Let's get you home." Taking her by the elbow, he guided her to the passenger side.

One block from the house, Winifred still wasn't sure what to make of his rejection. Maybe he'd seen the error of his way? Decided, at last, to travel higher moral ground?

"I'm moving in to your place." Russell broke the awkward silence.

A dry laugh tripped from her mouth. "You're very amusing."

"I'm not joking. You're not leaving my sight until I've dealt with those thugs. I hope you have a comfortable couch." Eyes on the road, he didn't even crack a smile.

"Absolutely not." Was he insane?

"This isn't up for discussion." He pulled into the open carriage house and shut off the engine.

"The town thinks I'm a trollop for yesterday's . . . public display. There is no way on God's green earth you're sleeping under my roof. Even though I don't fit the mold"—she flicked a glance at her ringless hand and hardened her tone—"I *am* a lady."

"I'm fully aware of that fact." His voice rumbled low and intense. The tangy scent of citrus hung in the air alongside his insinuation.

Heat filled her body. She told herself it was indignation.

"If you know another way to keep both you and your secret safe, let me know."

She didn't, and truth be told, she was already terrified at the thought of her and her mother being alone. She tucked her aching hand against her chest. "Momma won't allow it."

"My guess is she will when she finds out what going on. I assume you've kept everything from her—the debt, the thugs?" No accusation. Just a question.

"She's been through so much. I just . . . couldn't."

They sat in silence, staring at the slatted carriage house wall. Russell's wrists draped the steering wheel. His chest filled and emptied. Slow and steady. Confident. What must it be like to have no other care in the world than winning the next bet, the next race?

Maybe that was why she enjoyed his company. His carefree spirit rubbed off on her, made her forget her world was careening off the tracks. His present mood, however, was anything but carefree.

"Are you telling her, or am I?" Russell's no-nonsense question hovered between them.

Her teeth clamped down on her lip. She wanted to be angry, wanted to hate him for butting into her life and making demands. But it felt too good to be taken care of, to have someone else make the decisions.

"I'll tell her tonight."

Weariness consumed her, ate at her bones. She rubbed the heel of her hand against her forehead. "I can't think anymore. Whatever energy I've had to keep the family's reputation afloat, the shop doors open, food on the table, momma's heart from *completely* breaking . . . ." Her hand fell to her lap. "It's all gone." Her gaze dropped to her bandaged finger. Even her dreams were gone. The Los Angeles Chamber Orchestra was now as unreachable as her daddy's much-needed wisdom.

Fresh tears threatened, but she refused to give in.

"Come here." Russell stretched an arm across her back and tugged her toward him.

She welcomed the summons, not even feeling foolish at her shuddered sigh.

He rubbed her arm. "You don't have to worry about any of that while I'm here."

It sounded divine. But there were racetracks to conquer. Bets to be won. And she was just a besmeared wrench-turner with more baggage than any man could carry.

He was here, but not for long.

Present Day

The smoky, salty scent of bacon drew Meghan toward the kitchen. Steve sat at the dining table with his iPad and a near-empty plate in front of him.

Meghan looked at the yolk-smeared dish, then to the counter by the stove. "Any left?"

"No, sorry. I wasn't sure if you'd be up or even want any since you've been eating healthy."

"Mm." That was true. But part of her still bristled at the idea that he'd made himself a nice breakfast without offering her any. Wisdom told her it was her wounded heart looking for a target.

Lord, help me have a good attitude today. I don't like being in this place. I miss my husband.

She eased into the dining chair across from him. "So, are things slowing down at work yet?"

"Maybe a little."

"Good." She smiled. "Summer's here and I was thinking we should do something with the girls. Maybe take them to Disneyland, or drive down to San Diego and visit Sea World." *Remember how to be a family. Build some bridges.*

Steve cleared his throat, then scratched his ear. "Uh, I don't know. Maybe." His chest expanded with a deep breath, then he busied himself scraping the last bit of egg off his plate. He stuck the fork in his mouth as he riveted his attention back on his iPad.

Meghan felt her eyebrows pull together for a moment before she made a point of smoothing them. She didn't want to dissect his mood. Not today.

He scraped his chair back and took his plate to the sink. "Well, time I head out." Grabbing a can of root beer out of the fridge, he turned toward the door to the garage, then stopped. "I shouldn't be late tonight."

"Okay. I'm glad." She pressed her lips into a smile, then crossed to him. "Thanks for working so hard." Shackling all her raging concerns, she banished them from her outward expression. She drew in a breath and stood inches from her husband, wondering if he'd offer a kiss. Hoping he would.

He shifted his weight, then turned the door handle. "No problem." He flashed the briefest grin. One that lifted and fell so quick she would've missed it had she blinked.

Meghan reached out and grabbed the edge of the door as he took a step under the frame. "Bye." She bit her lip and gave what she hoped was a coy look. Batted her eyelashes.

"Bye." As he leaned toward her, Meghan's heart quickened. But his kiss landed on her cheek. "See ya tonight."

And then he was off.

Her throat swelled as he slid behind the steering wheel.

She closed the door and spun toward the mug tree. She needed a cup of tea.

As she waited for water to heat, she prepared her mental to-do list. She needed to go back and edit some of her manuscript, but first she had to vacuum the bedrooms and load the dishwasher. She hoped the girls would sleep in while she did the chores. Then she would take them to her mom's for a treasured "school's out" Grandma Day, while Meghan tried to make progress on this book of hers.

The wall clock ticked like a soundtrack to her life. She plunked the tea bag into the hot water and gazed out the kitchen window. A sun-bleached fence separated their yard from the neighbor's. She looked at it, knew it was there, but her eyes weren't focused on it. They weren't focused on anything. Silence smothered the house.

The chirping of her cell phone made her gasp, and the jolt sloshed hot tea over the side of her mug. She shook her head and grabbed a paper towel before reaching for her phone, which sat plugged in by the coffeemaker.

She crammed it between her shoulder and ear, wiping up spilled tea at the same time. "Hello?"

"Hi, Meghan. It's Curtis."

Her breath hitched. Hearing his voice on the line was strange . . . and wonderful. "Oh, hi."

"Hey—I really liked the chapters you emailed. You're a wonderful writer."

"Aw, thank you." Meghan moved her hand to her cheek, hoping to cool the heat radiating from it.

"I mean it. So, I've done some digging around and found the information you wanted, and I have some papers you'll want to see."

"That's great! But . . . Brooke and I aren't scheduled for the gym today, so . . . "

"I know, I'm not there either. I'm working at the office but I can drop them off if you want."

Her brain seized. Curtis here? In her house? Why did that idea scare her so?

"Or we can meet up somewhere during my lunch break if you prefer."

"Yeah, that's a good idea."

"The church?"

Relief sent the air from her lungs. But, relief from what? "That works. So . . . twelve-thirty?"

"Sounds about right. I'll see you then."

~~~

A peculiar sensation rolled around in the pit of Meghan's stomach on her way to the church. She chose to chalk it up to curiosity at what information she was about to get her hands on.

She flipped on her blinker and turned onto the church grounds, then pulled up beside the one other vehicle in the lot. Curtis emerged from his car as she set her brake.

Her stomach dipped at the site of him in a crisp suit. He'd never looked so handsome. Sky blue button-down mirroring his eyes, tailored suit jacket draping broad shoulders and tapering to a lean and solid torso. As she got out of her own car, she tried not to take notice. Or react. But she wasn't blind.

And, she was certain, he wasn't either. Had she disguised her assessing gaze well enough?

Cheeks on fire, she prayed he hadn't seen right through her. What would he think of her, a married woman, looking at him that way? But judging by the way he locked eyes with her, he'd noticed her reaction.
~~~

She rubbed her arm to chase off the tingling in her skin. "You, uh, sure look spiffy in that suit."

"Oh." He looked down at his clothes. "Yeah . . . gotta dress the part at the office." He shrugged and gave her an embarrassed half-grin that made her lips tilt.

Maybe Russell should be less cocky. This self-consciousness thing was incredibly attractive.

She sucked in a breath, acutely aware of his gaze on her. Why hadn't she worn something else?

His eyes flicked over the length of her. "You look nice today." His Adam's apple rose and fell. "Look at the definition in your arms." He smiled and squeezed her bicep.

Blood racing at his touch, Meghan laughed, hoping to dispel the sudden image of running her hands over his muscles. "Yeah, right."

"I'm serious. You've done great." Curtis turned toward his open window and leaned into his car. Meghan's eyes were drawn to drink in his form but she fixed her gaze on the church building as he bent over the front passenger seat. A light breeze blew a wisp of hair across her neck, raising gooseflesh.

He retrieved a sheaf of papers from a briefcase then stood and held them out. "For you, Madame."

She reached out to take them. Would their fingers graze?

They didn't, and disappointment filled her. With a mental gasp, she scolded herself and pulled the stack of documents into her arm.

He nodded toward them. "Hope these are helpful."

"I'm sure they will be." Why did he have to smell so good? She fought the urge to close her eyes and take a deep breath.

"This material was intriguing. I'm excited about seeing some family cameos end up in a book. Did you know that my great-great-great-grandmother was good friends with the proprietress of the hotel in your book—The Hotel Del Rey. She helped her get on her feet when she was a penniless widow. If it weren't for my family you might even say that hotel may never have existed. And then where would your racers be staying?"

"Wow, I didn't know that." She'd have to read up on that story later. "I guess she passed on her generous spirit."

"Nah." He shrugged. "But you should know I'm not going to let you quit until it's done."

Well, *this* sure was different. "My own personal sentry, eh?" She couldn't say she minded. How refreshing to have someone urging her on. Watching over her. Didn't hurt that it was her lead character.

"That's right." He grinned then cleared his throat. "Oh, I also brought you a little something." He grabbed a plastic container from off his dashboard and handed it to her. "Remember that killer guac I told you about?"

"Ooh. You've set my expectations awfully high. Hope it lives up."

"Me, too. And there's more where that came from." His gaze hit her straight on, then a grin lifted his tanned cheeks. "Well, I'll see you at church."

"Yeah, see you Sunday." Should they hug? No. "Thanks again."

"No problem." He opened his car door. "I'll wait for you before I pull out."

She smiled, feeling feminine and valuable all of a sudden. "Okay." She buckled up, dizzy with anticipation over the Jameson family journals. The gems she might find to work into her novel. And she had all afternoon to devote to writing.

Glancing down at the papers on the passenger seat, her forehead wrinkled. Curtis had attached a note.

Impressive, Meghan. You're amazing. I'm already a fan.

Meghan's heart hammered, and heat filled her belly. She glanced out her window, where Curtis sat in his car waiting for her to pull out of the lot safely before he left. He smiled.

She pressed her lips together and swallowed as she turned her key. Yes, she was eager to write. But now she was ravenous for something else, too.

So she shouldn't be thinking about Curtis.

She shook the thought away. She wasn't. Not really. His compliment gave her a boost, reminded her that, like Winnie, she was still a woman, with all the natural desires that came with the role. Made her long for her husband. And that was a good thing, right? Restorative?

Of course it was.

1916

Russell tossed on the couch and plumped the pillow beneath his head. Through the living room windows, dawn kissed the sky, dissolving any possibility of falling back to sleep.

From overhead floorboards, the whisper of feet reached his ear. Daughter or mother?

He tossed the sheet off his legs and sat up.

A lithe figure appeared at the top of the stairs.

The pulse in his neck ignited and throbbed. *Easy, killer.*

Winnie tiptoed down the dark steps, her nightgown swishing against her legs. Without a glance his direction, she continued toward the kitchen.

He gripped the sides of the couch to refrain from following.

A cabinet opened and closed, then a quiet, persistent scraping noise began and grew louder by the second. At a small pained exclamation, he jumped up to investigate, following the whiff of powder she'd left in her wake.

Wounded hand against her breast, Winnie hunched over a drawer, fighting it one-handed. A mass of curls blocked her face from view, but her calves and bare feet were exposed. The thin fabric of her gown far from concealed the rest of her outline. With reluctance, he averted his eyes and shuffled his feet to announce his presence. "Need some help?"

She glanced up then spun away, a hand flying to her loose hair. "You're awake! And . . . not dressed."

He looked down at his rumpled pants and sleeveless undershirt. "You didn't expect me to sleep in my shirt, did you?"

"You caught me off guard, is all." She inched back around, flicking her gaze between him and the door. Planning her escape route? Taking care with her pinky, she hugged her chest and gave him an apologetic smile.

Dim light from the adjacent window set her hair aglow. It tumbled around her face and shoulders in sensual disarray. An adorable sleep line creased her cheek and ended at the corner of her mouth. Last night, he'd turned down the chance to savor that plump mouth. For the life of him, he couldn't remember why. Something about propriety . . .

The skin between her eyebrows crinkled, and she moistened her lips as though she, too, were remembering the missed opportunity. "If I'd known you'd be awake already, I would have put on my housecoat."

To keep his gaze from wandering south, he stapled it to her eyes and grinned. "I don't mind." Not a bit.

"Good morning."

Russell and Winnie spun.

Mrs. Fisher stood in the doorway, wearing an ankle-length dress, a chin-high lace collar, and a scowl.

"Good morning," they replied in unison.

Mrs. Fisher's eyes narrowed at him. Had she read his rogue thoughts? He took a step back from Winnie, feeling much like a boy caught stealing a treat.

"Winifred?" She eyed Russell.

"I came down for an aspirin."

"I think we might be out." Mrs. Fisher's face softened as her gaze shifted to her daughter, then back to Russell. She jutted a finger toward the counter. "Can you open the drawer?"

"Yes, ma'am."

Winnie stepped away from the front of it. He caught her sidelong apology and lifted his mouth in a discrete smile.

His tug on the handle got him nowhere. He grabbed the drawer front around the edges and applied muscle. With a terrific screech, it gave way, jostling the contents. He removed it, and set it on the counter.

Winifred rummaged in it a moment then blew air through tight lips. "You're right, Momma. We're out, and Mr. Thomas doesn't open for another two hours." Creases formed on her brow as she walked stiffly from the room.

Fresh guilt stung him. *I'll just have to make it up to her.* It was a tall order. How did one make up for that level of fear and pain?

The drawer, for starters. He ran his fingers along the tracks under the counter. The one closest to the sink was damp. "Moisture's coming from somewhere. It's made the wood swell."

"Mr. Keegan." Winnie's mother stated his name with all the authority of a presiding judge. She stood several paces away, hands folded in front of her.

Russell straightened and gave her his full attention. "Ma'am?"

Her slippered feet slid one step closer, and his torso inched back. A hundred miles an hour in an open car, and he didn't bat an eye. One look from this woman, and the urge to hightail it nipped at his feet.

Interminable seconds passed before she graced him again with her tight, low voice. "I'm not quite certain yet that your motives for helping us are entirely pure, but seeing how the reason I slept the two hours I did was on account of your being here, I'll thank you for staying. But be advised. My daughter's inherited her father's reckless spirit, but I'll not allow her to be swept away by the allure of the races. Or a flashy racer. Do you take my meaning?"

In other words, don't touch Winnie. Don't go near Winnie. Don't look at Winnie. "Yes, Ma'am. But ma'am, in case you forgot, my Bearcat's out of the race."

She peered at him from the tops of her eyes. "I never forget anything, Mr. Keegan, and I never assume a racer is finished racing, no matter the condition of his vehicle. Now. Thomas Drug opens at eight sharp. You may take the car, and while you're there, I suggest you apologize to Boris for your behavior. Your conscience will thank you, as will I."

Russell swallowed a mouthful of pride, grateful Winnie had left the kitchen. "I agree, but I intend to take Winifred with me."

"I expect nothing less. She shouldn't be alone." Her hard gaze dropped to somewhere on his chest, and for the first time, he caught a flash of vulnerability. "Promise me you won't leave her alone. Not until this madness is put to rights."

A wave of protectiveness washed through him, solidifying his decision. Her mother's staunch backing was a boon he hadn't expected. "That's my plan, but they could just as easily come after you. You should come with—"

"You just take care of Winifred. I'll see to myself."

"I'm not sure that's safe."

She swatted the air. "I said don't worry about me."

The click of heels drew their attention to the doorway. Winnie entered dressed in a long, wispy skirt. Her white blouse was tucked in, reminding Russell that she had a waist and, beneath it, a nice set of hips. Her hair no longer hung in seductive waves down her back. A loss, for sure, but the loose, coppery bun that haloed her face accented the tone of her peachy cheeks. She was a peach he'd nibble any day.

Beside him, Mrs. Fisher's gaze burned his ear. He checked—

Present Day

What on earth—?

The garage door was opening. Meghan's head snapped up, senses on high alert. Bees buzzing in her belly, she moved the mouse to the Save icon, then closed her laptop. She trotted to the kitchen and gave the veggies a stir. Then she fluffed her bangs, adjusted her blouse, and pinched her cheeks. The doorknob turned and she pressed her hand to her stomach just before Steve entered.

She flashed a smile. "Hi."

"Hey, do I smell steak?" His mouth curved up.

"Yep. And cheddar mashed potatoes."

His brows rose high. "Sounds great." He pecked her cheek and stepped around her toward the hall. "Let me change real quick."

"'Kay." She bit her lower lip as he drifted down the hall. When he disappeared into the bedroom, she lit the candles she'd placed on the table and plated the food onto their best china.

He returned and paused in the entryway, eyes sweeping over the layout—the candles, the flowers, the placemats. His forehead crinkled, but a smile played on his lips. "Just two plates. Where are the girls?"

Meghan dipped her chin and looked up at him through her lashes. "I sent them to my mom's. Overnight. Sit down and eat, everything's ready."

He looked at her with a lopsided grin, then pulled back the chair at the head of the table.

Meghan seated herself to his left. She unfolded her linen napkin and smoothed it over her lap. "Shall we pray?" She held out her open hand, and he took it. Hope filled her heart as he said grace.

Steve lifted his fork to his mouth, closed his eyes and groaned. As he savored each bite of his favorite dinner, she mentally patted herself on the back. And when the meal was finished, she carted their dishes to the sink . . . and left them there for later.

"That was delicious, Meg. Thank you. I'm going to wash up."

"Take your time."

As soon as the master bathroom door clicked shut, Meghan dashed to her room and dug through her top dresser drawer. Whoa, she needed to get organized. Too many ratty socks, and underwear with elastic strings hanging off the waistband. She continued sifting until she found it.

The lingerie she'd worn on their honeymoon. Kept all this time and still in perfect condition.

She ran her fingertips over the delicate flowers embroidered into the silk. Like Steve had done when she'd worn this on their first night as man and wife. Heat crept into her cheeks. Even now, she flushed at the memory.

She'd been more than ready, and he was so gentle.

Seeing her in this tonight, the memories should rush back to him, too. Goosebumps rose on her skin as she slipped into the black- and rose-colored nighty. She hadn't been able to wear the sleek negligee in forever, but thanks to a certain handsome trainer—she blocked off the thought.

When the shower turned off, she dimmed the bedroom lights and prepared to pounce.

There's nowhere to go, buddy.

He'd hardly be a man if this desperate measure failed.

She moistened her lips as the door opened. Dropping a shoulder, Meghan tilted her head and met his gaze. "Hi," she purred.

Clad in a towel, Steve stopped short. One side of her mouth lifted as he took in the full sight of her. Water dripped down the sides of his face, and wet hair jutted out from his scalp. Eyes still roaming over her, he stood silent.

Meghan lifted her chin, wickedly pleased with his attention. Her breathing picked up speed as she sensed his yearning. At last. Steve's mouth closed and he swallowed. When he formed a response, his voice was low and hoarse. "Hi." His eyes lingered on her curves, and a vein in his neck pulsed.

She savored the erratic beating of her heart as she moved to him and ran her hands over his damp, bare chest. "How was your shower?" Reaching up, she traced the contours of his shoulders, then clasped her hands behind his neck and pressed herself to him.

"Good." His voice was barely audible and he cleared his throat. He released an unsteady breath as Meghan made trails up into his hair with her fingernails.

She trembled as Steve's palm found the small of her back, pulling her closer. Resting her hand on his jaw, she ran her thumb across the stubble on his cheek. Then, on tiptoes, she pulled his face down toward hers. She hovered close enough to feel the energy pass between them, for his breath to warm her lips. Mint mouthwash. Inviting. Parting her lips, she touched them to his, caressing his mouth with hers.

His kiss boasted a craving she hadn't awakened in a long time. Electricity sparked throughout her. One strong hand moved behind her head, cradling her as if she were once again the most precious thing in his life. His other arm encircled her waist and held her tight.

This was a familiar place. Home.

She slipped her arms under his and clung to his back, straining on tiptoes to get closer, kiss him harder. As she strengthened her grip and molded her body to his, Steve's muscles tensed. He held back, restrained his passion. His lips continued to move with hers, but a slight resistance in his body made things feel suddenly awkward. Back rigid, he rested his hands on her shoulders and stiffened his kisses as if putting on the brakes.

No way, mister.

Running her fingers down the smooth skin of his back, she encountered the edge of the towel tied around his waist. If he wouldn't put the pedal to the metal, she'd have to.

They were just revving up.

Meghan reached behind her head and tugged the cord on the window blinds to block out more of the sun. The shower started. She uncurled herself from hugging her pillow, rolled onto her back, and stared at the ceiling.

With a puff of her cheeks, she sat up and jutted her fingers into her hair. As memories of the previous night filtered through her mind, she sniffed and wrapped her arms around herself.

Oh, Lord, why doesn't he want me?

Her throat tightened, and Meghan pulled her knees to her chest and closed her eyes. His touch had been so . . . cold. Forced. His kisses devoid of passion no matter how she tried to please him. Instead of getting lost in the moment, loving her with abandon, he'd held her with such deliberate concentration she felt like a calculus midterm. Like it took effort for his mind not to wander.

God . . . I repulse him.

She gulped back the sob in her chest and straightened her spine. With a quick intake of breath, she swung her legs over the side of the bed and stood. Arms crossed in front of her, she yanked the nighty over her head and shoved it toward the back of her drawer. Then she pulled on her sweats to wait for her turn to shower.

Talk to him.

She shook her head then dropped her chin to her chest. She was too embarrassed. Humiliated. Besides, she *had* tried talking to him. And still she felt stranded in the middle of a vast desert. Tiny, thirsty, and forgotten. Even after the previous night's intimacy, she felt more alone than ever before.

Meghan busied herself muddling through a laundry basket when Steve emerged from the bathroom.

"Your turn."

"Oh, okay, thanks." She feigned concentration, as if searching for something in particular, and didn't look up at him.

"I'm going to grab a bagel real quick, then head out." He rubbed her arm as he passed, bending to peck her cheek. Like things were normal.

She shaped her lips into a smile. "All right. See you later."

As soon as he left, she started the shower. Pulling off her sweats, she stepped into the stream and shivered. She turned the dial, but nada. Hadn't she turned up the water heater again last week?

Maybe it was broken. She snatched the shampoo bottle and scrubbed like a madwoman, hoping to get out of there before the lukewarm water turned icy.

Who needed to be scrubbed and polished for a day at the beach anyway? She toweled off and pulled her hair into a sloppy ponytail, then donned her bathing suit for the first time that year. At least she wasn't bulging out of it like the last time she wore it. She wouldn't be gracing the cover of *Sports Illustrated* anytime soon, but she didn't fear the seams cutting lines into her hips either.

She pulled on a white, flowing skirt over it, and gathered towels and sunscreen, shovels and buckets, then loaded up the car with the beach supplies. Potato chips and Capri Suns for Faith and Zoey, and grapes and iced tea for herself.

All that was left to get into the car were the girls themselves. Meghan zipped over to her mom's and found them already in their suits, staring out the window like two puppy dogs. When they saw her, they disappeared from the window and soon flew out the front door and came barreling toward her before she even had the engine off.

"Whoa, slow down there." She got out of the car and giggled as her two darlings wrapped their arms around her waist. "Are you excited to see me, or does this have anything to do with the beach?" She rubbed their backs and kissed each head.

"Good morning." Her mother appeared in the driveway, coffee cup in hand and twinkle in her eye. What would Meghan have done without this woman? Always smiling, always giving.

"Morning, Mom." She wrapped her arms around her mother and held her a little longer than usual. "I hope these two didn't drive you crazy last night."

"Oh, no. Of course not. We had a wonderful time playing Go Fish and watching *The Sound of Music.*"

"You got them to watch that? I used to love that movie."

"I remember. You used to twirl around pretending to dance like Liesl." She placed her palm on Meghan's cheek and smiled. "We had fun."

Meghan knew she meant with *her,* as well as with Faith and Zoey. She grinned, then turned to her kids. "Girls, what do you say to Grandma?"

They were already buckling their seatbelts. "Thank you, Grandma!"

Zoey kicked her dangling feet back and forth. "C'mon, Momma, let's go to the beach!"

"I guess they're a little excited. I better get them to the sand. Thanks again, Mom."

"Anytime. Have fun."

Forty-five minutes later, the girls were running down to the shore and digging their toes into the damp sand.

While they splashed and ran from oncoming waves, Meghan reclined on a beach lounger soaking it all in. The beach brought so many memories. She and her dad used to hunt for the best seashells to add to their collection. The big ones with no cracks were a rare find. She didn't know why she hadn't gotten rid of them yet, but they were still in a little box in the back of her closet. Like a sad shrine to the childhood she could have had.

Trips to the beach weren't the same after her parents' divorce. Sure, her mom and grandma were willing to comb the shore with her, but it never felt right.

Did this day feel wrong to her girls, without Steve there with them?

She shook her head. Of course not. It was one day while Steve worked. Even with so many of these days beginning to rack up, it wasn't the same as knowing your dad wasn't interested in you anymore. Had replaced you.

She swallowed against the sting needling her throat. Steve's absence was more about her than their girls. Had to be. Seemed she couldn't hold the attention of any man in her life. At some point or other, they lost interest, distanced themselves.

"Mom! Mom!" The girls shouted and waved at her. Meghan dabbed her eyes and arranged her smile before jogging over to join them.

"Will you help us find sand crabs?"

"Sand crabs, huh?" A tradition she'd passed on to them from her own childhood. Meghan laughed. "Who's got the bucket?"

She walked to the edge of the water and dug her hands down into the wet sand, hunting for the creatures. A cold wave passed over her wrists, and as it went back out, she felt a squirming little critter in her fingers. "Ooh, look at this one!" Brushing the grit away, she showed off the crab before dropping it into the bucket. It buried itself into the two inches of sand on the bottom.

All three busied themselves with the quest, squealing with delight whenever one was found. Zoey dropped several, especially when she happened upon a "daddy" crab, whose larger claws seemed to freak her out. Sometimes Faith managed to capture it before it tunneled to safety, but others got away.

After about twenty minutes of digging, Meghan rinsed her hands in the ocean and adjusted her sun hat. "Okay, girls. You build a pretty one, and I'll take a picture when it's done." She grinned at her little beauties and turned to trudge up the beach.

Whoosh.

With a gasp, Meghan jumped back as a Frisbee passed in front of her and landed a few feet to her left.

"Sorry!" A man jogged toward her from the right. Deep tan, smooth chest, sun-bleached mop of hair. "I didn't see you coming." He tugged his earlobe, which was decorated with a small silver hoop. "Yeah, no, that's not true." A sly smile appeared under his somewhat crooked nose. "I threw it on purpose. Didn't know how else to come talk to you."

"What?" Meghan's laugh bordered on a snort.

He angled his head. "Want to join our game?" He jutted his thumb toward two men standing several yards away.

She pulled her head back. Okay, he wasn't joking. "No, I don't think so. But thanks anyway."

"Then can I get your phone number?" His eyes locked on hers, no trace of guile.

Meghan's eyebrow rose. Her tongue felt thick. "I . . . don't think my husband would be happy about that."

"Ouch." He shrugged. "Well, can't blame a guy for tryin'." He pressed his lips together in a half-cocked smile. "Have a great day."

"Yeah, you too." She continued up the slope a few paces, then looked back over her shoulder.

The man hadn't left his spot. As his eyes swept her form, his lips puckered into a small "o." He shook his head as his gaze traveled back up. When it connected with hers, he wiggled his eyebrows. "Can't blame a guy for admiring, either." He winked, then jogged back the way he'd come.

Meghan blinked. She should be offended. Furious for being treated like a piece of meat. Creeped out by the guy's overt ogling. His boldness.

But she wasn't any of that. Not even close . . .

She felt pretty. Sexy. Maybe even a little smug.

Seemed she wasn't so repulsive after all. Too bad Steve wasn't there to see the kind of attention she got from other men.

Lowering herself into her chair, she reached into her beach bag and pulled out her phone. After zooming in and snapping a couple pictures of the girls, she forwarded one to Brooke, then checked for messages. None.

She sighed. Though she loved watching her babies play at the beach, she felt isolated. And she longed for connection. The nagging loneliness seemed to rise with each wave that crested then collapsed across the vast ocean. Her iced tea was no longer iced, but she gulped it down anyway. She licked her lips and double-checked her phone. No missed replies, no calls. Scrolling through her apps, she launched Lex Linx. She hadn't intended to look for Curtis's name, but she was soon staring at it. Her eyes traveled to the green dot beside it. He was logged on.

Sinking her toes into the grainy grit until they found a cooler layer, she dashed off a greeting. *Hey, it's Meghan. Rare opportunity to log on today, and look who I happen to find.* She added a smiley face and waited for a response.

Hey, what's up? I'm on my lunch break, creaming a few unlucky souls. Gladly take you on next. You up for a whoopin'?

Her cheeks lifted. *Always ready to give one, if you're ready to take it.* He had no idea what he was walking into.

For the next fifteen minutes, they volleyed vocab and smack talk until Meghan's lead came dangerously close to threatening Curtis's manhood.

Whoa, there. I knew you'd have that author edge but even so, I underestimated you. A mistake I won't make again. LOL. Business calls, and I'm afraid any more of this is going to pummel my ego into the ground. But next time, I'll be prepared. Better watch out!

She bit back a laugh. *I'm shaking in my boots. Enjoy the rest of your day—if you can, after that embarrassing loss.* The giggle in her throat bubbled out.

"What's so funny, Momma?" Zoey appeared beside her, torso covered in sand.

She slipped her cell into her bag and looked over her daughters. "Just a game on my phone. How did you get so much sand in your belly button?"

Zoey looked down at her tummy and swirled a pudgy finger in her navel. "Faith buried me. Can we eat now?"

Meghan shook her head, cheeks lifting. "What am I going to do with you two?" She busted out the snacks and drinks and after little tummies were full, it was time to shower off and pack up. As usual, both girls nodded off shortly after she started down the freeway.

As she listened to the steady spin of tires on asphalt, Meghan sifted through her mental snapshots of the day. Crazy, wet hair framing freckled cheeks, fingers and toes and crabs all digging into the sand, an attractive man looking at her with hungry eyes. She drew in a deep breath, then reluctantly dismissed the memory with a shake of her head. Jetting a puff of air from her nose, she imagined Brooke's laughter when she told her the story. *That* would be fun.

But probably not as much fun as destroying Curtis in their next game of Lex Linx.

Chapter Eleven

1916

She was a peach he'd nibble any day.

Beside Russell, Mrs. Fisher's gaze burned his ear. He checked his thoughts, contrived what he hoped was a gentleman's neutral demeanor, and made a mental note never to be in the house alone with Winnie.

"How long will you stay?" Winnie lifted her lashes to him.

"As long as it takes."

"We'll all say a prayer it's resolved sooner rather than later." Her tremulous smile failed to reach her eyes.

He'd pray for the opposite. He shifted his gaze to Mrs. Fisher. "I'm no carpenter, but if you've got the tools, I could try shaving a bit off this track."

Another layer of steel peeled from her face. "That would be helpful. Thank you. Danny's tools are in the shed. You might find what you need there."

Time flew as he crunched on toast and tinkered with the drawer. At last, it slid without ado into its slot. With a grunt of satisfaction, he turned to find Winnie leaning against the opposite wall, her hand snug against her chest, her face serious and pale. He tossed the chisel on the counter. "You all right?"

Her gaze wavered with a shrug. "Boris should be opening for business in about fifteen minutes. Can we go now?" He didn't miss the tension in her voice.

But even in her desperation for relief, once they arrived at the drugstore, she refused to leave the car to avoid being seen with him in public—*especially* Thomas Drug.

Since he'd parked in full view of the drugstore's large windows, he allowed it. If she knew he was on a mission of humility, she would have insisted on being a witness.

Despite her snub, he did his best to clear her name, then bought her a soda and took it out to her, along with the new aspirin. She offered quiet thanks, and he settled back to watch her savor the beverage. When she was done, she took a deep breath and let it out through her nose. "It's feeling better already."

"Ah, that explains it." At the questioning cock of her head, he brushed the back of his finger down her cheek. "You don't look green anymore."

She rewarded him with the first full smile of the morning. Powered by that fuel, he drove them to the Del Rey Hotel to retrieve his belongings, check out, and pay up. When she, again, refused to leave the vehicle, he rounded the front of the car, opened her door, and gave her as stern a look as he could muster. "It's not safe here. On your feet or over my shoulder—either way, you *are* coming in."

"If you hurry, I'll be fine." She pressed her lips into a line and stared him down until he reached for her waist.

With a squeak, she squirmed past him and out of the car, teasing his nose with the trace scent of gasoline. "Fine, but we're not together. You're just the chauffer." She cast the words over her shoulder as she stalked toward the front door.

Slowing his steps, he lengthened the distance between them and admired her willowy gait. "Chauffeurs have it pretty good from back here." His sly grin weaseled its way into his voice.

She flicked a hard-boiled glance back at him and disappeared through the door. He followed, noted that she found a seat in the foyer, and took the stairs two at a time, slowing when he passed the forty-something proprietress.

He tapped the brim of his hat. "Morning, Mrs. Frazier. I'm checking out now, if you don't mind."

She rearranged her face into a broad smile. One less racer to contend with was always good news it seemed. "I'll prepare your bill right away."

He thought he'd made quick work of packing, but it wasn't quick enough.

Hand clutching her chest, Mrs. Frazier met him at the top of the staircase, her eyes wild. "Mr. Keegan, come quick!"

His heart faltered. Abandoning his suitcase, he pounded down the stairs.

Across the foyer, Silsbury gripped the wrist of Winnie's injured hand, holding it above her head.

Cheeks flushed, she stood on tiptoe and scratched at his fist in an effort to free herself.

Silsbury caught sight of Russell and rolled his eyes. "I thought you ditched this loser. You'd be better off with me, tootsie."

"Winnie!" Russell barreled into the room, blood pounding his eardrums. "Let her go!" He tried to wedge himself between them, but she shoved him in the chest with her free hand.

"Stay out of it, Keegan," she said through a clamped jaw.

Afraid his jostling pained her further, he backed up several steps.

A few gawking patrons, including Cooper, rushed from the adjoining dining room. Fire in his eyes, Cooper lurched toward Silsbury, but Russell threw an arm across the man's chest. They locked gazes, silent understanding passing between them.

Silbury's hard stance wavered. "Relax, boys. I won't hurt the pretty lady." His gaze traveled to her blouse and parked. "Winnie. I like it." He leaned to her ear and whispered at a volume that included Russell. "Do you reserve that name for your lovers? Or did your cheater daddy call you that, too?" He let out a guffaw, turning his head to laugh in Russell's direction.

Russell's fists clenched and a growl rose in his chest, but Winnie's reaction was swifter.

Her free fist sliced the air and caught Silsbury on the chin with a resounding crack. He released her and stumbled back several steps, then landed an elbow against a side table. A vase rocked, then crashed to the floor. The scent of lilacs filled the air.

Arms stiff at her sides, Winnie shook from head to foot.

Cooper grinned. "Couldn't have said it better myself."

Russell felt as stunned as Silsbury looked.

The man cradled his jaw, eyes bugging at Winnie. "You're insane!"

"Maybe I am, but Danny Fisher was *not* a cheater." Her volume increased with each word. "I'm not a floozy, and Russell Keegan is no loser. He could win that race on three wheels. But then, you know that, don't you? Otherwise, you wouldn't have bothered to take a swing at the Stutz!" She jerked an arm, and Silsbury flinched.

Laughter filled the room, Cooper's the loudest.

Admiration bloomed in Russell's chest. The woman could handle herself. The wrench-wielding thugs might not have come out as unscathed as one might assume.

"I have too much to do to be wasting my time putting you in your place, which happens to be dead last." She stepped around Silsbury, stopped in front of Russell, and winked. "Let's go, Mr. Keegan. You have qualifying rounds to prepare for."

His smile slid up one cheek. "Sure do." He offered his arm, and with a pointed lift of her chin, she took it.

He nodded to Cooper and led Winnie toward the door.

"I don't need two pinkies to fix the Cat," she said for his ears alone.

"This isn't over, Keegan!" Silsbury's shout followed them out the door.

Rage surged through Russell, but he forced his feet to move forward.

Winnie matched his anger. It radiated from her like heat waves from an overworked engine. She wore feisty well—all the way to the car, where she plopped onto the bench with a whimper and shook out her right fist.

Russell couldn't contain his chuckle as he returned for his suitcase and to pay his debts—including the vase. Mrs. Frazier looked more than relieved to see him go.

Back at the car, he examined Winnie's already swelling knuckles, then clicked his tongue. "Next time you plan to announce to the whole world you're going to fix my car and win the race, how about you *not* bang up your one good hand?"

She blinked in rapid fire, losing the fight to hold back tears. "That imbecile called my dad a cheater."

"Yeah, but you should have let me be the one to give him a right hook."

"I couldn't help myself. Silsbury's just so . . . so . . . "

"Trust me. I understand." Russell released her hand and closed the door. "But your mother won't."

Eyes closing, she tipped her head back and groaned.

His stomach dipped. "Look, ignore Silsbury and forget the race. He's not worth it."

She shook her head, knocking a curl loose from its pin. "He's gone too far. What he did to the Stutz alone is worth driving him clean off that racecourse."

"Let someone else do it," he said, even as his gut screamed, *Cream him*!

"No." Her quick, firm reply raised his brows. "It's *our* job. And if my mother heard what he said about daddy, she'd be on the warpath with me."

He understood the burning need to slash Silbury's ego. "We've got just a couple days. It'll mean late nights and early mornings, and you're down a paw. Are you sure you want to take on this fight?"

Her face tightened with determination. "You bet."

"How much?" At her squint-eyed warning, he laughed and held up a palm. "Just kidding."

"You better be." A smirk played around the edges of her mouth. "Like I said, the Cat was built for Corona. She's gotta race. And I'm not down a *paw*. Just a pinky." She winked again.

With each passing second, the idea of taking on the Circle grew more attractive. As did his mechanic. "Miss Fisher, I think I like you, after all."

Her rosy lips parted in a breathtaking smile.

Get the Stutz to the race on time? Possible. Keep his hands off this woman? Not so easy.

Before pulling out, he took in her profile. Looking every part the lady, she sat erect and stared straight ahead. Regal. Delicate. It was hard to imagine her in goggles and a leather helmet, changing a tire on the side of the road with cars zipping by at breakneck speeds.

She'd seen the races, knew what she was getting into, but should he make her stay in the pit anyway? As the engine rumbled to life, he shook off the idea. Everyone knew that a racer without a mechanic riding shotgun may as well not race at all.

Present Day

As Meghan pulled open the glass door of the coffee shop, the blast of cold air dried the perspiration dampening her brow. She missed the ocean breeze she'd grown up with. Corona summers were scorching. She unloaded her arms from their book-burden, and set down her laptop bag before stepping up to the counter.

The spike-haired young man on the other side smiled. "Hi, Meghan. Chai latte?"

"No, it's too hot today, Landon. I think I'll just have a black iced tea. Venti. And can you sweeten with honey for me?"

"You got it."

"Thanks." She paid, then sat at the little round table and pulled out her laptop. While it fired up, she arranged her notebook, pen, and phone in front of her.

Today, Steve was working from home and didn't mind her spending a few hours out of the house for library research.

Let's be honest. He never *seems to mind going all day without seeing you.*

A couple low conversations buzzed nearby, and a blender sounded from the far end of the shop, but a certain quietness seemed to override all of it.

Landon approached carrying her plastic cup of heat relief. "Here you go."

"Awesome, thanks." Meghan took a long sip of the cool drink, then leaned back with a sigh. Time to crack open the first book.

The Heritage Room of the Corona Public Library had proven invaluable for race information, and today she intended to pore over the resources she was able to borrow. Photos of Grand Boulevard as it appeared in 1916 had been enough for inspiration. But now she needed to know the nitty-gritty about the races from a driver's point of view.

Her eyes flicked to her phone screen, then back to her library book. Was he logged on? She scrawled some notes, tapped her pen against the table and bit her lip. The lure was too strong. She'd only be a minute.

Snatching her phone, she pressed a few keys and opened Lex Linx. A challenge from Curtis popped up immediately. Meghan allowed her smile to fully bloom. Nobody she knew was around to wonder why—another luxury of the coffee shop. Feet tapping the floor, she dove in to give him a smack-down on the game he refused to give up trying to beat her at. The man was a glutton for punishment.

Waiting for it to load, she took another long drink of her iced tea and scanned the next page of *Corona's Grand Street Racing*, amazed the article had been written by a high school senior. Having this information already compiled saved her weeks of work. Combined with the inside info she was getting from Curtis, she had more great details than she knew what to do with.

A text flashed behind the app—a smiley and message from Curtis. *Get ready for defeat.*

Ha! After weeks of fruitless effort he should know he was going down.

You mean yours? ;)

She'd make this merciful and quick—the conference was closing in fast and she had plenty to do. She couldn't afford to squander the cherished opportunity to get out of the house and work.

She had a fifty point lead when her phone rang with a call from Curtis. Forehead scrunched, she answered. "What are you doing?"

"Saving you."

"Saving *me*?" She snorted.

"Yeah. Can't let you use all your words on this game or you won't have any left for your book."

She laughed again and heard him stifle a chuckle across the line. "Let's be honest, you're saving yourself."

"What? No. If that's what you think, you don't know me at all."

"I know you well enough, mister, and that's exactly what you're doing."

"I'll never admit it."

"You don't have to." She lifted her straw to her lips. Yuck. Even sitting in the air-conditioned building, the ice had melted and left her with half-flavored water.

"I'll make you a deal. We'll strike this game from the record, and if you finish the next chapter by the end of the day, I won't make you do the tire lifts at the gym tomorrow."

"Hey, no fair. I'm *researching* today."

"Rules are rules, missy."

"Rules are made to be broken." Her laughter cut short first, then his, giving way to a heavy silence that made Meghan's breath go shallow.

Curtis cleared his throat. "Hey. I wanted to say that your advice about my sister was spot-on. She listened to me this time. She didn't say much, but she listened. I think I finally got through to her and we're going to work together on a plan for her health. With me acting like her brother, her support system, not—"

"Her personal health Nazi?" She quirked her lips.

"Yeah, exactly. So . . . thank you."

"You're welcome. And I know from my own experience you make a great support system, so I have all the confidence in the world she'll do well."

"Thanks, Meghan. Okay . . . back to the books, little lady. For both of us. I have to finish this rather boring brief before three. No more distractions for me."

"Excuse me? Who challenged who to the game?"

He chuckled. "Hey, you logged on. That was distraction enough."

Meghan dumped her stuff on the kitchen table, then popped open her most recent batch of the famous Jameson guacamole. Curtis was right; this guac was good enough to eat with a spoon. She let the smooth avocado slide over her tongue then shook her head. No more, or she'd have to ditch her new skinny jeans. She stowed it in the fridge then headed toward the master bedroom.

"I can't talk here." Steve's voice carried from the other side of the door, his voice low.

Her hand paused above the handle. Holding her breath, she leaned closer to listen.

"No, I haven't told her yet."

She covered her mouth with her hand.

"I will soon . . . not ready."

Meghan backed up a few quiet steps, then returned to the kitchen in a fog. She reached for her purse on the counter. Gripping the shoulder straps, she looped them over the hook on the wall then stood there, clutching the fraying handles. She swallowed, then moved toward the fridge and grabbed a bottle of water for her parched throat.

Who was on the phone? And what wasn't her husband telling her? A wave of nausea washed over her.

As the refrigerator door closed, Steve appeared, stopping short when he saw her. Meghan tipped her head and looked at him sideways.

His round eyes and shifting weight betrayed him. "Didn't hear you come in." He scrubbed his fingers across his forehead.

She took another drink from her bottle. "Well, here I am." She looked at him and waited.

His chest filled with a deep breath, and his whole body seemed to deflate as he released it.

Meghan's gut churned, and her throat clamped. "Steve, please. Tell me what's on your mind."

"It's nothing. I'm tired. Picked up three new projects, all due for delivery within six weeks. Which of course means—"

"Paperwork. Yeah. So . . . let me help." She stepped toward him, a sudden desperation swirling within. "Please."

His foot slid backward a fraction of an inch and felt like a thousand miles.

"No, that's okay. I got it."

She moved closer, tongue darting across her lips. "But it's no trouble. Together we can get it done in half the—"

"I said *no*."

Her mouth snapped shut. She swallowed, then nodded. "Okay. I'll clear my books off the table for you then, and be out of your way."

"No need. I'm going to head down to the office and do it there."

"I thought you were working from home today. All your stuff is already here. Why drive all the way to the office?" She hated the squeak in her voice.

"I'd prefer to do it there, that's all. I'll be home when I'm done."

Tears stung the backs of her eyes. She set down her water bottle and worked her jaw. "When will that be?"

"I don't know, Meg. I'll be done when I'm done."

Iron walls of anger armored her bruised heart. She drew in a breath through flared nostrils and nodded again. "Okay."

Though she felt far from lovey-dovey, Meghan attempted an embrace. Searched his face for some small glimmer of love. He graced her with a quick peck, but sadness—and guilt—filled his eyes. And burned her soul.

He slipped out through the garage, leaving her standing there.

Alone.

She crossed her arms over her chest, chin tucked. She should get used to being glossed over, but it never got easier. And new questions formed as she expelled a weary sigh. What was *really* going on with him?

He hadn't reached for her once since that humiliating night. It killed her inside. She closed her eyes and pinched the bridge of her nose. Losing weight, romantic dinners, seductive lingerie, none of it was making a difference with him.

And neither would topping the New York Times Bestsellers list. Self-confidence and accomplishments wouldn't help. She realized that now. She'd been a fool to think it could be as simple as making herself less boring. Their issues ran deeper, whatever they were. From here on out, Meghan's writing was for her own fulfillment. Nothing else. And that was enough.

She spun to face her pile of books on the table. Right now, her story world sounded awfully inviting. A welcome escape from the one she was trapped in.

Meghan drew in a 'start over' breath, pulled a basket of blueberries from her fridge, and settled into the armchair with her laptop and notes. She popped a berry in her mouth and set the container on the table beside her. Then she closed her eyes, let the real world fade away, and prepared to step back in time.

Her fingers fell into place on the keyboard.

`Hands on hips, Winifred stood back and cocked her head at the shiny, new cylinder plugs. Perfect.`

`Russell sidled up next to her. "Perfect. The cat's meow."`

`She glanced at him out the corner of her eye, a half-smile nudging her cheek upward. "My thoughts exactly."`

Her pocket buzzed and she growled at the interruption. Irritation laced her spirit as she dug her phone out of her pocket, but it dissipated when she saw the text.

Praying you get a lot of writing done today. But I'd rather be playing Lex Linx. — Curtis.

1916

Hands on hips, Winifred stood back and cocked her head at the new cylinder plugs, spark plug wires, and circulating pump—each in its place, and not a day too soon. The pit crew was due to arrive any minute. Tomorrow at ten a.m. the starter would fire a blank into the air and signal the beginning of the qualifying rounds.

Four days of hard labor had paid off, and now the Bearcat was almost . . . *perfect.*

Russell sidled up next to her. "She's perfect. The cat's meow."

She glanced at him out the corner of her eye, a half-smile nudging her cheek upward. "My thoughts exactly."

"But she always looks nude without the windscreen."

At his blunt reference to nakedness, Winifred fought the heat creeping up her neck. "She does, but her tires will thank you for the loss of weight. I'd say I'm surprised you go to all the effort to put the monocle back on after every race, but . . . " She rubbed a smudge off the grill then frowned at the empty spot where the fashionable—albeit broken—windscreen had stood. "I understand. You'll have to order a new one though."

"Already done. Since I couldn't decide on the color, I ordered two—one in silver and one in black."

She rolled her eyes. "Why am I not shocked?"

He bumped her with a sideways swing of his arm. "Aw, come on. Don't tell me you aren't excited to see which one looks better."

If she had his endless funds, she might have done the same. Still, it was hard to imagine living that way, tossing money around like water from a bottomless well. She shrugged. "You win."

They shared a smile, and Winifred's pulse fluttered. "Ready to start her up?"

"I've *been* ready."

As though on cue, they each lowered one side of the doghouse hood. When Winifred's side clunked into place, she lifted her gaze to find Russell grinning at her like a boy on the last day of school. He dangled the key in the air in front of him. "Wanna?"

"You serious?"

"You earned it, darling."

Darling?

His demeanor remained nonchalant, so she blew the term off as a chummy byword. Over the last four days, that *was* what they'd transformed into—chums. "Swell." She flipped her hand palm-up.

He tossed the key over the car, then jabbed his thumb toward the open bay door. "We could use a test drive about now. Too bad we didn't beat the sun." He jumped into the passenger's side.

Racecars didn't have headlamps, and driving in the dark was for saps—and fathers who thought themselves invincible. Her heart constricted; grief clawed at it. She moved the conversation along. "The sun will be the last thing to ever beat *this* beauty."

"You or the Bearcat?"

Leaning an elbow against the car, she struck a pose and batted her lashes. "Why, me, of course."

With his palm, he hammered the driver's seat and laughed. "Hop up, Gibson girl."

She climbed aboard and grabbed the wheel with both hands. The splinted ring and pinky fingers of her left hand pointed toward the hood. The whole hand throbbed from being overworked, but it didn't stop her from longing, for the umpteenth time, to feel the road radiating through the column of this powerful car. Maybe one day . . .

In the meantime, she had to wake up this beast of an engine and get the tires rolling, or there would be no qualifying rounds. Sweat dampened the wheel beneath her hands. This was it—where the rubber met the road.

Smug as a Sunday drive, Russell stretched out his legs and propped a lazy arm over the back of her seat. Did he feel no anxiety at all? The key to his racing success lay in whether she'd done her job and repaired the engine, whether the Stutz had any life in her at all. And there he sat, not a worry line on his face.

With watery legs, she pressed the brake then the clutch to the floorboard. She slid the key into the starter block, caught her breath, and cranked.

The car jolted as the engine turned. A beautiful roar filled the shop, and Russell whooped.

Winifred startled then laughed as he leapt from the car. In a flash, he'd rounded the back and appeared at her side. "Come here, you!" He grabbed her under the arms.

She squealed as he plucked her from the seat. When her foot left the clutch, the engine conked out—along with Russell's common sense. He held her against his chest and spun, still shrieking like a Native in a victory dance. Her feet flew out in a most undignified manner, but the reprimand she should have given was lost in her laughter.

"You did it, Winnie!" He stopped spinning and crammed his lips against her cheek in a rough kiss. "That's for being so clever. A peach is what you are. A real peach. You know that?"

If he expected a genuine answer, he'd have to wait until she caught her breath from the spin—and the kiss.

"Well, isn't this *perty*?" A strange voice spoke from behind Winifred. One of the pit crew, no doubt. Her feet hit the ground as Russell released her.

"Sam Hyatt, you dog!" He stepped around her, then clasped the taller man by the arm and dragged him in for a rugged embrace. "It's about time you showed your hide around here. Was wondering if you'd up and volunteered in the British army."

"You kiddin' me? If I join the war, it'll be because they dragged my hide over there. And it better be the Americans doing the dragging. There's no way I'll fight with the Bri—" Sam's eyes narrowed as he looked over Russell's shoulder and zeroed in on her, reminding Winifred who she was.

Four days in a garage with a man who'd come to accept—and, from all evidence, *appreciate*—her, had made her forget that, to society, she was a rebel. She went to the Bearcat to remove the key.

"I thought Win—Miss Fisher—was going to have to do your job, too." Russell guffawed, still riding the wave of exhilaration.

"Fat chance of that." Sam directed his words at her.

Key in her pocket, she used her sleeve to buff the steering wheel. Anything to delay meeting another man who resented her career choice.

"Where's Albert?" Russell asked.

"Right behind you, blockhead." Another voice joined the mix, drawing Winifred's gaze.

The fracas resumed its fevered pitch as Russell greeted the final member of his pit crew. "How was the train?"

Albert rubbed his plump stomach, shook his head, and groaned.

"He had to sit riding backwards." Sam chortled. "About upchucked all over me."

Russell ribbed Al. "You'd never make it in the mechanic's seat."

"Hey you two, I want you to meet someone." With a grin plastered across his face, he grabbed Al by the elbow and hauled him toward Winifred. Sam followed a reluctant five steps behind.

It took all her determination not to retreat into the shadows of the Stutz. Instead, she stood her ground and shoved her lips into a smile.

"Winnie, meet my pit crew, Sam Hyatt and Albert Williams." He turned to the men. "Al, Sam, meet Miss Winifred Fisher, best mechanic within a hundred miles." Eyes sparkling, he winked at her.

The wonder of his bold statement was lost in the humiliation that came with Sam and Al's gape-mouthed reaction.

"Don't you know how to greet a lady?" Russell smacked Sam on the back of the neck.

"Ow!" His gaze snapped to Winifred, and his Adam's apple bobbed in his scrawny neck. "Miss. It's . . . good to make your acquaintance." At the last second, he plucked his hat from his head, revealing a shock of startling blond hair.

Half-hearted, Al followed suit. "Miss." He nodded then glared at Russell, as though daring him to take a hand to any part of his body.

"D'you hear the Cat roar?" Russell asked his crew.

"Sure did!" Sam grinned. "When your telegraph came, we thought we were done for. But just now, she sounded ready to tackle the track." He raised up on his toes as though priming to race that minute. "How's the competition looking? Who've you pegged to watch out for? I hear Wild Bob's back."

Russell rubbed the back of his neck. "Yeah, Burman's always a threat, same as Price."

"You haven't heard?" Al asked.

"Heard what?"

"Price crashed into a palm during practice rounds today. Gas tank exploded."

Winifred's knees went weak. "Is he hurt?"

Al's gaze flicked her way, but he addressed Russell when he spoke. "They got him at the hospital in Riverside. He'll live, but they say his racing days are over."

"Never race again?" The horror in Russell's hushed question seemed to be shared by all the men, judging by their solemn nods.

An impromptu moment of silence fell upon them.

Winifred cleared her throat. "Why the long faces? He should be thankful he's alive."

No one contradicted her, but neither did they agree, as though considering whether death might be a better alternative to a life without racing. They stared at her, blinking, making her feel more foolish by the moment for having voiced her opinion.

Their silence grew into a thing of substance. It pressed in on Winifred, fed the insecurity that hovered about her like a hungry, rabid stray. Her eyes darted to Russell, but she couldn't make out his features in the shadow of his hat.

Why did he not back her up? His own father had died in the races, did he believe—

"Winnie's dad died in the last race," he said. "Hit a palm, same as Price."

His reverent voice cut through the cord of tension strangling her breath. She let it out in a rush.

He stepped forward and wrapped an arm around her shoulder in a sideways hug. "It's why she's here. Doing what she does. To honor his memory."

Her mouth formed a straight line as she bit back the urge to correct him. Let him say what he would to win the pit crew over.

By the slow, thoughtful nods Al and Sam gave, she conceded that he knew what he was doing.

Sam stepped forward, his head bent. "My condolences, Miss, along with my respect."

"And gratitude. She got the Cat back on her feet." Russell dropped his arm and rubbed his palms together. "Now, let's talk about the rounds. The road's the best there is—smooth and consistent. I don't foresee any particular trouble spots."

The pit crew closed in, forming a circle, which to Winifred's surprise, included her. Emboldened, she spoke up. "Tomorrow's supposed to be cool, so overheating shouldn't be a problem. The lack of fine tuning might be an issue. I would have liked to take her out for a good hard drive, see what bugs there might be to work out. But there just isn't time."

Al rubbed his chin. "We'll have to roll with the punches. Let's list what could go wrong and then decide how we'll handle each one should it happen."

Of its own accord, a smile crept up Winifred's face.

Two hours of head-pounding strategizing later, Winifred and Russell arrived at her front porch. She plopped onto the swing, grateful to be off her feet.

Russell joined her on the bench and shoved them into a hearty backward motion. "It's a good thing we're not doing practice rounds at the moment. I've worked you so hard, you might fall asleep and take a tumble. I'd hate to run you over."

A yawn overtook her. "You might be right. I'm too tired even to smile at that one." If she didn't get upstairs soon, the rocking of the swing might lull her to unconsciousness right where she sat. Falling asleep next to Russell wouldn't be an altogether unpleasant thing, but she imagined her mother might have a thing or two to say about it.

Her eyes drooped. "But, I've seen the races, and I've seen you drive. There's a good chance I'd take a tumble, sleepy or not."

His baritone became muddy in the haze of sleep creeping over her.

"Did you say something?"

"Yeah, Sleeping Beauty, I said there's no way I'll let that happen to—" The swing came to a jolting halt.

Wide awake now, she was surprised to find a scowl dominating his features. But his gaze had traveled beyond her. "I've seen that

Four-Ninety . . ." He stood and went to the railing just as a white Chevrolet turned onto their street. Its top cover was lifted and side curtains, drawn.

Winifred joined him, a prickle of dread working its way down her back.

He stood rigid, tension flowing off him in waves.

The car came to a halt in front of the Fisher home, and Winifred's dread turned into mind-numbing fear. Half her brain told her to make for the house and lock the door. The other, like a bystander at a pile-up, couldn't pull itself away.

The engine idled on a smooth hum, and the scent of exhaust drifted past with the wind. The driver stared at them through the glassless window, his identity impossible to discern in the dark. No matter. Winifred didn't need a face to know why the man had come.

Russell stretched his arm across her, nudging her backwards. "Get in the house."

Her broken finger pulsated, screamed at her to run, but her knees locked. How could she leave? "No. This is my fight. Not yours."

With startling reflexes, he spun toward her and drew to within a foot of her nose. "If they get past me, they might not stop at a finger." His words came out on a low snarl. "Now, do as I say."

The hairs on her arms stood on end. Even so, she stiffened and matched his tone. "I'm not moving from this porch. So you can just—"

Hinges squealed. The backdoor of the car swung open. The curtain had been drawn back, but the interior remained a yawning black hole. No one stepped out.

"An invitation to join the party, perhaps?" Russell murmured, thick on the sarcasm. His gaze flashed from the street to Winifred, then back. Fists balled, he stepped off the porch, then wrenched around at the waist to look at her, his index finger pointing down.

"If one foot touches these steps, when I'm done with those goons, I'm coming after *you*."

Russell stalked toward the Chevrolet and hoped he'd scared Winnie into staying put for once. There was no telling what evil lurked inside that black chasm, but better he confront it than her.

Taking a strengthening breath, he propped an arm on the door's frame and ducked his head to peer inside the car. A single silhouette occupied the backseat. Besides the shadow and the driver, there was no one else.

The *click-click* of a lighter preceded the spark and flame that illuminated the car's occupant. *Hastings.* A cigarette jutted from beneath his mustache. Hastings slid his gaze to Russell and lifted an oily smile.

Russell concealed a shudder. "What do you want?"

The lighter went out, dousing the car in near obscurity. "Good evening to you, too, Mr. Keegan." Hastings' chuckle rankled. "As promised, I've brought my new motorcar. Care for a ride?"

"I don't, as a matter of fact."

"That's too bad. Perhaps Miss. Fisher would rather come instead?"

Russell gritted his teeth, then turned to Winnie. "I'll be back in a few minutes. Go inside and wait with your mother." He climbed in and shut the door.

"Russell, no." Terror filled her voice as she teetered on the edge of the porch, her foot hovering over the first step.

He'd learned enough about Winnie to know she was contemplating following in the Lizzie. *Don't you dare.*

The driver worked the gearshift and pulled away from the curb, yanking Winnie from his view.

"My man, Domingo, tells me you're Miss Fisher's new guard dog." Hastings gave a long pull, and the tip of his cigarette glowed. Tobacco permeated the air with its cloying scent.

"Does she need guarding?"

"Beautiful women always do. Even feisty ones such as Miss Fisher. She's far too tempting a morsel to be left on the counter unattended. I hear she's already had a bite taken out of her."

Blood pounded in Russell's head, and he gripped the seat to keep from smacking the cigarette out of Hastings' mouth. "Your *man's* work?"

"I was referring to you, Mr. Keegan." Laughter filled the increasingly confining space. "Then again . . . " He leaned toward the front. "Domingo, you didn't sully the adorable Miss Fisher, did you?"

The driver twisted and leered into the backseat. A streetlight illuminated his crook-nosed profile. "Only in my dreams, Jefe."

Russell shot forward and took a fistful of Domingo's collar. "You filth! If you think you'll get away with hurting—"

He squealed and smacked at Russell's hand. "*Déjeme!*"

"Where's your bravado now, eh?" Anger devouring his self-control, Russell yanked the man sideways to better land a punch. "One way or another—" The car swerved, throwing Russell against the door before his fist accomplished its mission.

Domingo righted himself and straightened the wheel, narrowly missing a fruit cart parked on the side of the road. He rattled off a stream of Spanish, with *loco* being the one word Russell caught.

He grinned. *Let the man think I'm off my rocker.*

"Are you trying to kill us?" Panic swelled Hastings' voice.

Good.

An unpredictable man always had the upper hand.

Hastings sat forward and straightened his suit jacket. "Really, Mr. Keegan. I thought you wiser than that. 'The best revenge is to be unlike he who performed the injury.' Marcus Aurelius."

Russell snorted. "'An eye for an eye.' God Almighty."

"Aurelius also said, 'When you arise in the morning, think of what a privilege it is to be alive, to think, to enjoy, to *love* . . .'" Hastings' lips puckered around the cigarette; its glow bloomed poppy red. "What a pity it would be to lose those things. For a handful of dollars. That's all it is to a man like you, isn't it, Keegan? Money?"

The ride grew bumpier. Was he being taken to the desert, never to return? Either way, the man was ready to talk business. Russell could handle that, but it would be on his terms, not Hastings'. "Very well, here's how it'll go. You'll get your handful of cash. I'll bring it to your place. Day after the race."

Hastings gave a low, patronizing laugh. "And if you don't win?"

"I will. But that's beside the point. Wells Fargo said my money would be available April ninth. Two days ago, I put in an order to have it wired from Philly. As a businessman, you know these things take time."

His chin dipped in a slow nod. "April ninth it is, then. One day later, and Miss Fisher will suffer more than another broken finger." The car rolled to an abrupt stop. "Perfect timing, Domingo."

Russell's gaze swiveled out his window and, to his amazement, they were back at the Fisher home. Winnie stood on the porch much the way he'd left her, hands wringing, toes hanging over the edge.

"Good doing business with you, Keegan."

"I bet it is, you greedy buzzard. But chew on *this*"—he plucked the butt from Hastings' lips—"my money can hire brainless thugs, just as well as yours. Touch Winnie again, and you'll find yourself on the wrong end of a pair of pliers." Russell ground the butt into the upholstery, mingling the stench of tobacco with that of scorched leather. He tossed it in Domingo's face, then released the latch and kicked open the door. "By the way, nice wheels."

He banged the door on Hastings' shout of rage and didn't stop moving until he'd barreled past Winnie's questions and deposited her on the other side of her front door.

Mildred stood at the top of the stairs, hand over her mouth, eyes round.

Chest heaving, he slammed the bolt in place and reached for Winnie.

She flattened herself against him. It was impossible to tell where her trembling began and his ended.

"I stayed." Her hoarse whisper was jagged. "I almost got the Lizzie so I could follow, but I-I stayed . . . "

He stroked her hair. "You did good. And it's all over now. They won't be coming back. I promise." He prayed it wasn't a lie.

Present Day

"Hey, Meg, how's my girl?" Brooke tossed her purse onto the table and scooted into the booth across from Meghan. The smooth skin of her slender arms boasted a new, deeper, color.

"Pretty good, what about you? Boys driving you crazy yet?" She snickered and raised her teacup to her lips.

Brooke opened her menu and scanned the contents. "Yes, yes they are. Which is why I was thrilled to send them to camp this past week. Hard to believe I've had a quiet house for three days."

Meghan could get so much done with a week of solitude! She sighed. "Enjoy it while you can."

"Oh, I have been." A sly smile lifted one side of Brooke's mouth. She closed the menu and slid it away from her. "What are you having?"

"Skinny turkey club, and fruit instead of fries. You?"

"Asian chicken salad, light dressing."

"Ooh, yum. That sounds good. Oh, before I forget . . . " Meghan opened her purse and pulled out a pink plastic bag. "Here's your lipstick and bronzer. Not that you need any of that, you look like you just came back from a cruise to the Bahamas."

Brooke waved a hand in front of her, then took the Tara May bag from her friend. "I wish. I tan easy. But this is from a bottle. I don't want to look like I'm sixty by the time I'm forty." She stuffed the bag in her own purse. "Thanks. Did you do good at the party? Got enough for your conference?"

Meghan snorted. "The party did okay, but I never expected it to cover the registration. Anyway, I don't want to talk about the cost of this trip right now." She let her shoulders droop and ran her thumb along her cup.

"Steve still upset, huh?"

"We don't talk about it, but it hangs in the air like napalm." Along with a host of other triggers driving a wedge between them. Thank goodness for friends to keep a smile on her face.

The waitress appeared and took their orders just in time to cut off the questions on Brooke's lips. After she left, Meghan changed the subject. "How's Darren?"

Brooke looked up at the busboy delivering her glass of iced tea, and thanked him. Then she turned to Meghan. "He's good. Busy. But I told him he deserves some downtime, too. He gets back from camping on Tuesday and he's gonna play in the church softball game Wednesday. Want me to have him ask Steve to go?"

Ha! Like there was any chance in Hades Steve would agree. Meghan moistened her lips. "He can try. Not sure if he'll have any luck, but I'd love for Steve to make friends at church."

"We'll drag him out." Brooke winked.

If only it were that easy.

Their food arrived and Brooke stabbed some lettuce with her fork. Then she set it back down. "Hey . . . " She ran her tongue along her lower lip, and leaned forward across the table. "Didn't you say Steve went to a ball game with Paul a few weeks ago?"

Meghan's brows pinched together. "Yeah, why?"

Brooke cleared her throat and used her thumbnail to scratch at something on the table. "Just curious. We ran into Paul and Brenda in the parking lot of the Macaroni Grill the other night, and he invited Darren to a game. Said he hadn't been to one all season."

She pulled her head back. "What?" Meghan blinked at Brooke. Spirals of thought spun in a dozen directions, trying to find the path toward reason.

"Listen, don't freak out or anything. Maybe I shouldn't have told you."

In the background, ice clinked and silverware scraped on dishes. But Meghan felt oddly disconnected from any of it. What possible explanation . . . ?

She pointed a blank gaze at the plate in front of her.

Without a word, she bit into her sandwich. A hundred different emotions could have come to the surface—all of them fought for the right to. Combined with the phone call she overheard… What was she supposed to do with this revelation? Ignore it?

Lord, is that what trusting You means?

Wait, why was *she* the one doing all the praying? Weren't they both Christians?

"I see your wheels turning. Just pray about what to do, Meg. I'll pray for you, too."

"Don't worry, I will." She released a breath through her nose. She'd pray her husband would quit being a selfish lout and start acting like the head of their home—being a spiritual leader, loving her the way he promised.

She stewed on it all the way home. If the shift in their relationship was her fault, she'd fix it. She'd already tried. But maybe the problem was all *him*.

After entering through the garage and hanging her keys, Meghan headed to the computer on shaky legs. The question hounded her. Wouldn't leave her alone. She had to know.

After a few incorrect passwords, she logged into their bank account. Something she probably should've done a long time ago. Heart banging against her ribs, she entered the date of the supposed ball game, then listened to the blood pulsing in her ears as the page loaded. *Whoosh. Whoosh.*

Her arms went weak.

A bubble of nausea rolled through her stomach.

There on the screen, in black and white, was a withdrawal in the amount of $400.

What would he need with that much money? Meghan rubbed the skin between her eyes and tried to lasso her bouncing emotions. Was it possible? Was Steve . . . *cheating* on her? After all this time? Certainly not.

Was he?

Anger tumbled through her then evaporated in some hollow space in her soul. She didn't want to be angry. She didn't want to travel this road at all.

She logged out and turned off the screen.

Why had she looked? She didn't want to know, she'd rather be ignorant. Why hadn't she just left well enough alone? Blinking away tears, she took a series of deep breaths and fought her rising panic. Did he want to leave her? Was he choosing someone else?

What would she say to him? Would he storm out? The scene played out in her head. She couldn't survive that. They had to stick together, always. And if her girls lost their father . . . *no*. No, no, no! She couldn't lose Steve. Their marriage was suffering but she couldn't let it end!

Her fingertips pressed into the wood surface of the table. She'd keep her mouth shut. That's what she'd do. She covered her ears and shook her head. She didn't want to know what was going on. She'd pretend . . . endure . . . take any amount of pain so long as she wouldn't lose her marriage. She'd have to.

Oh, God, did she have to?

Lord, is it too late? Can you fix this?

She wrapped her arms around her waist and doubled over in her chair. She couldn't lose her family, couldn't lose Steve. She couldn't, she couldn't.

The conference was days away. How could she go with her life hanging like this?

She wiped her damp hands on her thighs, then stood and paced. The girls would be home from their friends' house soon. She had to think. She *couldn't* think.

Meghan planted her feet and formed fists. Okay. Maybe getting away for a few days *was* the best thing to do. That way, she wouldn't accidentally say anything to push her husband further away. She could clear her head, put her thoughts in order, regroup. She needed that. Besides, she'd worked *so* hard.

So there was no way she would back out now. No way on earth.

The house phone rang and caller ID displayed her dad's name. She groaned, turned off the ringer, and walked away toward her room. "Sorry, can't deal with you right now, Dad." Time for him to wake up, and she didn't want to hear any refrains from "Cat's in the Cradle" either. He just wanted her at that party for Patrick's sake anyway. He'd gotten his replacement child.

Plopping onto the bed, Meghan stared at the ceiling. Dad used to listen to all her whimsical tales. She used to dream of making him proud by becoming a real author. The kind he thought so highly of, whose books he displayed on his massive mahogany bookcase.

She gulped the little-girl hurt. Truth was, part of her still hoped he'd be proud if she pulled it off. Wasn't that pathetic?

Tears pooled in the corners of her eyes and rolled down the sides of her face toward her ears. She squeezed her lids shut and just breathed. Where was God? This wasn't supposed to be her life. The Bible said if anyone was burdened and heavy-laden, to cast their cares on Jesus. Wasn't that what she'd been doing, over and over again? Asking Jesus for help?

Weariness ate at her soul and tugged her toward sleep. Slumber pulled over her head like a blanket and when she next opened her eyes, more than an hour had gone by.

Shaking off her disorientation, Meghan moved to the kitchen to prepare dinner. She had just set a pot of water to boil when the girls arrived home. They headed to their room and Meghan thanked God for the reprieve. Her heart and mind soaked up the silence.

Twenty minutes later the garlic bread went into the toaster oven and the spaghetti noodles were drained. But Steve wasn't home yet, no surprise. She tapped a fingernail on the countertop, then pulled out her phone.

She dialed his number and he picked up on the fifth ring. "Meg."

His voice was strained and the background noises weren't the usual ones at the factory. Soft music drifted from his end of the line, and unfamiliar voices rumbled over it.

The hairs on the back of Meghan's neck stood on end, but she forced calm into her voice. "Hi. Uh, dinner is ready and the girls are getting hungry. When are you coming home?" She tried to keep her voice steady.

"I'll pick up fast food on the way home later. There's a problem I need to take care of tonight. Since I can't work this Friday."

She prickled at the not-so-subtle jab at her plans to leave. She cleared her throat. "I offered to help."

He released a sigh into the phone. "I know, but you can't help with this. Sorry. Give the girls a kiss for me."

Ending the call, Meghan pressed her lips together, ready to implode. She dumped marinara sauce into the noodles and grabbed plates from the cupboard, clattering dishes and silverware and not giving a hoot about the noise.

She jutted a hip and rubbed her forehead with one hand. At least this day was almost over. Her phone trilled with a text. Looking down at the screen, comfort stole over her heart and a smile teased her lips.

Curtis.

Like a chocolate brownie in her chopped liver day.

This week marks the countdown, right? You excited?

Despite everything, deep down a part of her still was. Especially with Curtis's support. *Yep. Thanks for all your help. =)*

No problem. You're gonna do great. Need anything else from me?

Her stomach lurched. She needed a whole lot more than what he could offer.

Such as?

Family stories, insider info, something that might inspire a scene for your soon-to-be award-winning book?

You've already inspired more than you know. Did she just open that door? She slipped her bottom lip between her teeth and waited for his text to come.

Oh? How's that?

She moistened her lips, uncertain why she was being so open. *My characters are often based on real people and, ahem . . . you, sir, are THE Russell Keegan.* Her fingers trembled as she hit Send.

Are you serious? Ha ha. Wow.

Did he think she was a freaky stalker lady? Her thumbs flew over the keyboard. *Does that weird you out?*

No, it's cool. Does he get the girl?

She paused, took a breath, then typed her reply. *I don't think she could survive without him.*

She could if she had to. She's stronger than she knows.

Her abdomen squeezed. *Because he makes her brave enough to face her deepest fears.*

It'll be interesting to see how it all plays out.

Her brain stumbled along with her tripping pulse. She blinked. *I should go now. Kids and all.*

Okay. Log on later to play LL.

She bit the inside of her cheek and keyed in her response. *I will. Good night for now.*

Good night, Meghan.

Sitting in the sparse shade of Jameson Park, Meghan adjusted her sunglasses and squinted across the field. Darren had just rounded second base. Tom cocked his arm, chucking the ball to third. It arched through the sky, momentarily disappearing in the blinding sun. It reappeared just as the baseman, another one of the elders, caught it and tagged Darren as he dove toward the base.

"Out!" called the ump.

Meghan laughed as hoots and howls erupted.

Men and women milled about, most unfamiliar to Meghan. Brooke, her two boys, and Meghan's girls charged, breathless, up the hill toward her.

Meghan smiled and tipped her head toward the diamond, where Darren was throwing his cap on the ground. He then scowled as he snatched it back up and came heading their way. "Your husband's not a very good loser, is he?"

"No, he's not. And Tom's got a great arm." Brooke laughed, then plopped down on the blanket. She stretched out her sleek legs and propped her hands behind her. "Hey look, there's Curtis." Brooke raised her arm and waved.

"Oh?" Meghan shivered in the warm sun and pointed her face toward the baseball game down the slope. But her eyes slid toward his approach.

Curtis arrived, wearing a gray T-shirt that hugged every defined muscle. The casual attire flashed an image in Meghan's mind of a lazy day in a hammock swing, resting her head on his chest. She squashed the longing, stuffed it in the garbage where it belonged.

He crossed his arms and smiled. "Hey, ladies. Having fun?"

"*I* am." Brooked extended her hand toward Darren as he approached. "Sit down, babe. Take a load off."

Meghan cast a smirk at Curtis. "How could we not be having fun at a park named for your family?"

"Hi, Mr. Curtis." Faith grinned. "Are you teaching us tonight?"

"No, Miss Ellie, not tonight. Just Sunday mornings. You have choir on Wednesdays, remember?"

"Oh, yeah."

Curtis tousled her hair and she giggled before racing toward a group of girls a few yards away.

Meghan shadowed her eyes with her hand and looked up at him. "Miss Ellie?"

He shrugged a shoulder. "Short for elephant, because she never forgets her Bible verses." A smile lifted one scruffy cheek and melted Meghan's insides. Curtis sat beside her and aimed his baby blues out across the expanse of the park. "Is Steve around somewhere?"

She shook her head. "Of course not. He was too swamped to come." Good thing her sunglasses hid the fire in her eyes. She didn't want to imagine what other plans he had that day.

Curtis offered a sympathetic quirk of his mouth.

Darren chugged a water bottle then replaced the cap. "Bummer. Will he be here for the service afterward?"

"Nope."

The silence scorched more than the ninety-eight degree air.

Curtis coughed. "I'm thinking of joining the game. What about you, ladies?"

"I'm just a cheerleader." Brooke crossed one ankle over the other.

Darren pinched her cheek. "Shoulda brought your pom-poms, then. And I would've loved to see you in your high school cheerleading uniform."

"Uh. No."

Meghan giggled, but stopped when Curtis looked at her with raised eyebrows. "How 'bout it, Meghan?"

"No, thank you. You go on, and I'll sit with Brooke and watch. It should be quite a sight—I've seen you in the gym, you might break the bat."

Did she say that? Oh, what was it about Curtis that dissolved the filter over her mouth?

Curtis's eyes sparkled, the corners crinkling with his smile. "You sure know how to inspire a guy to try."

Mere inches from her, his scent filled her senses and made her head spin. She grinned. Nothing wrong with smelling good.

"We'll try to make it a good show. Right, Darren?"

"Yup. Come on, buddy." Darren headed back down the slope as the teams began switching places on the field. Meghan moved her glasses to the top of her head.

Curtis lingered on the ground beside her. She felt her ear burning under his gaze. "You head out in the morning for your big conference, don't you?"

"Oh, that's right, you do!" Brooke shook her head like she was just waking up.

Meghan looked from Brooke back to Curtis. "Yeah. Kinda nervous."

"No reason to be, it'll be great. Make sure and keep me posted on how it goes." Eyes locked on hers, Curtis gave a slight smile then hopped up and jogged to catch up with Darren at the bottom of the hill.

She stifled a sigh. The sun was so hot, Meghan's shirt stuck to her back. But Curtis was like a refreshing breeze to her spirit.

Brooke cleared her throat. Loudly. "Break the bat?"

Meghan's cheeks burned. "It was a joke. Since he's a weight trainer. Get it?"

"Mm-hmm." She pursed her lips and lifted her eyebrows.

Meghan's eyes widened and she elbowed her friend. "Stop it, quit teasing."

"Okay, okay." Brooke lifted her hands in surrender, then set her gaze across the park. "You're right, though." Her eyes slid to Meghan, a smirk lifting her cheek. "He's one fine specimen."

Meghan's lips inched upward, but she said nothing.

Yes, he most certainly is that.

Meghan wrinkled her forehead as she pulled into the driveway and parked next to Steve's truck. She and the girls picked their way through the garage, then opened the kitchen door to a darkened living room.

She hung her purse on the hook then turned around. "Okay, girls, go get your jammies on and brush your teeth. I'll be right there."

"Can we watch a movie in bed tonight? Please?" Faith turned puppy-dog eyes on her, and Meghan cocked her head.

"There's no school tomorrow," Faith added.

"Yeah, Momma. Please?"

Meghan rubbed her neck. "If you girls can agree on a movie, then maybe. But you have to hurry and get ready for bed. With no fighting."

As soon as the girls tore off down the hall, Meghan moved toward her room. She stopped in front of the den. There, in the dark, sat Steve–staring out the window. He turned toward her, his lips a straight line.

Bitterness clenched her stomach and a sneer warped Meghan's mouth. Sure didn't look like he'd just walked in the door. He'd said he was too swamped with work to go to church. Where was he really? At the Hampton? A sour taste burned the back of her throat, and the accusations danced on her tongue. But she bit her lip and pivoted away, marching toward the girls' room and ignoring him.

After starting a Barbie DVD, she went through the methodical motions of tucking them into bed. With any luck, Steve would park himself on the couch to watch a game and she wouldn't have to talk to him. There were too many things she might say that could ignite a grenade she wasn't prepared for.

Tiptoeing away from the girls' door, she sighed her relief when she heard the TV on, and slipped into her room to pack.

This was the worst possible time for an emotional outburst. She should be practicing how to summarize her book when talking to literary agents, enjoying the anticipation of getting on a plane in the morning, relishing every part of this trip and trying not to add fuel to the fire. Instead she was stomping around, anger pulsing through her veins, hoping to avoid her husband for the rest of the night, the rest of the weekend.

She unzipped the suitcase on the bed and flung it open. *Devious man.* Two pairs of shoes went in first. *I'm not stupid.* She stuffed a zip lock baggie of jewelry into the pocket in the suitcase lid. *Doubtless a guilty conscious kept him from church. What was he thinking about in the dark? How to get out the mess he was in, or where to set up his next rendezvous?* Her eyes stung as she shoved things into her suitcase.

Steve's soft frame darkened the doorway. "Hey. How was church?"

She jetted a puff of air from her nostrils. "It was wonderful. If you'd been there, you wouldn't have to ask."

"Meg, you need to lay off. Quit giving me a hard time and getting mad every time I don't make it to another service or volunteer day or church softball game. I'm getting tired of it and I can't deal with it right now."

Meghan sucked in her breath. "It's not *just* church. You're selfish, Steve. An absentee father, just like my dad. You're missing out on everything. The spelling bee, the beach, Zoey's kindergarten graduation, *and* church. Did you even know Faith had gotten a new Sunday school teacher a couple months ago? Or that Zoey lost her second tooth last week?" She squinted her eyes at his reddening face. "Or were you too busy watching basketball on the couch to notice?"

He stared at her, a vein pulsing in his temple. He thrust his hand through his hair, then gestured toward the door. "There was a message on the machine when I got home. From Patrick."

Of course—classic avoidance. It's what he did best. She shook her head and turned back to her suitcase.

Steve sat down on the bed and seemed to deflate. "Look. Meg. Seems the kid is trying real hard to heal the rifts in his family, and this party is his way of doing it. You sure you don't want to go?"

Meghan's hand stilled on a red blouse. Why didn't Steve try mending the rifts in *his* family? Cocking her jaw, she whipped the blouse toward her and folded it, a bit too harshly, then shoved it into the suitcase.

She straightened and cut her eyes to Steve. "I'll ignore the fact you're changing the subject. Look, if Patrick wants to be friends with his big sister, fine. I can give it a go. But *not* this weekend. I'm not obligated to show up at their beck and call. I. Have. Plans. See?" She gestured to the suitcase and shook her head. "Plans that mean a lot to me. And my *husband* should be taking *my* side." She sniffed and gave him her back as she yanked open her dresser drawer.

His voice was laced with tension. "What are you talking about, sides?"

Meghan bit her lip until she thought it would bleed. "Nothing."

Steve turned her back around by the shoulders. "Don't say *nothing* after an accusation like that."

He stared at her, waiting. Did he need her to spell it out for him?

"You're supposed to support *me*. Not pressure me to do what *that man* wants. How do you think I feel when you take his side, a practical stranger?" Meghan swallowed, fighting to keep her eyes from rounding as Steve bent close to her face.

"I'm not taking Patrick's side, or anybody's." He pulled back as if wounded. Offended. "And I've always been supportive." He thrust his hand in his hair again and looked up at the ceiling.

She turned toward her suitcase. "You used to be . . . " Her windpipe pinched, shrinking her voice. "But not lately." Lately it appeared someone else commandeered his attention. She spun back around and searched his face, the silent question shouting inside her . . .

Who is she?

"What's the real reason you don't want me to go to this conference?" *Shut up, Meghan.*

Something flashed in his eyes. She saw it and blinked. Resisted the urge to cover her mouth with her hand. Holding her breath, she braced for his answer. But his gaze shifted and he said nothing.

Her breathing picked up speed. She couldn't keep up this charade. No more ducking the truth. She needed answers. Now. Tonight. Was it the Hampton? Another "ball game" with Paul? Would having the girls throw a wrench in his plans?

Meghan raised her brows and worked her jaw. If staring him down wasn't going to produce a response, she'd have to hit him harder. Where to start—the lie about Paul? The bank account? Or maybe his severe neglect of certain bedtime routines? Which would loosen his tongue?

She crossed her arms, primed and ready to hit him with all of it.

The door creaked open, snapping them both to attention. "Mom?" Faith shuffled over to her. "I forgot to tell you to have a good trip. I'll miss you." She hugged Meghan's waist, pricking her heart.

Meghan's throat constricted as she squeezed her daughter tight and planted a kiss on her head. Her sweet baby girl. "I'll miss you too, princess." She blinked away tears and blew out a breath. "Say good night to Dad. Be good for him while I'm gone."

"I know, I know. I will."

Meghan's eyes darted to Steve, but his were trained on Faith.

He tousled her hair, then pointed her toward the door. "Go on, I'll come tuck you back in bed."

Faith slipped out the door and Steve leveled his eyes on Meghan. "You know I wasn't thrilled with how this trip got planned. But I do hope it goes well for you." Two heartbeats passed and then he left the room without so much as a look back.

She released her breath and lifted shaking fingers to her forehead. Faith's interruption was for the best. She didn't want to go another round. Didn't want to sift through the scraps of the marriage they once had.

She'd been saved by the proverbial bell. Because with Steve in the crosshairs, it was her daughters who would take the bullet. And she'd almost pulled the trigger. If she didn't get it together, find the strength to set her own needs aside, she was going to destroy what was left of her family.

When the front door opened then closed, Meghan's head started spinning. She rubbed her temples. What was she going to do? What more *could* she do? Steve seemed determined to stay on a course that led them apart. Spiritually, emotionally, and physically. In every way she could think of, they'd become strangers.

Maybe that was how he wanted it.

She wiped the moisture from her eyes then dug through a basket of clean laundry looking for her favorite top. Sniffing, she grabbed a handful of clothes and tossed them onto the bed out of her way. She kept digging until her eye snagged on a piece of paper sticking out from the pocket of Steve's pants.

A note? A phone number? Did she even want to see?

She gripped the edge, hesitated, then began easing it out, eyes glued to the black letters against the white cardstock. A business card. Her heart pounded. The letters began to form words. With a gasp, she squeezed her eyes shut and shoved the card back into the pocket. *Law Firm of . . .* was more than she had strength to see right then.

So Steve wanted out.

Hands fisted, she took a series of deep breaths to expel the information.

Could she change his mind? Did she want to? Her eyes darted back and forth across the room as she tried to grapple with what she'd just seen. Could there be any other explanation?

Her gaze landed on the suitcase and she blinked. She couldn't process all this now. She needed time to think. Space. Maybe when she got home, she'd have the strength to talk to him.

Straightening her back, she moistened her lips, finished packing, and closed the case. Then she whipped out her phone and messaged the one person who could lift her spirits.

Rough night tonight, Curtis. Prayers appreciated.

You got it. Wish I could do more.

Me, too.

Chapter Twelve

1916

Russell eased the Bearcat up to the starting line, his heart keeping time with his engine's cylinders. This was it. The big day. Exceed a hundred miles an hour or go home a sorry man.

Curious onlookers milled about and congregated in the grandstands along the first half mile of the track between the curb and the endless row of pepper trees. A raised viaduct had been erected to allow people and even the occasional vehicle to cross the road. Still, batons in hand, guards policed the road to keep it clear.

The fresh-pressed, warm asphalt was perfume to his nose.

The Stutz purred, and Russell patted the dash. "Atta girl."

Four cars to the left, Cooper's number 8 Stutz puttered into position. Beyond him, the amateur and Winnie's shadow, Bobby Tidwell, strangled the steering wheel of his Sunbeam and stared straight ahead. Russell shook his head in wonder, but had to admire the bloke for trying.

Silsbury wasn't around. According to Cooper's reconnaissance, the double-crosser wasn't scheduled to tryout until later in the day, which, to Russell, was perfectly ducky.

Al swung his limber frame into the mechanic's seat. "Let's get this dame on the road!" He howled like a wolf, and Russell rolled his eyes. The man would be handy in a pinch, but he was no Winnie.

Russell tugged his leather helmet over his head then straightened his ears beneath it. Leaving the straps to hang against his throat, he reached for the goggles on the floorboard.

His pulse sputtered when he spied Winnie shimmying between the Bearcat and Wild Bob Burman's Peugeot. She tipped her cap at him. "Good luck, Mr. Burman," she hollered over the roar of half a dozen engines.

Burman flashed crooked teeth and gave her a two-finger salute. "Thanks, but don't need it!"

Winnie turned to Russell. Rosy-cheeked and windswept, she looked good enough to eat.

He leaned down to speak in her ear. "If I was a braver man, I'd ask for a good luck kiss."

"You don't want Fisher luck," she shot back at him. "Here, your gloves." She yanked them from her breast pocket and thrust them into his hand. Jaw hard, she eyed the front wheel as though gauging its air pressure.

"Relax, everything's just dandy. You've triple checked every hose and wire. This is the fun part." He popped her under the chin with his knuckle.

"Oh, I'm having a whoopee of a time." If she was shooting for sarcasm, she hit the bull's-eye.

"What's eating you?" he asked, annoyed with himself for being concerned about a woman's emotional state when he sat minutes from savoring the Circle's golden dust.

Her teeth clamped down on her lower lip. Then, on tiptoe, she tugged his sleeve until he brought his ear within range of her hushed voice. "It might be nothing to worry about, but this morning, I might have felt a slight pull to the right."

He moved back to look her in the eye. "You sure? I didn't feel anything."

"It wasn't much, but at top speed . . . "

It would be more noticeable. "Gotcha. I'll be on my toes."

"If I'm right . . ." She glanced over her shoulder at Burman, who was preoccupied speaking to the chief timer. "It'll work against you since the track curves the other way." Her brow puckered, as though in apology.

No way could she think it was her fault. She'd done a bang-up job, especially considering the time crunch. "It'll be fine."

A grim smile in place, she patted his arm, seeming hesitant to leave. Was she regretting his decision to have her sit this one out? Well, she'd just have to deal with it.

Foot on the brake, he nursed the gas pedal. The engine wailed, begging to be unleashed.

Out of habit, he turned toward Cooper who gave him thumbs-ups. Russell returned it and wished his friend all the best.

Winnie tapped his arm.

The wind shifted and blew a cloud of black exhaust over them, blocking her from view. She coughed, and when it cleared, he found her eyes were moist. The fumes, or something else? "Be careful. All right?"

Ah. She was worried about safety. He should have known. The last time a man in her life tackled the Circle, he never left it. "Four, five laps tops. I got this."

A dubious frown shifted her features. "And, Mr. Keegan, don't be rash."

He dropped his jaw in faux shock. "Who, me? I never do anything stupid."

"Says you." Her eyes narrowed. "I'm serious, Russell. No stunts." She spun and marched back to the sidelines and Sam, the keeper of the stopwatch.

Al sneered. "Who made her boss? Suffragette, I bet. They're all the same."

Russell crammed his hand into a glove. "Give her a break. She's worried I'll kill you."

Pallor swept over the man, and Russell laughed.

The last few minutes passed in a blur of excitement and dread. The first horn sent Pullen's Mercer barreling down the road ahead of them. His dust had yet to clear when the second blast sounded. Wild Bob peeled out, decorating the asphalt with a dual streak of rubber.

At the third signal, Russell's instincts took over conscious thought. The Cat leapt over the starting line. Wind and momentum beat against him in a familiar embrace. His bones vibrated, becoming one with the chassis and the road.

The Bearcat had devoured a good portion of the three-mile circle before Russell thrust her into top gear. She was pure power, but as Winnie predicted, her alignment was off. Russell compensated, but he felt their speed diminish.

Even so, Burman's Peugeot came in sight. The Cat was already closing in.

Russell grinned, and flying grit embedded itself between his teeth.

From the right, a woman waving an American flag darted around the barricade onto the Circle. Russell's arm jerked to the left. The Cat wrenched in response. He righted it, jostling Al from one side to the other.

Al's jaw flapped in indignation. The wind sucked away his words, but if Russell could hear them, he was certain he'd agree. The police had better step it up and keep the road clear, or someone was bound to get hurt.

They approached the second viaduct, the halfway point. Corona citizens waved from its rail, screaming and tossing flowers overboard. The car whizzed through a shower of petals. A heavy bud smacked Russell in the head. He ground his teeth. Racing in the center of a town was a new experience and one he wasn't sure he'd choose to repeat. The distractions and hazards were proving more than he'd anticipated, and this wasn't even the race—the day a hundred thousand were expected to swarm the Circle City.

The starting line reached them so fast Russell almost forgot to scan the crowd for Winnie and Sam. At the last second, she appeared out of the corner of his eye, jumping and shouting, which could be interpreted one of two ways. He chose to think positive.

Al twisted in his seat to look back at them then shouted in Russell's ear—something about "good time."

Russell nodded, relief easing his shoulders a notch. Positive, indeed.

Seconds later, the happy feelings were snatched away by the sight of number 8 nose-first against a swaying telephone pole. A lone tire rolled along the road then crashed into a storefront window.

Still behind the wheel, Cooper jostled a limp mechanic.

As the scene disappeared from view, dread crunched down on Russell's gut. Death wasn't uncommon on the racetrack, and Russell's no-accident luck was due to run out.

The intersection of East Sixth came and went as the Cat entered Burman's dust cloud. The Peugeot suddenly appeared just to the front right—too close for comfort.

The Stutz's alignment had worsened, and Russell tensed to keep her from veering into Burman. A new shudder worked its way through the steering column, becoming more apparent by the second.

Al pointed toward the left front then slashed his hand across his throat.

Tire's on the brink. And with the way it was shuddering, if they didn't get off the road fast, they'd be the next Earl Cooper.

Russell eased off the accelerator, and Burman pulled away.

The viaduct above the starting line materialized on the horizon. No more than a quarter mile remained, but Russell wouldn't risk it. Nothing rash.

Sweat trickling down his neck, he moved to the side of the road and took the Cat out of gear, letting her coast to a stop.

"I'm on it, boss!" Al bolted out of the seat and flung open the lid to the side-mounted tool box. He had the jack in hand before Russell could jam the brake into place and lift the goggles from his eyes. By the time he made it to the front of the car, Al already had her tilting up on one side.

Heat radiated from the hood in waves. When he bent to inspect the motormeter, a drop of sweat fell and sizzled on the grill. The meter's red alcohol had risen one-quarter of the way from the bottom.

"How's she coping?" Al spoke around the nut between his teeth.

"Beautiful."

"Russell!" Winnie's faint voice drew him around. She ran toward them, her cap off, her hair brilliant.

Speaking of beauty.

"The chief timer said"—a car barreled past—"and five."

"What?" he shouted back.

Still several hundred yards distant, she cupped her hands around her mouth. "A hundred and five! You did it. You're in!"

Present Day

Meghan sat forward in her seat, tingling head to toe as she listened to the keynote speaker give the address for opening session.

Prolific romance writer Peggy Robertson's wrinkled but joyous face filled with a smile that came right from her soul and took residence in her sparkling eyes. "Anne Rice, Stephen King, Sylvia Plath . . . you're just like them. They too started out with dreams bigger than Texas . . . "

Meghan bit her bottom lip and found herself wanting to whisper to Steve about her dreams coming true—until she remembered he didn't plan on being around long enough to see it happen. Her throat ached. Was she supposed to even be here right now? Should she be home begging Steve to love her?

A few murmurs and appreciative nods rippled through the crowd drawing Meghan's attention back to the here and now. Peggy was laughing. She crossed the stage and looked out across the room.

"It's a fair bet to say most of you are here because you feel compelled to write. And if that's you . . ." For a moment, her eyes paused on Meghan's, and then she spoke again. "You're supposed to be here. This time is for you. To get in touch with that Something bigger than yourselves. That Something or Someone who whispers every day, "You. Must. Write!"

Meghan gulped, eyes stinging and leaking a tear down her cheek right in the middle of a throng of authors. Could that message have been meant for her? From . . . God? Yes, this was where she was meant to be at this moment in time.

The tissue she dabbed under her eyes could hide the moisture there—but not, she was certain, the awestruck wonder that must be radiating from her. After all, she was sitting next to one of her favorite authors. And two rows in front of her was the famed Madeline Hawk with her agent, Brett Gherkin. For all her determination, Meghan realized she'd had real doubts about making it to the Northwest Fiction Conference. About her journey to becoming a real novelist.

She bit her lip to keep her tearful smile from reaching goofy proportions, and slid her fingers up her left arm. The pinch didn't wake her up. It was real—she had a name badge and a packet of conference information and everything. She didn't deserve this, but God had done this for her anyway.

The keynote speaker closed her message and stepped off the podium as the conference emcee approached the stage. She launched into a rundown of the rest of the days' events—writing workshops, critique circles, and most important . . . agent and editor appointments.

The tingles rushed back.

Less than twenty-four hours earlier, Meghan had been on an airplane, touching down on the tarmac and absorbing the wonder of looking out across a foreign landscape. Then arriving at the hotel and being handed a key to her own room where she'd be staying for three whole days. No cooking, no cleaning, no shuttling around town. No arguing with Steve. And now, she was minutes away from her first pitching appointment. Her stomach nosedived and she blew out a slow breath through puckered lips.

Oh, Jesus, be with me. She'd hate to have worked so hard, spent so much money, come this far, and then shoot an air ball at the buzzer.

She already may have fouled out in her marriage.

She pulled her cardigan tighter, chilled by the air jetting from the AC vent overhead—and the uncertainty of her future.

Today's troubles were enough to worry about. She chewed her lip and pegged her eyes on the head in front of her as she followed the throng out the doors of the Wilson Meeting Hall. She smiled at those who made eye contact and watched as the crowd dispersed, on their way to various writing workshops.

But she was due in the appointment room.

Prayers bounced from her lips like popcorn, sweat dampened her hands, and anticipation teased her senses as she waited for her turn to sit across from the senior acquisitions editor of River Press. Meghan glanced at the other writers around the room giving pitches and went over her own rehearsed speech one more time.

And then the chair was hers. She eased into it and displayed her shaky smile. "Hi, I'm Meghan Townsend."

The editor, Norma Wells, shook her hand. "Nice to meet you, Meghan. I'm Norma. How are you this morning?"

"Good, thanks. It's a pleasure meeting you."

"You too. Tell me about your book."

Meghan gulped. "Sure. It's about a racecar driver and a mechanic. Oh, first I'm supposed to tell you it's a historical romance." She let out a shaky laugh. "Sorry, I'm nervous."

Norma smiled. "It's okay, you don't need to be. Relax, I promise I won't bite."

Her pleasant face calmed some of the nerve endings firing throughout Meghan's body. She took a breath and started over. "Racing Hearts is a historical romance set during the Corona Road Race of 1916."

Meghan went on to describe the essence of her plot, then shared all her favorite twists and turns. Soon she was caught up in her story, nerves forgotten. Breathless, Meghan slammed on the brakes, shifted her weight, and put her enthusiasm in check. Had she rambled too much? Talked too fast?

But Norma's chin bobbed up and down. "Okay. That's good." She tugged on the bottom of her vest then reached across the table for the Pitch Sheet Meghan held. "May I?"

"Of course." She chewed her lower lip as she handed Norma the glossy paper, complete with a stock photo of a shiny red Stutz, and a black-and-white of the Starting Lineup of the 1916 race.

"Okay." Norma looked up at her. "Send me the full manuscript when it's ready and I'll take a look."

Meghan's jaw came unhinged, but she locked it back in place. "Really?"

Norma smiled like they were old friends. "Yes, really. It looks promising. My email address is right here."

Meghan's heartbeat returned as she took the business card offered. "Great! Thank you very much." She stood, then pumped Norma's hand. "Good chatting with you."

Meghan made sure she was a safe distance, around a corner, before she lifted up onto her toes and did a little Snoopy Dance. Her first request! And another appointment in less than 20 minutes.

According to her agenda, she was supposed to be at a session on Opening Chapters, but she was too elated to go to a class right then.

Not with another meeting to charge into. She found an empty recliner in the lobby and perched to type a message.

Eeek! An editor just asked to see my whole story!

She typed in her mother's number, started adding Steve's, then froze. No. She didn't want her parade rained on. She wanted a marching band to join her. She typed in Brooke, then added Curtis and hit Send.

The rest of the day passed in a frenetic whirlwind of note taking, craft studying, and feeling more and more at home among this group of crazies who kept company with imaginary friends. Her kind of peeps. By the time she entered the Wilson Meeting Hall for the next general session, she'd garnered a request for the first three chapters from one agent, as well as another request for a full. And by the time she unlocked her hotel room door that night and set her notebook on the desk, she was fried. Ready to conk out.

But first, she wanted to call and check in on the girls. And maybe even Steve, she was in that great a mood.

Zoey answered on the third ring. "Hello?"

"Hi, punkin."

"Mama!"

Meghan's heart leapt. "I miss you."

"Miss you, too, Mama. When are you coming home?"

A soft chuckle escaped Meghan's lips. "Today's the first day, sweet pea. I'll be home on Sunday."

"Oh yeah. I forgot. Guess what! Grandma bought us pizza for dinner!"

"She did, huh?"

"Yeah. And she said we could play Go Fish until Daddy gets home."

Meghan's stomach plummeted, her legs weakening. She forced her lips into a quavering smile. "Oh? That sounds fun. Where . . . where's Daddy?" She reached a shaky hand out toward a chair back, then eased into the seat.

"He said he had a portent meeting so that's why Grandma was bringing us pizza."

"Oh. Okay." She massaged her throat. "Well, you . . . you be good for Grandma then, okay? Tell Faith I said goodnight. I'll call again tomorrow."

"'Kay. I love you, Mommy!"

Her temples throbbed. "I love you too, baby. I have to go now. Night night."

All the way home from the airport, the weight on Meghan's shoulders seemed to increase. The conference had been a raging success, but behind it all was the burning question. How had her husband filled his time? She could think of a few answers to that question, and none of them were good.

She pulled into her driveway, cut the engine, and sighed. She pressed a hand to her aching chest, then hit the garage opener.

By the time both her feet hit the pavement, Steve was on his way out to meet her. Faith and Zoey raced past him, squealing. Meghan cast an assessing gaze over her husband, securing the iron cage around her heart. He was keeping secrets. And she was done being hurt by this man.

He offered a tight smile as he approached, then gave her a quick, stiff embrace. "How was it?"

She nudged her chin up. "Fabulous, actually," she deadpanned. "Don't suppose you want to grab my suitcase for me."

"Sure."

As Steve headed to the back of the car for her luggage, Meghan knelt to embrace her princesses. Both seemed to have their switches turned to "turbo," talking in fast-forward as they regaled her with all their news. Zoey wrapped her arms around Meghan's neck and didn't appear to be going anywhere any time soon.

With a smile that made her soul ache, Meghan rose, carrying Zoey and holding Faith's hand as they passed through the garage toward the kitchen entrance. She looked back over her shoulder at Steve, who seemed to be making a show of carrying her suitcase. As if it were a burden.

"Give me a break," she muttered under her breath. Why had she even asked him to do anything for her?

She wasn't sure what to make of him at the moment. He didn't seem angry, but there was sure no spring in his stride either. Was she supposed to forget the conversation they'd left hanging before she left? The answers she never got? Not that she needed to hear him say it in order to know.

He stepped into the kitchen after her, then set the case down with a restrained exhale. "I'm trying to take a half day tomorrow."

"Oh?" Did this mean something? A kernel of hope popped in her spirit whether she wanted it to or not.

"I tried to take the whole day, but Jones needs me to make sure the delivery trucks get loaded and on their way without any problems like there were last time, and we're expecting an inventory drop-off in the morning that I have to be there to sign for."

"Okay." She should be glad. Whatever Steve had been thinking of doing, maybe he'd changed his mind during her weekend away. Maybe he'd chosen her. But she couldn't muster happiness. She didn't feel anything, good or bad. It was like she'd been given a shot of emotional Novocain.

Her stomach churned.

She didn't trust him. Bottom line.

Meghan had had no clue what to expect when she got home, but this . . . whatever it was . . . was too little to go on in the way of renewing real hope.

He was waiting. She took a breath and tried to find something to say, but the ringing of her cell phone interrupted her train of thought. She slid Zoey down onto her own two feet and pulled her phone from her purse pocket. "Hello?"

Brooke's voice bounced through the line. "Are you home yet?"

"Just got in."

Steve moved to the living room and re-warmed his couch cushion. Within seconds, the TV roared with hoots and hollers, and Steve chuckled at some amazing "ally-oop."

Meghan snorted and left the room. Things would never change.

"So how did it go? When am I going to be the best friend of a published author?"

She chuckled. "It doesn't work that fast."

"Well, give me the scoop, the news, the skinny."

Meghan laughed harder, feeling the thrill of the weekend rush back to her.

She stepped into her room and closed the door. "It was amazing! There were so many people there, so much to take in. I got to meet a few of my favorite authors and they were so encouraging. Oh, Brooke, you would have loved the Awards Banquet last night. The room was gorgeous and everyone dressed up. Even me. I took pictures. The Debut Author Award winner had her sister there and it made me think of me and you. I totally pictured you in your six-inch heels and a swanky dress, clapping for me, your dear little friend."

"You better believe it. And how many people are totally clamoring to publish your book?"

"Stop it, don't get my hopes up too high. I got a total of three requests. One for the first three chapters, and two for the full manuscript. Which means I need to hurry and finish it—yikes!"

"You can do it. VBS starts next week so you'll have hours of silence to write in. Oh, Meghan, this is great news for you. Congratulations, girl."

Meghan smiled. "Thanks. This is big, but there's still a long way to go. Finishing the book, sending it, waiting to hear back, then even if they do like it they may want me to make changes, and at the end of it all decide not to offer me a contract."

Brooke groaned. "Why do you do that?"

"Do what?"

"Tally the hurdles and never enjoy the success. Don't be so afraid to enjoy your life, Meghan. This is a time to celebrate!"

"I . . . " Meghan nodded and looked up at the ceiling. "I don't know why I do that. I guess I just don't want to be disappointed." She'd had so much of that.

"Yeah, but if you always expect the bad then it's all you'll ever see. You're always going to have some disappointments, but this right here is a blessing from God. You know, 'life more abundant' and all that. Let me hear you squee!"

Meghan laughed under her breath. "Okay . . . squee." She did feel a thrill of excitement bubbling up in her chest.

"You can do better than that. Squeeee!"

Brooke's exclamation drew a belly laugh from Meghan. She closed her eyes and pulled the phone closer to her mouth. "Squeeeeeee!"

"Atta girl! Now go get yourself some champagne and maybe even some chocolate ice cream. Just this once."

"Diet rebellion. Wow, you do want me to let loose."

"It'll be good for you. Now go on, I'll talk to you later."

The call ended and Meghan bit back a smile. She would celebrate. But she'd stick with sparkling cider and a parfait. Through the closed bedroom door, she heard the basketball game still going strong.

Plopping onto the bed, she leaned back against the pile of pillows. She'd promised Curtis she'd share the details when she got home, but there was too much to say for a text. She dialed his number.

"Hey there, I'm back."

"Welcome home. How'd it go?" Excitement resounded in the lilt of his voice. Excitement to hear from her.

"Great! I have three requests for my manuscript! They all asked great questions and said it was a unique concept. 'Very promising,' one of them said."

Adrenaline pumping, Meghan gushed about the conference. "I learned so much. And got some great compliments on my story. You should hear the feedback I got. Oh, but first, I have to tell you about the opening session."

A chuckle sounded from his end of the line. "Whoa, whoa. Slow down there."

"Sorry." She laughed at herself.

"Don't ever be sorry." A smile colored his voice.

"I guess I'm excited."

"I couldn't tell," he teased. "I'm thrilled for you. And I want to hear all about it, but I'm on my way out to meet a client in a minute. Why don't we meet for coffee tomorrow and you can spill all the beans?"

"Coffee?" Meghan's pounding heart sputtered.

"Well, I'll have coffee. You can drink that tea you love so much."

"Chai."

"I know. Nonfat, double-foam."

She swallowed around the lump in her throat. Did Steve even know that? "I suppose I have time to talk books over a cup of tea."

"Okay, I'll see you at It's A Grind at . . . let's say ten a.m. ?"

"Sounds good." Too good.

"K, take care."

"You, too."

Her whole body tingled.

A cup of tea with Curtis? No biggie, right?

In the other room, the TV still blared. Steve argued with the ref. Meghan unzipped her computer bag, slid out her laptop, and fired it up. She had manuscript requests to fill, and there was no better time than the present.

1916

"Wrong one. Let's try a thirty-two." With the oil pan on the ground five inches from her ear, Winnie popped the wrench off the nut and extended it out from under the car toward Russell's feet.

He took it then dug around, creating a clatter while grousing about a lack of lighting.

She felt as cranky as he sounded. Every part of her ached.

Early yesterday, she'd determined the misalignment was due to a warped axle rod. Either the tow to the shop or Russell's reckless driving had been the culprit. As much as she'd like to blame the daring Mr. Keegan, she suspected the former.

He'd telephoned the Stutz shop in Los Angeles which, glory be, had the parts they needed. They'd spent the rest of the day driving there and back and had gone to bed long after the street lights had come on.

A mere two hours remained in the practice day. At seven thirty, the Circle would reopen to local traffic.

While Russell grumbled, she tried to stretch in the confining space. Joints popped like a repeating rifle, and she groaned.

Sam sniggered from where he'd stationed himself with a soda. "Don't you worry, Miss Winnie. This is man's work. No one expects you to keep up."

Russell cast a glance under the Cat in time to catch her eye-roll. With an understanding wag of his head, he passed her the thirty-two. "Ignore the narrow-minded fool. Just show him what you're made of."

"Who's the fool? I don't see a fool," Sam said.

"Me." Al's voice was garbled from whatever food it was he chewed. "For sitting here all day, listening to you beat your gums."

"Hear, hear." Russell clapped his hands in slow, melodramatic applause.

"You boys are going to be the death of me." She clicked the wrench into place then went about securing the last nuts. Pain seared her finger and shot darts up her arm.

"See, told ya." Sam's words boomed through the garage. "She's near death. Now tell me you've heard of a man dying from a day in the shop."

"Aw, dry up, already." A scuffle followed Al's whine.

"Put it down, Al," Winnie hollered. "Whatever you're about to throw at Sam, just put it down."

Al harrumphed, and Winnie grinned.

Russell stretched out on the ground beside the car, placing his head under it next to hers. "Two days, and you've already got 'em figured out." Heat from his leg spread warmth to her insides.

She riveted her eyes to the transaxle and ignored the bouquet of castor oil wafting off him. Her hand fumbled, and the wrench slipped off the nut. Since when did she associate the oil's smell with something other than . . . bad? A new train of thought was in order. "While I have your undivided attention, care to tell me how you got those gorillas off my back?"

"A little negotiating. Wasn't hard."

In other words, he'd paid her debt, which meant she was now indebted to him. Which was so much better than the alternative. "Thank you." She swallowed tears of relief and gratitude. "I haven't touched your cash advance, so I'll return it in full. The rest I'll get back to you sooner or later."

"Who said I forked over money?"

"No need." A bitter laugh shook her chest. Another trip of the wrench and her finger banged against the underbelly. "Ouch!"

"How you holding up?" The concern in his soft-spoken question elicited a weary sigh.

The creeper shifted beneath her, as though begging to be out from under the car. "I'm filthy and smelly and ready to call it a day."

"And the finger? Taken any aspirin since this afternoon?"

"No. That and a bath would be heaven right about now."

"How much longer?"

"Actually . . ." She wiped stray grease off the brake lines. "I think I'm ready for Sam to put the tires back on."

"The axel a snug fit in the gearbox?"

A tiny smile lifted her cheeks. She'd missed shoptalk, and soon, she'd miss Russell. Too late, she stopped herself from looking at him. His piercing blue eyes severed her breath. "A perfect fit," she whispered.

His lips spread in a slow, knowing smile. "Yes, we are."

Overheated and in sudden need of space, Winnie beaned him with the rag. "Let's get this baby on her feet."

Russell laughed and slithered out, rolling her out with him, then hooked a hand under her shoulder and lugged her upright. She didn't have the energy to refuse the help. Not that she wanted to.

Puffing air from tight lips, she took the rag he offered and gingerly wiped her hands. "I'm tuckered out, boss."

Russell turned to Sam. "Put that soda down and get those tires over here."

Wheels on, toe-in checked, and jacks removed, Winnie gave a satisfied nod and declared the Cat ready for a test drive.

Fifteen minutes later, she parked the Lizzie on Sixth Street as close to Grand Boulevard as possible.

In the passenger seat, Al twisted to peer at the long line of cars and wagons waiting for the Circle to open to local thoroughfare. Russell and Sam were in the Cat, somewhere toward the end of the line. "Traffic is awful in this town of yours."

Winnie smacked his hat down over his eyes. "Because of the race, dingbat." She squelched the motor and settled in to wait for the next scheduled opening.

The high-pitched squeal of engines faded in and out as the racers tore up the asphalt on the Circle. The wind shifted and a cloud of exhaust enveloped them. She coughed and wondered how the racers could eat dust for hours on end.

The six o'clock whistle blew from the corner of Joy and Harrison, announcing a shift change for the migrant workers. In forty-eight hours, the race would be history, and she and the town could resume life as usual. Life as usual? Without Russell?

Al elbowed her. "Why the droopy lips? Perk up. She's gonna run like a champ."

Engines rumbling and horses snorting, traffic inched past. When the Bearcat reached them, Russell punched Sam in the knee. "Give the lady your seat."

Sam complied then surprised her by holding her elbow as she jumped into the car.

On the Circle, Russell pulled to the side to wait until traffic was shut down again.

Clipboard in hand, the chief timer, Mr. Pendelton, walked up. "Mr. Keegan, glad to see you made it in today, but once the whistle blows, you'll have no more than ten minutes. We're shutting down early to let the trucks lay another layer of macadam."

Russell's shoulders dropped several inches. "I understand. Thanks for letting us know." He turned to Winnie, concern puckering his brow. "You best drive, then."

"Me?"

"You're the one who sensed a problem last time. Not me."

She raised her splinted hand. "Did you forget?"

His eyes softened. "I'll be right here, but I don't think you'll need help."

Maybe, but fear still gnawed at her insides.

"You'll be fine, Winnie. This isn't a race." An excellent point.

Of the few racecars on the circle practicing this late in the evening, none would be vying for position. And she'd seen to the Cat's safety herself. Short of another defective tire—which was improbable—nothing should happen.

And the idea of experiencing the Bearcat for herself held appeal. The entire Circle lay open before her with only friction to regulate her speed. "Move over, roadster."

A wry grin claimed his lips as he handed her the extra set of goggles and climbed out. "I figured you wouldn't protest overly much. Just don't get too attached." He circled the Cat and climbed into the passenger's seat.

Fifteen minutes later, she released the brake and wasted no time ratcheting up the speed. The accelerator was just halfway down, but the ride was already exhilarating. Unbridled power radiated through the steering column and into her body. Let's see what you can do, sweetheart. Palms already tingling from the vibration, she drove the pedal to the floor.

The engine responded, nailing her against the seatback. Under the strain, the Cat didn't so much as shudder. The smooth road passed beneath them in a blur, as though it didn't exist.

Winnie topped out the car's potential then tuned her hands and body to any unusual tugs. Nothing. Not a hint of a waiver. Flawless. She gave Russell a thumbs-up, and he returned it.

Time flew almost as fast as they did, and all too soon, Russell signaled to pull over.

When they stopped, he removed his goggles to his forehead. "Well?"

Skin chapped and hands trembling, she did the same and faced him, breathless. "Well . . . I'm afraid I'm hopelessly attached."

He threw his head back and laughed. "I would have been disappointed with anything less." He nudged her leg. "Scoot. I'll drive you home."

"What about the Lizzie?"

"Al's got it. Your mother invited the boys to dinner."

Extra time with "the boys"? Winnie withheld a whine. "How very kind of her."

Russell pulled up to the house and parked in front of the picket gate. Her bones creaked almost as much as the porch steps, but the smell of fried chicken lifted her spirits.

"I'm home, Momma!"

"Your bath is drawn and ready, dear. Dinner in half an hour," Momma said from the kitchen over the crackle of hot grease.

Sam emerged from the back of the house, wearing a petulant expression and carrying a glass of water and the bottle of aspirin. "You carrying a torch for the gal don't make me your new errand boy, Keegan. I'm not paid enough."

"I pay you too much, now quit your yapping and give the lady what she needs before I put you in Chester's old bed at the hospital."

"I'd like to see you try." Sam passed her the goods and left with a huff.

An eyebrow cocked, she turned to Russell.

He gave her an impish grin and shrugged, then pointed up the stairs. "Enjoy your little bit of heaven."

Winifred's own words echoed back to her. Aspirin and a bath would be heaven right about now. "A bath? Heaven, here I come."

Enjoy, she did. Relaxed, scrubbed, and feeling like a lady again, she slipped into a dress and joined the others in the kitchen.

Russell looked up from setting the table and froze mid-stretch.

Sam whistled, and Al hurried to unseat himself. He motioned toward his empty chair. "Here you go, Miss Winnie."

Her mother swiveled, took in Winifred's old outfit, and shook her head. "You boys act like you've never seen a lady in a dress before."

"Not this one, we haven't." Al patted the seatback until Winifred accepted.

Smoothing her skirt over her thighs, she focused on the one who mattered. Russell winked at her and deposited the last plate.

"You're all being ridiculous." A flush heated her cheeks. "Why aren't more places set?"

Russell picked up a picnic basket off the floor. "I told your mother you could use a leisurely ride in the country. She agreed."

"Quite reluctantly, I might add." Mildred pegged him with a killer expression, and his cheery smile wilted.

Winifred swallowed a snigger, as her mother came to her and adjusted a hairpin. "You've been working so hard, and I know how much you enjoy a ride just for the fun of it. You haven't been since . . . your father." Mildred spun on her heel and pointed a trigger finger at Russell. "You're to have her home by nine and not a minute later, or you'll find yourself on the porch swing tonight."

Paling, Russell nodded. "Yes, ma'am. Nine, it is."

Winifred laughed all the way to the Lizzie where she tossed Russell the key.

He snatched it out of the air and rounded his eyes in bogus shock. "Aren't you worried I'll warp an axel?"

"Psh! If you do, I'll change it. I'm perfectly capable, you know."

"So I've seen, and I thank you for freeing me to drive as fast as I please." Despite his bold declaration, he kept his speed under twenty through town, increasing it only a little when they reached the country.

Even with his care, the car jostled and lurched in a way she'd never noticed before. The Bearcat had ruined her perception of what a car should be able to do. Hopelessly attached.

He eased off the road where a lemon grove collided with the desert. Grass grew in patches beneath the trees where shade was abundant. "How about here?"

"It's beautiful." She inhaled the fresh citrus air then grabbed the basket at her feet, handing it to him before accepting his help down.

A blanket spread beneath them, they ate in relative silence, enjoying the calm and the satisfaction of a project completed. The desert stretched before them, rocky and barren. Beyond lay the foothills, from which swept a cool breeze. Winifred closed her eyes and savored it.

"I didn't think you could do it." Russell stretched out on his side, his head propped by his fist, his gaze more intense than she'd anticipated.

"I didn't either."

"You were bluffing?"

Gaze darting to the hills, she shrugged and failed to fight off a simper. "Maybe."

He laughed. "Unbelievable. Remind me never to oppose you in poker."

"Certainly." She passed him a saucy smile then sobered. "What's next on your racing calendar? After Corona."

Russell picked at a long blade of grass, allowing a comfortable silence to settle between them. At last, he tossed it aside, sat up, and brushed off his hands. "Not sure. Pop and I always had the next five races lined up, but since he died, this is all I've thought about. There hasn't been a future after Corona." His eyes traveled beyond the wasteland, beyond the jagged peaks spanning the horizon.

Seconds passed in silence.

"You're thinking about him, your Pop."

He blinked and drew a deep breath. "Every day."

Tears prickled. "I understand."

Their eyes met, and compassion softened his mouth. "I know."

She sniffed and cleared her throat. "Dreams are a good thing. You need to find another one."

"What about your dreams, Winnie?"

A bitter laugh cut from her throat. "They're irrelevant."

He shifted and looked her full in the face. "Horse feathers. What are your dreams?"

Her gaze fell to the two things that harnessed her future—the bandage holding the split against her broken finger and the oil that sullied it. She picked at the frayed edge. "I wanted to play first chair in the Los Angeles Chamber Orchestra."

"Winnie, I—" Voice breaking, he reached for her good hand and squeezed it. "I didn't know, didn't think . . . I'm sorry. Your finger will heal, and you'll play just as beautifully as before."

A tiny lift of her shoulder dismissed his argument. "Maybe. But that dream was a bust before those goons got ahold of me. I can't leave the shop, or Momma." She donned a brave smile. "Onwards and upwards, right? Just like you, I need to find a new dream."

Releasing her hand, he stood. A few paces away, he stopped, picked up a stone, and pegged a small saguaro with it. The cactus shook and coughed up a small bird that fluttered into the settling dusk.

"I know! Electricity," she said.

Nose scrunching, he gave her a sidelong stare.

"In the shop. My new dream."

"A noble goal, but can't you think of something better than that?"

"What's better than electricity?" She put on a cheesy grin, hoping to lighten the mood. "Now, let's think of one for you." A finger to her chin, she feigned deep thought. "How about five monocle windscreens, all in different colors."

Eyes closing, he twisted his features as though in pain.

Laughing, Winifred pushed off the ground and straightened the skirt of her dress. She chose a rock and bounced it between her hands. "Wanna make a bet?"

"With you? Wouldn't miss it for the world."

"Don't get too excited, gamester." She pointed at the saguaro. "I bet I can hit that white flower, the one halfway open, near the top of that cactus. If I do, I get to pick a new dream for you. If I don't, you get to pick your own dream."

"That's not how dreams work. People don't pick them for you."

"You haven't done such a great job on your own, now have you?"

Eyes narrowing, he jutted out a hand. "All right. Deal."

They shook, and she took aim at the flower. Stepping out with her left foot—just as her daddy taught her—she let the stone sail. With a thwop, it slapped into the base of the flower, sending it airborne.

Russell's lips parted, hung open, then closed with a breathy grunt.

"So, about that dream." Winifred brushed her hands against each other, all business now. "I propose you give up racing for a safer, more fulfilling life. Find a new hobby, a new ambition. Find a cozy, little house and fill it with children who adore you. You're young and full of zeal. Use those assets to do something meaningful. I'd hate to see so much potential splattered across a speedway." Out of breath, she sucked air. "There, I've said it. In case you had any doubt that I–"

"That you cared for me?" Heat lighting his eyes, he grabbed her dress at the waistline, and tugged her toward him.

What? How had he come to that conclusion? Talk of children?

But now that he forced her to think on it . . . he was absolutely correct.

I care for Russell Keegan.

A smile curved the edges of her mouth. She hadn't intended to express it, but, yes, she cared for him.

A rush of blood to her head left her hands tingling and her heart tripping to keep up with the revelation. "I was going to say that I hated the races, but . . ." She tasted her lips while eying his. "But . . . that works, too." Her gaze crawled to his eyes.

Their baby blue darkened with intention.

She swallowed.

Mouth lowering, his breath blew over her chin and tickled her throat. One hand ran up her back and clamped onto the base of her neck, tipping her head toward him.

Of their own accord, her arms wrapped around him. A treacherous shudder careened through her, and he tightened his hold.

Like a whisper, he brushed her neck with his lips. His hand began to tremble as he nudged the side of his face against hers and inhaled in tatters. "May I?"

Impatience clenched her fist around his shirt back. "You better."

Air left him in a whoosh, but contrary to what she expected, he moved slow and purposeful.

With maddening accuracy, he traced her cheekbone with kisses, moving lazily toward her mouth. When he found the corner of her lips, she turned toward him.

First contact was sweet and familiar, light and tender—far short of where she wanted to be. But Russell was in the driver's seat. Tension built within her as she waited for him to floor the accelerator.

Weary of his constraint, she pressed in, plying for more. Measured but strong, she led the way until he withdrew, his breath coming fast and furious.

"Good golly, woman. What are trying to do to me?"

She cocked a brow and slipped on a sultry smile. "Just pursuing my dream."

If Winifred had never seen a man hungry before, she did then. Although "hungry" didn't quite describe Russell Keegan in that moment. Ravenous, more like.

"It's electricity you want, is it?" By the promise in his tone, she knew to buckle up.

Present Day

Meghan's fingers barely kept up with her imagination. She'd been anticipating that kiss for ages and completely lost herself in Russell's strong arms—Curtis's arms. What would it be like to taste his lips?

Of course she would never know. But Winifred would get the full experience.

It must have been late when Steve interrupted her. "Aren't you ready for a break after a whole weekend wrapped up in that story?"

"Shhh. Please. I'm trying to concentrate." Concentrate, indeed. She could write a hundred kisses with Russell and never tire of it.

She finished off a paragraph and looked up at her husband as he headed to the bathroom. "The conference didn't make me want a break, it got me motivated to plow through it. I've got requests for the manuscript and I don't want to keep anyone waiting. This is a big deal, I'm . . . euphoric!"

"That's great, Meg, but it's after eleven o'clock." Steve jammed his toothbrush in his mouth and started scrubbing. "So how much longer are you planning to be up?" He spoke through a mouthful of white, drippy foam, then choked on a gag before spitting into the sink. Meghan recoiled. Romantic kissing mood, dead.

She shook off the image. "I don't know. I'm making a lot of progress and don't want to mess with my mojo."

Steve slurped water from the tap, spewed it, then wiped his mouth with a towel.

Meghan studied his weary face. Guilt pricked her conscience and her shoulders drooped. "I can go in the other room if it's going to keep you awake."

"If I'm not asleep in fifteen minutes I'll let you know."

After hitting the lights, he climbed into bed beside her. "Good night." He puckered up for the expected peck. Obviously they were back to pretending things were fine, so she obliged. Then he rolled onto his side, jostling the entire bed as he found his comfortable spot.

Nerves on edge, Meghan's jaw tensed as she waited for him to be still. When he finally pulled the covers over his shoulders and lay motionless, Meghan's writing took off again like a jet-powered racecar.

1916

If Winifred had never seen a man hungry before, she did then. Although "hungry" didn't quite describe Russell Keegan in that moment. Ravenous. And she was his prey, caught in his sights.

Like a startled doe, she reflexively tried to bolt, but he already had her pinned against him.

"It's electricity you want, is it?" By the promise in his tone, she knew to buckle up.

And good thing she did. When he shifted gears, her heels left the ground, and she found herself creating a new dream—one that involved Russell Keegan and a house full of children. Their children.

He smothered her mouth beneath his, stealing her air. She gasped, but when he eased off, she pursued him.

Breaking away, he slid his fingers onto her chin. "No, that zeal you referred to isn't always a good thing."

"I can handle it."

"I believe it, but that doesn't mean it's smart." He laid a kiss as soft as a sigh on the corner of her mouth. "You're a strong woman. You know that? For taking on the Cat, your dad's shop. The whole town, for that matter."

She breathed a laugh. "Sam doesn't think so."

Russell stroked her cheek and snorted. "Sam doesn't have room to talk. He wouldn't be caught dead in the mechanic's seat during a race."

"Good thing you have Al then, huh? Otherwise, you'd be up a creek."

"What are you talking about?"

"Al riding shotgun. Tomorrow."

He took an emphatic step away from her, his brows lowering. "Al's not riding shotgun."

Realization smacked her upside the head. Her hand flew to her chest. "Well, don't look at me, as though, as though—"

"As though, what?" His jaw inched forward.

"As though you expect me to—"

"But that's the mechanic's job. It's your job! Who else would ride? Sam and Al are great at what they do, but anything beyond changing tires and checking fluid levels? I don't think so."

"I never told you I would ride. Russell, you know I hate the races!" Another step back lengthened the distance between them.

"Of course you wouldn't tell me! It's understood. It's what a racer's mechanic does. We talked about this, before we even shook on it. I said you'd have to be tough and fast and—"

"In the pit!" She threw her hands skyward. "And yes I plan to be there, but if you think I'm going to put myself in that deathtrap and take a thousand spins around the city, all for a stupid race, you don't know me at all!" And that knowledge stung, as did her accumulating tears.

Hurt slackened his features.

Guilt tightened hers. The races weren't stupid to him. "Russell, I—"

He held up a silencing hand and took several steps backwards before spinning and striding into the desert where he kicked the fallen flower. Minutes ticked past as he paced.

When he returned, it was with determined steps. "I do know you. I know you loved your father. And that you hate racing because it took his life. I know your brother left you in a bind, and that's what forced you to go against your principles. At first. But now . . . things have changed. You've discovered being a mechanic is more than a paycheck. You love it. What's more, you're good at it. And we're good together, me and you. A perfect fit. Tell me I'm wrong." He spoke with unnerving confidence. And uncanny accuracy.

"You're right. About all of it. But if I'd known all along you intended to be flippant with my life, I would have jammed the brake on my heart." Her voice cracked.

He reached for her, cupped her face in his hand. "I would never hurt you, Winnie."

"Promise me you won't crash—promise my mother that the race won't take another person she loves"—she kissed his palm—"and I'm all yours." The ridiculous request hung between them like a thick, black cloud.

At his silent, crestfallen expression, she spun, tears tumbling, to pack the remnants of their evening and any future they might have had.

Chapter Thirteen

1916

Winifred sat straight up in bed, blood pounding in her ears, fear spiking her senses. The clock on her nightstand banged away the seconds. Sheet gripped to her throat, she searched the murky haze of her room for what had woken her.

Pain twanged her finger. Had the brute with the pliers gotten past Russell? The bedroom door remained shut. She shook her head.

Fear.

That's what had jolted her, but fear of what? She wasn't riding shotgun tomorrow, and the pits were safe, considering the alternative.

The back of her gown clung to her skin. Sweltering heat surrounded her, radiated from her. The sweat covering her body did little to cool.

She tossed off the sheet, and peeled away the damp fabric of her nightclothes. She didn't need a sleepless night. The race was hours away, and their day was scheduled to be begin long before the crowds arrived.

Lying back down, she forced her breath to even intervals and tried to empty her mind, but unease clawed at the edges of it. Had she forgotten something? Something to do with the Cat? An important part? *Of course not.*

Unbidden, the image of her father's body flying over a hood flashed across her mind. With a groan, she flung an arm over her eyes, but the illusion repeated, this time ending with him crumpling against the side of the Hanley's Seed and Feed. The vision was familiar and as clear as though she'd stood on the street corner that day and watched, instead of being tucked in bed. George had described the event in tearful detail, leaving her with a loathsome, full-bodied taste of it.

It began again.

"Stop it!" She slammed her arm onto the mattress.

Vision blurred by moisture, Winifred cast a glance out the open window where the lace curtains hung limp. Daddy had died under a full moon, much like the one winking at her through tree limbs and lace.

The moisture grew and spilled.

He and George had spent the week tweaking Bobby's Sunbeam, preparing it for the race. They'd worked late into the night when George convinced their father to let him take it for a test drive around the Circle. Daddy agreed. Perhaps to give his estranging son a bit more liberty? To salvage a failing relationship? Winifred might never know or understand why he would take such a risk, and without Bobby's consent.

The stroke of midnight had just sounded. The town was in bed, or should have been.

Without headlights, George didn't see the girl until they were upon her. He swerved, hurtled the Sunbeam over a curb, and into a palm. Daddy connected headfirst with the brick of a nearby building. An adjacent grassy lot spared George's life.

During the investigation, it was discovered the brake pads hadn't been changed as George had previously claimed. To the cops, he stated he hadn't gotten around to it yet, that he'd planned to do it the next day. Bobby's version on the police report said the opposite.

The investigator found the old pads had nothing to do with the accident, but it didn't matter. The gossips had latched onto that bone and refused to bury it. Whether Bobby felt he'd been cheated about the brakes or not, he never said—at least not to Winifred. He certainly hadn't gone out of his way to snip the grapevine.

She rose and padded to the window. Not a breath of wind stirred the stifling air. The heat was as suffocating as the memories—her errant, absentee brother; Bobby offended, wronged; her daddy and the wreck to their lives his death had caused . . .

Regardless of what the town said, it hadn't been the brakes that killed Danny Fisher; it had been the building. Nausea clenched her stomach. Like a scratched Victrola, the vision replayed. But this time, it wasn't her father who flew over the hood.

It was Russell.

Gasping, she swiveled toward the door. The urge to run to him, to make sure he slept sound—and safe—nudged her feet. She dug her toes into the rug even as fear dug its claws into her mind.

When had fear for her own safety morphed into fear for his? *When he kissed you senseless, that's when.*

She spun back to the window, bent, and clutched the sill. "He's not yours to worry about. He's a racer. It's what he does. Get a hold of yourself, Winnie," she muttered, startling herself with the use of his pet name for her. Eyes closing, she released her breath in a rush. She shouldn't care for him so much, and yet she did.

She cared about his dreams, his happiness, his safety. A deep inhale filled her lungs with hot, stale air as she tallied the reasons she shouldn't worry.

Russell Keegan, dubbed the most prudent driver in the American Automobile Association, had never crashed. The Circle had been declared the safest speedway in existence. She'd looked over every inch of the car. *It's ready. It's safe*, she tried to convince herself, but the fear didn't dissipate. Instead, it wrapped its steel fingers around her chest and constricted.

An angry sweep of her hand set the curtain to swaying. "Why doesn't anyone make these cars safer?" she demanded of the innocent branch staring at her through the window.

In the interest of less weight, racecars had no top, no doors, no safety belt—nothing to keep a man from becoming a human catapult. It wouldn't take much to make the Cat safer, just a few pieces of—

Winifred's fist flew to her mouth. "I can do that." With shaking fingers, she struck a match and lit her bedside lamp. The clock read thirty-seven minutes past midnight. Plenty of time.

She reached for her trousers, and for the first time in fifteen minutes, drew a full breath.

Awake by five, Russell visited the outhouse then entered the kitchen to the scent of fresh coffee. Mildred faced the stove and a hissing skillet. Already dressed, Winnie sat at the table, a mug encased in her palms. Her splint glowed white with a clean bandage.

They had yet to speak a word since the orchard, but he intended to remedy that. Soon. He'd lain awake long into the night chewing on everything she'd said, and he'd come to a certain conclusion.

"Good morning, ladies." The amusing, early morning croak in his voice didn't generate so much as a smile from Winnie, who had yet to look his direction.

"Is it?" Mildred replied without turning. "Help yourself to coffee. Do you want your eggs fried or scrambled?"

Stomach churning, he didn't think he could eat a bite, but he'd learned long ago a man couldn't race on an empty stomach. He cleared his throat. "Whatever's easiest, ma'am. Thank you."

He filled a mug with the hot liquid then chose a seat across from Winnie, who avoided his eyes like a motorist would a pothole.

The steam rising from his coffee had nothing to do with the sweat dampening his upper lip. He wiped it with the back of his hand. "It's too hot out, too early."

She said nothing. It may have been the deep shadows in the room creating the dark circles under her eyes, but there was no confusing the puffiness, nor the weary expression.

"Sleep much?"

She raised the mug to her lips and sipped before responding. "I got a couple hours."

Russell nodded and fell silent until Mildred set a plate of fragrant eggs before him. "How about you, Mrs. Fisher? Sleep well?"

"Not a wink." Her answer came swift and crisp.

Guilt washed over him. He wasn't paying these women enough for all the stress and inconvenience.

Mildred stood by him, twisting her apron between her hands and staring at her daughter, whose raised mug hid half her face. Brow puckering, she studied its contents.

"Aren't you eating anything?" Russell asked.

"I'm not hungry."

Mildred laid a motherly hand on his shoulder and kissed his cheek. "Be safe. You're in my prayers today." Without another word, she left them.

Soon, the squeak of the floorboards above their heads joined the periodic clink of his fork against the plate. Tension darkened the room.

Unable to stand it a moment longer, he set the utensil down, slurped his joe, and dove in. "This is killing me, Winnie. You being angry. I've done a lot of thinking, and . . . you were right." These women didn't need another tragedy. And Russell didn't need another victory, not at their expense.

Eyes still averted, she nibbled at her lower lip.

"Are you listening?" He wrapped his fingers around her wrist, drawing her full attention. Her eyes swelled with tears, spurring him on. "I'm sorry I even thought about putting you in danger. I'd rather lose a thousand races than win one and hurt you in the process."

"Thank you. For saying that. Racing isn't safe."

"I know. The course is no place for a woman."

Her throat lurched with a swallow. "Last night, I couldn't sleep. I kept seeing you flying over the hood and slamming into a building. Again and again, like a nightmare I couldn't wake from."

He increased the pressure on her wrist. "You worry too much."

"I'm not worried anymore. At least, not like before."

"Why not?"

Her chair scraped the floor as she rose. "Sam and Al will be wondering where I am. Come on, I'll drop you off at the shop on the way to get them."

Hours remained before dawn, but the city was already abuzz. Streams of motorcars and carriages entered Corona from every direction, already vying for the best parking. The ride to the shop took longer than expected, so when they arrived, the two fellows Russell had hired to transport their equipment were already there, waiting by a truck.

With the Lizzie's engine still running, Winnie unlocked the bay door and swung it open.

Russell motioned the men inside and toward the massive stack of tires, gasoline and oil cans, funnels, tools, and everything else his pit crew might need to keep the car on the road. With the men busy loading, Russell turned to find Winnie standing by the Cat and looking . . . guilty.

"Winnie?" He made a slow approach. "What have you done?"

Russell eased the Bearcat into the twelfth position he'd acquired by drawing the number from the referee's hat. Five rows back from the front and far right—the *last* row. He wasn't happy with it, but he would make do.

The sun beat down, heating the metal contraption into an oven. Heat undulated from the hood.

When they'd left the shop at eleven thirty, the thermometer had read a hundred and one. It had to be hotter now. The incredible heat would make this race unforgettable, if nothing else did.

He fingered the broad leather strap lying over his leg. The other half of the belt dangled over the side of the car, and both had been bolted beneath the seat to the car's frame. The straps weren't going anywhere unless the seats were removed, and there was no time for that.

It was Winnie's doing. Her unauthorized, middle-of-the-night doing—an attempt to keep him safe, she'd said. But what of her own safety? Had her experience with those pliers-wielding thugs taught her nothing? A growl rose is his throat, but he wasn't sure if he was angrier at her for leaving, or at himself for not waking.

As unwieldy as the belt was, he'd promised his thoughtful little mechanic that he'd wear it snug against his waist. However, he couldn't make the same promise for Al, who had been provided a similar safety measure yet had sneered at the suggestion of using it.

Smacking his chewing gum, the gas jockey-turned-mechanic sat to Russell's left. Winnie stood on his right, having just finished her final engine check. Seeming a thousand miles away, she stared into the sea of faces lining the track.

Crowds stood five and six deep, cheering and waving flags. He'd never seen anything like Corona. In other races, fans were kept at a safe distance. Here, he was square in the middle of them. It was exhilarating. Hearing his name, he turned in the general direction and waved. The roar increased.

Red, white, and blue ribbons decorated the front of every business and residence. A poster that read "Two hundred minutes of thrills by world-renowned speed marvels" plastered the windows of Hank's Bicycle Repairs.

"Pops, pickles, pears!" a vendor cried above the din. He lifted his tray to better squeeze through the throng that pressed against the wire barrier just beyond the sidewalk. Telephone poles swayed as young men and boys perched on their tops.

All to the delicious aroma of castor oil lubricating every warming engine.

Cooper approached.

Russell greeted him with a handshake. "Say, how's your Stutz?" He jabbed a thumb at the air behind him. "Your motor's purring again, I see."

With a hanky, Cooper mopped the sweat dripping down the side of his face. "The Beam is hardly purring, but she's here and that's what counts. I'm still not sure she's ready. A few hard-pressed laps should tell the tale."

Russell understood the heartbreak of a race spiraling down the drain and the frustration of being helpless to stop it. "You're the road race speed king. It'll take more than a misaligned crankshaft to throw you off this game." He gave Cooper's shoulder a hearty shake. "I'm glad you made it. No kissing telephone poles today, all right?"

He hopped out of the Bearcat, and sweat raced down his spine.

Silsbury's mocking laughter rang out from two cars over. "Giving up already, Keegan?"

Not even dignifying the man a glance, Russell shouted, "Better be on your dogs, big mouth. You've got a debt to settle, and I aim to collect."

"Come and get me, flyboy!" More laughter followed, and Russell ground his teeth.

Winnie slipped a cool hand inside his and squeezed. "Just ignore him."

Cooper laughed. "She beat me to it. I was coming over here to tell you more or less the same."

"Why? The jerk could use another strong right hook." Russell shook his fist.

"We'll make 'im choke on our exhaust instead," Al said from behind. "Let's get 'er moving!" The car rocked from his bouncing, and his customary howl pierced Russell's ear.

He caught Winnie's gaze then rolled his eyes heavenward, and for the first time all morning, her beautiful tinkling laugh filled the air.

"Seriously, now." Cooper's face fell into a mask of sobriety. "Thanks to this California sun, we got blowouts coming. Lots of 'em. Steady as she goes. And don't let Silsbury's egging or Burman's antics get under your skin."

The man meant well, so Russell played along. "Nothing stupid. Be deliberate. Careful. Got it."

"That's the ticket." Cooper popped him on the arm with his leather helmet, gave Winnie a crisp, playful bow, and trotted back to his white Stutz.

Winnie wound her way through the cars to the shade of a full-grown pepper tree and the rectangle of asphalt chalked out with the name Keegan. Russell's gaze traveled to the gas cans stacked under a makeshift awning. He did another quick mental calculation of the gallons of fuel to the number of miles ahead. There should be more than enough.

A keg of water stood next to the three stacks of tires, twenty-four in all. He just might go through all of it today—water and tires.

Sam made annotations on a chart. Winnie sidled up to him and pointed at something he'd written, her lips forming silent words. Moisture darkened patches of her shirt, and her hair hung in damp tendrils against her throat. Despite the harsh conditions, her posture remained erect, her spirits high. An extraordinary woman, if ever he knew one.

He slumped in his seat. She should enjoy the fruit of her hard work. She deserved it. And he deserved the luxury of sharing this race with her.

"I might not be pretty, but I'm every bit as useful as she is." A childish pout twisted Al's mouth.

"Wrong there, my friend. A good luck kiss coming from you just wouldn't be the same."

Al's face screwed up, and Russell sneered. "That's what I thought."

He started out to—hopefully—collect from the appropriate person, but Winnie's broad-shouldered friend, Bobby, appeared at her side first. Russell picked up his pace.

The amateur hadn't made the cut in qualifications, topping out at eighty-seven miles per hour, not that Russell had been surprised. What did surprise him was the smooch Bobby planted on Winnie's cheek—dangerously close to her kisser—right in the middle of the world, right in front of Russell.

Color flared on Winnie's cheek, mirrored by the anger pounding Russell's temples.

One eye squinted, Bobby nodded to him. "Mr. Keegan. May the best man win." *The pretty lady.* The unspoken portion of his statement was as clear as a starting pistol. Before Russell could respond, Bobby ducked under the wire and vanished into the masses.

So, he was entering into the ring, at last. Russell could respect that. Winnie was worth fighting for.

He stepped up to her, eyed her mouth, the corner Bobby had claimed, and scowled. Resisting the urge to wipe at it, Russell cupped her bent elbow in his hand and leaned close. "What was—?"

"Ladies and gents, citizens and esteemed visitors." A voice rang out from the starting line where Hastings stood, a megaphone pressed to his mouth. "Welcome to Corona, the Indianapolis of the West!"

A hair-raising chorus of cheers and shouts poured from the crowd.

When it died down, Hastings continued. "We more than rival Indianapolis; we top them. Only in Corona will you find such a smooth track, such an accumulation of talent, such adoring fans!" Again, the city roared, sending chills down Russell's arms. This was what he lived for—the electric excitement, the challenge to perform, to thrill.

"Despite the appalling shadow of a European war," Hastings said, "the nineteen sixteen acclaimed Corona Road Race is destined to make history, to forever live in the mind of each person present. Today, you will be blown away by these amazing speed-defying machines. Grab a soda and a bit of shade, if you can . . . " Laughter filled the arena. "And settle in for the ride of your life!"

Russell turned back to Winnie, but Hastings wasn't done. "Before the racing begins, I announce a very special request by our own Mr. Ian Jameson. A request I couldn't deny." Hastings stretched the megaphone toward a young man who jogged to the center of the road.

"Thank you, Mr. Hastings." He faced the stands. "On this most memorable of days, I dare to put a question to the lovely Miss Durant." Murmurs and soft exclamations of surprise rose from all around, including from Winnie, who put fingers to her rounded mouth. They knew something Russell did not.

"Mary?" Jameson extended his hand toward the burgeoning sidelines until a willowy young woman emerged, hands on her flaming cheeks, eyes bright and round. She *was* pretty.

When Jameson dropped to one knee, the town went silent as death. He set the megaphone in the dust, placed both hands over his heart, and bellowed. "Mary Durant, you fill my every thought and desire. No other woman comes close to you. My life would be meaningless if you did not go through it with me. Will you do me the honor of taking my hand in marriage?"

Miss Durant turned wide eyes to an older couple standing nearby. The woman, presumably Miss Durant's mother, dabbed at her eyes. The gentleman next to her gave Miss Durant an encouraging nod.

Her head spun back to Jameson, and then she waved her gloved hands in the air and squealed. She darted onto the road and into

Jameson's open arms where she laid a kiss on him that sent the stands into an uproar.

Determination settled in Russell's heart, stunning him. If there weren't a racetrack to conquer, he'd echo Jameson's statement, here and now.

"How beautiful." Winnie sighed, her mouth bent in a dreamy smile that weakened Russell's knees. Compared to Winnie, "the lovely Miss Durant" was a mop. Raising her eyes to him, Winnie as much as begged him to love her.

Love her?

It was true—they were a perfect fit. She filled his every thought and desire, and he couldn't imagine there being another woman who would ever match her.

"What were you going ask me?" Her question plunged him back into the present.

"Huh?"

"You had a question."

His mind reeled back to the Bobby's kiss. "I was going to ask you what was going on with that Bobby fellow."

Her brows shot up, disappearing under her oversized cap. "It was just for luck."

"I wouldn't want *his* luck, but I'll share mine." He pulled her close and narrowed in on her mouth, but when she presented her cheek, he stopped short.

"First, you come back to me in one piece. One piece, you hear? *Then*, we'll talk kisses." She gripped his shirt front with both fists.

"Five minutes 'til the pace car rolls!" The call sent a rush of panic through him. Life was short. Even shorter on the racecourse. Beyond the track, beyond this day, life was nothing. Unless this woman was part of it.

"Winnie, I—before I get in that car, you need to know . . ." The words stuck to his tongue. He backtracked. "I couldn't have gotten here without you. You've amazed me at every turn. Your skill, your stamina and courage. The fuel that will get me through this race is knowing that . . . you're at the end of it." At her soft as cotton, doe-eyed expression, his voice cut off, but the clock was ticking. He swallowed and forged onward. "Now, if you'll be ever so kind as to cooperate, I'll be taking that kiss."

"Now?" The word squeaked out of her.

He took her full on the mouth, putting Bobby to shame and raising whistles and catcalls. She blessed him with her cooperation, even giving back enough to set a smile on his face as he broke away. "When I'm done, there'll be more where that came from. Then we'll talk *more* than kisses. We'll talk new dreams."

Rosy-lipped and flushing, she nodded.

"Keegan, what's the matter with you?" Al shouted, much to the crowd's delight. "Give the mechanic a rain check, and get your sorry backside over here!"

Russell flashed a broad smile and tugged his helmet over his head. "My chariot awaits."

With deft fingers, she brushed his hair out of his eyes and tucked it under the cap, then, without warning, dashed ahead of him to the Bearcat. Whatever she intended to do, she'd better be quick.

His baby sat idling in her typical high-pitched, aero engine whine. A jaunt around the front of her to check both leather hood straps assured him they were secure. Winnie missed nothing.

He climbed into the bucket seat, reached for the goggles on the floorboard, and froze. Helmet and goggles in place, Winnie occupied the mechanic's seat.

Al stood next to her, arms crossed over his chest, chin jutting. "What do you mean, you'd rather have *her*?"

"Gentleman, start your engines!"

"Winnie, get out," Russell demanded, his pulse breaking a record.

She buckled the helmet against the curve of her throat and reached for the seat strap. Determination etched her features in stone. "No. You need me, and you know it. If an oil line breaks, what's Al gonna do? Put his chewing gum on it?"

"Aw, c'mon!" Al said. "You gonna let her insult me like that?"

But Russell could deny none of it. Ahead, the pace car eased into motion.

"Clear the field, Keegan," an official called.

She gripped his arm. "Like it or not, we're in this together, and I take full responsibility for my own safety."

It wasn't enough, but it would have to do. He couldn't part from her if he was paid the winning purse to do so. "Your mother will string me up and abandon me to the buzzards."

"Leave Momma to me. This is my decision to make. Not hers. Besides, it's high time I moved past my fear, and I can't think of a better way than to face it head-on."

"That's my brave girl." Unable to resist, Russell brushed a gloved thumb across her cheek, then reached for her seatbelt and cinched it tighter.

Al faked a gag, then threw his arms up in the air.

"These tires aren't gonna hold long, kid. Your kinda speed in the pit is what I need most. See you in a few laps." Russell released the brake and threw the car into gear. Gas spurred the engine, launching them on the path to hopeful victory.

Then again, with Winnie at his side, who needed a trophy?

Chapter Fourteen

Present Day

Meghan's car rolled to a stop in the parking lot of It's A Grind at 9:57 a.m. It would be nice to spend a few minutes with someone who wanted to have a conversation with her. Steve had wandered through the house that morning distracted and lost in his own thoughts, almost moping, until he left for work. They'd barely spoken a word. She adjusted the mirror and reapplied her lip gloss, then dusted her bangs across her forehead.

She tried in vain to get that kissing scene out of her head, but it was all she could think about on the way over.

She was quivering as she walked across the lot and approached the glass door. She took a fortifying breath, then pulled the handle.

There he was. Looking extraordinarily handsome.

Guilt needled her but she shook off the inner scolding. It wasn't a crime to be attractive, after all. That's how God knit him together in his mother's womb, and it wasn't her fault for noticing.

His eyes sparked with recognition when she entered his field of vision. He smiled, sending an electric current rolling down her back. "Hey, good morning."

"Morning."

"I already got your tea, so have a seat." He extended his hand toward the empty chair.

"Thank you. You didn't have to do that." Meghan hung her purse on the chair back.

He grinned as she took her seat across from him at the tiny table. "No trouble. I'd already stood in line."

Meghan glanced at the half dozen people waiting to order. "Thanks for sparing me."

"My pleasure." He seemed to study her eyes, his silver-flecked blues mesmerizing her.

After a few moments of mundane chatter, he crossed an ankle over his knee and lifted his cup. "So, tell me how the appointment went down. Am I gonna be on every bookshelf in America or what?" He took a sip of his latte and a little foam clung to his upper lip.

Her gaze zeroed in on his mouth and she cleared her throat. "I had more than one appointment, actually. I learned a lot. Got a lot of feedback. They liked the race setting. Some had to be convinced about my female mechanic but I guess I did a decent job making that believable. They all liked Russell." Her cheeks warmed but she continued. "I'm at the most exciting part of the story now, the big race, and I just hope I can deliver. I got three requests and I want to finish the manuscript and send it off in the next couple weeks."

"Wow. Exciting stuff, right? By the way, I got you something." He pulled out a small, cherry-red figurine of a Stutz Bearcat then looked her in the eyes, a soft grin lifting one slightly stubbled cheek. "I couldn't resist. I hope you like it."

Meghan felt her face go slack. She closed her mouth and stared down at the treasure Curtis held. The thoughtfulness nearly bowled her over, stinging the backs of her eyes. With a gulp, she reached out, and he placed it in her hand, his fingertips tickling her palm. "Curtis, it's perfect." Her voice fell to just above a whisper. "I love this." She met his gaze, knowing it would send her pulse racing. Needing it to.

He brushed his thumb along the blade of her open hand and Meghan's breath caught. She felt the heat that surely colored her cheeks.

He curled her fingers around the figurine. "When you look at it, remember you have friends who believe in you. Who are here for you."

His gaze traveled to her mouth for the briefest of moments. She could have imagined it. Must've.

She pulled her fist toward her chest, paused to memorize the look in his eyes, then tucked the Stutz into her purse. She lifted her cup, grateful it gave her something to do and somewhere to look other than at the enticing lips smiling at her.

"Thank you, Curtis. That means more than you know." She cleared her throat, casting off the headiness of the moment. Trying to gain some breathing room. The world was tipping and she desperately needed solid ground.

Instead she found herself slipping further.

"I think my husband is getting ready to leave me," she blurted.

He waited in silence, but his jaw muscle twitched and his eyes darkened with something that stirred Meghan in a place deep inside, a place she dare not venture.

Blinking rapidly, she shook her head. "Maybe. I don't know. I shouldn't be burdening you with this."

"It's okay, Meg. I told you I was here if you needed to talk." His brows came together. "I'm sorry if my reaction unsettles you. I'm just stunned." He shook his head. "I don't understand. How he could treat you . . . how he could even consider . . . " He blinked and leaned away. "What makes you think he's about to leave you?"

She stared at the tabletop. "It's just, I've tried for months now, but I can't compete with the TV or the endless factory paperwork on his plate. There's always some excuse." She gulped. "Something he's hiding. I even got this stupid makeover and I'm still invisible to him."

"I have a hard time believing that." He slipped his fingers around hers and squeezed.

"It's true. You're not there to see."

"No . . . I'm not." Was that disappointment that tinged his voice? "But you aren't invisible. Certainly not to any man living in a ten-mile radius with two eyes and half a brain."

She lifted her eyes to his tender gaze, her despair morphing into treacherous longing. He withdrew and leaned against his seatback again. "How can I help?"

"It's probably just a rough patch. I'll be fine." She dabbed a napkin under her eyes. "Really. Let's talk about something else." She straightened in her seat and smiled. "Have you seen the previews for Judge and Jury coming out this summer? Made me think of you."

He nodded, his blue gaze intense and probing. "Yeah, that looks good." He'd allowed her to escape the subject, but if he didn't quit staring at her that way, she was going to melt into a puddle of goo.

Seeming to read her thoughts, he took a sip of his coffee and pointed his face out the window. "There's a theater across town that's doing dollar movies this summer. Old black-and-white flicks. I plan on checking that out, too."

"Maybe I'll drag Brooke over there. I have to push her into things like that, you know." She pasted on a playful smirk. "Guess not everyone is as cultured and refined as myself."

"Guess not." A smile slid up one side of his face. "Well, if she won't go with you . . . maybe I could be your backup plan."

Her heart lurched and she hid behind her tea.

Twenty minutes later, she swirled the last sip around the bottom of her cup. It was already cold—she'd made it last as long as she could. She finished her drink, unable to deny it was time to go. Besides, Steve would be getting home soon if he was working a half day.

They exited and walked together toward her car. She opened the driver's side door, but hesitated before getting in. "Thank you for the Bearcat. And for . . . everything else." She looked at the pavement then back into his eyes. "You've been a good friend. I don't think I would've made it these last couple months without you."

Curtis stood on the other side of her open door, hands resting on the frame. "You're a gifted writer and an amazing woman. I'm honored to have a small part. Besides, I enjoy your company. We should do this again sometime."

"I'd like that." She squinted an eye against the bright sun as one beat turned into two.

"Meghan..." He came around the door to stand directly in front of her. "I'm sorry about all you're going through."

"Thank you," she whispered.

Arms opening, he invited her in. She closed the distance, letting him hold her, and found her cheek pressed against his neck. This close, Meghan felt his stuttering breathing and hammering heartbeat. It revved up her own as they lingered in each other's arms. Longing spun her head, her heart. If they had been anywhere other than a public parking lot, she wouldn't be able to resist brushing her lips along the soft part of his neck mere inches from her mouth, tasting his skin. She closed her eyes. His scent intoxicated her, and the arms around her were so strong. So protective. A new dream blossomed within her.

He released her, slowly, and offered the casual smile of an old acquaintance. But by the look in his eyes . . .

They both knew better.

Their gazes locked, and this time when his eyes parked on her mouth, Meghan knew she wasn't imagining it. Her heart shuddered, and she moistened her lips. Curtis lifted a hand toward her face and fingered a lock of her hair. Tucking it behind her ear, he traced his thumb along her cheek, his chest expanding then emptying again.

Meghan stared at him, heart thrashing, pulse hammering her eardrums, every inch of her body buzzing with electricity, pleading for his kiss.

His fingers stilled. Blinking, he curled his hand into a fist and stuffed it into his pocket. His Adam's apple bobbed. "I should go." He pushed the Unlock button on his key fob with a strained smile.

She nodded, chest heaving, head clearing. "Yeah." Her voice came out too breathy and she fumbled behind her for something to lean on.

He backed away, his expression masked, as if a curtain had come down to hide the desire she'd just seen in his eyes. And a part of her mourned.

Meghan stood dazed as she watched Curtis cross the lot and slide into his car. Then she got in hers and started the engine. He wouldn't leave until she did. As they each left the lot, he turned one way and she went the other.

She rubbed clammy palms across her thighs and tossed her head to move the hair away from her face. Setting the blinker to change lanes, she licked her lips then checked her mirrors, trying to focus on the road. Her tensed stomach muscles hadn't relaxed yet and she puffed out her cheeks in a mighty exhale trying to find normal.

She'd just recovered even breathing as she walked into the house. She dropped her purse on the counter and sank into the living room recliner, digging her hands into her hair.

Oh, Lord . . . please . . .

But Meghan wasn't asking for strength, or forgiveness.

She wanted permission.

To feel. To be held.

She jumped at the buzzing of her phone and her heart somersaulted when it was a text from Curtis.

Lunch tomorrow?

Her eyes were still pinned on the words when she heard the garage door go up. Before she could overthink it, she typed her reply:

Sure, where?

As promised, Steve had taken the afternoon off work the day before. Once home, he'd shuffled about the house, keeping busy with odds and ends he'd been promising to get to. He fixed a broken sprinkler head in the front yard and nailed down a length of baseboard that had been propped up for months. He even swept half the garage floor before dumping himself onto the sofa. And all the while, he'd looked . . . nervous. Distracted. Wouldn't meet Meghan's eyes.

She studied him, trying to crack the code for his behavior. It boiled down to this: either he was getting ready to leave, or he was getting ready to stay. And judging by the way he buzzed around her without a word, Meghan guessed the former.

More than once, he looked at her and opened his mouth to speak, then seemed to change his mind. After the third time, Meghan figured she already knew what he was going to say. Meghan, we need to talk . . .

She was ready for it.

Today he'd gone off to work early, with no mention of any more half days, or even being home for dinner. Meghan dropped the girls off at VBS at ten a.m. then returned home to get ready.

Belly fluttering, she stood in her closet pulling hangers from one side of the bar to the other. The sundress revealed too much cleavage, the ruffled tee was cute, but hid more than she'd like. She needed an outfit that didn't show too much skin, but still enhanced her figure.

She settled on a fitted, cranberry colored, scoop-necked top with off-the-shoulder sleeves. Her skinny jeans looked great with the open-toed heels she paired them with. And her smoky eye shadow was just understated enough to avoid looking like she'd tried too hard.

She twisted in front of her full-length mirror, assessing her backside. Better than a year ago, but she was certainly no Brooke. Well, she'd be sitting on it anyway.

She pressed a hand to her stomach as she finished evaluating her reflection, then spun away toward the front door.

Her heels clacked on the sidewalk as Meghan scurried to the car. Adrenaline pumped through her veins, awakening her to . . . life. Her cheek lifted with her tiny smile. Surreal, yet familiar, this rush. Like high school, or the days before the couch absorbed her husband and deposited a spare tire around his middle. Back when desire darkened his eyes every time he looked at her, stirring longing in every cell of her body, and when sharing his bed meant more than trying to find sleep despite the rattle of his snoring.

She started the engine, pulse throbbing in her ears, then looked at her front lawn. Hadn't it just been yesterday they were putting in their offer to buy this house? Dreaming of watching their children grow up here, gathering friends for summer barbeques, hosting Thanksgiving dinners?

Now look at them.

Blinking against the sudden sting, Meghan shoved her sunglasses onto her face, then put the car in gear.

Like her characters, maybe she needed a new dream, too.

She pulled away from the house, beginning the fifteen-mile drive to the restaurant outside of town.

She blew out a breath through tight, berry-stained lips. The light at Main Street turned green, clearing the way to the 91 Freeway onramp. Grand Boulevard, the once-famous racetrack, blipped past. How she longed to have seen it the way it was a hundred years ago.

Her purse released a buzzing song and she grabbed for it to retrieve her phone. Anticipation tickled her senses and lifted a corner of her mouth. With one eye on the road, she fished it out and mashed it to her ear. "Hello?"

"May I speak with Meghan Townsend?" an unfamiliar voice asked.

"This is Meghan."

"Mrs. Townsend, this is Dharma Matthews calling from Corona General Hospital. Your husband, Steven Townsend, was brought in a few minutes ago. I'm sorry to inform you he's been in an accident. You should come right away."

"W-What?" Meghan's strength melted away and she struggled to hold onto the phone. "What happened?"

"As I understand it, he was injured at work. The doctors will be able to answer your questions. Ma'am, do you have a way to get here?"

She gave herself a shake. "Yeah. Yeah, I'm on my way."

Injured at work?

Meghan dropped the phone into the cup holder in the center console, then cut across three lanes, ready to make a U-turn. A boulder seemed to land in her gut, then roll around. "Oh God, please let him be all right."

She was going to be sick.

The town zipped by in a blur, more from her tunnel vision than from speed. Images flashed of Steve spread out on a hospital bed with wires and tubes jutting from him. A steady beeping marked his heartbeat as he lay unconscious. And while he was being delivered to the emergency room, she'd been on her way to . . .

What exactly?

Her heart thrashed. How bad was it? What if Steve . . . She couldn't finish the thought. Hands trembling, she grabbed her phone and voice-texted a message to Curtis: I can't make it. Steve's in the hospital and I'm on my way there.

His reply came immediately: Is he okay? Are you okay? Lunch was probably a bad idea anyway . . . Let me know how I can help. I'm praying, Meghan.

Of course he was. Because that's the kind of man he was. Chest aching, Meghan texted Brooke and asked her to do the same.

Her heart and mind were pulled in a million directions as she sped toward the hospital. Would he be all right? What kind of horrible person was she? This was surreal. Where were her tears?

"Be merciful, Jesus. Please, God." She prayed it over and over.

Meghan gripped the wheel as she turned in to the parking lot. Then somehow, she was standing at the desk to ask about her husband. The woman at the counter was on the phone and Meghan's gaze dropped to the floor while she waited. Her open-toed heels stared back at her.

"Can I help you?"

She looked up. "Yes. I got a call my husband is here, can you give me his room number?"

"Name?"

"Steve Townsend."

Meghan scanned the line of hospital rooms while the receptionist retrieved the information. Which of these doors would she be going into? What would she find on the other side?

"Here it is. Okay, Mrs. Townsend, I need to ask you to take a seat in the waiting area right over here. The doctor will be out to talk to you shortly. Here, you can take this." She handed Meghan a plastic bag containing Steve's personal items—phone, wallet, car keys. "His clothing is still in the room with him." She smiled at Meghan. "Someone will be out to talk to you very soon."

"Thank you." Meghan turned in the direction she was pointed and tried to catch her breath as she walked down the hall.

She rounded the corner and found Steve's boss, Mr. Jones, pacing along the far wall. He must have been the one who brought Steve in.

Noticing her, he approached and embraced her. "Now don't worry, Meghan. I'm sure he'll be fine."

Meghan just nodded, dazed. "What happened?"

"He tripped and dropped his end of a pallet. His leg was crushed. There was nothing we could do, it pinned him." He rubbed the back of his neck. "I care about Steve. You know that.

Let's keep things cool between us, okay? I'm a reasonable man. As soon as he's back up on his feet . . . I'll sit down with him and hammer out this mess."

Meghan's brow furrowed.

"No need for anyone's temperature to rise. See if you can get him to back off, for the good of his own health."

"What do you mean?"

"Just what I said. I'm one hundred percent willing to sit down with him and come to an agreement. He can have that desk job he wants, first off. No problem there, under the circumstances. Okay?"

Desk job? Since when had Steve been trying to get off the design floor? Meghan nodded again, but nothing was making sense.

"And we'll figure out the rest. We'll sit down with Matt and I'm sure we can find a solution we'll all be happy with. Just have him back off for now."

"I . . . I'll try?" She was too confused to say anything else.

He exhaled. "Okay, good. Look, now that you're here, I need to get back to the factory. But call me with an update as soon as you have one, okay?"

She met his eyes and nodded again, her throat too dry to speak. He squeezed her shoulder, then left.

Numb, Meghan rested on the end of a chair and wrapped her arms around herself, waiting. It must be bad if they were sending out a "handler" to talk to her.

Her chest burned. What was happening with her husband back there? She hated being in the dark. Pulling a tissue from her purse, she wiped off her glossy lipstick. She rubbed her forehead, squeezing her eyes shut.

The cell phone in the bag vibrated. Meghan tore open the zip-locked top, swiped the screen on Steve's phone, and read the text:

Mr. Townsend, you missed our meeting. Please call to reschedule as soon as possible.

A client? Meghan typed a reply.

Steven Townsend was in an accident at work today and is in the hospital. You may wish to contact Corona Custom Sheet Metal with your questions. I'm not sure when Steve will be available.

More to the point . . .

She wasn't sure about anything right then.

Chapter Fifteen

Present Day

Meghan's eyes popped open at the sound of approaching footsteps. Her gaze travelled from the black loafers to the careworn face of the man wearing them.

He glanced from her to another woman on the opposite side of the room. "Mrs. Townsend?"

"Yes. That's me." She stood as he crossed toward her. "How is he?"

"I'm Dr. Tanner." He offered his hand, so she shook it.

"Meghan."

"Let's sit." He lowered himself into a chair, and Meghan followed suit.

"Is he okay?"

"We're taking good care of him. Mrs. Townsend, Steve had a large piece of equipment fall on him. From what I gathered, he was trying to move some sort of machinery with another employee. His back simply gave out, and his legs buckled and followed. His partner was unable to hold onto the load on his own and it toppled onto your husband. He sustained a radial fracture of his femur and crushed his knee. He will need surgery on that leg to put those bones back together." He looked at the chart in his hand, then leveled his eyes back on her. "The bigger concern is his spine. We're running tests now to check the damage."

His *spine*? The doctor's no-nonsense tone was both calming and head-spinning. Was she supposed to be able to keep up? *Focus, Meghan.*

"He's experiencing partial paralysis in his legs. But we don't know yet whether it's permanent. There's a good chance it isn't."

The oxygen level in the room seemed to plummet. Meghan pressed a hand to her stomach. Surely he wasn't saying Steve was paralyzed. She blinked at him. *God, please let this be a mistake.*

After a pause, the doctor continued. "Steve presented with back pain, which appears to have been a factor in *causing* the accident, not a result of it. We aren't sure yet if there's any further injury. Initial X-rays look clear, but we'll have more specifics in about forty-five minutes."

More waiting. Meghan ran her fingers over her eyebrow. "Okay. Thank you." How was she going to sit here that long without answers? She clamped down on her lip to keep it from quivering.

Dr. Tanner shook his head. "You know, with his back issues, he shouldn't have been lifting anything at all."

She stared at him as the question formed on her sluggish tongue. "What do you mean?"

His forehead wrinkled. "The herniated disk. The one he said has been causing him pain for months." He slid his pen into the clipboard. "Mrs. Townsend, either I or one of the other doctors will come talk to you as soon as the tests are finished. And then you can go in to see him." He stood and smiled down at her. "Try not to to worry. He's in good hands."

He walked away, leaving Meghan alone and confused. Thoughts zipped through her head. Bits of information, memories. All of Steve's time on the couch . . . his stiff embrace . . . could it all have been due to pain? Could it be that simple? Visions of the girls jumping onto his back made her wince. No wonder he'd snapped at them to get off. The final image of Steve laboring with her suitcase just days ago filled her with guilt and pity.

It didn't explain everything, but it was a start. But why the secrecy? Did he not even trust her enough to let her in on something so important? Meghan stared at the white tiles beneath her feet, going over everything she knew . . . and everything she didn't.

As she sat there lost in thought, Brooke rounded the corner and flew to her. Meghan got to her feet just in time to be pulled into her arms.

The comfort of a familiar face, a friend to share the burden, made something inside Meghan come undone. The tears came then, slow at first, then full-force. She shook in her friend's arms, while Brooke clung to Meghan.

Stroking Meghan's hair, Brooke whispered in her ear. "Jesus, take care of Steve. Heal him, please. Strengthen Meghan. They're a good family, God. Watch over them. Be with the girls—"

Meghan gasped. "Brooke, the girls! What time is it? They were at VBS."

"Don't worry; they're with your mom. I called her right away."

Meghan leaned away from her friend and exhaled. "Thank you." Though hidden under makeup, Brooke's eyes were swollen and red-rimmed, as if she'd been sobbing for hours. She wouldn't have been crying so hard over Steve, would she?

"What have you heard?"

Meghan pulled in a breath and told her what she knew. Then the two lowered themselves into the hard plastic chairs. Meghan dabbed her eyes with a tissue, wiped her nose, then leveled probing eyes on Brooke. "What is it, Brooke? And don't tell me *nothing*. I can tell when something is wrong."

Brooke gave a forced smile, then patted Meghan's hand. "It doesn't matter right now. Not while Steve is back there."

Meghan glanced down the hall in the direction the doctor had gone, her stomach churning. "Steve's going to be back there for quite a while, and it would be cruel of you to keep me worrying about you that whole time. So tell me what it is. Please."

Brooke looked at her, fear in her eyes. "Oh Meghan, you are much too good for me. I'm such a mess." She covered her face with her hands and broke down.

Meghan rubbed her back, disquieted by the burden she saw weighing on Brooke. She pulled out a tissue and handed it over. "Tell me what's the matter."

"You're going to hate me . . . " Brooke sniffed.

"No, I'm not. Now out with it."

Brooke straightened and wiped her nose with the tissue. "I don't even know how to tell you this so I'm just going to say it." Eyes pinned on the twisted tissue in her hands, she took a deep breath, then plunged in, voice low. "I've been having an affair. With Tom. Darren found out, and . . . I think he wants a divorce." Her shoulders jerked as she looked up into Meghan's eyes.

Meghan's stomach dipped, and shock robbed her of words.

What? When . . . ? How . . . ?

"My kids, Meghan." The words squeaked out. "They don't deserve this. I've torn apart their home. I'm the worst human being in the world." She covered her face again as sobs overtook her.

"Oh, sweetie . . . shh." Meghan wrapped an arm around Brooke and rubbed her shoulder. "You are *not* the worst person in the world. Believe me, I understand." Her voice cracked as her eyes welled up and spilled tears down her cheeks. She couldn't speak. Could barely breathe. Spots floated across her vision.

Oh, Lord, it could have been her.

The two sat for several minutes, wordless. Meghan touched Brooke's arm, drawing her attention. "How long?"

Brooke dropped her gaze to her lap. "Six months. Maybe more."

"I can't believe I didn't know . . . "

"Maybe if you had, you could have smacked sense into me. All I knew was how alive I felt with Tom. But now . . . " she lifted a shoulder "I feel like I'm dying." Her face twisted and Meghan took her hand. "I really do love Darren. He's so hurt. The look on his face . . . " she closed her eyes, sending droplets of moisture onto her lashes. "I'll live with that image forever."

"I'm so sorry, Brooke."

"I tried to cut things off so many times. But I was weak. I knew it was wrong, but as long as we were careful, I convinced myself nobody would get hurt. Stupid." She pressed fingers under her bottom lashes.

Meghan was afraid to ask the next question. "Did Darren find you . . . together?"

She shook her head. "No, thank God for that small mercy. He found an email I thought I'd deleted. A very . . . *personal* . . . email."

A text message buzzed Meghan's phone—her mother was praying and would keep the girls as long as needed. "Thanks" was all she could say in response.

At long last, Dr. Tanner returned. "Sorry to keep you waiting—I know you're anxious for news. Tests are finished. Steve won't be needing spinal surgery at this time. The paralysis looks to be due to swelling in the spinal column, and should resolve on its own within days or weeks. Afterward, he'll need physical therapy and he'll need to stay in touch with his doctor. I do recommend surgery for the herniated disc once this injury has healed."

"Okay." Meghan nodded, relief cranking her fears down a notch.

The doctor smiled. "We'll be keeping him here tonight, and his leg surgery will be performed tomorrow. You can go in to see him now. But I'll warn you he may be a little out of it. He's on a morphine drip. He's in room 212, right down this hall." He lifted a hand in the direction of a long hallway.

Meghan's eyes burned. "Thank you." She shook his hand, then looked at Brooke. "You don't have to wait. I don't know how long I'll be in there."

Brooke stood. "As much as I hate to, I need to go home and . . . find out what happens next." She sniffed, then pressed her cheek to Meghan's and gave her a squeeze. "Call me later and let me know how you're doing."

"Same with you. I'm praying for miracles."

Brooke's sullen expression held little hope. "I'd like one, but I don't deserve it." She adjusted her purse strap and gave a sad smile. "We'll talk soon." Then she turned and headed toward the elevators.

The heavy drumming of Meghan's heart as she walked down the hall nearly drowned out the sounds of machinery and voices. She drew in a strengthening breath as she lifted her hand to open door 212.

Steve lay in his hospital bed, tubes and wires jutting out of him and her heart constricted. She approached his bed, gaze riveted to his face. When she slipped her fingers into his hand and squeezed, his eyes opened.

She tipped her mouth. "You know, when you said work was killing you, I didn't know you meant literally." She studied his eyes—the soft brown eyes of Steven Townsend, varsity point guard, fierce protector, unclogger of toilets.

A single huff of a laugh blew past his lips. "Yeah, well, neither did I." He smacked his tongue on the roof of his mouth then blinked, lids sluggish.

A cup of water sat on a tray nearby and Meghan picked it up. "Thirsty?"

He nodded so she held it to his lips and supported the back of his head as he lifted it for a drink.

"Thanks." He winced as he settled back into his pillow.

Meghan bit her lip, recoiling from his obvious pain. "You're welcome."

A nurse appeared. "Ma'am, it's best he sleep for now. You can see him again later."

"The girls." Steve patted her hand. "Go home or they'll worry." He scarcely got the words out before dozing off again.

Meghan nodded. "Okay. I'll be back as soon as I can." She brushed away a lock of his sandy hair and kissed his forehead. His eyes remained closed, his breathing rhythmic.

The nurse ushered her out with an understanding smile, then closed the door. Meghan stood, wringing her hands. She'd go home for the night for the girls' sake. But not yet. For now, they were with her mother, and Meghan needed time to process.

She found a machine in the lobby offering hot tea. Earl Grey would work fine today. She lifted it to her lips with shaky hands as she found her way to the cafeteria. Finding a small table in a corner, she settled in.

Lord, he's in so much pain. Please give him relief. Touch and heal him.

Her mind turned to situations outside of his physical state, and a bevy of questions rose from her heart.

God, why didn't he tell me? How could he have shut her out of something like this? Misplaced, macho pride? Why had he pulled away from her after all they'd been through?

She drained her cup as her heart reached heavenward. But the hours of waiting stretched out before her and she needed a distraction. Lucky for her, she had one.

And a therapeutic one at that.

She ran out to the car and retrieved her laptop.

1916

They'd reached fifty miles per hour and the race hadn't even begun. Winifred forced herself to breathe, but could do no better than a series of quick, irregular intakes. And the scarf wrapped around her nose and mouth had nothing to do with it.

You've gone faster than this, Winnie. But she'd never had thirteen other drivers wishing for her demise, or the responsibility to keep a car running for three hundred continuous miles. One hundred laps. Two hundred and fifty minutes of terror. All for one trophy. And a twelve-thousand dollar purse.

The first lap neared its end; the starting line loomed ahead with Frank Lowrey on the sidelines, green flag dancing in the wind above his head. Waterman's Grandy Spec—playing the pace car—reached Lowrey, and the flag dropped.

The noise of a dozen engines, pressed to capacity, deafened her.

The drivers began vying for position in the pack, Russell among them. He moved in and out, around, and behind cars with a deftness and skill Winnie wouldn't have appreciated had she been in the stands. She'd seen races, but being behind the hood, feeling the heat and rumble of an adjoining car, took the experience to a spine-tingling level.

But even with Russell's deft moves and cheek-warping speed, Winifred knew the race hadn't begun in earnest. They were still at the rear of the tight pack.

The Bearcat's engine hummed with nary a shudder, carrying them in an effortless glide, and Russell had yet to unleash the beast. Winifred's chest constricted in anticipation of the moment, while her brain seized with fear.

He's never crashed. He's never crashed . . .

When he darted between two cars, she clenched her teeth and her seat, more grateful by the second for last night's ingenuity. Their speed increased, but Russell held a reasonable pace. By the end of the second lap, he had snaked along the inside of the track and placed them in fourth. Cooper drove among the lead cars, along with Wild Bob Burman. But where was Silsbury?

Winnie twisted and spotted the yellow grill of his Mercer. Trapped behind three cars, he swerved left and right, bullying them for an opening.

At lap three, he overtook the Cat on the left in the narrow gap between them and the curb, far too close for sanity and comfort. She leaned toward Russell and squealed. The wind snatched the sound, but still Russell flinched. Their speed fell away, and Silsbury left them choking in his wake.

Russell shot her a hasty glance. Even amidst Silsbury's exhaust, she caught the much-deserved warning.

Nails embedded in her leather gloves, she clung to the seat's edge and swallowed a mouthful of horror. Her little overreaction could have caused an accident. The full implications of her situation crashed down upon her. At these speeds, every tiny decision could mean the difference between winning and losing, life and death. Tears pricked.

What had he said about playing with the boys . . . ? If she was going to do it, she'd have to play by their rules, and she was pretty certain that cowering, squealing, and crying were against regulations. *Buck up, Winnie. You're in it for the long haul.*

For an eternal ten seconds, they pressed through Silsbury's cloud, blind. The instant they broke through the haze, Russell responded.

Her body slammed into the seatback as the motor's whine transformed to an ear-splitting pitch. Its vibrations carried through the chassis and into every bone, stamping its imprint on her body. Even without her hands on the wheel, the car spoke to her. Through the roar, the whisper of her name sat her up straight in the seat, and for a time, she lost track of their standing in the race. Transfixed, she listened to the engine, took in every fluctuation and hitch. Like a doting mother, she memorized the sound of its cry. Except the Bearcat was no mewling infant. She was dominion itself—raw and horrible—restrained by nothing but Russell's expert hand.

A flash along the sidelines snapped Winnie out of the trance. They swept past the starting line and Frank Lowry holding a placard that read Lap 13. Her brain jerked into gear. Had they gone that many already? Maybe she could do this, after all. An assessing glance revealed them driving alone, except for O'Donnell's Duesenberg some five hundred yards ahead. Were they that far behind the pack . . . or ahead?

A rhythmic bump and flapping sound drew Winnie's gaze to the front left tire. Misshapen, it threatened to blow. A hand signal clued Russell in to the situation. He eased to the right edge and held there for the extra three-quarters of a mile to their designated pit.

He brought the car to a jerking stop and engaged the handbrake.

Bystanders cheered. The boys atop the nearest telephone pole hooted and shouted, "Doing fine, Miss Winnie!"

She raised a weak arm, lips cracking with her smile. Mind and body, she hummed like an electric cable.

Replacement tire in hand, Sam greeted them with a scowl. "What sorta game are you playing out there? When are you going to serious about—?" The crowd, along with the ringing in her ears, drowned out the rest his words, but she was pretty sure he'd accused Russell of not driving to win.

He'd seemed serious enough to Winifred. Was he holding back?

Unbuckling, he turned to her. "Stay in the car." With a bound, he cleared the wheel and swooped around the front.

The car tilted as Sam cranked the jack. "What do you mean *get serious*?" Her throat scratched out the question. Someone handed her a canteen. She drank with greed, never taking her eye off Russell, who bent over the motormeter, a frown curving his grimy face.

"Get some water over here," he yelled, removing a handkerchief from his pocket. He threw it on the meter and began unscrewing.

With shaky fingers, she unbuckled then stepped from the car to retrieve the water he'd asked for. A knee gave way, and she crumpled to the stinging raceway. Heat penetrated the glove on the palm she used to catch herself. The knee of her trousers stuck to the melting asphalt.

"Winnie, I said to stay—watch out!"

She glanced up as Russell grabbed her by the shoulder. He yanked her to her feet and shoved her against the side of the car. Its frame dug into her back when he plastered his body over hers. An instant later, a car swept past, its wind sucking the breath from her.

The city hissed and booed.

With a whirl, Russell screamed after it. "Idiot!" He whipped back around. "Did anyone see that? He has the whole road, and he passes so close I can spit on him!"

"Don't worry, Mr. Keegan. He won't get away with it," a man shouted through the wire barrier.

By the time Winifred got a glimpse of the Mercer, its yellow tail was disappearing around the curve in the road.

"Silsbury?"

Face strawberry red, Russell deposited her in a clump on the floorboard. "Who else, sweetheart?" He stalked back to the motometer, where Al had arrived with a jug.

Scrambling upright, she boiled over like the water from their radiator. "He-he about ran me over!" Jelly legs beneath her again, she plopped back onto the seat. "Get a move on, boys. We've got a cheater to whoop." With a grunt, she tightened her safety strap until it bit into her thighs. "And Russell, if you're holding back because of me, we're gonna have words when this is over."

"Road's too hot," he hollered over the exhilarated masses. "Any faster and we'd be in the pits every three laps."

The Cat bounced as Sam released the jack and whisked it out from under the frame. "All clear!"

Rolling up his sleeves, Russell slid into the seat then reached for the gearshift.

"Safety belt," Winifred quipped.

"Yeah, yeah." His grin shone stark white against his smutty skin. With a racer's hustle, he strapped in and hit the road. Within seconds, wind and grit mashed her cheeks.

Halfway around the Circle, they zipped past Cooper, whose sidelined Stutz belched smoke and steam. Head in hand, he sat droop-shouldered on the sidewalk. But there was no time to pity him.

The laps flew by. Twenty, thirty, fifty. They hit each with more confidence.

Time and again, they passed Silsbury and his frantic crew swapping out frayed tires and sloshing water over a seething engine. Silsbury made up for the lost minutes by sprinting, which melted another set of rubber.

The tacky, roughened track abused tires like no other Winifred had come across, but as Russell foretold, a moderate pace kept them out of the pit. And the Cat had yet to require her skill. Winifred's diligence and care beforehand, combined with Russell's wise handling on the road, were the ingredients for an ideal racing team. *A perfect fit.*

She would smile at the thought, if the wind weren't already stretching her cheeks.

Another reason to smile came in the shape of the second place position they held behind O'Donnell's Duesenberg. At the Bearcat's last fueling stop, Sam had filled them in—Silsbury and Burman were their closest threats and neither could manage to eat up the two laps separating them from the Cat.

Rear end numb and brain rattled, Winifred's body screamed for relief. The clock ticked, the sun dropped, and the road began to cool. Russell took each lap faster and a shade more daring than the last. But no amount of wrecklessness could compare to Wild Bob, who passed the Stutz at speeds that warped his Peugeot, leaning it forward.

Russell shook his head as the Peugeot weaved through nearby vehicles—those many laps behind the lead cars. Before he disappeared around the curve ahead, rubber flew from his car. He'd be forced to pull over. *So much for catching up.*

Without warning, Winifred's torso flew the left, then—held in place by her safety belt—snapped back to the right. Pain seared as her head bobbled and lashed her neck. No time to baby it, she threw a glance over her right shoulder.

Silsbury! Between the Cat's right wheels, his front left tire churned mere yards from Russell's elbow. Fighting the steering wheel one-handed, he screamed and waved at Silsbury to back off.

But the Mercer pressed closer. Their left front wheel bumped along the curb for ten yards, twenty, thirty. The next bump could take them over and into the crowd. The intermittent screech drove nails of fright into Winifred's mind.

Bystanders scrambled.

The curb whizzed by in a dizzying blur. Instinct screamed to lean away from the sidewalk, the barrier, the rows of innocents. But terror stiffened her.

Both hands on the wheel, Russell eased right, toward Silsbury who mirrored Russell's move until their cars unlocked.

The curb grew smaller, and Winifred gasped for breath. The scarf sucked into her mouth. She pulled it down, wondering how Silsbury had managed to get them into such a predicament with no other cars nearby. Anger followed fast on the heels of relief. Russell was right. The man was an idiot.

Their speed decreased, and Winifred noted the uneven rhythm of their pace. The wheel that had kissed the curb spun with a minor, lopsided gate. Not tragic, but not good enough to get them to the finish line—as close as it was—with any sort of hope for a win.

Silsbury shot ahead. Was he still a lap behind? Winifred had lost track of where they were, who had passed them, how much farther they had to go. The near collision had felt like minutes, but it couldn't have been more than a couple dozen seconds.

The cords in Russell's forearms protruded as he fought to keep the car on a straight course. Less than a minute and they would reach their pit. She silently cheered him for his ability to keep the car in check while maintaining racing speed. He had to be exhausted, hurting, strained to the breaking point.

She longed to talk to him, to apologize for having considered not fulfilling her half of the bargain. They had shaken on being a team, and teams stuck together through the easy times and through those that required swallowing fear and making selfless sacrifices.

As soon as she was able, she'd wipe the soot from his face and tell him she thought the world of him. That no matter the outcome, she would always root for him. He would always be her hero.

Far ahead—beyond Silsbury, beyond O'Donnell—Al held high a sign painted with the words Last Lap.

The judges may as well engrave the trophy with the name O'Donnell.

Russell signaled for her to clear his way to move far right. She twisted at the waist to get a full view behind them—clear, for as far as the curve allowed her to see. Before she could form a thumbs-up, the distant wail of grinding metal reached her. A collision ahead.

An instant later, the Cat gave a terrible lurch to the left, tossing her against Russell's side. He slid with her weight. The instant before their wheel rolled out from beneath them, she spotted his safety belt lying limp.

A scraping noise filled air.

Before she could push off him, she was thrown against the opposite side of her seat. Russell slammed into her as the Cat tipped toward the left. His weight forced her headfirst over the edge. Slicing pain seized her gut, then released. Vivid and terrifying, the wheel-less axle came into view just feet from where she dangled. It dug a deep, crooked rut in the road. Gravel pelted her face and arms like myriad bee stings.

With a jarring thud, the careening Cat landed on all fours, jerking Winifred back toward Russell. But this time, when her chest landed in his seat, he was gone.

Chapter Sixteen

1916

Like a hammer, pain beat Russell's temple. The world tipped and spun as his body summersaulted through the air.

A voice called to him. He resisted, fleeing the pain that electrified every nerve. His shoulder blades burned against the hard, hot ground. He wasn't spinning?

Several smacks to his cheek popped open his lids. A cheer erupted. The brilliant blue sky stared down at him, along with a ring of unfamiliar faces.

"Mr. Keegan, can you hear me? Can you feel this?" A burly, whiskered man spoke into Russell's face.

He grimaced. "Who are you, and why are we holding hands?"

Laughter surrounded him. "He's going to be just fine, people," someone declared.

"You lay still, Mr. Keegan. Medics are on their way." The whiskered man used his hat to shade Russell's face. "They're taking care of Miss Fisher first, but you're—"

"Winnie!" Russell sat up, bumping the hat to the ground. A river of blood ran into his eye. "Where is she? Where's the car?"

"She's being taken care of." Hands grappled his shoulders, tried to push him down.

He swung at them, making enough contact to free himself. On his feet now, the road tilted. Half-blind, he took several stumbling steps, pushing objectors out of his way.

When his sight landed on the nearest car, he blinked to clear the blood and grasp the backwards scene. The auto lay belly up, wheel creaking around the axle, smoke pouring from its flattened hood, paint a dull, scratched gray. Was that the Cat?

Where was Winnie? Sluggish, his eyes slid left to a group of huddled people . . . doing what?

A clanging bell entered his consciousness. How long had it been ringing? He turned toward the sound. An ambulance barreled down the road toward him.

"Where is she?" Mrs. Fisher tore through the crowd, hysteria flashing in the whites of her eyes. "Winifred? Where's my baby?"

Yes, where's Winnie?

The ambulance came to a halt near the overturned car. Medical personnel leapt from the front. Two ran toward the huddle. Another swung around to the back and withdrew a stretcher.

"Mr. Keegan, you shouldn't be up . . . " He tuned out those around him, brushed their hands off him.

Fighting to clear the fog from his brain, Russell found himself ambling toward the scene.

Mrs. Fisher passed him at a dead run. Someone went after her, screaming for her to stop.

Russell followed, accepted the cloth pressed to his head.

A scream pierced his heart.

Ahead, the crowd parted and a loaded stretcher emerged carried by the two medics. They passed him at a trot.

He saw her then, arm swinging over the side, blood dripping from her still fingers. Curls were matted against the side of her pitted face. Half open, her eyes stared at nothing.

Pain slammed into his knees as they hit the pavement.

Mrs. Fisher hustled behind the stretcher then scrambled into the front of the ambulance.

"Russell? Russell Keegan?"

With a sluggish blink, he peeled his gaze from Mrs. Fisher, and directed it at the man down on one knee in front of him. "Yeah, that's me."

"You look awful. Let me get you to the hospital."

"Hospital?"

"That's where Winnie's going. You'll want to follow, I assume."

Russell gripped the man's elbow. "Is she alive? Do you know?"

The man wiped sweat from his pale face. "For now."

Relief sapped the strength from Russell's thighs. His backside landed on his heels.

The stranger hooked Russell under the arm. "Come on. We need to be there when she wakes up. And you could use a little help too. Seems like everyone else forgot about you."

"I'm fine." Now that he knew Winnie was alive.

"Sure you are." He hauled Russell to his feet and guided him through the crowd.

Someone stepped forward and volunteered to drive them to Riverside. Russell's guide accepted and within ten minutes, they were in the man's buggy bouncing along the lengthy country road toward the nearest hospital.

Winnie had just been taken down this road. Was she still alive? In pain? Her face . . . A vision of it, cut and bleeding, filled his mind, fisted his gut.

He should never have let her ride with him . . . should never have asked her to fix his car.

A groan rumbled his chest.

Orchards crawled past his window at a horse's canter. "Can't your animal go any faster?"

The driver looked over his shoulder at Russell on the back bench, pity softening his eyes. "Sorry, Mr. Keegan. Can't push her any harder in this heat. Must seem awful slow."

"You hurting much?"

Russell moved his gaze to the man sitting next to him. Hurting? Depended on his definition of the word. "I'll live." Were those tears in the man's eyes? "What's your name?"

The stranger's lids fell, and after a minute of silence, Russell figured he hadn't heard the question.

"George. George Fisher."

Russell angled his body toward George. "Winnie's brother?"

His short laugh dripped with bitterness. "The one and only."

Now that Russell thought about it, the man resembled Winnie. Same defined chin. Same copper hair, poking out from under his cap. "You come home on your own, or did my man finally twist your arm hard enough?"

"I wouldn't have come home on my own. But your telegram . . . " His voice broke. He cleared it. "Your telegram made me see what a selfish schmuck I've been. I had no idea things had gone so far south at home. And if I'd known Winnie had been—" He flicked a glance to the front bench, then left his thought hanging.

"When'd you get in?"

"Two days ago. Been staying at the Del Rey. Didn't have the courage to swing by, but I've been watching the two of you. At the practice rounds. Today. You work well together." A shadow of a smile lifted his cheeks.

"I'll drop you off at the door," the driver announced. "Then I gotta get back. Left the wife and kids eating sandwiches at First Congregational."

They met Mrs. Fisher in the lobby. Upon seeing her son, she twisted her face into a mass of angry lines. "George Fisher, where in heaven's name have you been?" She tore across the room, smacked him on the arm, then threw herself against him, bawling.

Russell stood by, awkward and uncertain, mind wandering to where Winnie might be and how he might find her.

"Sir?" A nurse touched his arm. Brows pinched with concern, she tugged him through a set of doors while calling out for assistance.

"Russell, wait!" Mrs. Fisher rushed toward him, then stopped a couple strides away. Her mouth hung open, indecision clouding her expression.

"How is she?" he asked whoever might answer. "Have you heard?"

The nurse was joined by another. "Sir, you've lost a lot of blood. We need to get you into a bed."

Mrs. Fisher took a step closer. "Not since we arrived. But before they took her back, she opened her eyes, and . . . " She licked her lips. "She asked for you." Fresh tears spilled from her chin. Her face crumpled. "You let her ride with you. What were you thinking? She's too precious to lose!"

"I know. I'm so sorry," Russell said with a voice knotted by grief and regret.

"It's too late for sorries. If I lose my sweet girl because of your display of stupidity—" Her jaw clicked shut. The tight line of her mouth quavered.

He nodded, his conscience flinching beneath the blade of understanding. Petty, trivial—that's what racing was. Every dream he'd ever had, every goal he'd ever strived for, crumbled in significance next to a person's life. *Winnie's life*. How many foolish risks had he taken?

Never again.

If she pulled through this, if she lived, he'd quit racing. As God was his witness, he would. He'd settle down. With her. Protect her with his life. Love her the way she deserved—selflessly.

He opened his mouth to speak, but every promise sounded shallow and ill-timed in his mind. *Too late for sorries*.

"That's not helpful right now, ma'am." The head nurse tried to intervene, but Mrs. Fisher pushed past her and wrapped her arms around Russell's neck.

He held her, hesitant to believe she was forgiving him.

After a moment, she pressed her lips to the blood-caked side of his face. "Thank you," she whispered. "For finding my boy."

Present Day

Meghan closed her screen, tears clogging her throat. *Racing Hearts* had proven a good diversion throughout her sleepless night, and somewhere along the way Meghan realized something . . .

She was a lot more like Russell than Winifred.

She'd had a specific track to take—for her marriage, for herself—and she wouldn't give up until she attained it. She'd been so focused on navigating her way through rough turns and potholes, squeezing through tight spaces, speeding toward a finish line she'd fashioned herself.

What she hadn't done was let God into the driver's seat. All her praying, she'd been asking Him to ride shotgun, fix up her rickety car, while *she* kept control of the wheel.

"I'm so sorry, Jesus." She closed her eyes, letting the words fall from her lips in a whisper. All along, God had wanted her to give Him control. To trust Him with her husband. With her hurts. With her heart. Instead, she'd tried to steer her own way out of difficult places and wound up veering completely off course.

Was it too late to get back on track?

A draft of cold air blew across Meghan's shoulder drawing a shiver. Already eighty degrees outside, but within the confines of the four sterile walls of the hospital, it was a meat locker. The computer on her lap provided a little warmth but she wished for a cardigan to snuggle into.

She closed her eyes, sensing God's presence. Surely, He was there. Always had been.

I will never leave you nor forsake you.

The truth of it wrapped around her like a robe.

Jesus was with her, loving her, and that was all she ever really needed. She had prayed for human responsiveness—judging her worth by the interest she garnered, yet largely oblivious to the interest of the One who mattered.

She hung her head. *Forgive me, Lord.*

Meghan blew her nose then whispered aloud. "Help me trust You."

She dug her fingers into the hair on the sides of her head, rubbing circles into her temples.

The girls were home with her mother, worried but not panicked. Meghan had put up a strong front for them the night before but truth was, she was scared for their family.

Please get us all through this. She still had hours to wait before Steve would be out of surgery and she prayed he'd be okay.

But what about *them?*

Could their marriage survive? Steve hadn't trusted her enough to tell her he'd been in pain, or that he'd been at odds with his boss. And she had been too caught up in her own hurt to notice the signs. Her heart had drifted toward another. How could he trust her now? But if they could give it one more chance . . .

Please, Jesus.

A nurse approached. "Mrs. Townsend? There's a lawyer here to see you."

A lawyer? Meghan's mind flashed to the business card in Steve's pocket. Surely she wasn't about to come face-to-face with her husband's divorce attorney, right here in the hospital!

"Okay." Fear raised gooseflesh on her arms. Had they no decency?

"I'll direct him here."

Moving the laptop to the chair beside her, Meghan prayed for strength. Hands clasped, she squeezed her eyes shut and clung to the heavenly cord between her heart and God's.

A soft voice interrupted her prayer. "Hi, Meghan."

At Curtis's cheerless greeting, her head snapped up. She blinked. "What are you doing here?" She flicked a glance beyond him.

"I have something for you." He took a step closer as Meghan rose to her feet. "Your husband missed an appointment yesterday."

She pulled her brows together and shook her head. How did he know that?

"I . . . I wanted to pull together some information for you about your legal options. For an on-the-job accident. And when I did . . . I found his file. Your husband is already a client at our firm. I had no idea."

Heat crept up her throat as the pieces fell into place. She bit her lip and nodded, humiliation making her feel small.

"I'm not part of the team working on this file, but . . . I had to come." Curtis looked around, shifting his weight from one foot to the other. "When they found out Steve was here, there was a lot of scrambling going on. I know it might sound bad, but this accident probably makes his case a slam dunk."

"His . . . case?" She shook her head, lost.

Curtis nodded, his beautiful eyes full of sorrow. "He'd retained legal services a couple months ago in regard to a business arrangement with the owner of Corona Custom Sheet Metal Corporation."

He'd put down a retainer? The withdrawal!

"Seems Mr. Jones was trying to renege the agreement for Mr. Townsend—I mean, Steve—to take ownership at the end of the year. He instead wanted to split the company, sending national accounts to his nephew while Steve maintained the smaller local clients. He claimed Steve's inability with the physical aspects of the job put them at risk of losing market share."

She lifted a hand to her mouth. Steve wasn't pursuing divorce?

But . . .wait . . . Mr. Jones wasn't turning over the business?

Deep pain clenched her stomach and stole her air like she'd been sucker-punched. Meghan's tear-filled eyes darted back and forth as she fought for her bearings. She lifted her questioning gaze to Curtis. Why hadn't she been told?

He shook his head, as though able to read her heart . . . like always. "His express instructions were to not call his house or speak with his wife about any of this unless it was absolutely necessary.

He, uh . . ." Curtis cleared his throat and looked down at his papers, voice dropping to a near-whisper. "He didn't want her to worry."

Meghan's breath whooshed out of her. Her mouth hung open as she shook her head, overwhelmed with more reality than she knew what to do with.

Curtis handed her a manila folder, mumbling something about circumstances falling under 'necessary.'

As she took the offered file, Meghan tried to meet his eyes, but couldn't. The desire to fall into his embrace and take comfort there filled her with immeasurable shame. Curtis hesitated, jaw set as his Adam's apple bobbed. A muscle in his forearm twitched, as though he might reach for her.

But he didn't.

After one last, heart-piercing gaze, he turned and walked away.

When he had disappeared, Meghan scooped up her Bible and laptop, along with her husband's legal file, and headed to the cafeteria. She still had hours to wait.

And she would need every second to figure out what to say to Steve.

1916

A long, meandering crack marred the plaster in the ceiling above Winnie's bed. It blurred. She squinted until it came back into focus.

She wasn't dead.

Russell . . . She shifted right, expecting to see him there.

Instead, her sight landed on a stretch of narrow beds. Above them, the evening sun painted a row of windows blood red.

Someone coughed. Another groaned. A woman called for water.

Hospital. The accident. Russell . . .

Her head flared with pain, as did the rest of her. She gouged the mattress with her fingers.

The sharp scent of antiseptic mingled with that of soot, stale exhaust, and . . . *castor oil*. She smelled like Russell. Her heart lifted then crashed. Would his scent be the last of him she had to cling to? Fear twisted inside her.

Heels clicked a presto rhythm on a hard floor. She tilted her head toward the sound.

"Look who's awake!" A cheery-eyed, capped nurse approached and bent over her.

"Do you know—" The words snagged on Winifred's dry throat.

"Be right back." The nurse stepped away then returned with a glass.

After a few sips, she tried again. "Russell Keegan, he was driving. Is he—?"

"Oh, your Mr. Keegan is as dashing as ever."

Winifred released the mattress.

"How are you feeling, dear? More than a bit sore, I'll wager." The nurse lay a cool hand against her neck.

"Like I got run over by a car." She couldn't contain the grimace.

"Almost! But they say a leather strap kept you right where you belonged. Not a broken bone in your body. Except for that finger. Nasty bump on the head though." She lifted a bandage on Winnie's cheek then gave a curt nod. "You're a lucky lady, you know. Others didn't fare as well." She patted Winifred's hand. "But you're going to be just fine. A few marks to remind you how brave you are, but other than that, right as rain in no time." A smile lit her face.

Winifred tried to emulate it, but gave up and closed her eyes against the shards of glass probing her brain. *Russell's safe, Russell's safe . . .*

The thought carried her back into darkness.

When she returned to consciousness, the pain had lessoned. Someone held her hand and stroked her tender knuckles, coaxing her lids open.

Her brother's crooked smile beamed back at her.

"George? Where in heaven's name have you been?"

He chuckled, then bounced forward and kissed her cheek. "Just what Mother said." The water glass came back into view. He helped her drink then set it on a nearby stand.

The liquid cooled her tongue and accentuated the taste of blood. She licked her lips and encountered several cuts.

He cocked his head. "You don't look so good."

"I don't feel so good."

"I thought you were a goner."

"I can say the same about you. Where've you been hiding?" The relief of seeing him alive and well couldn't mask the annoyance that he'd been gone. Abandoned them. Caused her so much worry and pain.

A shrug lifted George's thin shoulder. "Nowhere in particular. Anywhere that's not here. Any place I might find a job to pay off . . . you know."

Oh, yes. She knew. "And did you? Find a job?"

"Mechanics are always in need these days."

Male mechanics. She killed the snort before it escaped. And no need to ask what became of any money he'd earned.

The crack in the ceiling distorted.

"Don't cry, Sis." The bed dipped as he pressed closer. "I'm home now. I promise I'll do better. Be a new man. No more gambling. I'm through with all that. Gonna take care of you now. Mother says we still have the shop."

Barely. "It's good to see you, George. I'm glad you're home." She forced a smile and a glance his direction.

Cheeks drenched, he stared at her, eyes pleading forgiveness. His throat worked a swallow. "Mother went to grab a bite. I'll go see if she's back." He stood, slow and awkward, but made no move to leave.

"Prodigal's returned at last, eh?"

The taunt came from two beds over. Winifred didn't recognize the woman's voice, but who in Riverside County *didn't* know of them and their story?

Several joined in the woman's chuckle.

George's neck flushed, but he didn't cower. Instead, he raised his chin and his voice. "I'm sorry, Winnie. For everything."

Seeing was believing, but the apology was a step in the right direction. And something he'd never said before. Heat seared her lip as she smiled and split it. She raised a shaky hand toward him. "I love you, Georgie."

He took it and kissed her fingertips. "You're a peach. Know that?"

Russell's face came to life in her mind. Her smile grew. "So I've been told."

"Let me guess . . . " His eyes narrowed and his cheek lifted in a conspiratorial smile. "A certain world-renowned racer has been whispering sweet nothings in your ear?"

The desire to see Russell, touch him, know he was well, took root and burrowed deep. "Is he here? In the hospital?"

"Maybe." The tease should have been endearing.

Impatience took command. "Find out for me."

"Sure things, Sis."

He blew her a kiss and left, but it was her mother who entered moments later. Hair mussed and eyes puffy, she flew across the ward, sending up praise to Heaven as she went.

"I'm sorry, Momma."

Her mother took George's empty spot on the edge of the bed.

"I shouldn't have—"

"Hush. We won't speak of it. None of it matters. Not anymore. You're alive. George is home." A decisive nod of her head stamped a seal on the issue. "You just get your strength back, then we'll take you home and put our life back together. I've been thinking . . . " She brushed hair off Winifred's forehead. "We'll start a quilt together. How does that sound? We've always wanted to, and now with George running the shop, you'll be home and we'll have the time to . . . "

Her words faded into the background of Winifred's thoughts. *Quilts . . . George home . . . no more working in the shop . . . no more Russell . . .*

"What's wrong, sweetheart?" Her forehead wrinkled. "Is it your head? The nurse said you have a concussion. Shall I call her?"

Confusing fear twisted Winifred's stomach. "Where's Russell?"

"He's in another room."

Need pressed into Winifred's chest, suffocating her. "I want to see him. Before . . . before . . . " Before what? Thoughts and emotions tangled inside her pain-filled head. Try as she might, she couldn't identify them.

Her mother nodded. "You will. Maybe later."

Memories flashed—the dangling safety belt, his free-flying weight crushing her, the empty seat.

The empty shop.

Before he left Corona. Before he left *her*.

A rift cracked open in her soul and yawned wider with each frenetic breath. "Now. I need to see him now." Would it be proper to beg him not to leave?

She half-rose, tamping down sudden nausea.

Her mother put a hand to her shoulder. "What you need is to—"

The door at the end of the ward banged open. Russell's square shoulders filled its width. A bandage ran the circumference of his head. He still wore his racing clothes, stained with blood and road filth.

The room fell into a hush.

He scanned the beds. When his line of sight connected with hers, the crystal blue of his eyes shone against the grime darkening his skin. Brighter still was the longing she detected. Was she imagining it?

Even across the distance, she sensed the whoosh of air leave his lungs.

No, she wasn't imagining it.

Peace enveloped her, filled the cavity in her middle, eased her back to the mattress.

"Sir, you must go lie back down. We can't have you passing out in the women's ward."

Russell marched past the attending nurse. George followed, grinning like a kid.

Momma sighed. "I believe I've been passed over for a newer model." She brushed her lips across Winifred's brow then muttered, "He's growing on me, too." Before ceding her place to Russell, she riveted him with a commanding glare. "Call me if she needs anything."

"Yes, ma'am."

From the end of the bed, George winked at her, took their mother's elbow, and escorted her out.

Russell knelt beside her. He rested his arm on the sheet and picked up her hand as though it might disintegrate. "How are you?"

"According to George, I'm grisly."

He snorted, crisp and indignant. "You're beautiful."

"You're befuddled."

"I didn't get *that* banged up."

"Thank God."

Eyes shimmering, he pressed her palm against his rough cheek. Her fingers brushed the bandage on his head. Another strip of gauze encased his forearm. Fresh blood seeped through to its outer layer.

"What happened? You were there, next to me. Then you weren't. I thought—" A gnarl formed in her throat as she recalled the interminable moments it took for the car to stop tumbling. And the horrifying thought that Russell had been crushed beneath it. "Your belt. Why—"

"I forgot. At the last stop, I forgot to put it back on. Somehow, I was thrown clear of the wreck and ended up with a few bumps and scrapes. By then, we'd slowed enough to avoid skinning more of me than I did."

The irony was not lost on her—he'd come out unscathed despite not wearing the belt, while she—

"But you . . . without that belt, you'd be dead, for sure."

The truth unsettled her stomach. "Yes, you're right."

He closed his eyes, and she heard the apology before it rose to his lips. "Winnie, I—"

She slipped her fingers over his mouth. "No. It was my choice, remember?"

He jerked his head to the side, freeing himself from her grasp. "Let me say this. I've been too focused . . . blinded—"

"Stop. Everything is all right. No one died."

"Actually . . . " He studied her hand resting on the sheet, ran his finger over her greasy nail beds. Fatigue weighted his voice. "Wild Bob, his mechanic, a bystander. Haven't learned their names."

Each one was a mind-numbing slap. "Dead? Burman? The others, too?"

With a nod, he lifted his gaze. "Silsbury."

Silsbury. Dead.

It could have been us. It could have been me. One look into Russell's eyes told her his thoughts ran a similar course.

Silence descended between them.

Eyes closed, she tried to remember something, anything about the moments before they started swerving, but all that came back was the scream of twisting metal. "What happened?"

"I'm not sure." He shook his head and rubbed bloodshot eyes. "Burman never pulled over to change out a bad tire. It couldn't take the heat, you know. Blew out. He lost control, took the curb, mowed down a telephone pole, not sure what else. Or who. Others were injured."

Winifred absorbed the details, bringing to mind Burman's flapping rubber. "He never pulled over . . . " She mumbled. "And Silsbury?"

"Don't know. Got caught up in it somehow. Flipped."

"Like the Cat."

Russell's nod came sluggish, weary. "Like the Cat."

"We lost a wheel. And you . . . you were wonderful." Her hero. "How you kept the car straight for so long, enough to slow us down, avoid hitting other cars . . . " She shook her head in wonder. "Out there, you're a sight to behold. The best I've seen. You should have won."

"O'Donnell earned it. He was the better man with the better time." Through his brave words, Winifred searched for disappointment, for the utter failure she expected to find woven through his tone. Either her brain was too foggy to catch it, or there was none.

"Next time, right, roadster?" she tested. "How bad off is the Cat? Think we can put her back together in time for San Fran?"

He raked fingers through his messy hair. "Nah. She's done for. And so am I. My racing days are over. Never thought I'd say this, but"—he perused her, head to toe—"the alternative has more appeal. By far."

The stammer of her heartbeat made her breath catch. "The . . . alternative?"

"That's right." With a finger, he traced her eyebrow and cheekbone. "Something happened to me out there, Winnie. When I thought you'd . . . that I'd lost you . . . " He paused, hung his head.

"But I'm still here."

"Yes, thank merciful Heaven, you are." He lifted his chin and sniffed. "But if I *had* lost you, it would've been too late for me to see."

"See . . . what?"

"Everything." A breathy chuckle spewed warmth over her hand. "I've been a single-minded fool. Blinded by my own wants. Driven. Not considering the consequences or the toll pursuing my dreams would have on those around me."

Chest expanding with a gulp of air, he went on. "But I have new dreams now. Better dreams. Dreams that look beyond myself. And I aim to pursue them. Starting today."

New dreams? Would they take him from her? An involuntary swallow seized her throat. "What are you going to do?"

"Depends." His shoulder jerked with a shrug before he rose. "You're tired. I've stayed too long. Get some rest, Fred."

Panic swelled within her, so that his peck on her cheek almost went unnoticed. "You're leaving?"

Still hovering above her, he inhaled deep, then held his breath as though savoring her scent. A smile curved his mouth as he moved it to hers and grazed it with a feather-light touch. "Relax, beautiful. I'm not going anywhere."

Present Day

Meghan wiped the back of her hand across her cheek then continued typing, living out the scene on her computer screen. The buzz of lights, the tapping of keys, and a dozen monitors droned in the background. Through the cool, still air, hushed voices mingled with the scent of antiseptics. The stark white walls, the faces strained with worry . . .her surroundings fueled the sense she was in that hospital room in 1916—A bystander listening in as Russell bared his soul to Winnie.

Voicing Meghan's own heart.

Steve was still her hero. She saw that now. But was it too late?

Dr. Tanner approached and cleared his throat. Meghan wiped her nose and blinked before looking up at him.

"Mrs. Townsend, your husband is awake and alert. You can go in and see him now." He gave her a warm smile.

"Thank you." She drew a steadying breath then chewed her lip as she prepared to face him. How would this conversation go? For so long now, she'd been uncertain what Steve felt for her, or even what she felt for him. Whether he still had her heart. Truth was, he did. But so much between them had been damaged.

And she'd had a part in the communication breakdown.

Lord forgive her, she should have done things different. "Give me a clean heart, God. Before I go in there, wash me. All things are possible with You. Please . . .restore our marriage."

Still firing up prayers, she rose and gathered her things. Trembling legs carried her to the door and ushered her into Steve's room.

His eyes were closed, and his chest rose and fell in time with the beeping monitor. Wires and tubes still extended from his body. He lay there, so vulnerable. Broken. He'd run himself into the ground, literally. And in that, she recognized his strength. He'd carried so much for so long.

Stupid, wonderful man.

Meghan's heart was near bursting as she dumped her belongings in a corner chair, then lowered herself onto the edge of his bed. His lids twitched then lifted. He looked at her and she caught the glimmer of regret in his caramel eyes before he dropped his gaze.

Meghan reached for his hand and rubbed her thumb alongside the IV taped to his weathered, work-hardened skin. She studied the fine lines around his eyes, the little-boy expression behind his several days' growth of beard. "Why didn't you tell me?"

Steve's very soul seemed to reach out for hers. "I should have. I'm sorry. It's just that . . . after rolling the dice with that stupid software job and almost wiping us out . . . I swore it would never happen again. That I'd always provide for our family. And when the wheels started coming off this deal with Jones . . . " his jaw slid to the side, "I couldn't bring myself to tell you. I'd sunk almost everything into buying him out, took a pay cut in January . . . I don't want you to be afraid for the future . . . " He paused, swallowed. "But we're about to lose everything. Again."

She laced her fingers through his. "But I would've understood."

He shook his head. "I don't want your pity. Time's slipping away, Meg. We're not kids anymore. Nothing I set out to do for you has worked out. I can't face myself in the mirror anymore, how was I supposed to face you? I had to deal with Jones on my own, as a man. No matter what."

"Oh, Steve." She searched the depths of his eyes, seeing the power of determination behind the sorrow of failure. The misguided, silly man. He'd fought valiantly. For her. The penny-pinching, the absentee church work days, even the overgrown yard. It made sense now.

Her throat swelled, pinching her voice. "How did you bear the pain?"

"Lots of Excedrin." He released a short laugh. "I'm on prescription painkillers and have slipped out for physical therapy and chiropractic adjustments a couple times a week. But mostly I stayed off my feet as much as possible."

"Looks like you'll be off them for quite a while now." Meghan chewed her lip, vowing to never say a word about Steve lying on the couch again. "Don't worry about a thing. I'll make sure the girls are careful with you."

Despair reflected in his eyes. "Guess I'm not the same strong daddy able to toss them up onto my back for rides around the living room anymore."

"Wrong—" she resisted the tingle behind her eyes—"you're a very strong daddy. The strongest one I know." Meghan hiccupped as her tears came, realizing how lucky her girls were to have Steve. But for his stubborn pride, he was everything she could ever want in a man.

"I love you so much." She leaned forward, and he reached up with his free hand and ran his fingers through her hair, sweeping a tender gaze across her face.

"Me, too."

She lowered her mouth to his—the most tender, honest kiss they'd shared in years.

But their future was still muddy. There were things he didn't know. Her heart pounded as she pulled back a few inches, opened her eyes, and whispered, "No more secrets."

He nodded as if scolded, like she only meant him. Mouth dry, she studied their entwined fingers and spoke just above a whisper. "Steve, I *have* been afraid. Terrified I was losing you. That I wasn't enough for you anymore. I thought maybe . . . maybe there was someone else."

"What? No, of course not, Meg. Never." He set pleading eyes on hers. "You're all I've ever wanted. *I'm* the one who hasn't been enough." His brow furrowed and he pressed her fingers to his lips. "I've hated myself for failing at everything. Hated the thought of you realizing you'd married a loser. I don't want to be weak in your eyes." He shook his head. "Our life hasn't been what I promised when we were kids. I'm sorry, Meg." His gaze fell from hers. "You deserve better."

Her chest tightened. "We both do. Starting with total honesty." But where to start? "Steve . . . I'm sorry, too." She looked at the ceiling and exhaled a shaky breath, then faced him again. "I'm sorry I didn't look closer and see that you were in pain. I was too focused on my own. And I'm sorry I didn't tell you *exactly* what I was feeling, fearing. What I needed from you. Because . . . "

Terror pounded against her ribs, shredding her spirit.

Help me, God.

"Because I've been *so* lonely. Hungry for connection. And I didn't realize how much I needed that attention until . . . " Her tongue was so dry it wanted to stick to the roof of her mouth, but she had to say it. Had to disinfect the wound. "Until someone else started giving it to me." She closed her eyes to finish the rest. "And I enjoyed it. Far more than I should have."

She forced her eyes open and was met with Steve's stunned expression. He blinked, then flicked his gaze around the room. The beeping monitor increased its tempo as his chest rose and fell, and Meghan closed her eyes and prayed to weather the coming storm.

"Are you saying you . . . Meg, did you . . . ?"

"No." She licked her parched lips and stared down at her wedding band. "No, I didn't. I promise. But . . . I could have. And that scares me half to death." Tears dripped from her nose as she hung her head. "I'm so sorry, Steve. Please forgive me." She sniffed and fought the convulsion of her shoulders. "All I want is for us to face life together from now on. To trust each other again. Do you think we can we do that?" *Please?*

With a grimace, Steve straightened in the bed then cupped her face in his hand. "Meg, this is us. Of course we can." She leaned into his palm as he brushed his thumb under her lashes. Then he pulled her face toward him and placed a firm, declarative kiss on her lips. He rested his forehead against hers, not hiding his own tears.

He cleared his throat. "I can't say I don't have a truckload of questions, I can't say I'm not upset, but . . . one thing I can say is, I don't ever want you to feel lonely, Meg. That's on me too. I know I'm an idiot sometimes, but I don't ever want you to doubt that I love you."

"Yes, you *can* be an idiot sometimes. Makes two of us."

His mouth took on a gentle curve as he brushed aside a lock of hair from her forehead. "I'll do whatever it takes to get us back to where we used to be."

"Me, too." Meghan leaned her head on his shoulder and clung to him, allowing herself to both grieve and rejoice in the catastrophe they'd come through.

Thank you for stopping me, God. For giving us this chance.

They had a long way to go, but Meghan had more hope today than she'd had for a really long time. Since long before *Racing Hearts* had entered her imagination.

She sat back up and wiped her face. "Steve. I know I've spent too much time on this novel. But it's *not* more important than our marriage. I'm going to set it aside while we work through all this."

Steve shook his head. "No. I've been distracted and self-absorbed, stressed out . . . but I never intended you to give up writing. You've got to finish. You're too close to the end to stop now." He gave a half-smile. "This is your dream, right? Getting published, becoming a career novelist. It could change our life."

Meghan swallowed the fresh tears threatening to spill. Her heart was overflowing with raw emotion. Yes, she did want to be a novelist. But she didn't want everything in her life to change. She *was* happy with where she was at, and with the man she had.

She released her bottom lip from between her teeth and shrugged. "I just have to figure out the ending." She laughed.

"Slacker." Steve chuckled too, eyes sparkling. "Looks like I'm gonna have some free time on my hands. Maybe you could bounce some ideas off of me." His smile softened. "In fact, I hope you will. It'll be like old times."

"Yeah? That would be great." She kissed him again, etching this moment into her memory.

Chapter Seventeen

1916

Three hours in a hospital was about all Russell could handle. Three days should be excruciating, but when he arrived in the women's ward, Winnie appeared anything but ready to leave.

She sat on the edge of the bed, a loose-fitting, light blue dress disguising her figure. The map of scratches and bruises, pale skin, and ringed eyes belied the beauty he knew was beneath the layers of abuse and fatigue. Her calm, prim posture didn't deceive him, either. More than a headache fogged her eyes.

Whatever emotion plagued her, it tugged at his spirit, gnawed like a rat at his elation to accompany her home.

When he approached, she dipped her head and began picking at her fingernails. "Time to go?" Her voice was too tiny for his go-getter Winnie.

"George is bringing the motorcar around. It'll be another few minutes."

She flicked him a glance accompanied by a stiff smile.

He dropped into a squat, chasing her gaze as it fell back to her lap. Tipping his head, he peeked under the mop of loose curls veiling her face. "What's the story? You don't look as happy as I'd be if I was going home."

"I am. Just won't know what to do with myself when I get there . . ." A massive sigh blew a strand of hair from her mouth. "But I'm ready. I'll have to be."

"I see. Trying to figure out where you'll fit into the picture now that George is home?"

Her head snapped up, revealing a premonition of tears. "Yes, that's it exactly."

"I'm in the same boat," he said in answer to the how-did-you-know cock of her head. "Been racing all my life, but now . . ." Forearms propped on his knees, he spread his hands, palms up.

"Where will you go?" Her eyes widened with sincere curiosity.

Go? He'd told her he wasn't going anywhere. Hadn't she figured out that whatever life choice he decided on, whether grocer or gas jockey, it would include her?

How he'd love to make her understand, to join her on the bed, cocoon her, nibble away the worry creasing her mouth . . . if a dozen women weren't watching. He settled for a flirtatious wink. "Still working on it."

Color infused her cheeks, much to his delight. When the moment was right, he'd kiss her until she never again had to wonder about his future—their future. Assuming she'd have him.

He tapped her knee. "Heard something about a quilting project with your mom. That'll keep you busy. And, oh yeah, you're still in charge of family finances."

Brows arching, she sat a little straighter. "I am?"

"Yep. Your mother said as much to George right in front of me. Something about him needing to regain her trust. And yours."

"She's right on that count," she mumbled.

Russell withheld a nod. "So, see? Your hands won't be completely tied." She wouldn't be cloistered in the house, away from the shop. For a woman like her, such a thing would be tantamount to stalling a thoroughbred. "Come on. Let's get you out of here."

He took her small satchel and escorted her into the sweltering afternoon air.

George helped her climb into the back of the Lizzie, while Russell took the passenger seat. Outside of town and a good distance into the desolate expanse of road connecting Riverside to Corona, they rounded a curve and came upon a white car blocking the skinny, dirt road.

A white Chevrolet. Series 409.

"What the—?" George hit the brakes, stopping the Lizzie ten yards from the obstruction. Dust plumed about them.

Winnie sat forward and poked her head between them, eyes glued to the vehicle blocking their path. "That's the same car that . . ."

"What day is it?" Russell asked from between clenched teeth.

"Wednesday," Winnie offered, dread creeping into her voice. "Why? Russell, what's going on?" Fear drenched her words. She shrank in her seat and clutched the wrist of her broken finger to her chest.

His gut swirled into a knot. With the accident, the deaths, the threat to Winnie's life, he'd forgotten about his promise to Hastings. "I'm late paying up, but—"

"Late? You said it was taken care of."

"It was—I mean, it was going to be. It had been arranged, but then the accident happened. Look, I don't want you worrying. I'll fix this. It's not going to be a problem. You sit tight and let George and me take care of it." Heaven forbid she get worked up and do herself damage.

Another car drove in behind them. Russell peered through the back window at three Hispanics with faces far too serious for a simple afternoon drive.

He exchanged glances with George, whose pallor rivaled the Chevrolet. "You got any money on you?" Russell asked.

"Four bucks, seventy-five. You?"

"Less than that." But the bank should have the thousand he'd wired for. He flipped his wrist and checked his watch. "An hour 'til the bank's closed. Plenty of time."

A door opened on the Series 409, and Hastings emerged. He straightened his suit jacket and withdrew a cigarette case.

Winnie craned her neck forward. "Mr. Hastings? What's he—?"

"Not now, Winnie," George snapped.

Russell shot George a narrow-eyed reprimand. "He's the man your brother's indebted to."

Three others—all men of substantial size—climbed out and took up stations around Hastings.

Like a deflated tire, George slumped in his seat.

Winnie's gasps and sputters filled the back seat. "He's the one who broke my finger. Coward." She grabbed for her door handle.

"Stay put, Winnie." George killed the engine. "This isn't your battle anymore." He loosened his collar, and stepped from the car. Russell put his hand on the latch to follow, but Winnie grabbed his shoulder. "No. It isn't your fight, either."

"Listen to your brother and stay in the car."

He joined George near the Lizzie's grill.

"Well, lookie here," Hastings drawled as they approached. "Mr. Fisher himself, back from oblivion. Done letting your little sister take the licks for you?"

George bristled, lifted his fists, and strode toward Hastings. Russell reached to stop him, but a cry from behind spun them both around.

A sombrero-wearing ruffian had Winnie under the arms, dragging her backward from the Lizzie. Her feet cleared the running board and clunked to the dirt.

"Get your hands off her!" Russell was already en route. When he was halfway there, the man released her, but crossed thick, brown arms over his chest and, with a jut of his chin, dared Russell to interfere further.

"Mr. Keegan, you're needed," Hastings called. "Let Fernando do his job while we do ours."

He'd go when he was good and ready. "You all right, Winnie?"

"I'm fine," she shot back, gaze slicing to her handler as she straightened her dress.

He allowed himself a moment to study her—cheeks flaming, hands balled and trembling—then figured he wouldn't be satisfied she was truly fine, until he had her tucked into her house, safe and sound. Best get this over with.

Tramping back toward the Chevrolet, he passed George and prayed Hastings would see reason. He stopped within feet of the man's odorous cigarette and leveled an uncompromising glare at him. "I haven't been able to collect the money. But it's there. I'll have it in an hour. We'll meet in the parking lot of First Congregational at five fifteen."

Hastings snickered, then looked at the nearest amigo and laughed.

Russell's jaw seized. "You'll understand with the accident and Miss Fisher's brush with death, I've had more pressing issues to deal with."

The laughter ceased.

Cigarette between his forefingers, Hastings pointed at Russell, drawing so close, Russell could smell the smoke on his breath.

"I'll tell you what I understand." Hastings spit each frothing word into Russell's face. "I understand that Fisher here has owed me four hundred big ones for over a year, that you promised to settle up, and that you've failed me, too. I realize you're new in town, so let me help you understand something. One way or another, I always get what's owed me."

He flicked a finger, and two lackeys, blood lust written in their eyes, verged upon Russell, one on either side of him.

Hair standing on end and skin tingling, he swiveled toward the closest—a portly chap—and swung. The man lurched backward, but Russell's fist nicked him on the chin.

While the man teetered, Russell redirected, but the second came at him before he could complete his turn. Within seconds, his arms were locked behind him, his front exposed to Portly who had made fiery recovery.

"Quieto, imbecil!" Spanish poured into Russell's ear.

He twisted in the goon's grip. Before he could ready himself, a fist collided with his ribs. Once, twice, doubling him.

Breath whooshed from his lungs and refused to come again.

The ground charged him, and dirt coated his mouth.

Amidst the screaming pain, Winnie's cry zinged him into motion. He spat and pushed up to find George flashing his fists at another thug and Winnie in a head-long rush toward Hastings.

"Stop it! Stop it right now, you hateful man!" Judging by the flames shooting from her gaze, she intended to inflict damage.

George intercepted her, locking her in his arms. "Let Russell go. This is my debt," George said over her bobbing head. "If anyone's going to take a beating for it, it'll be me."

Holding his side, Russell reached his feet only to be seized again from behind. Spanish flew in every direction, frustrating Russell to no end. Groaning, he tested his strength against the man's and discovered he was no match. He'd have to either negotiate his way out or take the trouncing and hope he didn't end up in the hospital again.

Portly advanced. He rubbed his knuckles, and zeroed in on Russell's throbbing abdomen.

Bracing for the inevitable, he dragged his gaze up and down the lane. Did no one take this road, or had Hastings blocked it farther down to ensure he had no audience to his crime?

"Where's your heart?" Winnie shrill voice sailed over him. "Or are you enjoying this?"

Hastings lifted a hand and Portly backed down. A sickening fatherly expression bloomed on his face. "You're being unrealistic, Miss Fisher. Of all people, you should know the power of a man's—or woman's—reputation. Without it, he finds himself on a one-way road to the poorhouse. Sounding familiar?"

He strolled toward her, and Russell tensed.

"My reputation," Hastings continued, "dictates I follow through on my promises. Which works out well since such a policy ensures I always get what's due me." A lecherous grin grew beneath his heavy mustache.

A shudder rocked Winnie's body.

Russell strained to free himself. His captor had to weary soon.

"You'll be receiving notice from the bank within the week, informing you that your shop's assets are to be seized. And I believe I overheard Mr. Houser saying he couldn't afford to let you order baked goods on tab any longer. You just may find yourselves out of luck with a number of your creditors. In fact, I'd bet on it."

George's hold loosened, and Winnie stepped away, her jaw slack.

Russell blinked. Could he . . . do that?

The flush on Winnie's cheeks deepened. "You're a bully. Nothing but a bully with a pocketbook!"

"Am I?" Hastings' voice rumbled with threat.

"Yeah, you are." She stalked him, slow and purposeful. "And a coward, too."

"Quiet, Winnie!" Did she want another broken finger?

George followed, spoke low in her ear. She batted at him as though he were a bothersome cloud of exhaust. In Hastings' face now, she laid on the spite. "A coward who lets others do his dirty work while he sits fat and happy in his big, fancy car."

Tugging at her arm, George gave a nervous chuckle. "Never mind her, Mr. Hastings. She got walloped good. Isn't in her right mind. Let's you and me talk about this. Like gentlemen."

"You have no voice here, Fisher. Keegan," Hastings hollered. "Get control of this woman before I do something I'll regret."

Released, Russell stumbled forward then gained his footing and made tracks for Winnie.

She spit out a dry laugh. "Got a pair of pliers in that pretty car of yours? Go get them. I dare you!"

Russell cringed. Crazy woman didn't know when to muzzle it. "That's enough!" He wrapped an arm around her chest and pulled her away from Hastings, whose whiskers shook with rage.

She dug in her heels and fought to keep her place. "Those pliers are the most complicated machinery in the car. It's pretty on the outside, but under the hood, it's just as lazy and worthless as you are. Even the Lizzie could beat that jalopy." Her shrill laughter pierced the air.

Had she taken ill? While backing her up, he pressed his palm to her forehead. No fever.

George stood by, green in the face.

"You could beat him in the Lizzie, couldn't you, Russell? You're the best there is. I bet every cent I own, you could beat the socks off old Hastings." She tipped her head back to look him in the eye and passed him the faintest of winks.

His feet stilled. Half a second later, he latched onto her intent. "Of course I could, but now's not the time—"

Hastings exploded in laughter. A pack of brainless hyenas, his lackeys joined in.

"What's the matter, spineless? Afraid of a little race?"

Russell raised his voice. "You've said quite enough for—"

"A race, you say?" Hastings rubbed thumb and forefinger down his mustache. "A race between myself and Russell Keegan . . . "

Beneath the curve of his arm, Winnie's chest halted.

Eyes narrowing, Hastings closed the distance Russell had achieved. "You're on, Miss Fisher. A bet it is. What'll you wager?"

Winnie, you're magnificent.

She wiggled free and jutted her chin. "Whatever you want to throw at us." Couldn't Hastings see it was all bluster?

"Is that a fact?" Hastings sniggered and turned to Russell. "I say you and that piece of junk you call a motorcar can't make the circumference of my avocado orchard in better time than my

Chevrolet." He pointed out the scanty dirt road that wound through the trees and looped back to the main road. "If you win, consider all Fisher debts forgiven."

A worthy reason to race, and the exact terms Russell had hoped for. "And if I don't?"

A sly grin cocked Hastings' cheek. "All debts are doubled. Payable within the week."

It was a huge chunk of change. He eyed the old Lizzie and pushed air through tense lips. It would be tough. The Series 409 had a more powerful motor, but she was longer and heavier. Russell had countless hours of racing experience, but never on windy, pitted roads. It wouldn't be as sure a bet as Winnie had spouted. And her precious Model T would most certainly take a beating for it.

Their gazes connected. He lifted a brow, and she responded with a slight nod.

"It's a deal." He thrust his hand toward Hastings who shook it with gusto.

On his way to the car, Russell passed Winnie, whose crowing had faded to a tremulous smile. He returned it with a cocksure strut and a chuck on the chin. "I've got this, sweetheart. But there's a chance I might warp the axle." He pitched the words over his shoulder.

"Give it your worst."

Delighted with the return of her old, plucky spirit, he gave her a twelve-cylinder grin.

At the starting line that George had toed into the dirt, Russell revved the engine, and the Model T sputtered a protest. "Come on, baby." He adjusted the throttle. "You can do this. For Danny."

When she'd reached a more compliant hum, he took off, nursing the gas and easing her into speed. She thanked him for it by responding with unquestioning obedience. "That's right. Easy does it."

The rutted path whizzed beneath the car and imprinted itself on his bruised ribs. Amidst the distracting pain, he calculated the upcoming bend then hit it at close to thirty miles per hour. Rocks and dust spewed as the rear tires skidded in an arch.

Still in complete control, he stared down a long, straight stretch and floored the gas. The sun flickered faster and faster between rows of trees. Top speed of forty-five came in a heartbeat. Too soon, too slow.

On the left, a pothole leapt onto the path. He swerved and missed it by inches.

The next curve was upon him, this one sharper. He tapped the brake. A single tree stood at the end of the stretch, daring him to make the turn without smooching its trunk. He glared at it. Seven, six, five— The tree grew. Its leaves shook in a mocking wave. Hold, four, three, two—

Simultaneously, he rammed the clutch and brake. A wrench of the steering wheel sent the tires into another skid. Every muscle in his body tensed for a collision. When the rear stopped sliding and found traction, he downshifted and accelerated, propelled by a ray of hope.

The remaining grove passed in a blur of bark and leaves, and in seconds, the Lizzie devoured the finish line.

Steam burped from under the hood. On this bumpy road, there was no telling how the axels had faired. He parked and jumped out.

"One minute, thirty-seven seconds," Winnie called.

A pathetic number.

With her hanky, she brushed dust from his cheeks and nose then leaned in for a conspiratorial whisper. "Ready to watch him ruin his machine?"

Engine purring, the Chevrolet perched on the starting line. A smug twist to his lips, Hastings closed his door and peeled out, leaving a choking cloud of dust. By the time it cleared, Hastings was already accelerating out of the first curve.

Russell grimaced. It deepened when the Chevrolet galloped past where he knew the pothole to be.

Although the car was a distant blob flying between trees, Russell knew its speed was too great for the encroaching turn. "Slow down, slow down. Slow—"

The crunch of metal cut across the orchard.

Winnie buried her face in his shoulder. "I can't watch. Tell me what happens."

The impact hadn't sounded too alarming. "He'll be fine. Pulling out of it now." The car's engine emitted a high-pitched whine, and Russell imagined a rear tire lodged in a rut or behind an exposed root. The thought cued a smile. "Or trying to."

Several breaths later, the Series 409 rocketed forward only to sputter, stall, and roar back to life on the homeward stretch. When it limped across the finish line, George spun away from the man holding the watch. "Two, oh, four!" A series of whoops accompanied his one-man dance.

"You won. By twenty-seven seconds." Winnie's quiet voice filled with awe. "In the Lizzie. I can't believe it."

"From the sour apple expression on Hastings' face, I'd say he doesn't believe it either."

Winnie laughed and threw her arms around his neck.

Surprised, he stumbled backward and chuckled. "You're welcome!"

When she loosed him, they both turned to study Hastings, who inspected the rear of his car. "Think he'll stick by the agreement?"

"He prides himself on being a man of his word. He'll stick by it." A teasing smile quirked her lips. "Maybe betting has its place, after all."

Freed from the burden of debt, Russell's laugh came light and free. "Nah, it's not worth the pain." He embraced his ribs with one arm and Winnie's shoulder with the other. "Let's see if that racecar of yours will get us home."

Winifred lowered the pieced quilt square to her lap and raised her face to the warm morning breeze rustling the parlor curtains. It carried the tangy scent of citrus, and she took it into her lungs in a deep, invigorating breath.

The smog from the race had blown into the desert, and the rubbish left by the crowds had long been removed. The cloak of death, however, still hung over the city, dark and regretful.

Familiar with racing grief, Winifred chose to focus on the bright things in life—such as life itself, and the fact Russell hadn't left town. A week out of the hospital, and he still bunked on a cot in the shop, took meals with them, and dawdled with George, doing . . . who knew what. Working on cars belonging to new customers, she hoped.

She hadn't stepped foot in the garage since the day of the race. Partly because of her nagging headache, partly because her mother didn't seem ready to let Winifred out of her sight, but mostly because Russell had asked her not to.

He'd begged for an unconditional promise of seven days' complete rest. At the time, it had been easy enough to acquiesce, but as the week went on and her headache lessened, she'd begun counting down the hours to freedom. What she would do with her freedom was another matter altogether.

She twirled her grandmother's ring around her finger and pondered life's drastic, unexpected changes.

"Young lady, you haven't listened to a word I've said for the last five minutes." Momma set aside her own sewing and eyed Winifred with a mixture of annoyance and humor. "Here I am pouring out my heart about fabric patterns, and you're gazing out the window with a goofy grin and stars in your eyes."

Winifred blinked. Stars? Goofy? Not surprising. "Sorry, Momma. I was thinking about—"

"Russell Keegan. I know." Her mother's dull voice ignited giggles.

"I was going to say I was thinking about what to do with myself now that I don't need to work in the shop." She grinned. "Yours was a good guess though."

Eyes sparkling, her mother drove her needle into the patch of fabric between her hands. "As far as what to do, your possibilities are endless. The church has been asking for volunteers to help organize the donations going toward the war in Europe." She paused, and Winifred hummed a noncommittal response.

From beneath her lashes, her mom peered across the room, the corners of her mouth curving upward. "What about Bobby? He's pleasant company."

"That, he is." But a bore compared to Russell.

"There's always Los Angeles. You'll miss the cutoff for the tryouts for this year's chamber orchestra, but I hear a Philharmonic is in the works for a couple years from now. A hundred chairs they say—"

"Really? I hadn't heard." And little wonder since she'd had her mind buried in one distraction or another the last several weeks.

"You don't sound as excited as I thought you'd be."

"Funny thing. I don't feel as excited as I should be." Had she lost all hope of playing again, or had another, more appealing dream enveloped the first?

As it had the last months, the music stand stood empty in the corner of the room. She rubbed her splint. "It'll be another month before I can even consider picking up my instrument."

"But you will."

Winifred nodded. "The question is, how well?"

How well would be well enough for an up-and-coming philharmonic orchestra? How well would be well enough to make Winifred happy? Could she be content passing along her skill to others and performing for her family and friends? And Russell . . .

At the thought of him, warmth oozed into her soul and set her insides to buzzing.

Momma chuckled. "He's due to pick you up any minute, so if you—"

"He is?" Winifred popped to her feet. He never showed up before dinnertime. "Why? Where's he taking me?"

"My, my, aren't we eager?" Her mother's smile contradicted her dry tone. "I could have been talking about your brother, you know."

The distinct rumble of the Lizzie's engine drifted through the open window. Winifred dropped her sewing and darted up the staircase to powder her cheeks and secure her hairpins.

Gazing into the mirror, she groaned. "These scabs are atrocious." She slunk back down the stairs, reaching the bottom as the front door opened.

Russell blew into the house like a desert cyclone—hot and breathtaking. His golden skin shone with vitality. The acute blue of his eyes stopped her short. They swept the length of her, with blush-worthy boldness. "Hello, pretty lady."

Butterflies took flight in her stomach and left her speechless.

He strode toward her, plucked her from the second-to-last stair, and set her beside him. His cheek sprang into a half smile as he crooked his elbow and leaned in. "How 'bout a ride?"

"I—yes. I'd love that." Why was she stuttering like a swooning schoolgirl? "Where to?"

"The shop. Where else?" He winked and then tsked at her quirking lips. "Baby steps, darling. We'll take a drive in the country another day."

The mention of "another day" transformed the twist into a smile.

He proved wise about taking it slow. The short, bouncing ride to the shop jostled her brain to the edge of endurance.

When they parked, George came to the shop's open backdoor. He wiped his hands on a rag, tossed it to Russell, then swapped places with him in the driver's seat. "You're looking awfully chipper, Sis. I've got a few errands to run. Have a look-see. It's a top-notch job we've done while you've been lazing around." He flashed her a grin.

"He's right." Russell swung her door wide. "We only spilled the gas cans twice."

Laughter bubbled in her throat. "You two are incorrigible!"

As George drove off, she stepped into the office. The scents of oil, gasoline, and rubber wrapped welcoming arms around her. She kissed her fingertips and tapped them on her father's smiling photograph. "Hi, Daddy. I won't do it again. Promise."

Russell sidled up and withdrew a photograph from the pocket of his Norfolk jacket. He handed it to her. "My pop." The photo showed a trim gentleman, leaning against the hood of an older-model Stutz. Hands in pockets, ankles crossed, and wearing a wide, confident smile, he seemed every bit as self-assured and driven as his son. And there was no denying where Russell got his good looks.

"He was handsome." Winifred propped the picture against a book next to her father's frame. It seemed fitting. "He would have fallen in with Daddy. I'm sure of it."

"Bet you're right."

She pegged him with a sidelong glance, and a single lifted brow. "Bet?"

"Fine!" He threw his hands toward the ceiling, his cheeks twitching with what had to be a suppressed smile. "You're right. Sometimes it is just a saying. Happy now?"

"Depends." She fluttered her lashes and lifted a shoulder in a sassy shrug. "On whether or not you're going to hang around Corona."

Seeming not to have heard, he squinted past her into the dim shop. "What's that?"

Her gaze flitted through the office door to the bay where two unfamiliar cars straddled the pits. "The motorcars? Don't recognize them."

"No. On the counter, in the corner."

"I don't know. It's too dark to tell."

"Does this help?" A crisp click flooded the office—the entire shop—in light.

Winifred's hand flew to her chest. A brilliant bulb dangled above her head. Hurried footsteps carried her into the workspace where four others cast enough light to intimidate any shadow.

"Russell, what have you done? It's . . . it's . . . " She spun, taking in the place, seeing it as never before. Even on the brightest of days with the bay doors open, shadows had always reigned at the back of the shop. No longer.

Daddy would have applauded.

Every cobwebbed corner, every greasy smudge lay naked before her; every bicycle spoke and copper motor component gave a cheery sparkle; every tool winked from its nail on the wall; every tire in the stack flashed its tread; and every bit of it—dust and grease, copper and rubber—sent fuzzy goodness into her middle.

A long, dreamy sigh released from her lungs. "It's . . . perfect. Everything—the electricity, the shop. Better than when I left." She rested a palm on the black hood of the car to her right—a glossy Keystone. "New customers, even."

"Tidwell sent them our way." Russell's hushed voice brought her line of sight back to him. His use of "our" spurred a jolt of electricity down each arm.

A shudder rocked her.

Shoulder propped on the office doorway and hand on his hip, he observed her with an unusual seriousness. Eyes and black hair reflecting the artificial lights, he looked delicious.

She traced the car's copper grill with her fingertips. "It was kind of Bobby to recommend us." She tapped the closed hood. "What seems to be the problem with it?"

"Keeps stalling in second gear." Russell pushed off the doorframe and strode toward her. "George has had a little time to dig into it, but so far, he hasn't made any progress."

Winifred eyed the coveralls hanging from a hook on the back wall. Her fingers twitched to crack the hood. "My, how I've missed this place." The words popped out of their own will.

"Surprised about that?"

She surveyed the cluttered shop, her former prison. The money ledger lay sprawled atop the counter for all the world to gawk at. A scowl tightened her face. She remembered the markings in the accounts to be as ugly as the dust coating the violin case in the corner. This was the place that had shackled her dreams. Stripped her of her femininity and her standing among the townsfolk.

No, not the place. The book, the ledger. Before debt controlled their lives, the shop had been a retreat and sanctuary.

Her most precious memories had been hatched between these walls—where corset and societal rules did not restrict her. Daddy had taught her as much, and more. He'd taught her to appreciate the purr of a well-adjusted engine, the weight of a wrench in her grip, the satisfaction of a hard day's labor, the joy of making a customer happy.

She moved back into the office and picked up his picture. "Daddy, would you have been surprised I missed this dirty, old garage?" His squint-eyed smile met her with silence, but she didn't need to hear his voice to know his answer. He'd told her countless times over the years what he thought of her interest in mechanics.

You were born for this, Winnie. A real natural.

As she set down the frame, her ring captured the electric light and sparkled its approval. "I belong here. In the shop." The words squeaked past her constricting throat.

From behind, Russell wrapped his arms around her waist and rested his chin on her head. "Of course you do, and don't let anyone tell you different. Not Corona or your mom. Not even that little voice in your mind."

She rotated inside the circumference of his arms. "What about the violin? My dream to play in Los Angeles?"

He shrugged. "Do that, too. With me and George here to cover things, you can come and tinker as often as you like."

"Do both?" The idea sprouted wings and took flight. She could teach, practice and recondition herself for tryouts, and fiddle around under the hood anytime she got the urge.

"Wait. You said . . . you and George would be here . . . " Hope swelled within her.

"That's right." Eyes aflame, he trailed the back of his hand down the side of her face.

Prickles teased her neck as joy and gratitude competed for dominance in her chest. "Thank you, Russell. For pulling us—me—out of our hole. For intervening with Hastings, taking the punches meant for George . . . " As the enormity of her debt became clear, her voice grew small. "I haven't spent the advance for the repairs. I'll give it back. Returning the money hardly evens things up between us, but—"

He planted his fingers on her mouth. "That's just the beginning of how I want to provide for you. If you let me into your life. Your heart." When he tipped her face upward, her body leaned into him, as though created to respond to his touch.

"Consider yourself welcome."

His smile crinkled the edges of his eyes. "Shop aside, you belong here." His arm tightened about her. "Right here."

Heart running on all cylinders, she drew a ragged breath. "I couldn't agree more. But—shop aside—I could use a little more electricity. If you're willing . . . "

"Willing?" A saucy smile played around his mouth as he lowered it to hers. "Better buckle up, sweetheart."

Chapter Eighteen

Present Day

Comfort cradled Meghan's spirit as she replaced her Bible on the nightstand. How had she let life's busyness crowd out time reading the Bible? The sweetest part of her day now was her morning devotions—even on Saturdays. It was like she was discovering God for the first time. And He amazed her.

She gulped the last of her chai, then dialed Brooke. Her friend's bright voice answered. "Good morning."

A grin lifted Meghan's cheeks. "Morning to you, too. Just checking if we are still on for Tuesday."

"Hmm. Zumba, huh?"

"Doesn't it sound fun?"

"Yeah, I just wouldn't have expected you to suggest it. Didn't realize you were so adventurous. I had to twist your arm to start the weight training, and now, you're dragging me across town to this women's gym and signing me up for all kinds of crazy classes." A smile colored her voice. "I like it."

Meghan laughed. "Good." Brooke's positive mood was an answered prayer.

"Maybe Thursday we can give their spin class a whirl."

Meghan's lips quirked and she rolled her eyes. "Ha. Funny. But, yeah, sounds good." She stood and carried her mug to the kitchen sink. "So . . . how are you doing?"

A sigh carried across the line and Brooke's voice dropped. "Better than I would have thought a few months ago, but not great."

Meghan's heart twisted. She couldn't imagine having to live through Brooke's ordeal. Her own was difficult enough. Ghosts of regret still haunted her.

Pain laced Brooke's voice. "I don't know if he will ever trust me again. But for now, I'm just grateful he's willing to talk and keep the family under one roof. The counseling is helping, but it ain't easy. We need a lot of prayer."

"I hear ya with the counseling. Just, don't give up hope."

"Thanks. I'm not."

Meghan had hope for them. Because despite the heart-piercing stares and whispers among the congregation, Brooke hadn't missed a Sunday service in months. Asked to step down from the elder board, Tom had left his wife and slunk away in disgrace, but Brooke chose to cling to Jesus despite the shame every time she stepped into the sanctuary—and despite the shredded state of her marriage.

A shudder ran through Meghan. She'd come so close. Oh, how easy it was for lines to blur.

"I'm glad we're friends, Meghan. You . . . you're a great role model for me."

Meghan's eyes widened. "Brooke, you know that's not true."

"I just mean, the way you've turned things around. You and Steve seem closer every day. I just . . . pray I can have that with Darren again someday."

Brooke was right. Meghan and Steve were closer now. His injury had actually helped them. Even after his paralysis went away, he needed more help than he was used to, forcing him to be vulnerable. And it forced her to be the supportive one. Quite a role reversal—one that Meghan knew came from God.

"Steve and I have been out of our comfort zones with everything that's happened—and that's good for us. So, it's like they say: God never wastes our pain. As far as Darren . . . give it time. Just keep loving him."

"Thanks, Meghan. You're, like . . . awesomesauce."

"You're pretty awesomesauce yourself."

They shared a soft laugh, then Brooke cut in. "Oh, hey–Any news on your book?"

Meghan leaned a hip against the kitchen counter and released a breath. "It's been less than two months since I sent it out. Too soon for news I think. It's a torturous waiting game."

"I'd be climbing the walls."

"I am. But I've had plenty to keep me occupied. Steve's physical therapy three times a week, and school starting up again. Not to mention all the stuff with the factory."

"I'm glad you have distractions. And let me just say, once again, that Jones is one lucky man. I would've dragged his tail to court in a heartbeat, no matter how accommodating he suddenly became."

"You say that now, but if you were in our shoes you might reconsider. I mean, courts, judges, paperwork, lawyers? No thank you. Seriously, sticking to the original deal is all we want."

"I guess. But you're probably missing out on some great legal research opportunities for your next book."

Meghan's lips curved up. "I thought of that, but it's not worth the headache. We have enough paperwork as it is, now that we've got this ball rolling. We're up to our eyeballs with it. I can't even see our kitchen table anymore, no joke."

Brooke laughed. "It's kind of exciting though, right? I mean, owning your own business? That's huge."

"Yes. It is exciting." Especially because she and Steve were working on it side by side. "It's been a rough road, but in a convoluted sort of way, I'm glad. I don't think the business would've been such a blessing had it all gone smoothly. Might've made things worse, with Steve trying to shoulder everything alone. I think we're in a much better place now to handle it."

"I think you two will handle it like champs."

"Thanks for your vote of confidence."

The sound of the garage door opening perked Meghan's ears. "Oh, gotta scoot. I'll catch ya later!"

White clouds marbled the blue sky overhead, and Meghan filled her lungs with post-rain air. At last, the hot, sticky summer was showing signs of departure. She rested against the scrolling, wrought-iron chair back. Bright colored Spanish tile inlaid their table as well as the fire pit ten feet away.

Her thoughts turned inward, to all she had to be grateful for. Including Curtis, as surprising as it was. He'd quietly moved on to another fellowship, giving Meghan the space to repair her family.

Despite what almost happened between them, Curtis was a good man.

Human . . . but good.

Without safeguards in place, even good people could fall. Meghan had learned that nobody was immune to temptation.

She shuddered, then refocused her eyes. One look at her real-life leading man was all she needed to bathe her bruised heart in hope.

Seated across from her, Steve popped a tortilla chip in his mouth and crunched, then brushed his hands together. "Any more chips and salsa and I won't have room for lunch."

"Yes, you will."

He shrugged. "Yeah. I will."

A laugh escaped on Meghan's breath, followed by a shiver. She inched closer to the outdoor heater near their circular table.

"You aren't still cold, are you?"

"No, it's nice. Perfect, even." She pulled Steve's jacket tighter around her. "You're probably the one who's cold since I stole this."

"Nah. I'm good." He reached for another chip. "That jacket has always looked better on you, anyway."

Meghan relished the subtle compliment. She made a mental note to add it to her journal that night. "Thank you, I love it when you say things like that." She licked the salt from her lips and wiped her hands on her napkin.

He gave a nod, lips curving. "Noted."

Pointing out when Steve did something she wanted more of still felt awkward sometimes, but it was helping. As was her personal journal chronicling their positive interactions. She could be blind to the understated way Steve flirted with her. But in recent months, as his depression lessened, she'd been reminded what a charmer he could be.

A charmer and a rascal—in his own way, not like the men she wrote about in novels. Especially when she removed her expectations of what that looked like.

Their waitress appeared with their entrées and Meghan smoothed her napkin. "Ooh, thank you. Looks yummy."

"You're welcome. Anything else I can do for you, let me know. Enjoy!"

Meghan's mouth watered at the sight of her crispy tacos—steaming chicken jutting out from the sides, cabbage and pico de gallo piled high on top. She leaned forward and inhaled the delicious scent of cilantro. How long had it been since they'd come to the Mission Inn for a meal?

Too long.

She flicked a glance at Steve's dish—enchilada slathered in cheese. Feeling ornery, she stabbed the corner and tore it off, then popped it in her mouth.

Steve's eyes widened. "Careful. You may find one of your tacos missing next time."

She dipped her fork into a mound of rice. "You wouldn't dare."

"Don't be so sure." He stabbed at her plate, pulling a piece of chicken from her taco shell and shoving it in his mouth.

"Hey!"

He chewed around a smile and returned his attention to his own plate. "Warned ya."

The sound of scraping knives and forks filled the next few minutes as they dug into their Mexican feast. They'd talked about factory business over the chips and salsa, so now the rest of the afternoon was for just being together.

The counselor was right—the regular dates were doing wonders for getting them back on solid ground. Why had they never carved out the time to connect this way before? The power of communication was remarkable.

And dangerous. She stared at the ice floating in her drink. 'Just talking' had almost destroyed her marriage.

Meghan sniffed, then looked out across the enclosure, soaking in the image of the ivy-covered stone and tall, skinny palms surrounding them. Her eyes came to rest on the man sitting before her: Shoulders relaxed, comfortable. The fine lines around his eyes crinkled as he chewed, and the new gray at his temples blended so well with his blond that few would notice but her.

He caught her assessing gaze and tipped his head. "What?"

"Nothing." Her lips twitched upward and she snapped the mental photograph. She just had to mentally Photoshop out the enchilada sauce clinging to the side of his mouth.

Or maybe not. Real life was messier than fiction, but that was the beauty of it. Love was found in the mundane. The every day. The flat middle between the exhilarating highs and terrifying lows. It was found in socks with holes, in split ends and cellulite, in late work nights and unplugged toasters.

Steve cut into his enchilada. "Okay. So, let's hear about this new story idea of yours."

"Well . . . " Meghan's belly tingled as she launched into a story of mistaken identity, secrets, and war. Sharing it all with her husband sent a smile to her heart. Especially because he was actually paying attention. "The fun part will be filling in all the details."

He swept his tongue behind his molars. "War story, huh? What about Texas? Not the Alamo, that's been done; but there's always General Santa Anna's fear of water that led to his capture, or the massacre of Goliad." Forking another bite, he tossed Meghan some ideas for plot twists, chewing as he spoke.

She raised her brows and nodded. "Hey, not bad. Maybe you should write it."

"Yeah, right. You're the writer. I'm just the fan club."

She smiled at the compliment. "Aw, that's sweet . . . But don't get ahead of yourself. Publication has to happen before the fan club does."

"I'm not worried." Said with such confidence. He might talk with his mouth full, but he was still her champion.

Her journal would be full tonight.

The server cleared the plates and brought their desserts from the famed Casey's Cupcakes—Rockin' Red Velvet Razzmatazz for Steve, and Peanut Butter for Meghan.

Meghan took a bite of moist, peanut-buttery goodness, and groaned. "Oh man, I'm afraid of what will happen to my figure with the holidays approaching. But this is heaven."

"Meg, your figure is fine. So eat up and enjoy . . . But I wouldn't mind if you made that little groaning noise again." He wiggled his eyebrows and Meghan's cheeks ignited.

She glanced at the patrons one table over. "Steven Townsend, you're incorrigible!"

"Is that bad?" He chuckled and bit into his cupcake.

Meghan rolled her eyes and smiled. "Yeah." She shook her head as she popped the next morsel into her mouth. The embarrassment warming her cheeks did not keep her from savoring his attention. Somehow she enjoyed it even more now that she'd stopped looking to her husband to fill the deepest needs of her heart. God alone could do that.

Steve's love and affection were frosting—rich, chocolate fudge frosting.

"So, are you ready for pseudo-Thanksgiving?"

Her shoulders fell an inch. "As ready as I can be."

Why had she agreed to seeing her half-brother, Patrick, and their dad, for a pre-Thanksgiving gathering?

She shook her head. "I feel as nervous as a caffeinated Chihuahua. But I know it's time. Gotta stop burying my feelings, get it all out there and see if healing is possible." So in a few short weeks, Meghan would sit down for a meal with her father for the first time in over ten years. The thought made her dizzy.

"It'll be fine. I'll be with you." Steve reached across the table and enveloped her hand in his strong grasp, sending warm tingles dancing up her arm.

"I know," she whispered. "It's the only reason I was able to say yes."

"If things do head south, you know I have no trouble getting up and taking you home."

Meghan simply nodded. She had no doubt he'd do just that if necessary.

Their eyes locked and the world disappeared. Fifteen years of history—support, loyalty, good times and bad—collided into one spark sizzling between them. Steve ran his calloused thumb along the inside of her wrist and Meghan's pulse quickened.

He squeezed her fingers, cleared his throat and gave an impish grin before reaching for his water. "So . . . what time did you tell your mom we'd pick up the girls?"

The longing that darkened his eyes left no doubt as to what was on his mind. Meghan felt the fire licking her cheeks and warming her belly. "I . . . didn't give her an exact time."

"Interesting." He poked his fork into his crimson dessert, then met her gaze again. "You've seen the museum before . . . right, Mrs. Townsend?"

Meghan swallowed. "Why, yes I have, Mr. Townsend."

"In that case, you wouldn't be too disappointed if we skipped it today?" He raised questioning brows at her, and she lowered her lashes, feigning interest in her cupcake crumbs.

She raised one corner of her mouth in what she hoped was a seductive smile. The laser surgery for his herniated disk had made him nearly pain-free, and Steve seemed to be making up for lost time. But her phone rang before she could respond.

"Maybe it's my mom. Want me to ask her for extra time?" She smirked and pulled her cell out of her purse.

Her thumb hung in midair, eyes widening at the number on the screen. She knew that area code. She'd memorized it weeks—months—ago.

"Oh my gosh." She shifted her rounded eyes to Steve. "I think it's about my book."

Steve set down his fork. The phone rang again. "Meg. Answer it."

Meghan ran her tongue across her bottom lip and pushed a button. Forcing as much of the tremble out of her voice as possible, she answered, then listened to the agent on the other end of the line as best she could over the loud swooshing in her ears. "Mm hmm. Mm hmm. Okay . . . Thank you."

With a deep intake of air, she laid down her phone and raised her face to Steve's expectant eyes. "She said I should start a different project."

Steve's expression fell. He cocked his head, mouth twisting in quiet pity.

Meghan's stomach flopped. She couldn't stand it anymore. "She said to start a different project because . . . she can't wait to see more from me!" Her mouth stretched into an exaggerated smile and she tapped her feet under the table while drum-rolling her palms on either side of her plate.

When Steve's jaw fell open, Meghan squeezed her eyes shut and let out a tiny squeal. His chair scraped the concrete and next thing she knew, he was pulling her out of her seat and into his arms.

His warm breath sent goose bumps racing down her neck as he murmured in her ear. "Congratulations, babe. Let's celebrate."

Babe. She smiled and craned her neck to look up at him, soaking in the genuine joy exuding from his face. Eyes wet, she nodded. "Sounds wonderful."

After paying for their meal, Steve laced his fingers through hers and, with a slight limp, led her through the hotel vestibule and out into an inner courtyard. Topiaries accented the columned archways and splays of pink flowers hung from balconies overhead.

Meghan was ogling the view when Steve paused in front of a delightful bubbling fountain, slipped his hand to the small of her back, and drew her close. So close she felt the erratic beat of his heart. He lowered his head and nuzzled into her hair, the warmth of his breath on her neck making her shudder. Awareness of being watched froze her gaze. With the crook of his finger, Steve tilted her chin up.

"Steve, there's people around." Discomfort shifted her eyes to their left.

But instead of retreating, he leaned in. "I don't care. Let 'em watch."

He was trying. Maybe still not in tune with her comfort level, maybe overcompensating, but he was trying to love her better and that thought alone eased the tension from her body.

Letting go of her self-consciousness, Meghan's eyelids fluttered closed as her husband grazed his lips across hers. As she shut out the rest of the world, she felt delicious anticipation blossom until he pressed into her with a passion that transported her back to their wedding night. Hands buried in her hair, his kiss continued to deepen, making Meghan momentarily forget where she was.

He pulled back, leaving her breathless, then lifted her hand a placed a soft kiss on her knuckles. "Thank you, Meg. For helping me feel like a man again."

Understanding warmed her insides, and Meghan pulled her brows together, her sobered gaze tracing the contours of Steve's face. It wasn't only about her. She had to learn how to love him better, too. How to build him up.

Raising her chin, she flattened her palm on his chest. "And not just any man. My man. And I'm not ashamed of it."

Was that a tinge of red rimming his eyes? He coughed, then pulled her hand from his chest and slipped something onto her finger. "I was going to wait until Thanksgiving, but I got antsy."

Furrowing her brow, Meghan looked down to see the stunning emerald ring making its new home on her right hand. Diamonds encrusted the delicate double band, scattering rainbows as rays of sunlight hit it.

"Do you like it?" Steve bent his head of silky blond hair—thinning in the back though it was—and captured her gaze.

Her mouth dropped open and her throat pinched shut as Meghan bobbed her head, sending her hair bouncing around her face.

"I got it to represent a new beginning for us. I know things aren't perfect. Never will be. But I don't need perfect so long as you'll let me love you for the rest of our lives." He lifted a shoulder. "It can also commemorate the day you got a call about your book, that's fine too."

Cheeks stretched with a wide smile, Meghan looked down at her finger again, emotion robbing her of speech. Not because the ring was gorgeous, but because this man so deeply loved her. And she felt his love down to her bones.

Wiping moisture from under her lashes, she sniffed then looked up into the face of the man she'd loved since before she was old enough to know what love meant. Butterflies and breath-stealing kisses might come more seldom now than fifteen years ago, but he could still weaken her knees on occasion. And even when her toes weren't curling, what they shared together went so far beyond all of that. Could real life get any better than this?

Her heart raced faster than Russell's Cat as she found her voice at last. "I love you, Steven. Always have, always will." She took in the details of his face, then pulled his head down for more of his kiss.

A moment later, he leaned back and seemed to look into her very soul. "I love you, too, Meghan. Don't ever forget it."

Meghan drew in a deep, satisfied breath. Fictional romance would never hold a candle to the messy, imperfect, tenacious love she and Steve shared. The kind of love possible only when it came behind faith. "I could never write a love story as real as ours. No one would believe it."

But given the chance, she was sure gonna try.

The End

Being independent authors, we rely completely on the reader – that's you! – to get the word out about our books. If you enjoyed this book, won't you please rate the book or leave a review at an online venue, then recommend it to a friend? The more you tell others about it, the more we can write. And nothing would please us more than to put a new book in your hands!

APRIL W GARDNER

APRIL W GARDNER writes *history with a Christian perspective and a little imagination.* She is a copyeditor, military wife, and homeschooling mother of two who lives in Texas. She writes Christian historical romance with a focus on our Southeastern Native Tribes. In no particular order, April dreams of owning a horse, learning a third language, and visiting all the national parks.

Connect with April online at:
www.AprilGardner.com
www.twitter.com/AprilWGardner
Facebook.com/AprilGardnerBooks

April's latest release ***Beneath the Blackberry Moon*** is now available in both digital and print at major online retailers. It is often offered for FREE to her subscribers. Sign up today at aprilgardner.com!

The war was simpler before his enemy became a beautiful face with a gentle warrior's spirit he cannot resist. But what woman would have a warrior whose blood-soaked hands destroyed her life? Then again...does she have a choice?

MICHELLE MASSARO

MICHELLE MASSARO writes *contemporary fiction soaked in grace.* She makes her home in Southern California with her husband and their four children. When she isn't tinkering with words, Michelle enjoys old Rogers and Hammerstein movies, making kefir, and Sudoku. A new lipstick and a good French roast always make her happy.

Connect with Michelle online at:
www.twitter.com/MLMassaro
www.MichelleMassaroBooks.com
www.facebook.com/MichelleMassaroBooks

Newsletter: Sign up at michellemassarobooks.com
Subscribers always receive bonuses!!

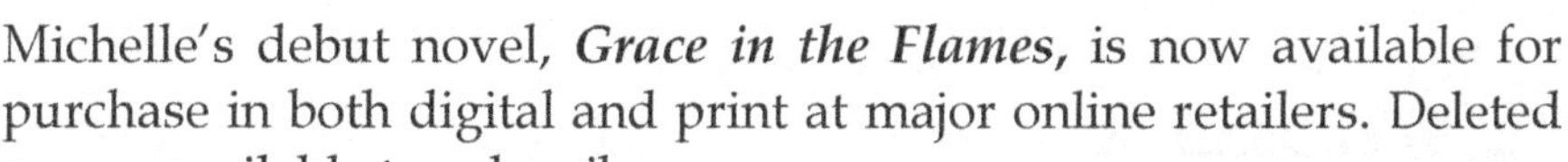

Michelle's debut novel, ***Grace in the Flames,*** is now available for purchase in both digital and print at major online retailers. Deleted scenes available to subscribers.

A deadly fire, a dangerous temptation, a desperate heart. When three lives intersect, God will ask them to do the impossible. To love Him *even if...*

Dear Reader,

Thank you for taking this journey with Meghan and her characters in *Better than Fiction* (BTF). For the curious among you, Michelle is the author of the contemporary storyline; April, that of the historical.

This story was a project five years in the making and is very near to our hearts for several reasons. It has allowed us to share our burden for the woman who feels forgotten by her leading man yet noticed by another... If that is you, you're on a tricky, slippery slope that ends nowhere good. Sweet sister, uproot those illicit thoughts, and put your eyes where they belong—on the Lord and the one He gave you. We know from experience how hard it is. Achingly hard. But through Christ, it's doable. And it's so very worth it!

BTF has also given two best buddies an excuse to work together, laugh together, create together. We do it seamlessly and with a harmony only the Spirit can produce. Ours is one of those rare friendships that comes along once in a lifetime and lasts just as long. It began in 2010 with a few random comments on a blog post. It journeyed into 2011 with the creation of our literary contest site Clash of the Titles, and continues today stronger than ever, as evidenced by the smashing release of *Better than Fiction*.

Will we write another story together? Maybe! Make sure you find us on social media, so you're not left out of the new-release loop. And have a look at the other books we've each written, now that you've sampled the flavor of our writing.

Another reason we've adored this project—it's given Michelle an opportunity to put a spotlight on her beautiful hometown of Corona, California, and its colorful past. In the spring of 2012, April flew to Corona to take a spin around that famous circle, dig into the library's archives, and stuff her face with In-N-Out Burgers. She left with a full tummy and a brain bursting with words screaming to be put on paper.

We took every opportunity to use recorded history and actual locations. After all, that's what makes this book so much fun! The BTF sites you'll want to visit in Corona include the following:

~The Grand Boulevard. Of course! Drive the entire circumference, making sure to stop at Main St., in front of Corona Fundamental Intermediate School, and snap a photo at Historic Marker #10. Once there, close your eyes and imagine Winnie slipping on her goggles and strapping in.

~Hunny's Café. Where Meghan skipped the Nutella crêpe and ordered an egg-white omelet, and you never know who might show up—last week, it was Kiefer Sutherland! You'll find all sorts of yummy goodness at Hunny's.

~It's a Grind Coffee House, where both Meghan *and* Michelle like to go to pound out their novels. Michelle introduced April to the spot during her visit and they sat in Meghan's favorite spot by the fireplace. To get in character, Michelle tried Meghan's chai latte. It's great! But she usually opts for the blended latte, or her trusty French Roast.

~The oldest church in the city, First Congregational Church of Corona, where sandwiches were served to spectators. (Historic Marker #2.)

~The Mission Inn, where Steve took Meghan for a romantic date at the Las Campanas Mexican Restaurant. Dine at one of their many high-end restaurants, shop the boutiques, or stay in one of their deluxe rooms. Don't forget to try one of Casey's Cupcakes!

~Hotel Del Rey (Historic Marker #7), where Russell bunked until he moved into the Fisher home. It currently sits in large container crates at Corona Heritage Park. Eventually, it will be rebuilt and used as it was during Russell and Winnie's day. Corona Heritage Park is itself a must-stop location for any Corona tour. Many charming weddings are held on their lawn, and you can meander through the small museum to see tons of memorabilia from Corona's racing heyday.

~"The brown corner" is located at Ontario and Buena Vista Avenue. Most likely, it is still there, empty, as it has been since Michelle moved to Corona in 2003. ☺ They may actually have finally removed the Coming Soon sign. They're not fooling anyone anymore.

~Jameson Park, where Meghan watched Curtis swing that batting arm.

~And if you're in town on a Sunday morning, you're invited to attend services at Living Truth Christian Fellowship. This is not the church Meghan attends in BTF, but her "Pastor Mike" is inspired by Pastor Michael Lantz, and Tracy Baber is still the children's choir director. Oh, and they do offer donuts for those with a sweet tooth—or who need to break hard news to someone.

Also of note are the actual historical characters mentioned in the book. They are "Wild" Bob Burman, Earl Cooper, Mrs. Frazier (hotel proprietress), Mr. Pendelton (chief timer), and a fictional representative of the city's Jameson family (the man who proposes marriage before the race, as well as Curtis). The Jamesons are still represented in and around the city of Corona and their fascinating family is well worth digging into.

If your appetite for nostalgic Corona has been whetted, you can find lots more to savor at the Corona Historic Preservation Society webpage (corona-history.org) and The Corona Public Library Heritage Room site (coronapubliclibrary.org/localhistory.aspx). Thanks to their resources, our imaginations were able to spring to life in brilliant color.

And the imagination is a *wonderful* thing… as long as it doesn't lead your heart astray.

Much love,
April and Michelle

READING GROUP GUIDE

1. What do you most admire about each of the characters? What are their greatest flaws, and how are they displayed in the story?
2. If you had to pick one character to see more of in another story, which would it be? Why?
3. Do you consider Meghan's actions and/or thoughts toward Curtis to be an illicit affair? Why or why not?
4. At what point did Meghan start on her downward slide?
5. Did Meghan do everything in her power to make things work with Steve or was there something else she could have said or done to repair their rift?
6. Name various points and ways in which Meghan could have stepped onto a more righteous path in regards to Curtis.
7. Do you see Curtis as a genuine Christian? Why or why not?
8. Which of the three—Meghan, Curtis, Steve—do you believe to be most at fault?
9. What was the difference between Brooke's situation with Tom and Meghan's with Curtis? Is one more wrong than the other?
10. Have you ever experienced a chronic sense of neglect? If so, how did you handle it?
11. Winnie and Russell both lost their dads. Were the characters' attempts to keep their memories alive healthy?
12. Meghan dreamed of being passionately loved by her husband and of being published. Winnie dreamed of playing in the orchestra; Russell, of winning the Corona Races. What is your greatest dream? What strides are you making toward achieving it? Have you taken God into account while working toward it?

13. Men receive a bad rap for their wandering ways, but women can be just as unfaithful. The difference is that our infidelity occurs mostly in a place only God can see—our minds and hearts. Have you ever found yourself devoting your thoughts and emotions to a man other than the one God intended for you? If so, what have you done to correct it?
14. Did you enjoy how the stories were woven together? Which aspect of Racing Hearts did you think most reflected Meghan's current situation?
15. Did you see Meghan in Winnie most or in Russell?

ACKNOWLEDGEMENTS

April and Michelle have spent five years working on this story, but we've had a lot of help along the way. We'd like to say a special thank you to the following people:

First, to our families, for the patience and enthusiasm you've shown these many years. You never doubted, and that's meant the world to us.

To Mary Bryner Winn, for connecting us with the Corona Historic Preservation Society and singing the praises of our book to other Corona lovers.

To the folks at the Heritage Room in the Corona Public Library, for helping us wade through a mountain of research.

To Karen Ball, for helping make the manuscript sing.

To our early readers for your feedback and encouragement, especially to Christine Tamm, LMFT, and Nancy Kaiser, pastor's wife, for your valuable insight into the slippery slope of emotional affairs.

To "the Sams" - Sam Lipot and Samantha Wilson, for dressing up and becoming Winnie and Russell for our front cover. Meeting the characters was so much fun and we couldn't have asked for better models.

And finally, to Jehova Rapha, healer of hearts, for showing us the way.

Made in the USA
Las Vegas, NV
20 June 2021

25108559R00215